JEM,

A Fugitive *from* London

DELANEY GREEN

Jem, a Fugitive from London

LOC number 2016940696

ISBN-13: 978-1533030528
ISBN-10: 1533030529

For Sam, who shows me every day what magic can do.

CHAPTER 1

NOVEMBER 1758

A Matter of Perspective

The shrunken space in our belly sends us aloft. We ride the updrafts. Watch for wings.

There. Flutter. Pigeon.

In our bones we feel the distance, the wind. We climb.

The bird's beating wings excite us. We time its flight; we know where it will be when we fall on it.

We tuck our wings. Earth takes us. Wind sleeks us. Our eyelids slide up. We are death falling. A foot short, we turn bottom-down, legs and talons out to strike. The pigeon's spine cracks. It falls.

We glide down, land, scan for thieves. Nothing moves in the open, but our neck prickles: Something watches. We spread our wings over our kill. We scream a warning.

The pigeon is warm. We straddle it, grasping it between our feet and pulling feathers until we reach sweet, warm skin. We tear off a bite, swallow. Life blooms in our blood. Our trembling eases. It is good.

Still…Something lurks.

We seize our kill and launch into the air, find a tree, wedge the meat. Watch.

A black bird on the horizon grows larger as it flies toward us. Raven. Thief. We raise our wings to warn him off, but he circles our tree. Turns a loop in the air like the fool acrobat he is. He flies round and round, too close, turning, tumbling, tormenting. His antics cannot lure us from our kill, but we are wary: he is twice our size.

We dig in our talons. The raven swoops over us, scuffing our head with his wings. His feathers reek of the carrion he eats. When we do not abandon our kill, the raven flies an arc and comes for us, leading with his beak. We scream and push off. Our anger drives us up. We will fall on the raven from above and take back what is ours.

But the raven does not steal our pigeon—he chases us into the sky. He follows so close we cannot get enough distance to dive. When we try short swoops, he pecks our breast, our wings, anything he can reach.

We slash at the raven with a taloned foot. He nips our wing. We scratch and pummel one another. Our battle rages across the sky. When his huge wing cuffs us, we tumble head over tail. We flap wildly for balance. The raven harries us all the way to the smoky warren of men that spreads on both sides of the river like a burned field.

Breathing hard, we labor up to try another dive. Speed is our only advantage. The raven doesn't follow. He has caught a current of wind and sails below us like a shadow. We have him now. We tuck our wings. Earth takes us. Wind sleeks us. We are death falling—

We falter when rushing air wedges between us like a hot knife, catching an edge and tugging. Light flares in the widening split. Motion stops. Heart stops. Breathing stops. She leaves me!

She? Me?

Before I can find her again, the Light that tore us apart snares me and pulls me over a whirl of gardens, walls, streets, animals, people to a stone house with windows like square eyes, and the Light—

yanks me through a window set in the stone...

to a human lying on a cloud...

to the edge of skin. No, no, not what I want I...

...have no wings, no way to stop, I plunge into a body with bones dense and flesh thick and naked and stretched impossibly long. Frantic, I tumble up and down this body, looking for a way out, but the skin shuts me in. I soar head to toe, lost, until

the body warms. It knows me. It draws me into gaps and breaks and holes, and I know this body, too, like I know hunting between earth and sky, and

—I know the feel of this face. This tongue that knows the taste of bread; I know it. Somehow, somewhere, some time before, I have felt this heart beating and these lungs breathing. I ease into spaces that feel familiar: hands, lips, knees. Like rain falling on sand, I seep into this body. It holds only me, alone. It is heavy. It is anchored to the earth.

* * *

"I saw her eyelids flicker." A woman's voice. Something warm around my hand. "She feels different to me now. Jem? Jem, are you there?"

Something smelled sour. Me. I opened my eyes to a silhouette framed by light from the mullioned window. As my vision cleared, I saw a fire flickering across the room. A woman sat close by the bed in which I lay, my hand clasped in hers. Red hair straggled out from the woman's cap. Great dark circles bloomed under the blue eyes. I knew the face. Knew the valiant heart that pumped blood into the hand. *M…Margery.*

"Jem?" she said. "Thank God!" She shouted over her shoulder to another woman nearer the door, "Mrs. Pierce, run and tell the doctor Jem's awake!" The woman hurried out in a rustle of skirts. Margery placed a hand on my forehead, ran it down my cheek, and said with tears in her eyes and a trembling smile on her lips, "Oh, Jem, we were so worried."

"What happened?"

"You've been…ill."

"I—is there water? My throat hurts. My mouth is so dry."

Margery poured a glass of water and helped me sit up. She held the glass to my lips. The water soaked into the parched places inside, knitting me more tightly together.

A man in shirt sleeves and waistcoat dashed in, his unclubbed hair flying.

His rumpled breeches looked as though he'd slept in them. His fierce eyebrows met over the bridge of his nose, and when I saw them, I thudded all the way back to myself suddenly, like falling on ice. *Dr. Abernathy. My master. What had happened?*

"Jem!" he said. He pulled me into a fierce hug, which proved whatever it was had been very bad. When he set me back, his face wore the focused look he gets when we're examining a patient. He felt my pulse, looked into my eyes, checked that all my limbs moved and functioned. His eyes met Margery's over my body, and he said, "She can't do this again."

"I know it," Margery said.

"I can't get sick again?" I said.

Dr. Abernathy's eyes widened. "Sick? You weren't sick."

"Margery, you said I was ill."

"And so you were, laid out in that bed for three days."

"What did I have?"

"What do you remember?" Dr. Abernathy asked.

Why were they dancing around whatever it was? "I—all I remember is a dream that I could fly. It was wonderful—I loved it. I wasn't by myself, though, I was with…somebody. We were flying together. We killed and ate a pigeon. It was so good we were shaking." Margery's fingers flexed, but when I looked at her face, she gave a wobbly little smile.

The doctor said, "I see. What were you doing before you had the dream?"

I said, "The last thing I remember before the dream was being in the garden. I saw a bird so high up it was a dot, and I—" I stopped. I whispered, "Margery, please tell me it was only a dream. Don't say I flew with a bird again." My eyes fixed on her face. She bit her lip.

"Apparently that is exactly what you did," Dr. Abernathy said. "Mrs. Jamison tells me you somehow or other sent your mind into a pigeon two weeks ago and rode the bird to the top of St. Paul's."

Margery said, softly, "I told him about the pigeon when we couldn't wake you. You didn't have a fever or an injury, but you were laid out on the garden path like a dead man. So I suspected you might be flying again."

"You should have told me the first time you flew," Dr. Abernathy snapped.

"Well, I didn't try to fly," I said. I plucked at the sheet. If she'd lived, Mum would not have liked to hear I'd flown, twice now. She'd told me our family magic was a curse. Which it certainly seemed to be.

"We were all busy two weeks ago, doctor," Margery said, "what with the Lord Mayor's Show and such. And then Patch tried to kidnap her the very next day. We've had plenty and enough to worry about. But, yes, we should have said something, because now you've gone again, Jem, only this time, you were gone for three days."

I frowned at the square of window above Margery's head. "Three days?"

"And for three days you lay there like a corpse," Dr. Abernathy said, his mouth pinched.

Margery wrung out a cloth and wiped my face. She said, "You wouldn't eat or drink. Finally, the doctor put a tube down your throat like they do at Bedlam for the force-feeding and poured down water and gruel."

"That's why my throat is raw."

"It was that or watch you die," Dr. Abernathy said, his voice gruff, "which I will not allow." He shut the door and came back. He cleared his throat. "Mrs. Jamison and I have a drastic solution to this flying problem of yours. We want you to go to Cornwall to Mrs. Jamison's grandmother, who can teach you to manage this flying business."

"But I don't want to go to Cornwall," I said.

"Jem, you are a human being, not a bird," Dr. Abernathy said. "You are a unique, *single* female, although you pretend to all the world that you are my apprentice, and a male, which is a deception I am beginning to question. If you spent more time indoors with female pursuits and less time out of doors, perhaps you'd be less likely to—do what you did."

"Forgive me, but that's a mad thing to say, doctor," Margery said. "Sewing and cooking won't keep Jem on the ground, and it's not being outside that causes trouble. Jem needs to learn to control her Sight." She turned back to me. "That's why we want you to go to Cornwall—just for a little while. Granny Kestrel flew with birds and never got lost. She can teach you how to manage that, and…oh, lots of things."

"You want me to go away?" I said to Dr. Abernathy.

"No. I don't." Dr. Abernathy sat on the bed and gripped my shoulders. "But I think you should." He said, his face very white, "Look at me and listen. It takes a long while to starve to death, but you know that a human body expires in three or four days without water."

"I know."

"You have seen what happens to people who do not drink enough water."

"You're talking about James," I whispered. My baby brother had died of the putrid sore throat eight months before, and he'd been so dried out he'd looked like an old man when we'd buried him. Mum had died the same week. I swallowed.

The doctor continued, "You can't know how hard it has been for Mrs. Jamison and me to watch your body lie in that bed drying up, knowing there was not a thing we could do except force-feed you." He lifted the skin on the back of my hand. It stayed pinched. "See? You're severely dehydrated."

"I'm sorry," I said.

"I'll not allow you to die, Jem. I'm afraid you must go to Cornwall." Clearly, he didn't want me to go, which was comforting, but my magic gave him no choice.

Margery had told me my magic, my Second Sight, was a gift, but at this moment, it seemed to be a curse, just as mum had said. The Sight *had* let me talk with Mum's ghost before she went to Heaven, but that was only for a few minutes. I hadn't seen Mum since. The Sight had let me see sickness inside our patients, which was medically useful. But Second Sight gave me bad dreams at night. It had tipped me out of my body twice, and now it might force me out of

London.

My unhappiness must have shown on my face. Margery took my hand in hers. She said to the doctor, "She's not leaving for Cornwall this minute. After all, she did come back both times she flew. P'raps she's found her own way to come home." She turned to me. "Jem, how did you come back from the pigeon the first time you flew?"

I tried to remember. I'd been crushing coffee beans for Margery on the back step of Mr. Galt's apothecary shop when a pigeon landed close by and fixed his pretty red eye on me. I'd looked at his eye so hard it seemed that was all I could see, and then I'd felt myself pitch toward the pigeon, and suddenly I was on the other side of the red eye looking at myself stretched out in the alley. When Margery had stepped out of the shop to check on me and the coffee beans, the pigeon—with me aboard—had fluttered up and away.

"The pigeon and I weren't…together," I said. "He was afraid of me. I…I wanted to come back to myself right away. I kept thinking about my own face and the feel of my hands. I felt a tug, like being pulled by a rope. I came back fast."

"Was it the same with the falcon? Were you pulled back?"

"There was a raven," I said, "a big black one. He attacked us. We were diving at him when we—came apart."

Margery said. "How did you do that?"

I recalled the glorious weightlessness of flight, the openness of all the sky I could ever want to fly in, every moment of *now* all my own. The rush of air as I dove toward a fluttering target, the last-minute thud and crack. The terrifying moment when I lost my other half. "We flew up so we could attack him from above, but when we dove at him, a Light wedged between me and the peregrine and peeled us apart, and then it pulled me through that window," I placed my hand on my chest, "into here."

"A bright light pulled you," Margery said. She looked up at the doctor. "There it is again. Jem, I think you made a tether all by yourself."

"A what?"

Margery pulled a crumpled letter from her pocket. "What you just said matches up with what Granny Kestrel says. I wrote to her the day you told me about the pigeon, and she wrote back straightaway."

She scanned the letter. "Where is it? Here: 'Your Jem must keep a tether betwixt her body and her mind. She must see the tether when she flies and keep it in sight. If she loses it, she must leave the bird that moment and go back or she might not find her way home again.' Jem, you said you were snared by Light." I nodded. "Did you make a tether?"

"How could I make something I never heard of?"

"This is a disquieting conversation," Dr. Abernathy muttered. He paced to the window.

Margery said, "I know this is difficult for both of you. Jem, I told you that when I was little, I went with the mice on the moor."

"Yes."

She smiled a sad little smile. "Well, I nearly killed my mother with worry. I was only four years old. She'd go to look for me and find me asleep on a tussock. She'd call and call and finally I'd wake up with stories about burrowing underground and all the delicious insects I'd had to eat, and she'd go crying to my da that we had to move to the city so she wouldn't lose me to the beasts."

"A legitimate concern," Dr. Abernathy said over his shoulder.

"What's that got to do with a tether?" I asked.

"Da asked Granny Kestrel for help. She told me to make a picture in my mind of something I cared about: my mother or Da or herself. She said when the mice called me, I should think of that thing, to keep seeing it with one eye, as it were. She said if the mice ever wanted me to stay with them for always, I must imagine that thing grown so large it was the only thing I could see."

"And?"

"And that link I made, that tie to my family, Granny said was called a tether."

Dr. Abernathy grunted. There was a knock on the door. Mrs. Pierce stuck in her head. "Shall I bring up a tray now that's Master Jem is awake, sir?"

"I—yes, but let me come and tell you what to put on it," Dr. Abernathy said to us. His glowering eyes flicked over me briefly when he went out. I had caused him a lot of trouble. I felt like a raisin, all squeezed down to nothing. If I couldn't manage my Sight, he'd send me to Cornwall for my own good—but what if Granny Kestrel's training didn't take even if I did go to her? What if I never got enough control over my Sight to come home?

"He hates me."

Margery said, "Don't be daft. Dr. Abernathy isn't angry with you, Jem. He was frantic. I don't think he slept more than a handful of minutes these last three days. Nothing in his precious books talks about a human flying with birds."

"I know. I've read the same books. But the Sight isn't just flying. I told you one of the lions in the menagerie at the Tower pushed into my mind and showed herself tearing out a man's throat."

"Yes, you told me. I think I prefer mice." Her mouth smiled, but not her eyes. "I think the mice invited me to burrow around with them when I was little because I—I heard them, and they heard me. I think they knew I was lonely—Dylan and Alfred had each other, but this was before Mum had my sister, Nessa. It could be your soul is ranging out like mine did, looking for…companionship, maybe."

"I don't feel lonely."

"The heart wants what the heart wants, Jem," Margery said, " and the mind doesn't always cooperate. At any rate, Da moved us to London. Mum was glad to be away from the wild, and there were other things for me to think about, for after Nessa came Tessa and Jory and all the rest. And my Sight got layered over and things piled on top, and after a while I couldn't remember how to See any more."

"So you ignored your Sight until it went away," I said. "Why hasn't that worked for me?"

"Your Sight may be too strong. Sight is passed down from a parent to a child. You know how some children look like a great deal like their parents and some don't? Sight is like that: it's strong in some but not in others." She leaned in close. "Jem, I wouldn't be a true friend to you if I didn't warn you: if your Sight is this strong, there could be consequences if you keep pushing it away."

"Like what?"

"It's hard to say. The Light is your birthright, a gift knitted into every part of you. Shutting it out makes you…not quite yourself. But whatever that might look like, I can't say."

"But Margery, even if I go to Cornwall tomorrow, I still need some way to fend off the magic. It's a long journey with birds and animals and fish all the way from here to there."

"True." A tiny line formed between Margery's eyebrows, and she said, "Very well, then, let me give you the same help my granny gave to me: have you something or someone you love more than anything?" Her blue eyes in her white face were like bits of sky.

"Yes," I said, "You. Da and Mum and Jamie are dead. They can't call me back. All I have is you. You are my heart."

She pulled me into her arms. "Oh, my sweet girl. Such a time you've had of it in your short life. Very well: if seeing my face can keep you safe and on the ground, then use me as your anchor. If you feel yourself yearning for the sky, put my face before you." I felt less shuddery in her arms, less scattered. Safe. Home.

"This is nice."

"And yet I feel sad, Jem."

I pulled away. "Why?"

She began to finger-comb my hair. She said, "Because you don't want what I would give anything to have back. There's no doubt that Sight sets a person apart from others. It's hard to be different. Still, losing my Sight was the worst thing that ever happened to me except for losing my husband at Culloden."

"Truly?" It didn't make sense that anybody would prefer seeing visions and being yanked into birds over being normal.

"Truly. I might someday find another man to marry, but my Sight is gone for good."

"But with your Sight gone, you don't have to worry about flying away."

"You're right. Without Sight I can't fly. I can't spin a line betwixt myself and any living thing and speak to it by touch. I can't see into the future or nestle in so close to plants I can feel them growing."

I stared. "Sight gives you the power to do all that? Can Granny Kestrel do those things?"

"Aye. That's what she'd teach you. And that's what makes me sad, that you would spurn a gift like that."

"Oh." It sounded like a fairytale. What if *that* were my life? Did I want it to be? If that were my life, could I be a doctor as well? *No,* I told myself. *If I could do all those things, I would be too strange for London. Too different.* Margery's blue eyes were so full of hope that I hated to disappoint her. But I had to. As gently as I could, I said, "Well, I'm grateful Granny Kestrel taught you how to help me stay safe, but all the same, I don't want to meet her."

"Why not?"

"Because if I met her, I'd be in Cornwall instead of here, and here is where I want to be."

"Don't forget, you still have to convince the doctor," Margery said.

"Convince me of what?" Dr. Abernathy said, opening the door for Mrs. Pierce, who bore a tray. "Thank you, Mrs. Pierce," he said, "you may go. Close the door." He waited until her footsteps retreated, then he turned back to us. "Well?"

"I don't want to go to Cornwall," I said.

"I don't want you to die," he answered. "I win. Drink your broth."

"Margery thinks I can resist my Sight."

"That hasn't been working, as we all know," he said. "Pick up your spoon."

The broth smelled lovely, so I obeyed. "I didn't have any tools to help me before, but now I do." I spooned up some broth. It was delicious. "Mrs. Pierce didn't make this, did she," I said.

"No. She ordered it from the tavern. Mrs. Jamison, explain what Jem means when she talks of tools."

Margery explained how I planned to block my Sight. His eyebrows mashed together above his nose, so Margery said, "Remember, doctor, this approach has worked for her before. Remember when she told Patch 'Don't see me' and he didn't? I'll teach her how to hide in her mind as well." She set down my empty bowl on the tray and took hold of my hands. "Jem, can you imagine a—let's see, how about a cave?"

I recalled a little cave I'd played in back home in the woods near Lamesley. For some reason I couldn't remember now, I used to hide in the dark just around the first bend. "All right. I've imagined a cave to hide in," I said, "Now what?"

"If your Sight comes on too strong, imagine yourself in that cave with a blanket over your head. Stay there until it feels safe to come out. Go there now so we know you can do it." She paused. "Well? Open your eyes and tell me."

Her voice seemed muffled. I opened my eyes. Everything in the room seemed duller, like at night when something red looks gray and something yellow looks white. "It's so dull. I can't see colors very well, Margery."

"And there's a consequence," Margery murmured. She sighed. "Well, I seem to remember the world going gray for me too, but it didn't last forever. You should be able to see colors again. Eventually." Dr. Abernathy crossed his arms over his chest. "Doctor, you can order Jem to go to Cornwall, and part of me wishes you would. I would love to see what Jem could become with proper training."

"But?" he said.

"But a person with Sight must want it, and Jem doesn't," Margery said. "So there we are." She paused. "Just remember, Jem, if you ever change your mind, you must promise to tell us so we can send you straightaway to my Gran. Otherwise, you'll end up like me."

"I should be delighted if Jem ended up like you," Dr. Abernathy said. Margery's eyes flew to his face. "Er…that is…without Sight." He fixed his eyes on me. "All right, Jem: I am willing to have you try these new techniques to control your Sight provided you agree to go to Cornwall immediately the first time you…get lost again. Do you agree?" They waited.

"Yes. Thank you, sir."

So it was that, for the foreseeable future, I must be vigilant. From now on, I mustn't look when a flock of pigeons on the wing turned in unison to settle on a rooftop like snowflakes, or when a peregrine's wings kissed the clouds. I must keep Margery's face fresh in my mind. I must keep my wits about me. *I can do it*, I thought.

CHAPTER 2

DECEMBER 1758

Sour and Sweet

Nothing is harder than not looking at something. If you hear a noise at night, even if you're afraid, you have to look. If everyone is craning their necks at something down the way, you crane yours to see what they've caught sight of. Most people turn away when they realize they've spotted something foul: a rotting dog carcass full of maggots, a mouthful of blackened teeth, a puddle of dead fish left on the bank of the Thames.

I don't turn away, usually. Even the first time I found the doctor in the cellar dissecting a cadaver and wanted to run, part of me wanted to look. Ugly things are good for learning.

But if vile things are hard to turn away from, imagine how much harder it is to turn away from things like a blue sky or a thrush singing in a tree or a flock of swans on the water. That's what I had to do. I kept my head down when I went out and watched the path ahead of me. I counted out loud when the birds sang their morning greetings to the sun, and kept myself close to my hidey-hole, both prisoner and gaoler. I didn't like it at all, didn't like facing the world with my heart closed, didn't like feeling as though I walked about swathed in cotton.

I chafed under my self-imposed restrictions. When I ran errands for Dr. Abernathy, I allowed myself to look in the shop windows on Bond Street and the bustle of Piccadilly, but whenever I came to a place that might have any kind of animal, especially birds, like a square with a patch of garden or even a row of trees, I made myself count out loud or sing. I made up stories. This behavior garnered notice, so to avoid being pegged as a lunatic, I started carrying a folded piece of paper in my hand as though I were a messenger so thick he had to mumble his directions over and over. I felt like a poor player on the stage, but it worked. Fewer people paid attention to me. Once, when I stopped to buy a penny tart to eat on the way, the girl who sold it pointed at my paper and said, "Instead of eating tarts, you should hurry along and deliver that. Y' might pick up a coin for your trouble if y' do."

I no longer spent Mondays at the apothecary shop helping Margery make medicines in case Patch was watching the shop. He'd already tried to kidnap me once, and we didn't intend to give him a second chance. Not going to the shop, however, meant the doctor could give me other things to do. I cut bandages and wound them, and I cleaned instruments with vinegar after his calls so they would be ready for the next call at a moment's notice. Vinegar is not my favorite smell, nor was it Mrs. Pierce's, so she did not allow me to disinfect the doctor's tools in her kitchen. The only good thing about working with vinegar was that my headaches eased. I thought the odor must carve paths in my brain so air could get in. I didn't ask the doctor about it, because then he would know I had headaches and have something new to worry about.

What the doctor called my disinfection station sat on a table in the dusty, unused parlor off the doctor's front room. I frequently had to step over to the window to get away from the vinegar smell, which is where Dr. Abernathy found me when he came in one Monday at dinner time.

"What are you doing over there, Jem?" he asked.

I returned to my table. "Breathing, Sir."

He came closer, waving his handkerchief before his face. "It is pungent, isn't it? Why don't you work over by the window and leave it cracked open? Put more coal in the grate. You'll be able to finish faster if you don't have to keep getting up for air."

Behind his back, I rolled my eyes. "Thank you, I shall," I said. "But your tools look perfectly clean without being dunked, see? Look at this shiny lancet; I haven't even put it in the basin yet."

"Put it in. Give it a good soak."

"But the vinegar stinks, sir." I waved my hand before my face. "Badly. Why do I have to do this?"

"You told me you and Franklin looked at scrapings from your teeth under his microscope," the doctor said. "What did you see?"

Had he even heard what I'd said? "We saw animalcules swimming around."

He nodded. "A Dutch scientist named Van Leeuwenhoek saw the same animalcules under his microscope fifty years ago and discovered he could kill them with vinegar."

"Your tools have animalcules on them?" I dropped the lancet into the vinegar.

"It's possible. One of Franklin's friends here in London took an egg yolk, mixed it with water, and put half the solution in a phial all by itself and the other half in another phial along with a thread he'd dipped in a rotten egg. He stoppered both phials shut. In a few days, he saw that the yolk stoppered up with the bit of thread went bad much faster than the yolk in the other phial."

"So…if I didn't disinfect your tools, animalcules that jump onto them from one person might jump off them to another person?"

"It's possible. Franklin showed me a letter from an acquaintance of his who thinks smallpox is caused by animalcules. What if every sickness is caused by animalcules?"

I thought of all the dirty beds and instruments I'd seen, all the blood and corruption on other doctors' hands at hospitals, all the filth and rot in the streets. I said, "If that were true and could be proved, everything would change." I looked at my basin. "Every doctor in town would do this. The whole city would smell of vinegar."

"Precisely," he said. "But it is not proved; it is merely a suspicion of my own. Still, I should rather err on the side of caution, wouldn't you?" He gestured at my array of tools and my basin of vinegar. "Let's move this over to the window so you can carry on."

That night the doctor took delivery of a cadaver for medical study, and the next day in the cellar I learned how to sew up a cut in its arm. It was juicier than sewing cloth. The doctor insisted we disinfect our hands with vinegar afterward, and I decided the smell of it wasn't as bad as having animalcules from a cadaver swarming all over me.

I'd had no chance to talk any more about animalcules with my teacher, Benjamin Franklin of Pennsylvania; he had cancelled my weekly lesson for three weeks straight. The Penn family's lawyers had told him that their clients made the laws for Pennsylvania, that the Assembly, Franklin's employers, had no power to do anything, and that the Penns wouldn't talk to Franklin any more. And so Franklin devoted his days to writing stern letters and meeting with influential people. He had no time for me. The last time I'd seen Franklin had been in the middle of November just after Patch tried to kidnap me outside the apothecary shop. When I'd told Franklin about Patch—I called him "Patch" because he wore an eyepatch over one eye, but he called himself Mr. Duncan—Franklin had said, "Dear me, Jem, this is a difficulty. Why, this Patch fellow could be anywhere. What if he followed you here? That wouldn't do at all."

"I know."

"Craven Street should be a bolt-hole to which you can retreat where Patch wouldn't think to look for you."

"Margery thinks he might leave me alone now that he's tipped his hand."

"Doubtful," Franklin said. "In my experience, a person who is up to no good and stands to profit by it doesn't give up the game if the profit is great enough." He rang the bell for Myrtle, and when she came, asked her to bring tea. "The converse also is true, Jem," he said.

"The converse?"

"Some men are loath to help others unless there is a profit to be made by it. For instance, the only member of the Privy Council with half a brain and all of a heart is the Earl of Mansfield. The rest of the Privy Council does not appear to understand that Americans are Englishmen who live across an ocean but retain their rights as Englishmen. England takes our money and goods but closes her eyes to our needs. Their disdain concerns me."

"Are they rude to you?" I asked.

He rubbed his eyes with his fingers and sighed. "They suffer me, Jem, they suffer me, but worse than that is the way they look down their noses at me whenever I have an audience with them as though I were a naughty schoolboy. Such scorn does not bode well for future relations between the Colonies and England."

When I left Franklin that day, he said he mightn't be able to meet with me again for a while, as he had to deal with "matters of diplomacy," which meant making trouble for the Penns. He'd asked if he could look at my cameo under his microscope—he was like a magpie that way, always noticing things he wanted to hold on to for a while. I'd expected to get it back the next time I saw him, but I hadn't seen him since mid-November.

I fretted about the cameo. Whenever I looked at it, I pictured it nestled in the hollow of my mother's throat and saw her smiling face just above it. The cameo was my only memento from when I'd had a family, the only token I had of my mother. I wanted it back.

During Advent, Dr. Abernathy and I sat one evening in the doctor's front room, he catching up his casebook and me copying into my own book a recipe for bitters: watercress (a peppery green that grows in streams), wormwood, angelica root, meadow crocus, and horseradish steeped in distilled gin. Bitters are good for gout, and the doctor wanted Margery to mix up a fresh batch for Violet Campbell, the Dowager Duchess of Glencoe, his sister Janet's mother-in-law. The doctor would see the lady over the Christmas holiday, for he planned to spend a week with his sister's family. It was a long time for him to be gone, but Chelsea was close. If a patient needed him, he could return to London quickly. I presented a problem, because I didn't want to go.

"Don't be ridiculous, Jem," he admonished. "Of course you will come with me."

"But it's only a few days, sir," I said. "If there is food in the larder and coal for the fires, I'll be fine. I can read. I can study. I can stop at Craven Street and get my mother's cameo back from Mr. Franklin."

"No, you can't visit Franklin. He is going to the Shipley's'—he's got a parcel of paints for their little Georgiana." He looked up from his casebook. "Why does Franklin have your cameo?"

"He thought it was interesting. He wanted to look at it under his microscope."

"Surely Franklin has enough to do without needing to hold your treasure for ransom."

"He doesn't want a ransom," I said, "he just wants to look at it once it's clean."

"Why didn't he clean it with vinegar straightaway so he could look at it without having to keep it?"

"I-I don't know." *What is Franklin about?* "Maybe he doesn't like to use vinegar. Many people don't."

The doctor started to smile, but he pursed his lips instead. "Well, let me know if you want me to remind Franklin to give it back. As far as Christmas is concerned, I'm afraid you cannot stay here alone. Mrs. Pierce will be with her own family. What if something should happen if I were gone and you were here alone? What if Patch somehow found his way here? What if a bird landed on the walk?" He narrowed his eyes and said, "I must say, it seems odd that you want to be alone at Christmas."

"I don't want to," I said as I smoothed my fingers along the barbs of my quill. "But I shall have to be a boy round the clock. What if someone learns the truth? Wouldn't I have to leave you, then?"

"So that's it: you're afraid my sister's family will find out you're a girl."

I bit my lower lip.

"Jem, my sister has four boys. I imagine you will spend much of your time with them, and I shall ask my sister if you may have your own bedchamber. We adults will be too busy to pry into your affairs, I can assure you. So your secret is safe. I've already written to my sister about you. You're coming. And that is that!"

To be honest, I wasn't entirely sorry that Dr. Abernathy insisted I spend Christmas with him and his family, because celebrating the holiday in a big house might take my mind off what Christmas reminded me of every year: change. Two years ago, I'd spent Christmas back in Lamesley with Da and Mum and James. By the next Christmas, Da was dead and we'd moved to London, so I'd spent the holiday with my mother and brother and Margery's family. This Christmas, Mum and James were gone. Since the age of eight, it seemed, my losses were measured out for me every Christmas.

A lesser difficulty was that Mum had taught me proper manners—for a girl. I needed instruction. I said, "Sir, would you...teach me how to behave at your sister's house? Your sister is a lady. I'm not certain what I should do when I'm introduced. Do I bow? Do I kiss her hand? How should I behave around the duchess? Will I dine with the adults or with the children or with the servants? How should I excuse myself to leave the room?"

The doctor frowned. "We have been lax in your social training, haven't we?"

"We've been busy," I mumbled.

"Still, I should have thought," he answered. "Put down that quill before you strip off all the barbs. Now then, first things first: My sister, Janet Abernathy, married the younger son of the Duke of Glencoe, who has a secondary title, the Marquess of Luddingham. The family name is Campbell. The titles work like this: the duke's older son, Trafford Campbell, is Lord Luddingham until his father dies, whereupon Trafford becomes the duke. The younger son, my sister's husband, is simply Lord Richard Campbell, and so my sister is Lady Richard Campbell, or simply Lady Richard. But she prefers Mrs. Campbell."

"So I may call her Mrs. Campbell."

"Yes."

"What may I call him?"

"He prefers Lord Richard. Now, stand up." I stood and faced him. "When you are introduced to him, shake hands. When you are introduced to a lady, if she offers her hand with the back facing up, like this, she expects you to take it lightly in your own hand and bow over it. Kissing the hand is not required. If the lady offers her hand with the palm facing to the side, like this, she expects you to shake it, very briefly and gently, combined with a slight bow of the head. Let's try. I shall play my sister."

He faced me. "Janet Campbell, may I present Jem Connolly, my assistant. Jem, this is my sister, Mrs. Campbell." He held out his hand, back up. I bowed over it.

In a high-pitched voice, he said, "How do you do, Mr. Connolly?" I giggled.

In his own voice, Dr. Abernathy said, "The bow was good, Jem," he said, "but you will be expected to speak as well. If she says, 'How do you do?' you repeat the same back to her. If she says, 'Pleased to make your acquaintance,' you can say, 'The pleasure is mine.' But, really, you don't have to worry about Janet. She's a kind woman. All right?"

"Yes, sir."

"Now, then, the duchess prefers to be called 'Your Grace.' That is also the proper form to be used by persons who rank beneath her, which means you and me."

"Isn't it different for you? You're a member of the family."

"I generally call her 'Madam,'" the doctor said. He smiled. "She can be quite direct in her speech, but don't let it bother you. I shall leap in if she decides to question you, which she might well do. I amuse her. She approves of Janet, and, by association, Janet's brother. One can hope her good regard will extend to you. As for whether you'll dine with the adults or with the children, let's wait and see what Janet has decided, all right?"

"All right." In case I dined with the duchess, I reviewed what I knew about using cutlery; basically one started on the outside and worked in. If only Mum were here to help me!

Christmas Day fell on Monday, so the doctor said we would depart for his sister's home early on Saturday morning. We would attend church at St. Mary Abbots on Sunday, and I could visit the grave that held my mother and my baby brother, both dead of the putrid sore throat last April, just eight months ago. I still hadn't got used to their being gone. Even now, whenever I learned something interesting, for an instant I thought I must tell my mother—and then had to swallow past the lump in my throat when I remembered that she wasn't there to tell.

Before we went to bed, the doctor surprised me: he asked me to stand on a piece of paper so he could trace round my feet. He said he'd give the outline to a cobbler in Chelsea so he could make boots for me. "The boots will be your Christmas present," Dr. Abernathy said. And that stopped me short. I had no gift for him or Margery or Mr. Franklin!

The next day was Friday, when the doctor usually set me a case to study in the morning. In the afternoon, if the doctor didn't need me to accompany him to London Hospital, Mrs. Pierce often gave me some unpleasant task to do such as scouring her cooking pots with sand. I hurried through my case and scrawled a note about my whereabouts at the top of my diagnosis. Then I sneaked upstairs before the doctor came home for dinner—and before Mrs. Pierce gave me a job. I filled my pockets and shoes with some coins I'd squirreled away and slipped out to the shops to buy Christmas presents.

It might seem odd that a person my age would buy a Christmas present for an adult, because usually it is the other way round, but I wanted to show my appreciation to my mentors. Without the doctor and Mr. Franklin, I might be in a workhouse. Without Margery, I would still think my visions meant I was going mad. Instead, I had a great deal of freedom for a girl, I was learning medicine, and I had a home. Best of all, the doctor hadn't said anything more about sending me to Cornwall. So I gladly spent a few coins on Dr. Abernathy, Mr. Franklin, and Margery.

For the doctor, I bought a book of six poems by Mr. Thomas Gray. Each poem had pictures to illustrate it, and the pictures weren't of veins and lumps like his casebook, either. One picture showed a swimming cat atop the title, "Ode On the Death of a Favourite Cat Drowned in a Tub of GoldFishes." The bookseller read the poem out loud in a rumbly voice much nicer to listen to than the vicar's (which was high and thin). The bookseller's shiny bald head caught the light from the lamps as he read out the last stanza of the goldfish poem so loudly everybody in the shop turned their heads:

From hence, ye beauties, undeceived,

Know, one false step is ne'er retrieved,

And be with caution bold.

Not all that tempts your wandering eyes

And heedless hearts, is lawful prize;

Nor all that glisters gold.

A lady standing with a gentleman said "Hmph!" and laid down the book she'd been perusing. She floated toward the door. Her gentleman friend tipped his hat and winked at the bookseller before dashing to hold the door for her.

When they were gone, the bookseller bent over his rounded belly, looked at me over his spectacles, and said, "Let this be a lesson to you, young gentleman."

"Lesson?" I said.

"Beware the wiles of women!" the bookseller said.

"But, sir…isn't this is a poem about a cat?"

"On the surface, the *surface*! If one wishes to appreciate poetry, one must dive be*neath* the surface like a leviathan, for a poem will not yield its treasure to any but the bold. You see here the word 'Beauties'?" I nodded. "That is a reference to the *fe*male of the species."

"Oh." I looked closer. "It says beauties have wandering eyes."

He nodded, laying a hand on my shoulder. "Beauties are *women*, dear boy, and this poem conveys the e*te*rnal difficulty of our sharing the Earth with *them*."

I wanted to laugh. If only he knew what I was! I said, "Females have heedless hearts?"

"*Every* female I have ever *met* was *heed*less." A laugh bubbled up from my belly, but I managed to hold it in. I bought the book and looked forward to telling the doctor about the bookseller. Dr. Abernathy and I hadn't had a great deal to laugh about together, considering the deaths in my family and our line of work, so I thought poetry might be a nice change.

For Mr. Franklin, I bought a live box so we could look at insects. He'd brought his live box out to Mrs. Stephenson's garden to release the spider he'd been looking at, but when somebody came to call, he got distracted and forgot to bring the box back in, and Mrs. Stevenson's housemaid Myrtle tripped over it and broke it to bits.

For Margery, I bought two yards of a pretty, light muslin sprigged with tiny flowers. I planned to cut it into circles, large and small, about thirty in all. Thick embroidery thread in a simple running stitch around each outside edge would make a little sack that she could open and close—thirty little pouches she could sell herbs in. I'd have to send her present by messenger because we still weren't sure if Patch had stopped spying on the shop, but at least Margery would know I was thinking about her while we waited to find out whether it was safe for me to go back. And she would know I loved her very much since I was willing to pick up a needle and thread for her sake.

For Mrs. Pierce, I bought a paper of lemon drops, which I gave to her when I got home. I didn't think they'd sweeten her temperament, but I hoped they might make her forget I'd sneaked out of the house. It didn't work.

The following Tuesday morning, before Dr. Abernathy and I went on our weekly visit to Bedlam, a messenger delivered a letter from Margery. The doctor frowned at my jumping up and down in the foyer and made me stand still before he would read out the message, which said:

Dear Dr. Abernathy and Jem,

I should be most grateful if one or both of you could drive me and Mr. Galt to the Chelsea Physick Garden on Wednesday, the thirteenth. Mr. Miller sent word to Mr. Galt today that two boxes of specimens have come from Mr. Bartram in Philadelphia by Captain Lyon. Mr. Miller is eager to open them, but he has invited Mr. Galt to be present when they are opened, which Mr. Galt has long desired. I hoped that you, Dr. Abernathy, might be willing to drive us to Chelsea with your horse and trap, if you have no pressing business on that day. And so, this letter is addressed to both of you: Would you care to go to Chelsea on Wednesday? If not convenient for either or both, please to inform us of same.

Your most humble and obedient servant and friend,

Margery Jamison

Dr. Abernathy said, "John Bartram is Franklin's friend. He sends seeds and roots from America to Chelsea. Well, I can't go to Chelsea tomorrow, I've a lecture." He looked at me. "But I don't need to ask if you want to go."

"Could I?"

"I suppose, since Patch hasn't been seen or heard for weeks. Still, you must drive to the back of the shop. Don't show your face in the street. Take Giselle. I can catch a hackney to my lecture. You're not worried about driving the horse?"

"Not at all. She and I are good friends."

I didn't tell him Giselle and I had an understanding, because I knew Dr. Abernathy felt uneasy about my perambulations outside my body. Still, my connection with the doctor's horse was different from the other connections I'd made with animals, because Giselle kept herself *to* herself. She kept the two of us separate.

I'd discovered my link with Giselle by accident two weeks before. The doctor and I had just settled into the trap for our weekly crosstown journey to Bedlam to see our usual patients when the doctor exclaimed, "Oh! I've forgotten Lady Emily's *Chronicle*. I must fetch it or we'll both catch the sharp side of her tongue." While he dashed back into the house, I waited in the trap and felt a sudden longing to see Margery. Giselle perked up her ears and set off round the square.

"No, Giselle," I said, reaching for the reins, "we're to wait for the doctor," and she walked all the way back to our door. The doctor stood there waiting for us.

"What was that?" he said, getting in.

"I don't know, sir. She just started walking all by herself. I didn't touch her."

"None of that, my girl," he said to Giselle as he settled himself and took up the reins. "I decide where and when we go," and off we went to Moorfields. As we passed Smithfield Market, near the apothecary, I thought how easy it would be to detour to see Margery—and at Pye Corner, Giselle tried to pull north toward Smithfield and the shop instead of continuing east. The doctor got her turned, but I began to wonder whether Giselle and I had formed a connection like the one I'd briefly suffered with the lions in the Tower of London menagerie, and had, I confess, enjoyed with my peregrine. If the horse and I had connected, though, it didn't feel the same. Giselle didn't push or pull or make herself known in any way. She felt like somebody you didn't expect to see turning up at your door.

When we got home that day, the doctor left me to unharness Giselle. When she and I were alone, I decided to test whether she could hear me. First, I put Margery's face before me, to guard against Giselle's…taking me. Then I laid my hand on her shoulder, and the joy in her heart flowed over me like moonlight on a path. I imagined her—I saw her—running free in the green hills back home in Lamesley. Her ears pricked up, and she swung her head round to nudge me with her nose as if to say, "Let's go, then!"

Yes, I thought, *she* can *hear me*. So she must have heard me before now, even though what I got from her was big feelings more than specific ideas, rather like seeing the light of a fire through a blanket. Was Sight somehow leaking out of me? I conveyed to Giselle that we were not going to Lamesley, and her head turned back to her oats. She became a horse again, just like that, and I couldn't even feel her any more. Could I learn to turn the Sight on and off like that?

Maybe domesticated animals knew humans so well they had no desire to link with us and blocked us out, but wild animals came close to Sighted people like me out of curiosity and couldn't keep clear of us. Maybe that was why I'd flown with the pigeon and the falcon, especially if I were leaking Sight: they'd been lured by my magic, and we had melted together like one raindrop running into another on a windowpane.

Or maybe each animal reacted to Sight according to its own nature; shy animals had to be coaxed, but predators like lions barged in as though they had the right to do whatever they pleased. If that was how it worked, perhaps I could let down my guard in the city when I met animals accustomed to humans. They wouldn't wonder what I was. Wild animals would be the ones likeliest to flee— or to shove in—*if* my theory was correct.

How could I test my theory? If I made a tether, could I try communicating with some animal other than Giselle? Just a bit?

Now, at last, I understood why Margery wanted me to go to Cornwall. It wasn't only to keep me safe inside my own body. Margery wanted me to explore my magic, and she thought I should want it, too.

Now that I knew it was possible to contact somebody like Giselle without being taken away, I *did* want to know more about my Sight. If only there were some way for me to learn without having to drop everything and go to Cornwall.

CHAPTER 3

DECEMBER 1758

A Snake in the Garden

On the morning of the thirteenth, I harnessed Giselle and we headed into the dawn. When we got close enough to Smithfield Market to smell the manure on the breeze, Giselle turned off and headed straight for Galt's Apothecary Shop. I pulled my neckerchief up and my hat down and drove Giselle round to the back. Margery's potted plants were gone (hauled indoors for the winter, I guessed). A big, new barrel, the kind they call a hogshead, stood beside a heavy new door inside a new wooden doorframe that replaced the old one Patch had kicked in. My heart fluttered like a bird, I was so glad to be back.

Margery opened the door before I knocked. "Abernathy is here, Henry," she called over her shoulder. She glanced up at the trap, then said, sounding a tad disappointed, "Isn't the doctor coming?"

"He had a lecture today," I said.

"Oh. Have you plans for Christmas?"

From inside, Mr. Galt called, "Did you lock the front door, Margery?"

"Aye, I did," she shouted, "and I put up the sign as well. Come along."

"We're going to Dr. Abernathy's sister's for Christmas," I told Margery.

"Good. I was worried that you might be all alone, the two of you." Mr. Galt came out then, his hand groping along the doorframe. Smooth as butter, Margery placed his hand in the crook of her elbow and helped him into the back of the trap. I folded a blanket round his legs while Margery locked the back door, and I stole a glance at Henry's face. His head bent toward me but his cataracts had turned his eyes white. His eyesight was very bad, which was why Margery had moved from her father's house to the room upstairs where I used to live.

Frowning, I helped Margery in, hopped up, and clicked my tongue at Giselle. Off we went along Holborn, back the way I'd come, all the way to Tyburn Road. When we drove along Hyde Park, Margery exclaimed, "Oh, I always forget how nice it is to get out of the smoke and noise. Even in winter, I do love to get out in the air! All right, Henry?"

"Fine," Mr. Galt said. "Well, young man, I never did have a proper talk with you. You're up and down Margery's stairs before I can grab you for a gabble. Jem is your name, I think?"

"Yes, sir." *Good thing he doesn't recognize my voice,* I thought. It wouldn't do for Mr. Galt to find out I was Jenna Connolly, the little girl who used to live above his shop. He would be hurt I hadn't told him straightaway, but, as Franklin says, "Three can keep a secret if two of them are dead."

"Surname?"

My mind went blank as water. "Abernathy," Margery answered. "Jem is a distant relation, isn't that right?"

"I-I'm from the north," I stammered.

"I see. Going to be a doctor, then?" Mr. Galt asked.

"I wish to be one, sir, but there is a great deal to learn."

"Abernathy must keep you hopping from sunrise to sunset, for we haven't see you at the shop since the Lord Mayor's Show," Mr. Galt said. "Is Abernathy afraid you'll be snatched off the street again?"

"P-possibly, sir."

"How goes it with the doctor, Jem?" Margery said.

"I am learning something new every day," I said. "I learned last week how to sew up a cut. The doctor asks me once a week or more to diagnose a patient's problem out of a book. He's got me disinfecting his tools with vinegar."

"I thought I caught a whiff of vinegar!" Margery said. "Still, vinegar's not as bad as asafoetida, I daresay. Watch out, Jem, here comes a carriage, and the driver's taking it right down the middle of the road."

"Giselle, left, please," I said. "Nothing smells as bad as asafoetida."

"Fleet ditch does," Mr. Galt said. "If you're as busy as all that, Jem, why did Dr. Abernathy give you leave to drive us to Chelsea today?"

"He says Christmas is coming and the use of me for a day as your driver is his Christmas present to you. He knew you wanted you to see Mr. Miller open the boxes from America."

"How kind," Margery said.

"I doubt I'll see much," Mr. Galt said, "but I hope Miller lets me sit close so I get a whiff as they open each one. Smellin' them boxes is as close as I shall ever get to the Colonies, I daresay. But you, Margery, you could still go to America, if you'd a mind to."

"Me? No, not now," Margery said. "and what should you do for a helper if I did, hm?" To me, she explained, "Mr. Jamison and I thought to try life in the Colonies, but when he died, I hadn't the courage to go by myself."

"America's all wilderness with cities hanging on to the coast like sailors to a spar when their ship goes down," Mr. Galt said. "'Tis too wild for the likes of me, but the lad here might do well there once he's got his learning in. Would you like to go to America, boy?"

I said, "Maybe someday. I know an American gentleman, a Mr. Franklin, who hails from Philadelphia. He says it is just as pretty as London, and cleaner besides." Margery nudged me and eased her finger up to her lips, but it was too late.

"You know Franklin?" Mr. Galt said. He leaned forward and stuck his head between me and Margery. "I used to know a sweet girl who had lessons of that very gentleman. Oh, the things they got up to."

Now what should I say? I didn't want him to know Jenna and I were the same person. My mouth dried to dust while Mr. Galt waited for a response. I couldn't have spit out two words just then if somebody had held a knife to my throat. Margery blurted, "Dr. Abernathy is acquainted with Mr. Franklin too, don't you recall, Henry? No doubt Abernathy thought Jem should have science lessons. Is that it, Jem?"

I sucked in air and wheezed, "Yes, the doctor arranged for me to have lessons with Mr. Franklin."

"Hm," Mr. Galt said, and sat back. Margery commandeered the conversation, leaving me to guide Giselle and calm my pounding heart. We drove south along King's Road. Giselle smelled the river and picked up her feet. Water is a magnet for a horse that's been working, but I didn't need a special bond with Giselle to know that.

Margery told me to drive Giselle to the gate of the Chelsea Physick Garden nearest the river. We handed the reins to one of the gardeners, who asked how long we intended to stay. When Margery told him Mr. Miller had invited us specially to see Mr. Bartram's boxes opened up, the gardener said he'd water Giselle while she waited for us and that he hoped to see the boxes opened himself.

"Mr. Bartram must not send boxes very often if getting one is such an event for everybody," I said as we walked through the garden toward Mr. Miller's study.

"It's to do with the shipping season," Margery said. "Seeds come on in late summer and fall. Bartram's got to gather them, package them, and send them, but very few ships sail the Atlantic in winter. Then there's the war as well. When the French seize our ships, Mr. Bartram's seeds and roots go with the rest of the cargo to France."

"They don't seize many, my girl," Mr. Galt said, "and for every ship they take, our navy builds two more."

"That's as may be, Henry," Margery said.

"Give us your arm, boy," Mr. Galt said to me. "I've forgot how these paths turn." Our feet scuffed up a few wet leaves, but I didn't have to worry about Mr. Galt slipping on snow or ice because the garden's being next to the river and inside high brick walls kept it warmer here than the rest of the city. It was so warm in the garden that the tips of green leaves poked out of the ground in the most sheltered spots.

"I wish I could come here more often," Margery said.

"What are those big trees over there?" I asked.

"Those are cedars of Lebanon that have been here almost since the garden started, some seventy-five years, I think. See that building underneath?"

"The one with big windows facing the river?"

"Aye. That's a greenhouse where they keep the tender plants that came from countries that never have winter. It's heated when it's cold like this."

"With stoves?"

"On each end, yes, and the heat is sent snaking up the wall through a curved flue. If you put your hand on the bricks, you'd think they'd been sitting in the sun all day."

"Can we move along?" Mr. Galt said. "I'm cold."

"Oh, aye, sorry," Margery said, and we began walking again. "But what I love about the greenhouse is the hotbeds. Mr. Miller's built beds inside the greenhouse some four feet deep, filled with tanner's bark. He's got steps going up from them like theater seats all the way to the ceiling."

"What is tanner's bark?"

"Bark from oak trees," Mr. Galt said, "Miller gets it from leather tanners."

"It gives off heat as it rots, just like a dung heap," Margery said. "Mr. Miller puts pots of tender plants right in the hotbed and less tender plants on the steps leading up and out. The whole greenhouse stays warm all winter as the bark rots away. I'd like to try tanner's bark in that big barrel outside Henry's back door if nobody claims it."

"I thought you'd put the barrel there yourself," I said.

"No, it just appeared there one day," Margery said, "but I put my plants on it over the summer and nobody complained, so I don't complain either."

We arrived at Mr. Miller's study, a large room with floor-to-ceiling bookcases and a row of windows along the south wall looking out on the garden. Several trees stood in pots at the windows, including living lemon trees with real lemons growing right on them. Lemons growing in winter! Long tables arranged end to end ran the length of the room. Two microscopes perched at either end like gargoyles, surrounded by a litter of leaves and stems and seeds. In the middle, two wooden crates sat side by side. Seven apothecaries in their black robes stood near the boxes, along with four gentlemen in very fine wigs, all of them talking and laughing as though they were at a party. I counted sixteen people besides us, including five gardeners in aprons and caps.

When we walked in, a gentleman with a long nose and pudgy cheeks, very plain clothing, and no wig bustled over to greet us. "Henry Galt, I'm delighted to see you again," he said, pumping Mr. Galt's hand.

"And I, you, Philip Miller," Mr. Galt said. "You know my assistant, Margery Jamison, and this here is Jem Abernathy, who drove us here."

"How do you do?" Mr. Miller said. "Mrs. Jamison, would you care to sit beside Henry, right next to the boxes? The boy can stand, I think?" Mr. Miller led Mr. Galt and Margery to chairs, and I stood behind Margery.

Sylvanus Bevan, an apothecary friend of Mr. Galt's, came up to shake Henry's hand, then asked, "Mrs. Jamison, how go your studies?"

"Well, thank you," she said. "I'll be ready for my test."

"We're looking forward to your joining the Worshipful Society of Apothecaries." Mr. Bevan tipped his head to Margery, then turned to Mr. Galt. "Now, don't you go haring off before the main show," Mr. Bevan said, referring to Henry's having to miss the Lord Mayor's parade last fall when I'd run to tell him Patch had kicked in the back door of the shop.

"Not likely, Mr. Bevan," Mr. Galt said. "I've put up a door of good English oak, so the next thief who tries to kick it in will break his foot."

"Better his foot than your head," said Mr. Bevan.

Mr. Bevan returned to his place when Mr. Miller took his place and cleared his throat. "Welcome, friends, to the opening of the first Bartram's Boxes of the year of our Lord, 1758." Everyone applauded. "A special welcome to our hon-

ored guests, the worthy apothecaries on whose behalf we keep these gardens."
The apothecaries inclined their heads whilst Mr. Miller and the other gardeners
(and me and Margery and the gentlemen) applauded again. Mr. Miller laid a
hand on one of the boxes and said, "I have had these boxes under my roof for
five days, and I must confess it has been difficult not to open them."

"You're certain you didn't eke out the nails the minute the boxes come, just to
have a look?" asked Mr. Bevan. Some of the others chuckled.

"I was tempted," Mr. Miller said, smiling. "Mr. Wilmer, if you please?" A
gardener stepped around the tables to a stack of paper, a quill and a bottle of
ink. "Mr. Wilmer will keep a record as we unpack each box, and Mr. Johnson
will take each item and place it on the tables. I ask that everyone wait until all
the items are placed before stepping forward to examine them." He took up a
lever and carefully began to loosen the boards on both boxes. The nails creaked,
which told me they must have been wetted on the ship. "Collinson lost a large
shipment of boxes to the French this fall," Mr. Miller told us, "and our share
was lost with them. So I am glad Mr. Bartram sent these two boxes as a postscript or we might have gotten nothing at all until spring."

Mr. Miller finished and set all the boards aside.

"Aha!" he said. "A letter." He broke the seal and read out the letter,

27 September in the Year of Our Lord 1758

> *Greetings, Friend Miller, along with my prayers that*
> *these boxes find their way to thee. Mr. Collinson writes that he*
> *copyed out my last letter to thee, so I trust thee found it conge-*
> *nial, though I had no reply to it.*

Mr. Miller looked up from the letter. "The poor fellow. I wrote back to him
straightaway. My letter must have miscarried."

>*I am much obliged to thee for the books thou sent*
>*by Mr. Collinson, especially the copy of Hill's Herbal, which*
>*inspires my Billy to produce the drawings I herewith enclose on*
>*each packet of seeds to illustrate what thou may expect when*
>*each plant is mature.*

"How delightful!" Mr. Miller said.

>*I sent six boxes to Mr. Collinson in May, but he*
>*writes to tell me they did not arrive and asks if I have forgotten*
>*my old friend. Please convey to Mr. Collinson that I am ever*
>*his friend, but that friendship cannot bridge the chasm created*
>*by war. I fear Captain Lyon's ship is taken by the French.*

"I say!" Mr. Miller interjected. "How I pray this war would end so we might return to civilized communication!"

"Hear, hear," said Mr. Galt and a few of the others.

>*The seed I send in these boxes is divided by type, to*
>*wit:*

>*Seeds of Toxicohendron as thou requested, but be*
>*warned the seeds and plant carry oil that produces a rash that*
>*spreads and itches. I cannot imagine why my friend wishes to*
>*plant this noisome plant, which we call poison sumac, unless it*
>*be to provide forage for birds, which seem to suffer no ill effect*
>*from consuming it. But other plants are good forage for birds*
>*without causing harm to man. I beg thee to reconsider planting*

Toxicohendron, for once it doth take hold, it be harder to root out than sin.

Mr. Johnson took the packet of poison sumac seed by the tips of two fingers and placed it at the far end of the table.

Seeds for Gale Asplenifolia which we call sweet fern. It makes a berry good for scenting candles.

Seeds of evergreen Helliborine, which thou requested, along with Ladies slipper root and seed. Ladies slipper seeds germinate in Oak leaf litter but thou mayest not see seedlings for more than a year and, if it grow at all, it may not flower for five years. Pray, be patient. Share with Mr. Collinson if his be poorly, as it is his favorite.

Seeds of Lobelia cardinalis, thy favorite, and Golden Ragwort, good for lung ailments.

"I want some of that ragwort," Margery whispered to me. "It's good for women's ailments as well."

Mr. Miller lifted up another layer of moss, gave it to Mr. Johnson, and said, "Mr. Johnson, pray fetch a pair of bowls to hold the cones. Bartram has sent seeds of, let me see…yes—of the red cedar and the black birch."

After Mr. Johnson had filled the bowls, Mr. Miller continued,

Also bark of the Basswood, which the Natives use for bandages. Of roots I send Phlox maculate, Sweet William, and Sassafras root, which makes a fine tea, and roots of Ink-

berry. It likes wet, boggy places. Thou needest male and female both for flowers, which, if found by bees, makes a flavorful amber honey. This, too, may not germinate until the third year. Again, I urge patience.

Mr. Miller continued to read and to unpack until both boxes were empty, making sure Mr. Galt got a whiff of everything. "And that is all of the samples and seeds, my friends." Two of the gentlemen stepped toward the tables, but Mr. Miller said, "I have a little more of Bartram's letter if you would care to hear it?"

The gentlemen inclined their heads and stepped back. One drummed his fingers on the head of his cane. Mr. Miller smiled and read again,

Of patience: This day I measured my young Striped Maple which I brought out about seven years since from beyond our Blue Mountains and had advanced one foot in height. This year it shot three foot eight inches whereof it is delicately striped with white and red. Four inches farther the white gradually diminisheth from whence the remainder is a fine red to the top. Last year's shoot is a silver strike on a light green and the other year's shoot is silver on dark green. James admires it exceedingly.

Per a comment from Mr. Collinson that sending all the seeds in a box were too much trouble to separate, which remark greatly troubled me, as I had collected them over several hundred miles' travel, had dryed, pack'd, box'd and shipped them, all so he would have them to hand for his intimate

friends: I have packed all in sphagnum moss and all separat-
ed out and labeled as well with my Billy's drawings. If this
arrangement doth not please thee, pray inform me what thou
wouldst prefer, and I shall endeavor to find the time to comply
despite my efforts from sunrise to sunset to keep garden and
family thriving.

    Best regards and may Thee be Blessed with health
and heart. Thy Friend,

                          J. Bartram

Whilst everybody applauded, I whispered to Margery, "Mr. Bartram sounds cross."

Mr. Galt murmured, "Our Mr. Miller is so keen to get his hands on plants that he sometimes speaks to Bartram like he were a servant."

"Why, Henry, how do you know that?" Margery asked. She leaned closer.

"Because I just heard Bartram's letter read out, Margery," Mr. Galt whispered, the fug of his bad breath seeping into my nostrils, "and he talked three times about patience. I can put two and two together."

Mr. Miller smiled over his letter, then tucked it away as he said, "My friends, that is all. Please come and have a look at Billy Bartram's drawings, which are quite remarkable. Mr. Wilmer will write down which seeds you would like to try, and we shall do our best to accommodate you. I do recommend, however, that you allow us to grow the plants you want, as conditions here allow a bit more control over the result." Everyone dashed to the tables, the gentlemen and apothecaries fingering the packets and roots and the gardeners keeping watch. I wanted to look at the pictures Mr. Bartram's son had drawn, but with everyone gathered round the tables like a flock of crows on a carcass, I saw I must wait.

"May I go look out of the window?" I asked.

"I'll go with you," Margery said. "All right, Henry?"

"Aye, go," he said. Mr. Bevan moved to stand near Mr. Galt and began to describe one of Billy Bartram's drawings.

We wandered over to look out of the windows at the sleeping physick garden. We spoke of plants—the ones Margery had seen here in Chelsea before and the new American ones we'd learnt about today—until Mr. Miller joined us at the windows. "Mrs. Jamison, didn't you want to look at what Bartram sent?"

"I do, yes, but there's rather a crowd," Margery said. "I thought I'd wait a bit."

"We aren't used to having ladies with us on these occasions," said Mr. Miller. "My colleagues have quite forgot their manners. I shall ask them to make way for you."

He turned toward the group of men, but I had an idea that I thought would please Margery more.

"Excuse me, sir," I said. "If you please, may Mrs. Jamison and I take a turn through your greenhouse, the big heated one there, until these gentlemen have seen all they like?"

"Certainly, but you must let me show it to you myself," Mr. Miller said.

Margery turned a delighted face to him. "Would you? We should hate to take you away from your guests. It's no trouble?"

"Not at all," Mr. Miller said. "Mr. Wilmer can answer any questions our guests might have, and I rather wanted to make a place to start growing the inkberry, especially as it takes three years to germinate."

"I should tell Mr. Galt where we're going," Margery said.

"I believe Mr. Galt is occupied with Mr. Bevan," Mr. Miller said. We looked over at the two old apothecaries, Mr. Bevan leaning down to listen and Mr. Galt punctuating whatever he was saying with his hands. Mr. Miller offered a quick word to Mr. Wilmer, offered his arm to Margery, and off we walked into the chilly gray day, toward the greenhouse. The closer we got, the warmer the air became. By the time we got to the door, the air near the greenhouse felt more like March than December. Mr. Miller opened the greenhouse door and showed us in. I breathed deep. The air smelled of green, growing things, a dense aroma as if all the scent above a whole field of growing grain were concentrated inside four walls. Breathing the stink of London day after day, I'd forgotten what it was to take in air as green as this. Outside, a gardener trundled a wheelbarrow, his breath puffing out in clouds. Inside, we breathed summer.

Mr. Miller said, "As you can see, we have our most tender tropicals embedded in the tanner's bark. Hardier plants sit on these other shelves." He moved a few pots. "And here is a perfect spot for the inkberry."

"What is this tree with red berries?" Margery asked.

"A coffee tree," Mr. Miller said, walking to stand beside her, "and these seedlings are *Chinchona pubescens*."

"Jesuit bark for malaria! Do you think they'll grow here?" Margery asked, but before he could answer she gushed, "Oh, a pineapple!"

Mr. Miller beamed at Margery's pleasure. "Mrs. Jamison, it is most gratifying to have a visitor so pleased about what we do here, especially one who is so pleasing herself," he said. Margery blushed and moved on, to the end of the table, where a door stood just slightly ajar.

"With such wonders in this room, I can hardly imagine what you have planted in the next," she said.

Mr. Miller's eyes moved from Margery to the door.

"Impossible," he said, "I locked that door myself only yesterday, and no one else has a key." He darted in, and we followed. "Wait here, please," he said. "This is the poison house, where visitors usually are not permitted."

In front of me, level with my eye, a lush plant bore long, trumpet-shaped white flowers and spiny pods, some small and some large. I reached out to test how sharp the spines were and poked my finger.

I stuck it in my mouth and dropped my eye to the plant label, which read, "*Datura stramonium*, Thornapple, Devil's Trumpet."

"Don't touch anything," Mr. Miller said over his shoulder as he pulled on a pair of gloves. "Some of these plants are toxic as well as medicinal, depending on the dose, as I'm certain you are aware, Mrs. Jamison."

I peeked at my finger. It showed just a drop of blood. I stuck it in my pocket.

Mr. Miller paced down the row of plants, gently pushing leaves out of the way and examining pots. He talked to his plants as well. "Who disturbed you, eh?" he said, and "Hello, my dear, all right there?" and "You look fine" as though the plants could hear. I smiled up at Margery, but she was focused on our host. She wasn't smiling.

When I looked back at the *Datura* plant, though, the flowers grinned too, and the way they gave off perfume told me they were laughing along with me. Mr. Miller kept talking to the plants down the row, and the *Datura* began to quiver with mirth, so when Mr. Miller shouted, "Dear heaven, look what somebody's done to you," we both guffawed.

Mr. Miller's head whipped around, and Margery said, "It isn't funny, Jem."

The *Datura* quivered even more.

"It isn't funny," I said to the plant. Margery frowned.

"I should say not, young man," Mr. Miller called. "The plants in this room were brought here at no little expense and are propagated with no little difficulty, some of them before I began working here, and that's thirty-six years ago. It is my responsibility to preserve them in trust for the next generation. It is not funny in the least that someone harmed them."

My face burned. "No, sir," I said, and turned my back on the *Datura* flower. He spewed perfume at me. "Stop doing that!" I said to him over my shoulder, my lips smiling and my throat aching to laugh. My stomach clenched with the effort to keep myself in check.

Margery bent down and hissed in my ear, "What's gotten into you? My granny talks to plants, and so do I. You talk to Giselle. It isn't that unusual to talk with something that isn't a person."

"I know, Margery," I said, "I can't help it. He's laughing too."

"Who?"

"Him." I pointed at the *Datura* plant. "It's his fault."

Margery frowned and put a hand on my forehead. "What is wrong with you?" she said.

The *Datura* plant watched me with a saucy grin. I crossed my arms; he tipped two leaves and flapped his flowers like wings. That's when I realized he was trying to get me into trouble, so I decided I'd best go somewhere else. I tip-toed to a jolly fat fellow at the end of the poison row. He was bursting with sap and wore a natty red flower. "How d'ye do?" I said. "Say, your cravat is askew just a bit, shall I fix it for you?" and I reached out a finger to help him.

"Jem! Don't touch that!" Margery shrieked.

I pulled back my hand. "But his cravat is crooked."

"His what?" She turned her head to shout, "Mr. Miller, I'm sorry, but can you come? Something's wrong with Jem."

She ran to meet Mr. Miller, and I finally could wheeze out the bellyful of humor that was choking off my air. The two of them danced over, wavering like reflections in bad glass. Mr. Miller peeled the gloves off his hands, and I felt something warm hold my head back and my eye open. Words tumbled out of his mouth like bubbles, but each bubble popped straightaway so I heard what he said.

"He's been exposed to something," Mr. Miller said to Margery. "Boy: did you touch anything in here, anything at all?"

I pulled my finger out of my pocket. "That fellow poked me before we got acquainted, but he's the only one," I said. I whispered, "I don't like to tell tales, but he was laughing before, too, it wasn't just me."

"Show me who you mean." I walked on water to the *Datura*. He wasn't laughing any more.

"I'm sorry," I said to the plant, "but you shouldn't laugh at Mr. Miller." The *Datura* pretended he didn't hear me.

"Good Lord, it's the *Datura*," Mr. Miller said. "It causes hallucinations. We must get him out of the poison house."

"Come, Jem, out we go," Margery said.

"But I haven't met everyone yet," I said, wiggling my fingers at the fellow with the cravat.

"They'll understand." She pushed me through the door and out of the poison room, and then through the outer door, away from the greenhouse, to the cold air on the path. "Breathe, Jem," she said, and so I did.

But as I took in air, I saw, far out over the woodland garden, a giant gray snake drifting between the trees like a bank of fog, its head the same level as my own. I could not make my mouth shape the word, so I thought "*Look*," hard, at Margery. If Giselle could hear me, maybe Margery could too, but her voice and Mr. Miller's ran on and on under the roaring in my ears.

As I watched, the gray snake winding through the trees stopped. Its giant head turned. Its black eyes lit up by red lightning fixed on me like a basilisk in a story. Its tongue forked out of its mouth—once, twice. Then its head sank down, and the snake slithered out of sight. *Why do they keep a snake in their garden*, I wondered. *Or a basilisk? A basilisk will kill all their plants.*

The next time I became truly aware of my surroundings, we were back in Mr. Miller's library. Margery held a cup of water to my lips. Mr. Miller stood with his hand over his mouth. Mr. Galt's lips were moving.

"—take the boy in there!" Mr. Galt's words bubbled from his mouth.

"Henry, really, how was Mr. Miller or I to know Jem would nick herself on a *Datura* spine?" That was Margery. Why was she shouting? I pushed the cup away. My ears were not working properly.

"Margery, please don't shout," I said.

"Sorry, Jem," she whispered. "Are you all right?"

"What happened?" I said.

"You had a reaction to *Datura stramonium*," Mr. Miller said, "and quite a violent one. I might have guessed it when you laughed so rudely, as hysteria is a symptom of overdose, but I had just discovered the door to the poison room had been tampered with and half my valerian plants pulled up by the roots."

"Will sh—he be all right? How serious is it?" Margery asked.

Mr. Miller said, "Jem is talking, so he probably didn't take in much poison, but I've never heard of a reaction that came on so fast. In Jamestown, soldiers ate *Datura* in a salad, and their reaction came after dinner."

"What reaction?" Margery asked. "What happened?"

"For eleven days they behaved like lunatics," Mr. Miller said. "One blew a feather up in the air for hour upon hour, another sat in a corner like a monkey, stark naked, making faces at the rest, another kissed and pawed his companions and sneered in their faces. They were all confined, of course, and when they came to their senses, they could not recall a thing."

I said, "I won't be seeing things for eleven days, will I?"

"How many fingers am I holding up?" Mr. Miller said. The fingers appeared to be pumping and deflating like a bellows.

"Five?" I said.

"Correct. I should advise watching the boy and giving him plenty of fresh water and exercise. The Jamestown soldiers ate the stuff, but the boy here only got a small puncture and smelled the flower. He didn't ingest anything."

"I feel fine," I said, and I didn't tell them about the snake in the woods, for I realized it must have been an hallucination. How could there be a giant snake inside the Chelsea Physick Garden, much less a snake that turned to look directly at me?

We didn't speak much on the drive back to the shop. Margery drove Giselle. I wanted to tell Giselle what had happened, but she didn't care to listen. Mr. Galt dozed in the back, and Margery divided her attention between me and the road. Once, Margery murmured, "Jem, today's trouble with the *Datura* is yet another reason you should go to Granny Kestrel. What if the doctor brings home something on his shoes or I mix up a concoction for him using some new plant, and off you go again? It is dangerous not to have a proper hold on yourself!"

"I know, Margery. I shall think on it."

"You need to do more than think. You need to go! Are you well enough to drive home?"

"Giselle knows the way," I said, hoping the horse wouldn't balk. Back at the shop, Margery helped Mr. Galt into the shop and dashed back out to hand me a little pot.

"This is bilberry jam," she said. "A customer traded it for medicine. It's good for the eyes. Eat a spoonful when you get home and another later today until your eyes are back to normal." I took the little pot and stared at it. "Why, what's wrong, Jem?"

I took a breath. "I used to pick bilberries for Mum when we lived in Lamesley," I said. "She made this same jam."

Margery's eyes softened, and she patted my knee. "Well, thinking of your mother will certainly help you too." At a crash inside followed by angry muttering, Margery said, "I'm sorry, Jem, but I must see to Henry." Before she shut the door, she added, "I miss you, Jem. Terribly."

Home, Giselle, I thought, *oats,* and to my relief, she started. On the way home, my thoughts drifted, but they got stuck on Mr. Galt's anger about my being exposed to the *Datura.* It seemed rather out of proportion for a boy that was only an acquaintance. But then, he'd always had a soft spot for two little children who'd lived above his shop and spent long hours alone while their mother worked. He'd fed us and let us keep him company. It was cruel of me to have gone away, supposedly to work for a seamstress, but not to have written a single letter to let him know I was all right. I decided I must write a letter from Jenna to Mr. Galt and send it to Margery, asking her to tell Mr. Galt she'd paid the shilling postage. I hoped it would ease his mind about me as much as writing to him eased my conscience.

When I got home, I fed Giselle and brushed her. My mind had cleared. I sat down in the study and wrote,

Dear Mr. Galt,

Please forgive my long silence, but I have been very busy in my new situation. I have found a home with a good and kind master and am learning many useful things that I hope will stand me in good stead when I am grown. I shall never forget the kindness you showed to me and my mother and Jamie when we lived above your shop. Do you remember the time we gave a bit of raisin to Jamie and the time I helped you clean your shop? Please give my regards to Margery and Dr. Abernathy, if you see him. Once again, thank you for being my friend. I pray for you every night.

Your most affectionate friend,

Jenna Connolly

Then I scooped up a spoonful of Margery's jam and popped it into my mouth. The tiny, tart bilberries swimming in sweet sauce called up a clear, sharp memory of Mum and Da and I taking baskets to the hills outside Lamesley to pick bilberries. Da worked steadily, but Mum and I ate as we went. When Da came to us with a full basket, Mum's was only half-full and mine had only a handful of berries strewn across the bottom. Da had laughed at my purple teeth. "Someone's got into the winter jam aforehand, Mary, I think," he'd said to Mum, setting aside my basket and tossing me up into the air. When Mum smiled, he laughed even harder. "And it looks like she's got an accomplice."

I swallowed my bilberry jam medicine. It was more bitter than I remembered.

CHAPTER 4

DECEMBER 1758

I Play the Mouse for a Christmas Cat

We set out for Chelsea on Saturday, the trap jolting in and out of the frozen ruts in the road. I felt sorry for Giselle as we traveled west and nervous about playing my part the closer we got to Chelsea. We arrived at the Campbell home before dinner, and a pack of boys poured out of the house like ants out of a nest, shrieking and laughing and reaching up for Dr. Abernathy. He swung up the smallest in one arm and pulled in the other three with his other arm. I shouldn't have been surprised that he was a much-loved uncle, but I was; he usually was so earnest with me. Janet Campbell in the doorway wore a mother's smile to see her darlings showered with affection. It made me think of my own mother looking on fondly as Mr. Galt played with Jamie, so very long ago, and I took a deep breath before I stepped down from the trap. One servant took our bags and another led Giselle to the stable.

The doctor set down the smallest child, Trafford, unwound the others from his legs, and reached out a hand. He pulled me forward to meet his sister, who looked down kindly on me. "Mrs. Campbell, may I present Jem Connolly, my assistant, about whom I've written," he said.

"How do you do, Mr. Connolly?" said Janet Campbell.

I bowed over her hand. "I am glad to meet you, Mrs. Campbell. Thank you for inviting me to your home."

"We are pleased to have you. I only hope my boys leave you a little time to yourself. They have been clamoring all day in anticipation of the arrival of an older boy who can play pony with them." I looked down at the merry red cheeks of four little boys and couldn't help but remember my own dear brother's face laughing up at me.

One of the children grabbed my hand and pulled. "Come on, then," he said. The doctor nodded, and off I went to play Snap with the boys. Snap was a race-horse whose fortunes Da had followed, loving horses as he did. Snap had won his fourth race two months before Da was killed.

* * *

At dinner, I sat with the adults. The children ate in the nursery. I'd enjoyed playing with the boys, but with four of them and one of me, Snap needed a rest. Sitting with the adults, though, made me a bit edgy. I concentrated on my cutlery, stealing glances at the others to make sure I was doing everything cor-rectly. It was pleasant to sit with dinner companions who carried on a relaxed conversation and didn't want to ride me pick-a-back: the doctor; his sister; his brother-in-law, Lord Richard Campbell; a vicar, the Reverend Jessup; and Mrs. Campbell's mother-in-law, Violet Campbell, the Dowager Duchess of Glencoe. Her Grace was the one who had the gout.

The table was done up prettily with holly twined around white candles and silver chargers shined up for the holiday. We ate puree of parsnips with duck, crimped cod, mincemeat pie, pullets with oysters, Scotch scallops, tarts and custards.

I let the adults' conversation lap around me, lulled by its easy ebb and flow, rather surprised that a meal in a grand house wasn't that much different from my meals with the doctor. But then, just as a servant began to serve a syllabub, I felt someone watching me. I glanced up into the steady eyes of the duchess, who wasn't even pretending to eat. If eyes were forks, I'd've been skewered. Why was the lady watching me? Was I supposed to be talking? Had I spilled food on myself? Across the length of the table, I felt her bubbling like a pot of stew on a stove. She called out, "So Mr. Connolly, where are you at school?" Everyone quieted at the same time and turned to me. I blinked.

Fortunately, the doctor stepped in. "Mr. Connolly follows Mr. Defoe's prescription that a man can educate himself. Jem studies with me at present."

"Really, Dr. Abernathy, surely a good school would be more appropriate," the duchess said.

"We shall look into it," Dr. Abernathy said.

"And what of your people, boy?" the duchess asked.

"His people are from the north of England," the doctor said.

"Are they the Lancashire Connollys?" she asked.

"Mr. Connolly's family is from County Durham, I believe," Dr. Abernathy said. My heartbeat slowed. I gave a slight nod at the doctor, who eased back in his chair.

"Are they any relation to the Conollys of Ireland? My daughter Anne is married to the second Earl of Danby, whose sister is married to the nephew of Speaker Conolly of Ireland."

"The Irish Conollys you speak of spell their name differently," the doctor said. "One *n*."

"Really, Dr. Abernathy, you might let the boy speak for himself," the duchess said.

"I don't think we're related, Your Grace," I put in.

The duchess sighed. "I see." She lifted her wineglass. "Perhaps yours is another branch of the family." I smiled, but I felt like an idiot. I had no idea. Clearly, the duchess put great stock in family connections. She said, "Tell me, Dr. Abernathy, where you found an apprentice so inclined to let you do all the talking. My own sons were not so inclined at that age."

"Now, Mother, we were the most dutiful and polite of children," Lord Richard said, laughing.

The duchess switched her eyes from me to her son and held his gaze while she sipped from her wineglass.

Dr. Abernathy gave me a slight wink before he said, "Mr. Connolly and I met in London through a mutual acquaintance, Mr. Benjamin Franklin, the ambassador from Pennsylvania. Perhaps you've heard of the gentleman?"

The duchess sniffed. "Indeed I have. My son had Thomas Penn and Lord Granville for a hunt this fall. At table, they said that Mr. Franklin was quite vociferous in advancing his pet projects in the Colonies. The colonists must be pleased that their interests are so assiduously attended to."

From there, the conversation shifted to the prosecution of the war, and I listened with half my attention. The other half focused on the duchess, who, having left off asking after my history, had not left off watching me. I caught her peeking at me over her glass more than once, but she was not the least perturbed when I caught her staring: she just smiled like a cat admiring a canary. She was enjoying herself. As for me, I felt like all eyes were on me, even though there were only two.

After dinner, the doctor suggested I have another romp with the children before bed. I quickly stood to leave the table, but my Sight flared at that moment, and I felt duchess's curiosity sparking toward me like Mr. Franklin's electricity. I glanced up. Her eyes glowed like little twin flames behind gray glass. She called out, "Good evening, Mr. Connolly."

"Your Grace." I bowed.

"Good night, Jem, sleep well," said the doctor's sister. "Ring for a servant if you need anything."

"Thank you, Mrs. Campbell, I shall." I escaped, but I knew the duchess was not done with me.

The next day and the next, and for all the days we visited, I felt the interest of the duchess focused on me wherever I went. She drew and repelled me at the same time, which put me in such a state that I avoided altogether any room she occupied. But on our last day, whilst playing hide-and-seek with the boys, I stepped into the parlor where the duchess sat working at needlepoint. "Ah, Mr. Connolly—I have been hoping to have a little talk with you," she said, and patted the chair beside her. I was trapped. I edged forward, and she watched me come, her needle poised above her work. I bowed.

"M-may I look?" I stammered. She turned the frame so I could see a nearly complete picture done in red and blue and gold of a parrot, a leopard, and a lion.

"I-it's very pretty," I said.

"It occupies the time. Please sit." She poked her needle into the lion's paw. I sat.

"So, Mr. Connolly," she began, "I trust you have enjoyed your holiday?"

"Very much, thank you."

"My grandsons certainly enjoyed your company. I wish I'd had the opportunity to get to know you better."

"I'm…sorry. The time has flown."

"Tut, tut, Mr. Connolly: you have been avoiding me. Don't bother to deny it."

I said nothing.

"I see you intend to be circumspect. Well, I had to speak with you before you left. To the point then: you say your people are from County Durham?"

"Nearby, Your Grace."

"But your father is not from Lancashire."

"No, Ireland."

"I see."

I thought if she believed I wasn't connected to anybody important, she might let me go, so I added, "My father's family were farmers, Your Grace."

But rather than ending the conversation, my statement prompted a question. "Did they breed horses?" she asked. "My son breeds horses, you see. He imports Irish mares—at an extravagant cost, it seems to me. But he insists that an Irish mare and an Arabian sire will produce a winning bloodline. He hopes to produce a racehorse that is both resilient and light of foot."

"Forgive me, but I know nothing of horses. My father did. In fact, he told me once that his family bred some of the best horses in all of Ireland."

"But your father is deceased. Your mother too."

I swallowed. "Sadly, yes."

"I confess that I am surprised your father's family did not claim you and carry you back to Ireland to live with them. It must have been a disappointment to them that you chose England and medicine over Ireland and horses."

Oh, she was a sly fisherman. If she couldn't get answers with one bait, she would try another. She meant to make me reveal more about my family. But over the week, I'd had time to think, so I answered, "My father always wanted the best for me, Your Grace, and I am better suited to the study of medicine than to the breeding of horses. My parents set by my apprentice fee before they passed." (That was true, although the money Mum had hidden away for me lodged then at Freame & Barclay, collecting interest rather than lining Dr. Abernathy's pockets.)

"What can you tell me of your mother's people?" *No*, I thought, *the duchess isn't a fisherman. She's a lancet, sharp and sure.*

But the doctor and I had discussed one afternoon whilst the ladies were napping what I would say if asked about my mother. I took a breath to tell as much truth as we'd decided the duchess needed to hear. "Alas, madam," I said, "my mother passed some time ago, and our family connections were somewhat muddled. Father's people came from Ireland, as I said, and mother's people from County Durham." I let her digest the information. "My father worked as a collier, you see."

Since I'd lived in London, I'd learned that colliers ranked little better than Robin Hood's merry men. That would stop her interrogation. Indeed, her eyes frosted immediately.

"Your father was a laboring man?"

"Yes."

"Not interested in the family breeding business?"

"More interested in my mother, madam. She was a laundress. They met in County Durham after Culloden, and he stayed to be with her." I hoped she would pick up her needle now and send me away.

She leaned back. "A laundress and a collier, eh? My, my—how you have come up in the world." She smiled. I relaxed. Then she said, "You're from County Durham, you say? I don't suppose you have any relations in Newcastle?"

My heart jumped. Newcastle lay just north of Lamesley. I kept my face still. "Not that I know of. Why do you ask?"

"It doesn't really matter, I suppose, but I have a story to share that will help you understand why I have been watching you this entire week. Oh, don't look so guilty—of course I knew you'd noticed my regard, and perhaps you were unnerved by it. If so, I do apologize. I'm not a dragon set on devouring you. I simply have been rather impatient while waiting for a chance to speak privately with you. May I tell you a story?"

"Please." It was my turn to sit on the edge of my chair.

"When you hear my story, Mr. Connolly, you will see why I was so interested in where you came from. So: some twenty years ago, the duke and I were in Edinburgh for an autumn tour. We had stopped for the night with dear Lady Stair, who told us there was to be a public execution the next day, which my husband wanted to watch. But the man who was to be executed, a Captain Porteous, was instead murdered by a mob of Scots that very night."

"What had he done to anger the mob?"

"Only defended king and country!"

"From what?"

"Smugglers. This Captain Porteous was to hang at dawn, but apparently the local hounds suspected the government would commute the sentence. The Scots are a very suspicious people, always jumping to conclusions before getting all the facts. Don't look at me like that, young man. I married a Scot, so I should know."

"Of course, Your Grace."

"We were awakened by noise in the street. We looked out of the window and saw the mob bearing the captain all trussed up like a Christmas goose. They dragged him away and hanged him, if you can believe it. Barbarians."

"I am sorry to hear it," I said, but my expression must have conveyed my confusion: how did this story explain her peculiar interest in me?

The duchess said, "I tell you this grisly tale because we had heard that the Duke of Newcastle and his family were arriving the next day. Naturally, Lady Stair was all turned about by the murder, so my husband and I decided to leave the next day so she wouldn't have to entertain two sets of guests, especially since the mob had roiled by her very door.

"We were being handed into our carriage the next morning when the Duke of Newcastle arrived with his wife and daughter, unaware of the tragedy. My husband stepped over to inform him about the mob's activities the evening before, and I glanced over at the duke's daughter looking out of her carriage window. I saw her as clearly as I see you now." She fixed her gray eyes on my face. "Mr. Connolly, I must tell you that she and you are so alike you could be twins."

"Oh?" My heart beat faster, but I held myself very still.

"Clearly, however, from what you have told me, it is impossible that you are connected to the duke's family." She peered at me. "Mr. Connolly, are you quite all right? You're as white as paper."

"I'm fine, thank you, Your Grace. I expect I'm tired. Your grandsons have a great deal of energy."

"Please accept my apology for detaining you."

"Don't even think of it. It gave me a chance to catch my breath. I'm glad you were interested enough to speak with me, and I apologize if it seems I've been avoiding your company."

"Forgive an old lady's curiosity about those who swim within her family's influence. The world is changing so quickly now that I shouldn't be surprised if a tinker marries a countess before too long." She picked up her needle. "Good day, Mr. Connolly."

I bowed. "Your Grace."

I stepped out. My heart raced. *Porteous. Edinburgh. Duke of Newcastle.*

Autumn 1736. I memorized the details so I could share them with Franklin. They might mean nothing, or they might be important clues if he ever got round to investigating my origins, as he'd said last May he intended to do.

CHAPTER 5

JANUARY 1759

A Mystery Acquires a Sleuth

Weeks after I'd hoped to resume our lessons, Franklin finally sent word I could come back to Craven Street. I was glad to go, but I found him in an irritable frame of mind. The city-wide celebrations we'd enjoyed in August and September once we heard the news that England had won Louisbourg from the French had made Franklin (and everybody else) expect the war to end soon. But the war dragged on. Franklin's letters to and from home continued to miscarry because so many ships were taken by the French. It drove him mad. He needed to communicate with Philadelphia, but he never knew whether a letter would arrive safely or be stolen by the enemy.

One letter that *did* get through to London from Philadelphia reported that Pennsylvania had been ordered to provide more militiamen to fight the French and Indians. "They still haven't paid the militiamen who volunteered last time," Franklin grumbled to me. When Franklin complained, the Lord President of the Privy Council told him that colonials must obey anything the Privy Council ordered, for members of the Privy Council had their power directly from the king. This seemed reasonable to me, as everybody must obey the king, but Franklin complained about that, too. "Americans would be delighted to obey the Privy Council," he grumbled to me, "if obligations were applied fairly and equally on both sides of the Atlantic, but they are not.

"I am to go before the Privy Council next month to speak of the anger of the natives, whose lands are being encroached upon by settlers," Franklin said. "The Penns do nothing to halt the incursions, to their eternal shame. I truly think Pennsylvania would be better off if it were taken from them and given back to the Crown."

"Would you go home if that happened?" I asked.

"The Assembly still would need someone to negotiate for them with the king, Jem," he said, "and I am the likeliest candidate for the job." I was relieved to hear it, for I enjoyed my lessons (when I could get them). Still, since we were talking of it, I had to ask something I'd wondered about since we'd met, "Don't you miss Mrs. Franklin and your friends?"

He sighed. "I do. But I cannot summon up the heart to leave London. If I go, I might never return. My contact with my London friends might be reduced to a handful of letters a year, and then reduced to one, and finally to nothing but memories."

"One could say that about your Philadelphia friends, now."

He took off his spectacles to clean them. "Indeed one could. But a man can be in only one place at a time, and, for now, the place I can do the most good for my country—and for myself, truth be told—is London." He settled his sparkling spectacles on his nose. "Now then, you and I have business of our own to conduct."

"Concerning my mother's cameo?"

"Correct. I had it cleaned, and the goldsmith explained some surprising things about it that deepen the mystery of your origins." He pulled down a book from his case and opened it to reveal a hollow cunningly carved out of the middle. "Dreadful waste of a book," he said, "if it were a good book." He reached inside and handed me a lump wrapped in velvet.

I peeled back the velvet. The cameo shone like new. "I've never seen it look so well," I said, "which reminds me: Dr. Abernathy said we could have cleaned this with vinegar. Why didn't we?"

"I didn't want to risk damaging it. The jeweler used simple soap and hot water."

I hugged the cameo to my heart. "I am so glad to get this back! Where is the ribbon?"

"The goldsmith may have discarded it, for it was tattered and filthy. Jem, I do apologize for the delay. You see, shortly after you entrusted your cameo to me, the Penns' lawyer delivered their answer to my request for aid to Pennsylvania—which was *no*—and I suddenly had more to do than I wished. It simply seemed more expedient to take your cameo to a professional, but your piece had to wait its turn for attention. Still, I think you'll agree it was worth the wait once you learn what the goldsmith told me about the tiny marks on the gold."

"You mean the initials?"

"More than that. The initials are easy, you saw them yourself, but this piece has four of them rather than the usual three: *M, P, H,* and *A.* Underneath is a faint inscription: *to our daughter Mary on her 16th birthday in the year of our Lord 1742.* Your mother's name was Mary, was it not?"

"Yes. Mary Anne." I squinted. "I never noticed that inscription before."

"It was grimy. Your mother's married name was Connolly. What was her maiden name?"

"I don't know. She never talked about her family."

"You never saw a letter, not even from her mother? Nobody said a word?"

"No, nothing."

"We can't be sure this cameo was created for your mother rather than found or purchased in a shop by her or your father until we gather more information, although having the names match is a good start."

"How can we gather information?"

"Like this." He lit two lamps and put them on either side of the microscope. Then he slid the cameo under the lens, and raised the eyepiece to focus it.

"Here, look," he said. I settled at the instrument, amazed as always to see tiny things in perfect detail. "First, you could have sat for this cameo portrait yourself, we noted that last time we talked of it. Notice the remnants of dark brown paint in the carved curls of the hair. The specks of color left in the eyes appear to be blue rather than green, and your mother's eyes were blue, were they not?" I nodded. "But your father's eyes were green?" I nodded again. "Well, Jem, you are the child of two parents, and the characteristics of the parents combine in the child. I wonder which parent you got your stubborn streak from—judging by the lady's chin, I would guess your mother?"

I sat back, surprised and irked. "Mr. Franklin, why do you say my mother was stubborn?"

"Tenacious, then."

My face heated. "*Ten* means 'hold,' and *cious* means 'full of,' so a tenacious person is still full of holding on to things. So you are still saying my mother was stubborn!"

Franklin laughed. "I see your Latin lessons have taken hold."

"She wasn't stubborn," I mumbled.

"She was a courageous person who never gave up; is that better?" he said.

I sniffed. "Somewhat."

"This conversation demonstrates a key skill of the diplomat: the careful substitution of a neutral word for a fiery one. *Tenacious* and *stubborn* and *never giving up* are all slices from the same cheese," he said. I opened my mouth, but he continued, "Jem, don't be offended. If your mother hadn't been tenacious, you might not be either, and our social experiment with you might never have begun in the first place. You might be toiling in a mine in Lamesley."

Keeping hold of something isn't such a bad thing, I decided. "Fair enough."

"Being tenacious requires more than the courage to do something difficult, Jem; it also requires the ability to stay the course even if the end result isn't guaranteed." He muttered, "And I ought to know." He clapped and said, "Shall we carry on? Turn over the cameo and put it back under the microscope so you can see the marks on the back. Focus on the upper edge of the frame. Do you see the letters *I* and *C*?"

"Yes."

"After that, you should see a woman's head, a lion with outstretched paws, three tiny castles arranged in a triangle, and the letter *C*."

"I see the marks! They're so tiny—like flyspecks. I never would have guessed they were letters. What do they mean?"

"The marks tell where and when and by whom the item was made. The lion and woman convey that the gold was properly assayed, as does the three-castle mark. But the three-castle mark also tells where the piece was made."

"Where?"

"Newcastle."

My heart lurched. "That's the big city north of Sunderland."

"Correct. It's just north of County Durham."

I wasn't sure I liked the way so many clues were pouring in after I'd known nothing all my life. What if we actually found my family and they lived so far away I'd never see anybody in London, not ever again? I was *tenacious* enough—ha!—to want to get to the bottom of the mystery, but uneasy about going on. Still, I suspected Franklin would not give up the chase at this point. I said, "Mr. Franklin, I learned something at Christmas that you should hear," and I told him what the duchess had said about Captain Porteous and the Duke of Newcastle's daughter.

Franklin listened, and then sat back and just looked at me. "That is extraordinary," he said, "for there is a twenty-year gap between you and the duke's daughter. On the other hand, physical resemblance alone doesn't prove a connection; I have been told more than once that thus-and-so a gentleman in London could be my twin. Poor fellow." He tapped his finger on his lips and said, "But it is curious." He shrugged. "On the other hand, the dowager duchess may have eyesight like mine."

"So she might be mistaken." He nodded. I set my eye to the microscope again. "What is this line of numbers and letters? What does *I C* mean?"

"The first two letters are the initials of the craftsman who wrought the gold, though he mightn't be the same person who carved the cameo. But the gold-smith told me when he was an apprentice thirty years ago, a lad came down from the north who stayed for a year, then went home again to set up his own business. The lad's name was Isaac Cookson, and he still runs his business out of

Newcastle. Based on these initials and the location and the time, I believe Isaac Cookson made this piece."

"You can tell all that from these marks?"

"I can indeed."

"Then what does the big *C* at the end mean?"

"It tells that this piece was created in 1742. What year was your mother born?"

"She was twenty-one when I was born, and I'm eleven now, so she was born about thirty-three years ago, so"—I did the sums in my head, and my heart wobbled again. I looked up. Franklin waited. I murmured, "Mum probably was born in 1726."

"And 1726 plus sixteen is—"

"—1742." I sat back.

He cleared his throat. "Let me summarize what we know. Based on the many very specific details that complement one another, not least of which is the way you said your mother guarded this piece, I think we can conclude that this cameo was given to your mother on her sixteenth birthday, and that these initials were your mother's initials before she married your father and took the name Connolly."

"What about Captain Porteous?"

He regarded me over his spectacles with a look I couldn't quite read. "I know something of that story. The riot certainly took place, but we've no reason to believe the unlucky captain to be allied with your family. We can pursue the tale later if we need to know more. What the tale does do, Jem, is mark the date the duchess glimpsed your double." I looked into the eyepiece again. How could such tiny marks create possibilities I hadn't even considered ten minutes ago? Because, of course, the marks might mean that Mum had come from a wealthy family in the North, a family that might want me back. I looked at Mr. Franklin, who said, "Well, Jem, have you anything to add?"

I said, "According to this cameo, Mum's name before she married started with *P*."

"Or *H*, or *PH*. Which means if we figure out the name, we can find your grandparents. If they live."

He waited.

I stammered, "Y-you want to know if you should go on."

He nodded.

"I-I can't imagine how we would find them. I never met them or saw them or heard their names."

"Which in itself is odd, don't you think? Another thing odd about your cameo—considering your mother's poverty—is that it is an expensive piece: the face was carved from ivory, the backing is onyx, this oval bezel that holds it all together is gold. If your mother had such a costly piece, why would she keep it rather than selling it to feed you and your brother, unless it had sentimental value? Furthermore, what parents could spend money on a piece like this in the first place? Making this cameo would have required payments to a carver and a jeweler and a goldsmith—it would have cost a great deal."

A whisper of a memory blew into my mind of my mother smoothing back my hair after some childhood bump or other and murmuring, "One day, my darling, perhaps you will live in a fine house with servants, and there'll be horses to ride, and a pretty river to look at, and you'll never be hurt or hungry or cold." I'd let my mother's lovely dream soothe me at the time, especially as my hurt was not as bad as my tears made it out to be. I said to Mr. Franklin, "I don't know if this is worth mentioning, but a long time ago, my mother spoke of a house I might live in one day, a big house with servants. You don't think she was talking of a real place?"

"It could be a place she lived in before she married your father," Mr. Franklin said. "Someone with money had this cameo made for your mother; that is my operating theory. Yet why would a widow with two children in tow *not* return to wealthy parents? Why would she choose to be a lowly laundress in London instead? It is a puzzle, Jem, and I am not content to leave it unresolved. May I have your permission to carry on with my investigation?"

I'd always wondered where I came from, why we had no relatives. On the other hand, I liked my life very much just the way it was, except for not being able to go to the apothecary shop any more—and having to guard against my Sight carrying me away. I said, "What if you find out I have grandparents who want me back? What if I meet them and don't like them? Could I stay with the doctor?"

"I can't say, but I can't imagine grandparents wouldn't want a long-lost grandchild returned to them. And what if they *do* have money? What if you are an heiress? Or even a peer of the realm? Money and a title can be useful."

"A girl can't inherit, only a boy."

"Not necessarily," Franklin said. "The rules are complicated, but it was explained to me that if the title was created by writ, and if you are an heir of the body, the title may include the right for a female to be a peeress in her own right. So, depending on what the writ says, you could inherit."

"What if I don't want to inherit?"

"Let's not put the cart before the horse. We needn't worry whether a female can inherit since we don't know your identity. But would it be so bad to come into money?"

"It isn't the money I'm worried about. It's all the changes." I looked again at the cameo under the lens. I inspected the faint lettering on the back. I would rather not solve the mystery if doing so would ruin my life. On the other hand, I might never again have such an excellent sleuth willing to find out something I'd always wanted to know. Besides, I didn't have to do anything if he found my grandparents; as near as I could tell, they hadn't made any effort to find me.

I leaned back. "If you want to find out who my mother was, go ahead. But whatever you learn, you must promise to tell it to me first and let me decide what to do about it before you tell anybody else."

Franklin frowned. "That is a complicated and weighty promise. What if we learn your grandparents want you back? If I had a secret grandchild, I most certainly would want to know about it. Would you break your grandparents' hearts by never letting them know you live? And here is another thing to think about: would you risk someone else learning the truth and bringing charges of kidnapping against the doctor?

"No, Jem, if I were to find your grandparents, you would have to tell Abernathy. If you don't agree, I shall cease my inquiries." He handed back my cameo and said, sadly, "I suppose your mystery must never be solved."

What a choice: let Franklin give up and never find any blood relations I might have, or let him keep going and risk the family I'd cobbled together! "What about this," I said, "if you find out I have a family, can you give me some time before you tell anybody else?"

"I promise not to divulge anything to anyone until it is confirmed beyond a doubt."

"Done." I stuck out my hand, and we shook on it. He seemed more cheerful than he'd been when I'd arrived, no doubt due to his having completed at least one successful negotiation.

"May I take the cameo home now?" I said. "It's all I have of my mother."

"Of course. I can make a copy of the face and inscription right now, and a rubbing of the frame too." Franklin got out a bit of lead, some thin paper, and ink and pen. First he put the paper over the cameo's face and gently rubbed lead on the surface, much as one might make a rubbing of a carved inscription. He copied the design of the frame the same way. Then he wrote out the inscription on another part of the paper along with a description of the face on the cameo. He made notes about the size and the bits of colored paint. When he was done, he wrapped the cameo in its bit of velvet and handed it to me. I dropped it into my pocket.

"What will you do first?" I asked. "How will you solve the mystery?"

"We know you lived in the north, near County Durham."

"Yes. In Lamesley."

"I plan to travel this summer to Scotland to visit a mutual friend of mine and

Dr. Abernathy's, Sir Alexander Dick. On the way to Edinburgh, I shall stop in Lamesley and make some subtle inquiries. Is there any person in Lamesley who might know something about your family?"

"Nan Knowles lives there," I said. "After Da died but before we came here, she and my mum spoke of a woman in town who had the brass to speak right up to Sir Henry's man after the explosion. Mum told Nan, 'The woman can't go back,' and Nan said, 'It's not just the lady and her sweetheart in a croft on Bonnie's Bank,' and Mum said, 'The lady burned bridges when she left.'"

Franklin said, "What a remarkable mimic—you sounded as though you were a hundred years old. I must say that, to me, it sounds as though the woman who needed to go somewhere was your mother."

"Why do you say that?"

"Your mother said the woman couldn't or wouldn't go; Mrs. Knowles said the woman wasn't alone, which suggests children. Now, why would a woman and children need to go somewhere? The mine had just exploded; presumably, the sweetheart was killed and the woman was widowed."

"But lots of men died that day besides my da," I said.

"But doesn't it seem odd that they would be discussing this nameless woman, and that shortly thereafter, your mother brought you and your brother away to London?"

"I suppose so," I mumbled.

"Nor did you go to your mother's family when your father died, which indicates, as your mother said, that bridges may have been burned. I shall try to speak with your Mrs. Knowles this summer." He wrote her name on his paper. "In the meantime, I shall continue my investigation here in London."

I clasped my hands behind my back to steady them before saying, "Sir, are you sure you want to go to all this trouble? I'm curious, but I'm rather…afraid to find out the truth."

He put his hand on my shoulder. "Jem, listen to a piece of advice, for you'll be as old as I am more before you know it. Last summer, I visited Ecton, the village where my ancestors lived for two hundred years before my father emigrated to America. I went for curiosity, just to see it. I'd been perfectly happy knowing only one thing about Ecton, that my father chose to leave it.

"And yet, Jem, walking the streets my father had walked, reading ancient family records in the church, getting a sense of myself in connection to my past—it meant a great deal to me. I felt like I lived inside a kind of magic made of blood and stone and time. I still feel like a walking, living link between the past and the future." He tilted up my chin. "So, if even a small part of the satisfaction I felt can be yours, Jem, I should like to help you find it. May I?"

"Of course. I'm not a little child any more." Brave words, but part of me still wanted to run the other way. Another part of me reasoned that knowing the truth was better than living in the dark. And, I grudgingly admitted to myself, the same principle applied to my Sight.

Let Franklin do what he could and go on from there.

CHAPTER 6

FEBRUARY 1759

Soundings

It was a wet winter. The heavy fog kept out the sun and kept in the vapors. Sickness seemed to drip from the very air. Some of our patients asked whether the sickness was caused by the great comet that Edmund Halley had predicted would come back, and which we'd seen in the sky since Christmas. Dr. Abernathy replied that if the comet caused illness, why did people get sick in years the comet wasn't in the sky? The frowns he got in response confirmed the low opinion people have about logic.

The doctor and I ran from morning to night, and Margery could hardly keep up with the demand for chest plasters and other medicines for complaints of the lungs. One or more of her siblings helped now and again, but, she wrote, she missed my help, as Mr. Galt had to be given tasks he could do by touch. Margery wrote that he sat by the door waiting for customers and shook their hands when they came in. He told her he did it to "give 'em a sniff and a listen" as a way to identify them. But sitting near the door put Mr. Galt in a constant draft. Over that whole winter, he breathed cold, wet air. He coughed constantly. He lost weight.

One morning when Margery came down, she found Mr. Galt lying in his bed with his bedclothes soaked through with sweat. He burned with fever. He barely breathed. He was too weak to cough, and his breath rattled in his chest. Alarmed, Margery got him comfortable and sent a boy to fetch Dr. Abernathy, who gave me leave to come along.

Margery whisked us inside the back door instant we arrived. A furrow carved itself between Dr. Abernathy's brows when he saw Mr. Galt lying like a gray ghost in his bed, wasted away to nothing. While she'd waited for us, Margery had made a mustard plaster for Henry's chest, using ground mustard seeds and flour and water spread on cloth, to break up the matter in Henry's lungs so he could cough it up. Every time he coughed, he grimaced with the pain of it. How had he gotten so ill so fast? Margery had written of it, but seeing my friend gasping for air was a horror. It seemed as though he were ebbing on a tide.

Dr. Abernathy carefully removed the mustard plaster and set it aside. "I'll put it back in a moment," he told Margery. The doctor wiped off the residue on Mr. Galt's chest and bent over him. He looked in Mr. Galt's eyes and mouth, and then placed the middle fingertip of his left hand on Mr. Galt's chest and tapped that finger with the middle finger of his right hand.

"What are you doing?" I asked.

"Is that your boy, Abernathy?" Mr. Galt gasped.

"Yes."

"Hello, Mr. Galt," I murmured.

"The boy shouldn't be here," Mr. Galt wheezed. "If I've got what's going around, he could catch it."

"He and I have seen sick people all winter, so I don't think it likely that one more will hurt him. He has a remarkable constitution. Lie back, please." He tapped on his finger again in a different spot on Mr. Galt's chest. "Look here at what I'm doing, Jem," Dr. Abernathy said to me. "It's a new technique they're using in Vienna to see inside a man by using sound."

"How can you see sound?" I asked.

Dr. Abernathy said, "If I tap on a full cask of wine, it sounds different from an empty one. The sound of a healthy lung when tapped is different from the sound of an unhealthy lung. A dull sound indicates the presence of a mass under the surface; in the case of a lung, it's likely to be fluid. A more resonant sound indicates hollow structures full of air. Put your finger here and try it."

"The boy shouldn't touch me," Mr. Galt said, raising his hands to push me away.

"Hush, Henry, the boy needs to learn," Margery said. "The doctor will guide him."

"Come, Jem, try it and tell me what you think," Dr. Abernathy said.

I placed a finger on the bony chest. Mr. Galt's wispy white hair draped over his pillow. His saggy skin puddled into his sheets. Before, when I'd seen him moving about in his apothecary robe and cap, I hadn't thought about his age. Seeing him now, helpless and breathless, struck me a shocking blow. Whilst I tapped his chest, Mr. Galt's clouded eyes stared at the ceiling. A dull thud sounded from his chest.

My eyes shot to the doctor's. "His lungs are full," I said, alarmed. "How do we empty them? He can't breathe." A man who can't get air will die. Henry Galt couldn't get any air. My old friend could leave this earth without my ever getting another hug from him. The shop bell rang. Margery hurried out.

"The mustard plaster will help him expel the fluid," Dr. Abernathy said, replacing it. Mr. Galt wheezed. He coughed, a long, racking cough that must have hurt dreadfully judging by the look on his face. I took his hand in mine to steady him through the spasm, and I didn't let go when he tried to shake me off. He sank back when his fit ended, limp as a fish in a basket. "Rest now," Dr. Abernathy told him.

The doctor unwound my hand from Mr. Galt's and jerked his head to indicate I should go with him to the front room of the shop. Margery was just tying twine around a package, which she handed to a woman bundled into a red cloak with its cowl pulled over her head. The woman's head bobbed at me and the doctor, then she hurried out. Margery came round the counter to meet us near the door beside the chair Mr. Galt usually occupied.

"What is it?" Margery said. Her eyes searched his face.

The doctor shook his head. "How long has he been losing weight?"

Margery said, "All winter at least. Maybe before."

"How long has he had that cough?" the doctor asked.

Margery said, "Henry's always coughed. I put it down to the nasty things he works with. But it got worse—when?" She whispered, "Did he cough when you lived upstairs, Jem?"

"Not like that," I whispered back.

Dr. Abernathy said, very quiet, "I'm afraid I know what this is. In times past it was called scrofula, but nowadays we call it *phthisis pulmonalis*. Dr. Morton's book calls it consumption."

Phthisis took off scores of elderly people every day in London, especially those crowded together in poorer neighborhoods. It usually passed from one person to another in the same household, then it spread through their neighborhoods, and it even lived on in the clothing of the dead. Dr. Abernathy said the Spaniards and Italians burned the belongings of those who died from phthisis so others wouldn't catch it. Judging by our experience, fully a fifth of Londoners who died had been taken off by phthisis.

And Mr. Galt had it. Margery put her hand to her mouth and shook her head.

Dr. Abernathy said, "I see you understand, Mrs. Jamison."

"I do," she said. Tears stood in her eyes.

"Then you know there is no cure."

Margery nodded, and the tears spilled down the front of her dress. The doctor put a hand on her shoulder.

"I am sorry, Mrs. Jamison."

She nodded. The doctor handed her his handkerchief, and she sank into Mr. Galt's chair. Dr. Abernathy shepherded me to the other side of the room. He looked out of the window and said, softly, "Jem, should a doctor tell his friend he has an fatal illness"—he paused and swallowed—"or should the doctor soften the blow?"

As a rule, Dr. Abernathy soldiered through every horrible case we went on, sometimes snapping at shiftless caregivers, usually instructing me and others as he tended the sick, but always defaulting to a calm manner. He'd said a physician should strive to give his patients a reasoned diagnosis untainted by emotion. I'd followed his lead as best I could, even though I'd had to leave a sickroom on occasion. But Henry Galt was dear to both of us, and we felt—lost, I suppose, as our minds had snagged on Henry's diagnosis. We were attached to him. It was hard to be calm.

It was hard for me to speak, too, but I cleared my throat and said, "Well, sir, doesn't it depend on the patient? Perhaps we can tell Mr. Galt your diagnosis and let him work out for himself what it means while we decide what to do for him." I blinked away my tears and quoted the doctor to himself, "Some do get better, you know."

He put a hand on my shoulder. "Yes. I know." He sighed. "Thank you, Jem, you're right, of course. Watch the shop for a moment, will you?" He turned to Margery. "Mrs. Jamison, if you would go in with me, please?" and they went to Mr. Galt's bedside to tell him the hard news.

I stepped behind the counter, upon which sat a scale for measuring, an oil lamp, the big prescription book, and Mr. Galt's model of a human head carved from ivory. Above me, the bottles and stone jars I'd cleaned a year and a half ago displayed a new, light coating of dust. Outside, weak daylight that filtered through the clouds was too feeble to lend a sparkle to anything. All was dull, dull, dull.

I couldn't imagine Galt's Apothecary without Mr. Galt in it. My hands closed into fists. If only death were a physical person I could kick and strike and chase away from me and mine for always. My blood sang with the need to pound something, but there was nobody to pound. Death wasn't stalking Mr. Galt; all Death had to do was wait for him. Dr. Abernathy came out.

He said, "Jem, I hesitate to ask you—no, I would forbid it if it weren't so critical—but what do you think of coming back to help nurse Mr. Galt until… of coming back?"

I swallowed, hard. "I should be glad to help, but can you spare me?"

"I shall have to. Mrs. Jamison cannot take care of Mr. Galt and the shop by herself."

"What about Jory? Or Alfred?"

"Her brothers will help, of course, but they have their own work."

"Of course I'll come. Will Mr. Galt allow it?"

"He must."

We went back. Dr. Abernathy said to Mr. Galt, "We shall do all we can to make you comfortable. If you wish, Mrs. Jamison, I can spare Jem to help you care for him, but you both must take great care to avoid contagion yourself by not breathing overmuch the air he exhales. You must keep yourself and Henry clean and dry. Give him milk."

"I can make a tisane out of peeled barley," Margery said. "Maybe put lungwort in it?"

"I don't want the boy," Mr. Galt blurted. "Me and Margery'll be fine without him. Her brothers'll come." His words shocked and hurt me. Margery's eyes widened.

"But you need the boy, and so does Mrs. Jamison," Dr. Abernathy said.

"Keep him away, I've said!" Mr. Galt barked, and then he launched into another coughing fit.

Dr. Abernathy said, "Henry, Mrs. Jamison cannot do all, handle all, alone, not even with the help of her brothers. Your customers will find another apothecary if Mrs. Jamison cannot meet their needs. Jem will come and mix medicines, and let that be an end to it."

Mr. Galt opened his mouth to protest yet again. The bell over the front door jingled.

"You see, Henry?" Margery said. "We have to stay open, but I can't see to customers and to you as well. The shop will fail if I don't have help." She raised her voice to call out, "I'll be there in a moment."

"Henry, I can alleviate your concern about contagion," the doctor said, "if that is your reason for not wanting the boy. These two will use vinegar every day to disinfect."

Margery headed for the doorway. She murmured to the doctor, "God bless you" and went out.

So it was that I went back to working at the apothecary shop under unhappy circumstances. Rarely, I minded the shop; usually, I mixed medicine at Margery's big table upstairs. Mr. Galt didn't like me near him, but many days found him too weak to fight me off. So, sometimes I wiped his face; other times I fed him, or read to him, or helped Margery position him so he didn't get bedsores. Mr. Galt had a cloth tied over his mouth the second time I came, I suppose to keep his bad air to himself. His white eyes staring sightlessly above it made him seem a phantom.

He detested the smell of the vinegar we used to disinfect. He hadn't minded the shop's odors when Mum and Jamie and I had first come to him, but losing his sight seemed to have improved his sense of smell. Margery told me to dilute the vinegar with water to make it less pungent, but Mr. Galt turned his face away and actually growled at me whenever I brought the cloth anywhere near his nose. One day he shouted "How many times must I tell you to go away?" and summoned up enough strength from somewhere to bat my arm and to keep batting away at me. He knocked the basin to the floor and the vinegar splashed all over my legs and boots and the floor.

"Now look what you've done!" I scolded. "It's bad enough this room hasn't been dusted since your grandfather lived here, and now I've this awful mess to clean besides!"

He settled back on his pillows. "Let's see you do it, then," he said, and turned his face away from me.

Immediately, I regretted my outburst. "I'm sorry, Mr. Galt," I said, but he wouldn't look at me.

On a day in late February when I entered the shop through the back door, I found a horror: Mr. Galt coughed and gasped as Margery held his shoulders. Every cough sprayed blood on her arms and smock.

Blood spattered the front of his nightshirt. Blood spattered his bedclothes and the wall beside the bed. Blood dribbled from his mouth.

"Jem, help me. Hold him up." I ran to oblige. Margery pulled off his shirt. I gasped: Mr. Galt had wasted away so that he was nothing but a skeleton wrapped in skin. Margery fetched a basin and rags.

"What happened?" I said.

"I heard him coughing," Margery said, "a nasty, deep, wet cough. Then he cried out. So I ran down, and found him like this."

"Sorry…Margery," Mr. Galt wheezed. "Jem…go…home."

"Shh. Quiet, old man," Margery said. "Don't excite yourself. Jem, make tea." She quickly wiped the blood off her arms and the front of her smock, and cleaned his face. Then she whipped off the bloody sheet and used it to wipe the wall, and set a bolster behind Henry so he could sit up. She said, "There now. Lean back—that's right. Let's cover you. I'm going up to make you some medicine. I'll be right back."

I already had assembled the tea things and put the kettle on. Margery dashed up the stairs.

Mr. Galt sucked in air and said, "You'll find a teapot in yon cupboard, boy,"—he sucked in more air—"tea leaves on the table."

"I have everything, Mr. Galt," I said. "The kettle's already on." I'd watched him make tea a hundred times in my other life while James sat on my lap and we chatted about silly nothings.

From the bed came his voice: "Now, how'd you know where my tea things lie, young sir?" he wheezed. "Margery didn't tell you. I never did." His breathing was better now that the coughing spell had passed. He pointed a crooked finger in my direction. "Is there summat you want to tell Old Henry? Summat you maybe should have told him long afore now?"

"Sir?"

"Jenna." I froze. "Aye, Jenna: d' you think I can't hear any better'n I can see? No, Jenna, my own dear girl, the hearing gets better when the sight gets worse."

I felt my heart pound in the sudden silence. He knew. Henry knew that

Dr. Abernathy's boy apprentice, Jem, was really the little girl who'd once lived upstairs, Jenna Connolly. My mouth dried up. "How long have you known?" I said.

"I wondered the first day," he said, "and I wondered more after our visit to Chelsea. I knew after that, especially these last weeks when you've come. Why d'ye think I've covered my mouth all this while? To keep from breathing on you, that's why!"

My stomach clenched. I felt desperately ashamed. I said, "You didn't say anything."

"I were waitin' for you to say it was you," he said. "Why'd you keep silent?" His quavery tone showed me just how much I had hurt him by keeping mum.

Keeping my secret from Henry had eaten away at me like a worm eating away at a woolen coat. Pretending to be a boy whilst going about with the doctor didn't bother me because, to our patients, I was just an extra pair of hands. I was nobody special. But Jenna had been the granddaughter Henry Galt never had, just as Margery was the daughter of his heart. I'd known he missed me, but I'd been afraid he would disapprove of my costume, afraid he might tell somebody that I still lived in London.

Now that my secret was out, I saw that my hurting him was worse than exposure, because Henry had nobody to love but me and Margery. Henry Galt loved me. He'd worried about me and waited for letters that never came, except the one at Christmas. How he must have wondered and waited and longed to be greeted and loved.

I felt a wretch. I wanted the floor to open up and swallow me.

I said, "I didn't know how to tell you. And then it seemed you didn't notice, so I thought to spare you. I was wrong to keep the secret. I'm so sorry, Mr. Galt."

He lay there looking in my direction with his clouded eyes. I went to the bed and knelt beside it. I took up his hand. It was as light as a child's.

I said, "Oh, Mr. Galt, how I've missed you! Remember what fun we used to have? Remember how we cleaned everything that first day we met? Remember how James and I used to sit with you when Mum was out? Remember Christmas dinner with Margery's family?"

One of the furrows between his eyebrows eased. A little smile tugged at the corners of his mouth. He said, "I remember all of it, Jenna, every minute."

"You saved us, Mr. Galt. I can never repay you for that."

He shook my hand up and down like an aspergil and said in a gruff voice, "There, now, don't cry Jenna, dear. There, there. Why don't you tell me why you're dressed that scandalous way? Why've you been coming all these months pretending to be a boy?"

"I'll tell you everything, Mr. Galt," I said. I sat on the edge of the bed and spilled my secrets. "Dr. Abernathy and the rest wanted to apprentice me to a dressmaker. Think of it: I would have been shut up in a dark room sewing tiny stitches all day, every day, for years. I would have never seen the sun. I would have never been let out. I would have been a prisoner, Mr. Galt."

"Terrible," he said.

"I wanted to run away, but then I found Brian Abernathy's old clothes and tried them on."

"The doctor's dead son? Abernathy approved of this?"

"No! Dr. Abernathy was angry. But after I helped him on a case one night, he and Mr. Franklin decided to conduct an experiment on me."

"Experiment?"

"They decided to see if a girl could serve the doctor as well as a boy could. If I could do it, the doctor would keep me."

"And you did well, that I know without your telling me," he said.

I smiled. "I did. And now I'm learning how to be a doctor."

"But, Jenna, you'll never be let to be a doctor," Mr. Galt said.

"That's what they said. Maybe things will change by the time I grow up. Even if they don't, I'll still be able to help people. I can make medicine. And Mr. Franklin is teaching me Latin and science."

As he listened, his wrinkled mouth opened and closed. His concave chest moved hardly at all. He looked like a fish tossed ashore and left to gasp out its last. Mr. Galt had never hurt me, but the thick shell I'd worn to keep myself safe had kept him out, and that had hurt him.

"I've loved coming to work with Margery because it meant I could see you too. Can you forgive me, Mr. Galt?"

The corners of his mouth tilted up a bit. "I can and I do, Jenna," he said. "I'm just that glad to have you back." I reached out to embrace his frail shoulders.

"Stay back," he said, trying to pull away, but he had no more strength than a baby.

"One hug," I said, "please, just one so I know you've truly forgiven me."

"Quick, then," he said and pulled me in. His breath still smelled like ten dead cats with rotten teeth, but it didn't matter as much as it once had. His forgiveness was balm for my guilty heart.

He pushed me away, and I made the tea. We heard Margery's feet on the stairs. She'd pulled off her smock. She brought barberry and mint pounded fine and mixed with honey, which she gave to Henry with his tea, and it seemed to help. He lay back to rest, his breathing easier.

We tiptoed out. I told Margery I'd confessed who I really was and that Henry had known all along. She let out a great lungful of air and said, "Oh! I'm ever so glad, Jem. I wondered if he knew—he was just full of questions about Abernathy's boy. You and him being chums again is better medicine than anything I could mix up. Can you wipe the counter while I sweep?"

I dusted the ivory skull. "I hope it's good medicine for him, Margery. Oh, I do hope so. But—his lungs are full of holes where the air cannot go."

She stopped sweeping. "How do you know that, Jem?"

"He hugged me, and I felt his lungs. They're like wool cloth chewed by moths."

She leaned her broom on the counter. "Jem, you do realize it was your Sight showed that to you."

"Yes, I-I know."

She set my polishing cloth aside and took hold of my hands. "Darling Jem, how I wish I was good with words so I could find the ones that would persuade you to go to my granny in Cornwall and let her train you."

"How could I go now with Mr. Galt sick, along with everybody else in London, and you needing me to help with the shop?"

"Well, as to the shop, I spoke to Da about my brothers helping out a bit more. I think Da will allow it so long as it don't interfere with Dylan's learning perfumery. Nessa might come, or Jory. So that's good."

"But if I'm not needed here, I shall have to return to my duties with the doctor," I said.

She let go of my hands. "And you don't want your Sight anyway, I know." She took up her broom again and jabbed the bristles all along the edge where the bottom of the counter met the floor, dislodging clots of dust and dirt. Was she angry with me?

"I have been thinking about that," I said. She turned. Her eyes sparkled with tears. She wasn't angry, she was unhappy. "Margery, please don't cry. I—can I tell you a secret? You know my Sight used to just come and take me. Ever since my peregrine, I have practiced hiding, like you taught me, when I felt it coming. But I think my Sight—leaks."

Margery leaned her broom against the counter. "Leaks?" She dabbed her eyes with the corner of her apron.

"Yes. Giselle can…hear me even when I'm not trying to talk to her. I was thinking about you one day whilst I waited in the trap for the doctor, and she started walking here, all by herself. But she doesn't try to…to take me. So now I don't hide up here all the time" —I tapped my head—"I just, well, keep watch. I decide for myself whether I'll go or stay."

Margery stared. "You're managing your Sight on your own?"

"I'm trying. I was thinking I might try to make a tether."

"And you haven't had any trouble? You promised to tell me if you did." I shook my head. She pulled me in. "Jem, that's wonderful. I'm so glad to hear you haven't given it up entirely. But Jem, Second Sight is nothing to play with. Sight comes from—well, I don't know exactly, but the way Granny Kestrel talks, Sight is Life itself."

Then I got a flash that made me tremble with hope. "Margery! Could—can the Sight put right something inside a sick person? Could Granny Kestrel show me how to use the Sight to heal Mr. Galt?"

She eased me back, her face sober. "Sight doesn't work that way, Jem. I'm sorry. But Granny could teach you other things about it you couldn't easily learn on your own."

My heart landed in my boots. I shook my head. What good was it to feel the great, free spirits of lions if I couldn't let them out of their cages? What good was it to fly with birds if I couldn't live in the sky? What good was it to be able to See Mr. Galt dying if I couldn't See to his getting better, too?

I study and I work and I try, but sometimes I just don't understand anything.

CHAPTER 7

MARCH 1759

Intrigue on Top of Complication Woven into Confusion

My helping to care for Mr. Galt did not excuse me from duties I performed for Dr. Abernathy. I fretted about Mr. Galt on the days I wasn't there and Margery's brother took my place, but Margery promised to send word if Mr. Galt took a turn for the worse. So it was that on a day I didn't go to the shop, the doctor assigned me the tedious task of winding bandages by hand. He'd taught me to lap three or four layers over my thigh, roll up those layers in a tight cylinder, then wrap the loose end of the bandage several more turns around the whole. The end result was something that looked like a fat white finger.

Mrs. Pierce didn't like things strewn about the front room, including me, so I worked in the parlor. I'd cleaned a spot by the parlor windows for my disinfection station, and that's where I rolled bandages. True, the windows needed a wash, but the morning sun shone bright enough for me to see. On a day in early March, when I'd just finished my sixth bandage, I heard the bell, then voices in the hall, then in came Mrs. Pierce, who had still never shown in her face or manner that she recognized me as the girl who'd stayed there the previous April. Either she didn't know or she didn't care—or she was glad to have a dogsbody to scour her pots and empty the chamberpots every morning or build up the fire in the doctor's bedchamber. The only thing that seemed to have changed for Mrs. Pierce was the quantity of food she indifferently cooked.

"Mr. Franklin," she announced, "would you care to receive him in the front room?"

"No, thank you, I'll see him here. I have to finish this for the doctor."

Her eyes flickered over the dust covers and me in my little island of cleanliness. She sniffed and opened her mouth. Behind her, I heard a voice say, "Is Jem in there, Mrs. Pierce? Thank you," and Franklin himself came in. Mrs. Pierce bobbed her head and closed the door behind her. There could be only one reason Franklin had come to see me. I stood.

"You must have found out something," I said without preamble.

"Well, hello to you as well."

"Sorry, Mr. Franklin. Hello. Please sit down." I eased a dust cloth off a chair and pulled it over to my table. "Shall I ring for tea?"

"Perhaps not. We wouldn't want to inconvenience your Mrs. Pierce. She seemed a bit put out when she had to answer the door." He sat. "Is the doctor in? Perhaps he should hear what I have to say."

"No, sir. The doctor has gone to St. Bart's and left me here to see to his bandages."

"May we speak while you work?" Franklin asked. He watched me roll for a moment, then took up a short strip of cloth. "I might as well help you. It will pass the time and I shall acquire a new skill." He began to roll. "Jem, I've come to tell you what I've learned about your cameo and your mother. It isn't much, and I am not sure if the family I found is yours. I also heard a curious story at St. Paul's Coffeehouse after I'd seen the records of peers and land holdings and so forth. You need to hear it."

He leaned in, "And let me tell you: it is no small feat to examine the records. They are great dusty books that one must have permission to look at. Such things should be a matter of public record. People have a right to know the legal owner of a piece of land, but the lawyers will have their hand in every affair." He frowned at his rolled bandage—it was sloppily done—but he added it to my pile and started another. "The sheer number of records made it seem that finding anything useful would be too time-consuming."

"I see." I decided to re-do his bandage later.

"But then a kindly clerk brought a book to me, published by a friend in Pall

Mall that listed the present peerages and showed their coats of arms."

"Peerages?"

"It seemed a logical place to start, given my suspicion that a wealthy person had commissioned the cameo, although it is true that not all peers are wealthy. The symbols in the arms and heraldry of the great families were so fascinating, I lost track of my task until the clerk came to offer assistance."

I braced myself. "What did you learn?"

"There is some confusion, since we're not sure what the letters on the cameo stand for. In a monogram, usually, the letter of a person's surname is wedged between the letter of the first name on the left and the letter of the middle name on the right. In your case—what is your middle name again?"

"Marietta."

"In your case, your monogram would be *JCM*."

"Connolly in the middle?"

"Correct. If a monogram is what we have on the cameo, its former owner's initials are *MPHA*, so *PH* would be the initials of the person's last name. But are these initials? Could the letters stand for a family motto—"More Powerful Hearts Arise" for example? If a motto, is it in English or Latin or French? Added to the range of possibilities with regard to the initials is some doubt about your mother's place of origin."

"What do you mean?"

"The book told who came from where according to region, but your mother could have traveled to Lamesley from anywhere, so she may not have come from the north in the first place." His bandage-winding slowed. "But I decided to focus on the northeast near Newcastle, because I had to start somewhere, and your Christmas story about the Porteous riot suggested a focus."

I tried to listen patiently. Usually, Mr. Franklin laid out information like he laid out experiments for the Royal Society, step by careful step. On the subject of family, I lacked the patience for careful steps—I wanted to know *now*.

Franklin said, "I found five families in the north country that are candidates if we operate on the likely theory that the letters stand for names. Two were Jacobites whose property was confiscated. A third family had four sons. Of course, the eldest is set up to inherit, and the other three will have to live upon his pleasure or go into the military or hope to receive something from their father, which some families are starting to do nowadays. I know that is my intention when I go home. I haven't a lot of property, but I'm no longer certain William would appreciate my library, so I may not leave it to my son at all. It may do more good as part of the stock of Philadelphia's lending library—"

"Mr. Franklin, I beg your pardon, but what did you learn from the books?"

"*Doctor* Franklin, if you please." He beamed. "Last month I was awarded an honorary doctorate of laws degree by the University of St. Andrews. I received notice of it just a few days ago."

"Sir, what an honor. Congratulations!"

"Thank you. I had not looked for it, but I confess that I enjoy the prefix *Doctor* added to my name."

"As would I."

He looked at me over his glasses. "That's as may be. If there be pork in the trees one morning, or reports of devils with frostbite in the Strand, you may yet be allowed to practice medicine."

I wrinkled my nose at him. *Why* could he not get on with his story? "You were talking about a fourth family? What of them?"

He dropped his bandage and pulled some notes from his pocket. "The fourth family is in a sorry state. Through bad management and dissolute heirs, not to mention taxation, the estate is whittled down with only a few servants in the house and the most meager of flocks and tenants. I believe they are nearly ruined. An unmarried son stands to inherit, so the father is trying to marry him off to a bride who can bring in a suffusion of cash to prop up the family finances and get the estate on solid ground again."

I blinked. "You learned all this from the book?"

"Dear me, no. The book lists only names. I got the extra information from the helpful clerk I mentioned earlier, a gentleman who knows a great deal about the peers of the realm and is delighted to share it—certainly, it is not correct to gossip, but public censure with her thousand eyes and thousand tongues divulges every least crime or foible."

"Sir?"

"Gossip can be useful." Franklin took up the end of a longer bandage and looked at it. I started it for him. "You know, Jem, this is relaxing," he said. "It allows me to talk and think and yet do something useful with my hands. Idle hands are the devil's tools."

Winding bandages was taking up too much of his attention and producing rolls I'd have to do over. "Dr. Franklin, what was the gossip about the fifth family?"

He smiled. "That is where I stumbled on to something interesting. I was invited to luncheon only last week at the Foundling Hospital, where Thomas Pelham-Holles, Duke of Newcastle, was also at table. Several people tried to engage him in conversation, but he seemed disinclined to converse. I asked a dinner companion why the gentleman was so reserved."

"And?"

"And my dinner companion said the duke was concerned about prosecution of the war. The Austrian and Russian armies were moving to join forces, which would be disastrous for Prussia."

How does the war relate to me or my mother? I wound my bandages very tight and ordered myself to stay calm while I waited for an end to Franklin's tale.

"The reason I tell you this is that my dinner companion related a story about the duke that may touch on you," Franklin said.

Finally!

"He said there had been a tragedy in the family some ten or eleven years before. A beloved daughter had fallen from her horse and broken her neck and was buried on the family property. The tragedy deeply affected the duke and the duchess. Now, Jem, we come to it: you may be their daughter's child."

I stopped winding. In a hundred years, I never would have made such a leap. My mind whirled like a flock of birds, then settled on simple logic: "I can't be the daughter of a girl who died."

"Unless she did *not* die." His eyes sparkled; his tale had hooked me good and proper, even though the idea that I was related to a duke was—absurd.

Franklin continued, "When I brought this tale back to the gossipy clerk, he confirmed that the girl's death was the official story but that rumors had been swirling about for years that the girl had run away with an inferior person, and that the duke wished to avoid a scandal, so he put about the story of her tragic death."

"An inferior person! But…can someone do that? Lie about a death?"

"People can lie about anything. But, you're right, it's unlikely that an important family would feign a death, if only because their comings and goings are known to their retainers and to others in society." He snatched up one end of another bandage. "Jem, I am quite enjoying this! I should like to roll bandages with you again, if I may."

"You are welcome to roll bandages with me any time. What were you saying about the duke's daughter?"

"The daughter who allegedly died and was buried was named after sister queens. The clerk thought it arrogant of the duke and duchess to use the names of two royal personages."

I waited. "Dr. Franklin, what were the names?"

"He showed me the entry in the book. Queen Mary ruled before her sister, Queen Anne."

He must have heard the *thunk* of my heart. "The girl who ran away was named Mary Anne?" *No*, I thought. *That girl can't be my mother.*

He stopped rolling his bandage and looked at me, his brown eyes intense. "Jem, do you grasp the enormity of what I am telling you? The father of the girl who fell off a horse, the Duke of Newcastle, is at present First Lord of the Treasury and advisor to the king, and *that* is the man who may be your grandfather."

My fingers stopped moving. The *shush-shush-shush* of my heartbeat sounded loud in my ears. I shook my head. "No, no, no," I said, "that can't be true." I saw a series of images in my memory as though I looked at them in a book—after Louisbourg, a man in the market exclaiming, "Newcastle sent orders for two Corporations to be made drunk!"; Margery reading to Mr. Galt about our taking Fort Duquesne from the *Gentleman's Magazine* with a portrait of the duke staring out from the article, all long wig and long nose and black eyebrows; Dr. Abernathy alternately criticizing the ongoing war and praising Newcastle's skill in raising money to fund it. I dropped my bandage and pressed my hand to the table. I could not be connected to an important man like that.

"But if you *were* connected," Franklin said, "it would be a scandal that could change the outcome of the war."

"Why do you say that?" *Why is it so close in here?* I tugged on my cravat.

"Newcastle is the chief financier of the war. He persuades bankers to loan money to the Crown for the war effort. If he were found to have a daughter who ran away with a stable boy, that would be bad enough, but if it were found that he had condoned a false burial—well, I don't know that the bankers would even see him. Powerful people deplore scandal." He brushed at his sleeve. "And if Newcastle could not persuade the bankers to loan money, what would happen to Prussia? To Pennsylvania? What would the future bring?"

His head shrunk to the size of a doll's, and I heard his next sentence as though my head had been plunged in a tub of water, "Jem, are you all right?"

No, not plunged in a tub of water—immersed in a tunnel of it. As sudden as blinking, as sudden as falling down a hole, Franklin's face disappeared. In its place, a succession of images swirled around me as though I were trapped inside a glass sphere spinning in a whirlwind—

horses and cannons and carts tumble above and below and beside me
red coats mass on a plain like a puddle of smoking blood
a hand sweeps papers off a desk

a soldier in Prussian blue collapses, and a painted arm raises a tomahawk, and boys and girls and men and women disappear—pop—like stones dropping into a pond

forests burn and oceans bubble and great iron birds fly high without flapping their wings and drop eggs that explode when they land

—and everything spun so fast it stole my breath, and when I next could see, I lay on the floor and Franklin stood above me staring down with eyes wide as Giselle's when somebody drops a crate of bottles in the street. My stomach churned. "I'm ill," I said, and Franklin fetched my vinegar basin and put it on the floor beside me. The nausea rumbled my stomach as if I'd eaten spoiled meat. I blinked and swallowed and fought to keep myself from vomiting.

The spinning eased as I got more air into me, but I gasped like a fish tossed to shore. Franklin said, "What on earth was that? Where did you go? Your eyes went black as night, and you stared into space, and then you measured your length there on the floor." I shook my head. I couldn't quite talk yet.

He helped me into my chair, then spread my eyes wide to look at them. He chafed my hand between his own. "I had a dizzy spell," I said. "Sometimes that happens." *Air in. Air out. Breathe. What was that? I haven't been hiding myself, that's what. Giant iron birds?*

"Does Abernathy know about these—these spells?"

The room still spun. "No, that is, it never happened before quite like this."

He drummed his fingers on the table, saying, "I hope your dizzy spell doesn't mean you're getting ill. I have been well all winter."

"I don't think you need to worry about getting sick," I said. "I'm not ill." Franklin pursed his lips. "Truly." I took a deep breath. "Er, you won't tell anybody about—my mother and the duke, will you?"

"Nothing is confirmed yet, so no. All of these…intersections…could be coincidence." He pushed aside the bowl of bandages and placed the basin on the table within easy reach. "Still, I think your case bears further looking into," he said. "The duke keeps a house in Surrey and another house in Lincoln's Inn

Fields. He and the duchess host parties attended by the cream and the crumb of society. I have written to the duke on the strength of our mutual interest in the Foundling Hospital and received from him a vague invitation to call on him. I shall accept his invitation and explore the mystery further." He looked to me for a comment. I didn't know what to say; I was just glad to be sitting up.

I picked up my bandage but put it down again so I could grip the edge of the table. I still felt dizzy. *Air in. Breathe.* "Why would the duke talk to you about his daughter?"

Franklin fanned his hands as though dispersing smoke. "I wouldn't speak to him about his daughter even if I did get a chance. It's far too personal. But the man at the Foundling Hospital dinner who told me about the daughter said a family portrait at Newcastle House was unbalanced, as though something—or someone—had been painted out."

I said, "You want to see the portrait."

He nodded. "The duke and duchess invite friends and enemies alike. I'm not sure into which category I would fall, but, as I said, I already have a foot in the door."

He would go to Newcastle House, I knew he would, even if I asked him not to. This mystery had seized his imagination—and if this story were true, Dr. Franklin would have leverage over a powerful man. He would know a secret that could tumble the duke from power— *No! Don't think about the future again!* I slammed my mind into its hiding place and changed the subject. "If you did go see the duke, what would you say to him?"

"Nothing about you—that's certain. If I could speak with him, I would remind him that American militiamen helped British regulars take Louisbourg from the French and that we've been routing the French ever since. Pitt thinks if France loses her North American colonies, she'll be easier to defeat on the Continent. America is key to England winning the war and all of North America besides."

"Winning the war would be good." I set the basin back on the floor.

"Good for England, most assuredly." He peered at my face. "Your color is coming back."

"I feel better."

"Good. I also would remind the duke that America is on England's side. Before I go home, I need to know England is on our side."

The last shreds of fog in my mind melted. "You're going home? When?"

"Not just yet, Jem. But I may be called back. Indeed, my wife already has called me back. Several times. The Penns won't see me. Some gentlemen here look on me as a mosquito buzzing in their chambers. Frankly, I've been focusing on your mystery because it's a distraction from my own attempts to lobby men who would rather talk about their gout than about the Colonies." He stared into my face with a little smile on his face. "Imagine! I might be tutor to Newcastle's own flesh and blood."

"Please don't say that. It's—it's like a bad novel. No, it's like a bad dream. Why would my mother keep something like that a secret?"

"Perhaps she didn't want to be found. Perhaps she wanted her life with your father to be…undisturbed."

"Maybe you should stop making inquiries," I grumbled, pulling the bowl of bandages closer. "I don't want anyone to wonder why you're poking your nose into this old story."

"Dear child, I haven't been a diplomat for all these years without learning something about the art of subterfuge. I'll be circumspect as a church mouse."

I looked at the bowl of bandages. Winding seemed pointless now that trouble stood on my doorstep. I said, "Oh, Dr. Franklin: what if it's true?"

"Let's not put the cart before the horse. The duke may want his dead daughter to stay dead—and let's not forget that she may actually *be* dead. Frankly, it seems improbable that a peer would condone a false burial just to cover up his daughter's elopement. Let us be patient until we know more."

"It's so complicated it makes my head hurt."

"Then let us wrap your head in a bandage," he said and proceeded to do so.

"You look like a drunkard the day after a brawl," Franklin said. He laughed, then tossed down his bandage and declared he'd had enough of bandage-winding and had learned all he could from it. He wished me good day and left to find something more stimulating for his active mind. Unfortunately, the bandage did not muffle the hammer in my head that had redoubled its pounding, although I preferred the pounding to the sickening visions that had laid me out on the floor.

* * *

Dr. Franklin's talk of my family reminded me that I hadn't visited my mother's grave since Christmas. So, shortly after his visit, on an afternoon which presented me with no pressing duties, the doctor gave me money to hire a hackney to take me to Chelsea where she was buried.

It was a sunless day like most days in March, cold, damp, and drizzly, so after I bought pink carnations at Covent Garden, I hired a hackney and asked the driver to wait.

I laid my carnations by the headstone. Fat raindrops spattered mud on the pink petals as I stood beside the grave talking to Mum and my baby brother, Jamie.

I told them I was well and that I enjoyed my studies. I told James for the hundredth time that I was sorry and that I would do everything differently if I had it to do over again. I told Mum Henry Galt was sick but that Margery and I were taking care of him.

I told her about an essay by Dr. Johnson in *The Chronicle* about how the passing seasons mark the passing of time in our own lives, and how we should give joy to others before it was too late. The essay had made me think of Mum, and of James and Da, and of all the things I could have and should have done for them while they were alive. Things I could never do, now.

I stood beside the grave thatched with dead grass, overhung by dripping branches, and I told them if I could have them back for just one day, I would make it the most joyful day they'd ever known. "And Mum," I whispered, "Dr. Franklin thinks the Duke of Newcastle is your father. Is he?" I waited for… what? A sign? A peek of Mum's face?

Nothing happened. I got no answer. I saw no vision. No second chances for me.

The chill wind whistled in the branches, a shower of sleety rain coated my muddy flowers, and the anxious whinny of the horse that waited for me in the cold reminded me that life is for the living no matter how much we might wish to hold open a door for the dead.

CHAPTER 8

SPRING AND SUMMER 1759

The Sweep of Time

We knew Mr. Galt was going, but expecting him to die didn't lessen the shock when he did.

On April 7, I went to the shop. It was a pretty day, the sky that sweet shade of blue that belongs to springtime. New leaves on the trees and the scent of blossoms on the air cheered me. Margery met me at the back door of the shop with red eyes and that lost expression I'd seen often enough on caretakers' faces to know why she wore it. Behind her, Mr. Galt's form lay still under his coverlet. I watched Margery's face and held my breath.

"Henry died in the night," Margery said. "I listened for his coughing as I've done all these weeks, but I didn't hear it. I thought he was having a good night." Her eyes filled. "I should have been here when he breathed his last." I tried to step around her to see for myself. "Jem, he's gone. Best to let him be."

My lips trembled. "I should have told him who I was from the beginning. I could have had so much more time with him."

Margery pulled me in. "That's life, isn't it?" she said, sadly. "You never do all you should do or can do until it's too late." I looked past Margery's arm to the bed. Henry Galt hadn't been my kin, but he'd been what I'd imagined a grandfather might be: kind, snappish, funny, wise, and, sometimes, smelly. He'd forgiven me my breeches even though he didn't like them. He'd forgiven my not telling him who I was. Like a grandparent, he'd forgiven everything without a second thought, because he loved me. Safe in Margery's arms, I let the tears fall.

At Mr. Galt's wake, Mr. Bevan told how one day when the two of them were still journeymen apothecaries, Mr. Galt was given the task of cleaning oil out of their master's favorite ceramic dish. They both wanted to be off somewhere (Mr. Bevan didn't say where, but he winked at us). To speed things along, Mr. Bevan set the dish on a flame and dumped in potash—and fire leapt up and singed Mr. Galt's eyebrows. Picturing Mr. Galt without great, bushy eyebrows was nearly impossible considering they'd stuck out like bird wings ever since I'd known him. I smiled at the story like everybody else, even though it squeezed my heart.

Because Henry Galt had never married. He'd had no children. His will mentioned only one person: Margery Jamison. To her, daughter of his heart, he left his shop.

After the funeral, Dr. Abernathy and Margery and I went back to the shop for a sad little cup of tea. I saw Mr. Galt everywhere: sitting at the door, squinting at his book behind the counter, sleeping in his bed in the back room. I saw a healthier version of him lifting up Jamie, smiling at my mother, scowling at me from under those bird-wing eyebrows, wiggling his fingers as he spun a thought. Pulling on his beard as he and Dr. Abernathy debated a treatment. Buttering a slice of bread for me. Giving my shoulder a squeeze. Laughing at my jests. A thousand thousand kindnesses. There never had been—no, nor ever would be—anybody like Henry Galt.

Margery sent a letter to us three days after the funeral, saying she'd decided to clean the shop top to bottom and asking whether Jem could help. I wanted to help; it seemed one last kindness I could do for Mr. Galt. Dr. Abernathy gave me permission to go in for a few Mondays until we finished the job, so long as I used the back door and stayed out of sight. When I knocked on the back door and Margery came to unlock it, I saw she'd already begun to clear out the back room. "We must burn or disinfect everything," Margery said. "That's what's done with phthisis."

We took out bits of paper and dried crusts of bread and started a fire in front of the big hogshead. We burned Henry's clothes and bedding on Dr. Abernathy's advice, and I found it very hard, for I kept seeing the man inside the clothes. In the folds of the garments, I smelled nutmeg and sulphur. But we fed it all to the flames. I mixed bucket after bucket of vinegar water to wash down Mr. Galt's back room, walls and floor and even ceiling, which made me appreciate having to do only a quick dunk of the doctor's tools at home. Fortunately, the weather had warmed so we could open the back door, and Margery opened the front as well once I'd gone home for the day.

Over the next several Mondays, Margery and I cleaned out the rest of the shop. She cried and sighed by turns as we worked. Margery moved the skull to a shelf high on the wall, where it kept watch over the counter. She found the letter I'd written to Mr. Galt at Christmas tucked up in the heart section of his big prescription book. She offered the letter to me, but I said we should leave it there to mark Henry's place. Margery's eyes got teary when she said she would do it.

When we got to the bottles and drawers displayed high above the counter, I said, "The day we moved in upstairs, Mr. Galt fetched a ladder and made me climb up and down dusting and polishing all of these."

"I wondered why they seemed cleaner than the rest of the place," Margery said.

"The bottles were clotted with dust," I said. "The labels were brown and partly peeled off and I couldn't tell what was inside because the ink was faded, and the language was Latin anyway. I asked Mr. Galt what was in the bottles, and he said if I opened them to find out, I'd have to clean them." Margery barked a laugh. I squinted at the bottles. "I probably could tell you what's in them now that I know more Latin."

Margery surveyed the rows and rows of bottles. "Jem, truly, I doubt I'd use a thing from up there." She heaved a sigh. "Leave them for now. I'll go after them a little at a time. Otherwise, I'll be cleaning bottles straight through to Christmas."

We cleaned and organized Henry's array of tools. Margery clucked and exclaimed ("Aha!" and "Ooh, look at this!") as we went along, glad to find a small portable hearth and bellows, a small cauldron, a crucible, ladle, tongs, scissors, hammer and file, some of which she hadn't seen in a long time. We found and cleaned flasks of different sizes, earthen pots, a large flat dish with sand in it, funnels, sieves, and filters. We cleaned the windows.

When Margery finally moved her own herbs downstairs and set up her living quarters upstairs, the shop looked almost as bright and airy as if it had been newly built. Margery put fresh medicaments on the shelves. She put pots of herbs in the big front window as well. Now, instead of smelling like nasty chemicals and old wood and Henry Galt himself, God rest his soul, the shop smelled like Margery's herbs.

I said I wished the doctor would have his parlor cleaned too, but that he'd shut it up when his wife and son died and left it that way.

"Whatever for?" Margery asked.

"Mrs. Pierce said it was his wife's favorite room, so he doesn't like to stir up memories."

"I suspect Mrs. Pierce just doesn't want to take on the job of cleaning it."

"She does tend to conserve her energy."

"Which is a polite way of saying she won't do a lick of work if she can get out of it. One of these days I may pop over to Cavendish Square, and you may invite me in for tea. And then I may attack the parlor with a broom and a mop, and then your dear doctor can see that it's foolish to live in a tomb, the great black-browed ghoulie."

I laughed. "Come soon, Margery."

Once we'd set the shop to rights, I thought my Mondays with Margery were done. But when I reported to Dr. Abernathy that we'd finished cleaning and that he should come and see how nice the shop looked now, he surprised me by suggesting something altogether different. "What would you think about going back to Mrs. Jamison once a week?"

I felt my mouth drop open. It was a moment or two before I could say, "Really? Do you think I could? What about Patch   Mr. Duncan?"

"Nobody has seen him in six months. It might be he has given up and gone back in disgrace to his employer," Dr. Abernathy said. "It might be he's been sacked. I probably don't have to ask if you want go back," he added when I threw my arms around his neck. I'd been dreading the end of my cleaning duty because it meant the end of my time with Margery. "Jem," he gargled. "Loosen your grip." I stepped back. He straightened his cravat. "Thank you. You still must keep your wits about you. Be aware of who is around you. Use the back door to the shop. Keep out of sight."

"I shall do everything perfectly," I said, "and nobody will bother me. Margery does need me, you know, even though she doesn't need me any longer to help her with Mr. Galt." When I said the name out loud, I went quiet. The doctor poured me a tot of brandy but drank it off himself when I reminded him I didn't like it.

So it was that something good followed on the heels of something bad. It seemed to be the pattern of my life: when Da died, we came to London; when mum and Jamie died, the doctor took me in; when Mr. Galt died, I got Margery back in my life. Perhaps it was wrong of me to think of life this way, but I believe every person lives inside a circle and takes notice of life outside the circle only when it shoves in. Perhaps people can't help focusing on themselves.

For me, Mr. Galt's passing closed one door but opened another: one day a week, I could be just *be*. With Margery, I didn't have to watch my manners or my technique or my posture or my voice. I didn't have to recite numbers to keep birds at bay. Once inside the shop, I didn't have to watch the streets for Freddie's red hair or Patch's gray coat. Margery knew everything about me. She knew I had Second Sight and what to do if it took me. Sometimes I wondered what might have happened if I'd gone to Margery's granny for training, but I let it go.

Spring turned to summer. Once a week, I walked to the shop and did whatever needed doing. On a balmy May day when I'd poured some melted goose grease into a trencher, I set it aside to cool and just sat watching Margery. We were making a burn salve that day of comfrey root, some bayberry bark she'd got out at Chelsea, beeswax, and the goose grease. I asked Margery what goose grease did to help burns.

"Nothing, really," she said, "but grease or tallow or beeswax makes the medicine stick to the injury."

"So the real medicine is whatever you mix in with the grease."

"Aye." She continued to grind the bayberry bark and comfrey root.

"Margery, do you have a recipe for your salve so somebody else could make it?"

"I don't need a recipe. I know how to make it."

"Yes, but if there were a recipe, somebody a long time from now and far away from here could make it."

"After I'm dead and gone?"

"Well, yes."

"What good would that do me?"

"It would be good for medicine, for the world, for sick people."

"That sounds like too much work for too little profit." She kept circling her pestle round and round.

"Could I make a book of your recipes?"

She leaned the pestle on the side of the mortar and flexed her fingers. "Thinking of setting up shop, Jem?"

"No! Not at all! I would never—"

She laughed. "Of course you wouldn't, Jem. I was foolin' with you." She took up her pestle again.

The idea seemed too important to give up. "Margery," I said, "could I write down your recipes?"

"What for?"

"If more people made medicine your way, fewer people would be sick."

"Wouldn't that let your Dr. Abernathy out of a job?"

"No, because half of his patients don't do what he says anyway."

She laughed. "I suppose you can write down my recipes if you want to. I don't know how a book would serve others, for each wise woman does things her own way, and apothecaries have their own books. But p'raps I shall have a daughter one day that would like to take over the shop. It might save her some time learning recipes if they was handy in a book." She smiled down at me. "And if I don't have a daughter, p'raps it will be you who takes over my work."

That sounded fine!

"You know, Jem," she said as she knocked the contents from her mortar into the trencher of goose grease, "you likely could make a fine doctor if only women were let to do it. You have a quick mind and a strong and steady hand. But you'll never be let to be one. P'raps when you get older, the doctor might let you work as my apprentice."

"As a girl?"

"Aye, as a girl."

"Thank you, Margery. I'd like to stay with the doctor a bit longer."

"Suit yourself, but one day you'll grow yourself a bosom, and you might change your mind." I looked down at the table. I did not want to think about growing up. Margery pulled a bit of hair out of my eyes, then shrugged and said, "Well, the offer's open until I get me a 'prentice of my own."

"I'll bring a blank book next time to write down your recipes, shall I?"

And that's what I did. Some Mondays instead of mixing compounds, I just wrote down recipes as she dictated them. Sometimes she would say, "It's a lump as large as an egg but a pigeon egg, not a chicken egg—I think—oh dear, I'll have to make some up before I can remember how it goes," and she would do so. Soon she had to purchase more bottles, for she couldn't clean out Henry's quickly enough. My little book filled with recipes for healing.

* * *

The weather warmed. On a Monday in mid-June, Margery unlocked a cabinet in which she kept her most valuable ingredients: saffron, gold, Jesuit's Bark, raw opium, ambergris. She took out a large earthenware container holding a pungent brown residue. "Opium," she said. "We'll use only a little. Here, you mash these plantain leaves to begin with."

"What are we making?"

"An elixir for the bloody flux. It comes every year, and I want to make medicine ahead."

"But people won't start getting the flux for another month or so."

"When people start getting sick, there are so many of them, I can't keep up." She got out honey, gum Benjamin, aniseed, licorice, blackberry leaves, and oak bark. She poured some wine into a flask. "When that lot is mashed, show me first and then dump it into the wine, then I'll add the rest. This will take the morning, but once we set it to steep, you and I are going over to the doctor's house."

I stopped mashing. "In Cavendish Square?"

"Does he have another house?" She smiled.

"But the doctor is out today."

She smiled. "As I'd hoped. We'll be able to take everything outside and wallop the dust out."

"We're cleaning the parlor today? Who'll mind the shop?"

"Dylan's coming. He can sell simple things and take orders. He'll lock up for the evening if I'm not back. Go on—mash."

Evening? How long did she plan to stay at Cavendish Square? Margery's proposed mission made me nervous, but I focused my attention on mashing plantain leaves and writing the recipe in my book. I mashed and wrote, mashed and wrote. Eventually, we combined my plantain and wine with the contents of her mortar and stoppered the lot in a big stone jar.

When Margery's brother came in, he smelled of cinnamon and orange. I said, "Mm, what have you and your father been making today, Master Penhaligon?"

"King's Honeywater," he said.

"That's the one with two dozen ingredients," Margery said. "Glad it's you making it and not I."

"And I'm glad me and Da and Nessa got it mixed this morning or I couldn't've come," Dylan Penhaligon answered. "Anything I need to know?"

"Just the usual: get the money before you hand over the package. You'll have to lock up as I won't be home until after closing." Margery loaded coins into her pocket and we left. Nerves spoiled my pleasure in what should have been a fine day for walking. I hadn't asked the doctor's permission to bring Margery home. I wasn't sure he'd like her meddling.

At home, I was glad not to see Mrs. Pierce's hat on the hall table. *Gone. Good.*

Margery sailed in like somebody deciding whether to buy the place. She gave a sniff, then headed for the kitchen.

"What's here?" she said. She rummaged in the larder, emerging with a dish of raisins and a heel of bread. "The man should be ashamed," she said. "No wonder you have headaches: there's no food in the house. Don't you eat?"

"Of course we eat. The doctor is very good to me. For dinner we stop at a tavern between patients, and we sometimes stop there for tea as well, or we buy a loaf of bread on the way home. We do eat, very well, we just don't eat here every day." Thank goodness Mrs. Pierce was not at home to hear this criticism of her paltry pantry.

"Still! A grand house like this and hardly a crumb to eat—it's a disgrace." She continued to rummage, and I felt uneasy. Margery had questioned me in the past about what I ate and what cleaning was done and did I get any sunshine and what was in the larder and the like. Today, it seemed, she'd come to inspect everything, starting with the pantry. I shifted from foot to foot as she opened drawers and cupboards. When she said, "Where's the parlor, then?" and sailed out, I followed.

"This way, Margery." I opened the door to the dark, high-ceilinged room with its sooty fireplace, blanket of dust, and faint odor of vinegar. "We don't use it," I explained. "Well, I do—I clean the doctor's instruments over here by the window. I wind bandages. But in the evening after dinner, we use the front room."

"How can you see anything?" she said. She batted at the drapery panel I'd tied back. A cloud of dust swirled in the light from the window. "And how clean can his instruments get with all this dust?" She fanned her hand in front of her face. She surveyed the room. Dust coated all: chairs, carpets, mantel, pictures. "It will take time to set this to rights," she said. She pointed to an armchair. "That first."

"I really don't think—"

"This is the work I've set for us to do today, Jem Connolly, and I shall do it with or without your help," Margery said.

"Fine, I'll help." We moved the chair to the garden. Margery found a broom and began to beat the chair. Clouds of dust puffed up. "Now, you beat every inch of this," she said, handing the broom to me. "Keep hitting it until no more dust flies. Then we can take a damp cloth to it. If it doesn't rain"—she looked up—"and I don't think it will, we can leave it out to air."

"But what if the doctor comes home?"

"I can manage Dr. Abernathy, never fear. Besides, he may like coming home to a pleasant, cheery fire and a soft chair and a piping hot supper. He might forget that his parlor is supposed to be a tomb for the dead."

"Margery!"

"Well, it's going on ten years that the place has been shut up, isn't it? Didn't you say it hadn't been touched since his wife died?"

"Yes, but—"

"But, your granny's eyeballs. I'm sorry, Jem, but once a man lands in a rut, it takes gunpowder to get him out." She grinned. "And today, I'm Guy Fawkes." She marched back inside.

All the furniture we could move went outside. My job was to beat the dust out of it. After half an hour, when I felt as though I'd never be able to lift my arms again, Margery came outside bearing a wicker carpet beater with a long handle. "Here, try this," she said. "I found it in with the fireplace tools, of all things. It's for carpets, but we can use it on the furniture, too. Besides, I need the broom." The beater made the job easier, and soon I'd beaten the dust out of all the chairs, with much of it landing on me. I looked like a gray ghost. We moved the rug outside, and I beat that too.

When I went in to fetch a damp cloth, I stepped into the parlor and couldn't believe how bright it looked, for Margery had found a ladder, taken down the draperies, and cleaned the inside of the windows. She'd seen a boy outside, paid him to fetch a carter, and sent off the draperies to be cleaned, though even with extra payment for immediate service, they wouldn't be done for two days. While I'd been outside, she'd wiped up most of the dust and swept down the cobwebs.

"Oh, good, you're here," she said. "Run out and see if you can find a sweep to clean the chimney."

"Margery, how are you paying for all this?"

"Your doctor is paying for it, my dear. The bills will be sent to him."

I swallowed. What on earth would the doctor say when he came home? Would he be angry or would Margery roll over his objections like a wave over pebbles? I ran out to look for a sweep.

When I returned with the chimney sweep and his boy, I found Margery struggling in the doorway with a clean armchair. I ran to help her, but the sweep scooped up the chair and placed it where Margery pointed.

"La, aren't you the strong one," she said, and the man blushed.

"This here fireplace the one to be cleaned then, Missus?" the sweep said.

"It is, sir, and if you please, it hasn't been cleaned in ten years," Margery answered.

The sweep laid down a large cloth all along the front of the fireplace. His boy, so small he seemed more imp than boy, watched with his tiny arms crossed on his breast. Soot blackened his clothes and face. With the cloth in place, the sweep grasped the boy's shoulder and pushed him toward the fireplace saying, "Up you go, then." The boy slipped off his shoes, the better to grip the sides of the chimney with his little black toes. Up he went.

"Ready," the boy called down.

The sweep handed up a long-handled brush with bristles spread in a flat circle, then stuck his head close to the fireplace opening and boomed, "All the way to the top, mind."

"Aye, sir," the boy's high voice echoed down. The sound of brushing soon echoed down the chimney, while soot pattered down to the hearth.

Meanwhile, Margery and I moved the rest of the furniture back inside, keeping it well back from the sooty cloud near the fireplace. The sweep helped with the furniture, blushing whenever Margery complimented him on his muscles. The sweep didn't seem that marvelous a specimen to me, but every time Margery jollied him along, he hauled in another piece of furniture. When it was all in, she gave him a glass of water, and fetched another for the boy when he climbed back down. The only thing white on the little boy were his two eyes. Margery paid the sweep out of her own pocket. They took up their floor cloth, the sweep tipped his cap to Margery and winked, and then they left. "Shake it out down the road, if you please," Margery called after them.

Then she turned to look at the sunlight shining through the windows. "Jem, can you wash the outside of the windows whilst I scrub the floor? Heaven knows when anyone last took a cloth to those panes." And I carried out the ladder and did that too.

When we finished, we looked at one another and laughed. My clothes were so gray I looked like I was made of dust. Margery took off her cap, and the hair that had been protected underneath tumbled out a pretty, coppery red. She looked like a torch.

"Well, we are a sight," she said. "Are you hungry?"

"Famished. But, Margery, why were you so saucy with the chimney sweep?"

She smiled. "Let's clean up a bit and have a nice tea at that inn on Tyburn

Road and I'll tell you. Would you like that?"

Before we left, we took one more look at the parlor, and I felt a kind of pride that we'd made such a difference. I hoped the doctor would remember that cleanliness is next to godliness. Perhaps Dr. Franklin would visit oftener now. Margery could visit too. We could all be friends. Then I had a thought: what if Margery and the doctor were to spend more time together as a couple? Could something come of it? Ever since the peregrine incident, whenever the doctor came by the shop to take me home, Margery's face lit up the moment we heard Giselle in the alley. Could I nudge along a friendship between them?

The inn gave us a delightful tea: sticky buns, clear broth and slices of beef, and young cider to wash it down. Margery said, "Now then, Jem, to answer your question about the chimney sweep: men must be managed, and with a man, a carrot works better than a stick. Even Philip Miller personally showed us his greenhouse when I was sweet to him, remember? So let me tell you how to manage the doctor when he comes home. He is a proud man. Like most Englishmen, he's always right."

"No, he isn't."

"He believes he is, and he believes it's his right to tell others what to do—and that includes you and me, my dear Jem, on account of our being girls."

"But, Margery, he does listen to me. It's true he doesn't like me to question him, but usually he thinks about what I said after he's done being vexed with me for disagreeing with him. And he did decide to keep me when he could have made me go."

"I think what decided him about you was that Dr. Franklin was on your side."

"No, Dr. Franklin argued against letting me stay."

"Of course he did. Because he thought you should stay."

"What?"

Margery sipped her tea, her blue eyes sparkling over the rim of her cup. "Oh, Jem, men are contrary creatures and Franklin knows that because—well, because he's a man, but a different kind of man, and very clever. Franklin argued *against* you so Dr. Abernathy was forced to take up the other side and argue *for* you. Then Franklin graciously gave in and got what he'd wanted in the first place."

My jaw dropped. Franklin used the same strategy for my lessons! I said, "How do you know that? Have you met Dr. Franklin?"

She'd said, "No, but he's an ambassador, isn't he? His job is to jolly people into giving him what he wants. Dr. Abernathy eventually came round, didn't he?" I nodded. "Now, it may well be that the doctor knew what Franklin was about and argued with him just for the fun of it. Men do that, too. Or the doctor might have wanted you to stay in the first place, but he were arguing against it to teach *you* a lesson—didn't you did say you tried on Brian's clothes *before* the doctor gave you permission?"

"Yes, so?"

"So keeping you on tenterhooks might have been Dr. Abernathy's way of letting you know who's the master here."

"But I… but that's…Wouldn't it be simpler if everyone just said the truth, straight out?"

"You didn't tell Henry straight out that you were Jenna." I poked at some crumbs on the table. "I know you had your reasons. Other people have reasons for holding back the truth. For me, figuring out what people mean or truly want is half the fun of knowing them." I sighed. "Don't worry about it, Jem, we all have to learn how to be people. Now then, I *know* the doctor is pleased with you, so we'll use that to calm him when he sees what we've done."

"What should I say?"

"He'll be irked when he sees the parlor, p'raps because he didn't think of having it done himself. Persuade him to have a glass of wine and some food. Food always mellows a man. Sit quietly by making pleasant conversation—but not too much of it. Don't speak of all we did. *Do not* talk about him getting the bills for it. Just let him be peaceful. He'll soon see what we did was a kindness."

As we finished our meal and bought supper for the doctor, I decided I was glad we'd cleaned the parlor, and I hoped Dr. Abernathy would be glad too.

* * *

Dr. Abernathy's displeasure when he saw the parlor was monumental. He said, "You had no right" and "How dare you presume?" As for Margery, well, I was glad she wasn't present to hear the things he said about her, although she likely would have laughed at "impudent hussy."

He grumbled until finally I said, "Sir, we can't get back the dirt. We can't stick the soot back on the chimney. The carpets and furniture have been cleaned, and I'm certain the filth has washed away to the river. The draperies were sent out to be washed; the drapers will put them back up the day after to-morrow, but they'll be clean too, I'm sorry to say. Since we can't get back all that dirt, may I bring you a glass of port and you can sit beside the fire and drink it?"

"You are impertinent. And just where did you get porter?"

"Margery bought it. She said a gentleman doctor that worked hard saving people's lives should be able to sit of an evening with a small glass of wine be-side a nice fire, and that it was little enough thanks for so great a service."

He narrowed his eyes. "She did not say that."

"She did, sir." Margery had made me memorize that little speech until I'd got it down perfectly. I added, "Please sit, sir, the chair's been beaten and cleaned. The fire is cheerful, isn't it? I'll pour the wine and fetch in your supper directly."

The doctor sat and looked at the fire. He said, "It's been ten years since I sat in this chair."

I handed over his wineglass. "It's nice, the fire, isn't it?"

"Mm. I suppose, though we hardly need a fire on a day like this."

"Shall I bring in a bite to eat?"

He narrowed his eyes. "What are you about?"

"Sir?"

"We always dine together on whatever's in the larder."

"Margery and I had a late tea. You must be hungry, though, and your dinner is ready. I am your servant, after all." *And you catch more flies with honey,* I thought, as I scurried off to the kitchen for the food Margery had bought for him.

So far, so good: I'd got him to sit and have some wine. For the next step, I carried cutlery and a plate to the doctor with slices of rare beef, a slab of fresh bread, and an apple tart. I set everything on the little table at his elbow. I said, "Here, sir. Supper."

I sat in the other armchair while he cut and chewed and became more cheerful.

By and by, he swallowed the last bit of apple tart and took a swallow of wine. He said, "Jem, I appreciate what you did. This room is more pleasant than I remember. I don't object to its being cleaned. I do object to your not asking me first."

Now for the last bit. "Margery was afraid you'd tell us not to bother, but she said a man who works hard should have a place to find a bit of peace at the end of the day. She said we should fix up this room as a present for you because there was nobody to think of your welfare but us."

He paused with his glass halfway to his lips. "She said that?"

"She said more, but that's the gist of it."

"She took time away from her own business and her own affairs to put this room to rights with no thought of payment or reward." I nodded. He walked his glass of wine to the window and looked up.

"What are you looking at?" I said.

"Just looking for pigs flying overhead."

"Sir! You know Margery yourself, you know how kind she is, always thinking of others. P'raps she's especially tender toward you because you've given me a home and a trade. She wanted the cleaning to be a thank-you for what you've done for me."

"Hm," he said, and he brought his glass to his lips. "Clearly I must have words with Mrs. Jamison. She's a fine apothecary, and I know she meant well, but she should not come barging into my home and turning everything topsy-turvy."

"Please don't scold her, sir. I know she meant only good."

"I never scold."

My mouth flew open, but I snapped it shut. "Of course not," I said, and forced my mouth to smile.

He fixed his eyes on me, then his own lips formed a little smile. "Well, perhaps now and again."

The tension eased out of my shoulders. My face relaxed. We spent the rest of the evening before the fire while he told me about his case in the country that day and I told him all that Margery and I had done. I left out the part about her flirting with the chimney sweep.

* * *

Just as Margery had predicted, mid-July brought an outbreak of disease. The bloody flux struck an area southeast of Cavendish Square near Broad Street, and once one person found out Margery's plantain elixir provided some relief, we made batch after batch of it. The doctor and I carried bottles of the stuff with us, but he often sent me running back to Margery's shop for more. In May, when we'd seen Dr. Franklin at a Foundling Hospital concert, he'd suspended my lessons for the summer as he planned to travel to Scotland. I felt some relief that he was out of town during the epidemic but some trepidation as well, as he planned to stop in Lamesley and County Durham on his way north.

In August, busy as she was, Margery had her examination before the Worshipful Society of Apothecaries. Afterward, she said Mr. Galt must have spoken highly of her to his brother apothecaries, for they were most cordial to her. I said perhaps they'd heard how she nursed him at the end. At any rate, Margery passed her test and became a full-fledged member of the Society.

Between my work with the doctor and with Margery, and fetching and carrying and running medicine to every corner of the town, I had little time to worry about Dr. Franklin's plan to hunt for my family in the north. But once the miasma of our London summer blew away and our battle against sickness slowed, I began to wonder (and to dread learning) what he had found out.

CHAPTER 9

SEPTEMBER 1759

News from the North

Franklin did not send for me; instead, he turned up at the doctor's house, hale and cheerful. I sat him in the parlor and ran to make us tea, as the doctor had gone out to one of Dr. Hunter's lectures and Mrs. Pierce had gone to market.

When I brought in the tea tray, Franklin stood with his hands clasped behind his back, looking out of the window. "You know, Jem, it's the strangest thing: I look forward to travel, but when I've been gone for a few weeks, I can't wait to come back to London. Then when I'm back here, I start to think of all the other places I want to visit."

"How was Scotland? Did you stop in Lamesley?" While I poured the tea, he told me a funny story of a traveler whose little dog got loose and was trounced by an innkeeper's cat. He said his new acquaintance David Hume, the philosopher, occupied himself these days with the writing of a history of England and listened keenly to Franklin's perspective on emigration, since Dr. Franklin's own father had left England for America, but his son had come right back.

"Jem, this summer gave me six weeks of the densest happiness I have met with in any part of my life," Franklin said.

"We had a rollicking summer with the bloody flux," I said. "It's clear you had the better bargain."

"A hundred times over." He peered at my face. "How are your...spells?"

"I haven't had a one since I last saw you, but I do have headaches."

"Hm. Strange." He looked around. "Is this the room you and your friend transformed this spring? It certainly sparkles."

"The doctor told you about it?"

"He said Mrs. Jamison could win the war tomorrow if the army allowed women to fight."

I laughed. "Did he? He's probably right. It was a job to clean it."

"My family believed doing hard work for no pay builds character, so I'm no stranger to thankless, dirty tasks. If I had a shilling for every time I skimmed rendered tallow from boiling cauldrons of fat in my father's shop, I would be a rich man. I believe now"—he winked at me—"though I certainly did not believe it then, any more than my William does now, that hard work builds character."

"How is William?" I didn't ask about William out of interest. I hadn't cared for Franklin's son when we'd met. He lacked his father's warmth; indeed, he'd nodded when we were introduced but hadn't said two words to me. More than anything, I wanted to hear what Franklin had found out about me—but Margery said polite conversation required me to ask people about their own interests before introducing my own. So, I showed courtesy to Dr. Franklin, thereby tormenting myself.

Franklin's smile faded when I said William's name. "My son was good company this summer. He copied out our ancestors' gravestones and behaved respectfully. But now that we've come back to town, he has taken up again with young men who have more money than sense." He sighed and sipped his tea. "I shall so miss the civility of a proper tea when I go home."

My cup clinked into its saucer. "You're going home? When?"

"I should have gone long ago when the Penns stopped talking to me. Pitt won't see me, either. At the same time, I can't make myself go. Whenever I think of parting from my friends, my feet refuse to take me to buy passage on a ship. I can walk five minutes in any direction here and find a genius to talk with." The doctor's clock chimed the half hour. Franklin set his cup in its saucer. "I have an engagement this evening, so let me tell what I learned about you this summer."

This was it. The sun shone in the windows, my tea cooled in my cup, and the clock quietly ticked the minutes by, all perfectly down-to-earth things that seemed skewed, somehow, as I waited to hear news that might change my life. Franklin pulled a folded piece of paper from his waistcoat pocket and opened it.

"First, Jem: whether your mother is the central character in this story, I cannot say with certainty. I think it likely. But you be the judge.

"I called on the Duke of Newcastle, Thomas Pelham-Holles, at his hunting lodge, Clumber House, near Sherwood Forest. His wife had accompanied him to see whether and how the property might be improved. What I learned there was told to me in bits and pieces by servants in the house. Over a pint in the village tavern, I heard more from a gentleman who'd got the story years before from a maid. Ready?"

No, I thought. "I think so," I said.

"Very well. In the summer of '46, a black-haired young man appeared at Clumber House leading a limping horse, astride of which sat the daughter of the Duke of Newcastle. Both the lady and the horse had been hurt as a result of the lady assuming the horse was willing to try a jump it hadn't seen before. The horse was not willing. Lady Mary fell."

"The daughter's name was Mary? Like my mother."

"Yes. To continue: in gratitude for the young man's rescue of his daughter, Newcastle hired the man to work in the stables, work the young man obviously knew. The new groom set about to heal the horse's bruises.

"Lady Mary felt guilty about causing her horse's injury, so she visited the horse in the stable. Naturally, she visited the groom at the same time. The horse recovered at the same pace as the lady, but by the time both were fit again, Lady Mary and the groom had fallen in love. There was no chance they could marry. Indeed, the duke already was casting about for an appropriate son-in-law. But then Lady Mary found herself with child."

"Oh! By the groom? That was bad of her," I said.

"Not bad of him too?" Franklin said. "Don't forget that it takes two to make a bargain."

"Did they marry for the child's sake?"

"No, I've said they couldn't. A lady marry a groom? Impossible. Lady Mary refused to name the father of her child. The duke thought the father was one of the nabobs who fluttered about the Dukeries—four ducal seats are close by in the area—but he never suspected the groom. The duke redoubled his efforts to find a suitable man for Lady Mary to wed so she could pass off the child as her new bridegroom's. The duke locked Lady Mary in her room, only allowing her out to parade her before a number of potential husbands. She refused all of them.

"Lady Mary got word to the groom about her situation. They waited until the duke was out on a hunt entertaining a prospective suitor. Lady Mary bundled up money and jewelry and books, and she and the groom escaped on the horse that had started everyone on this path in the first place, along with a second horse belonging to the duke."

"It's like a story in a book!" I said.

"It is a bit like *Pamela*, isn't it? Well, the lady and her swain reached the nearest village, Worksop, where they sold Lady Mary's horse, bought a drab and a cart, and paid to have the duke's horse stabled and sent back to the duke the following week."

"Why didn't they send the horse home the next day?"

Franklin smiled. "To give them time to get away, of course."

"Weren't they clever! Then what?"

"That's all anyone could tell me."

"But I want to know how it ends!"

"You forget, Jem: this may be your story. *You* may be how it ends. You may be the child she was carrying."

All my pleasure in his story flittered away. "*Me?* B-but...I...that's impossible. I can't be Lady Mary's child."

"Why not?"

"I wasn't born in Worksop, or even in Nottinghamshire. I was born in

Lamesley."

"The city of your birth doesn't matter. A woman can travel a good distance in the nine months before she gives birth. Your mother easily could have traveled from Nottinghamshire to Lamesley, or to London, or to anywhere else." I parted my lips to tell him he had it wrong, that what he suggested was preposterous. But the words wouldn't come. My mouth had dried to dust.

Franklin held up a hand and said, "Hold. Let me point out some areas of intersection between you and the actors in this story. The daughter was described as having dark curls and skin like milk, and that describes you precisely. The groom's eyes were a clear green; everyone commented on that."

I muttered, "My eyes are somewhat greenish."

"My dear, they're green as grass. In terms of temperament, the Duke of Newcastle can't bear to be on the losing side of anything. He fears public disgrace more than death. Like him, you don't like to lose."

"But—the duke and I aren't the only two people in the world who don't like to lose. And that isn't true of me anyway." He looked at me over his spectacles. "Besides, thousands of people in London have dark hair and pale skin. None of that proves I am the child of Lady Mary and the groom!" I crossed my arms over my chest. "I don't want to hear any more, if you please." I realized my crossed arms signaled stubbornness, so I shoved my hands under my knees.

"You must hear the rest," Franklin said, his tone brooking no argument. "Most interesting to me," he said, "is a story told to me by the lady of the house, the Duchess of Newcastle herself, Henrietta Pelham-Holles, the evening before I departed Clumber House. I share the lady's story because I believe it pertains to you.

"It was the evening before my departure to Scotland. I sat at the desk in my room writing letters, and who should come tapping at the door but Her Grace's lady in waiting? She said the duchess wished to speak with me in her chambers. I followed the maid, who opened the door for me, slipped out like a shadow, and closed the door behind her. The duchess sat in an armchair that had been moved away from the fire. She gestured me into another chair, which I pulled back from the flames as well. "It can be too hot when one sits too close to a fire, wouldn't you agree, Dr. Franklin?" she said, and she said it so strangely that my eyes immediately flew to her face.

"'Please sit,' said she, 'Forgive this intrusion on your privacy, but you are away tomorrow, and there hasn't been a moment when I could speak with you privately. I have a few questions for you, but they are not for the duke's ears.' I sat.

"She said her lady in waiting reported to the duchess that I'd made inquiries about her family's history. The duchess insisted I explain why. I can tell you, Jem, I was nonplussed. I certainly couldn't reveal your existence to the lady, for I'd made a promise to you. Yet the lady clearly felt disrespected, and she was my hostess to boot, so I had to offer some sort of explanation.

"I told her I'd been researching the peerage in London, which was true. I said I'd met the duke at a reception and recognized his name from my cross-referencing, which was true. I said I'd been in casual conversation with someone about the family portrait at Newcastle House in London, which seemed unbalanced, and this person said a daughter had been painted out. So I'd asked the servants about the matter, not wishing to upset the lady herself."

"What did she say?"

"She seemed to relax. She said 'Forgive me, Dr. Franklin, for suspecting evil motives. There was so much talk about our family twelve years ago.' And then, Jem, she told me an astonishing story.

"She said the family had given out that their daughter, Mary, had died twelve years before and that the Bishop of Durham himself conducted the funeral and recorded the death, but that the servants might have told me a different story. I confessed they'd said Lady Mary ran away.

"Then she said, 'I suspected as much. What they didn't tell you is that I am the person who let Mary out.'"

I gasped. "The duchess went against the duke's wishes?"

"She did. She told Mary not to write until she was settled. When Mary didn't write, the duchess hired a man to find her. She initially sent him to London, assuming Lady Mary and the groom would seek a Fleet marriage, since if their banns were read in County Durham, they would be found. Then she sent her man to Scotland. She bought notices in newspapers and sent letters to major employers and port authorities. She asked her most trusted servants to spread the word to servants in other houses that if Mary went into service, the duchess would pay to receive word of it."

I felt as though I were a lone tree in a field with stormclouds boiling toward me and lightning slashing in my direction.

"The duchess said the summer before last, a foreman at Ravensworth mine sent word that he'd met a woman who seemed out of place in a mining village—"

"—please stop," I whispered, seeing in a flash where this story was going.

"—and that this woman spoke well and wore an expensive neck bob. The duchess sent her man there, but the woman had left Lamesley before he arrived. The village wise woman said the woman went to Cumberland."

Relief flooded into my heart like the sun breaking through clouds. "Then the woman in Lamesley and Lady Mary can't be the same person," I exclaimed, "because when we left Lamesley, we didn't go to Cumberland, we came straight here. So the duchess's daughter can't be my mother!" I leapt to my feet.

Franklin said, "What if the woman with the necklace *was* your mother, and the village woman sent Her Grace's man on a wild goose chase? What if she sent him in the opposite direction from London to protect you?" He pressed his forefinger to his lips in thought, and then he said, "I'm afraid there is more that rather clinches it. Sit down. The duchess said her man had found a boy in London last fall—in November, she said—who might have been Mary's child, but the boy gave her man the slip." I looked down. My heart *shush-shush-shushed* in my ears.

Franklin continued, "Setting aside Her Grace's story for a minute, don't you find your mother's secrecy very curious? Why did your mother work as a nameless washerwoman when she clearly had an education and could have opened a school, at the very least? Why did she hide you and your brother in tiny lodgings in an unfashionable part of town? It is as though your mother wanted to disappear off the face of the earth."

"I don't know why."

"I think I do. Listen to the rest of the story."

I didn't want to hear any more. Every sentence he spoke, every question he asked, was like a brick in a prison wall. And I was behind the wall. But he kept talking.

Franklin said, "The duchess confirmed that Lady Mary took all her own jewels, all the money she had, and too many of her books. The books must have slowed them, but apparently, the daughter loved to read." I pressed my lips together. Mum loved to read.

"After she told me her man had failed to find the woman in Lamesley, the duchess wept. Her shoulders shook with her passion, yet she made no noise even though tears flowed down her cheeks like downspouts. I have seen somebody else in this room weep in the same way."

"But, Dr. Franklin, if I were the duke's granddaughter, Mum would have said so," I insisted and felt traitor tears prick behind my eyes.

"Not if she were happy in her life with your father. Not if she feared the duke's retribution. After all, he'd locked her up as though she were a criminal. She might not have wanted to live under his roof again. She might not have wanted you and your brother to grow up in his household." He patted my arm. "There now, Jem, there's only a little more. Be brave." He pulled a balled-up handkerchief out of his pocket but didn't hand it to me. "When the duchess had herself in hand, she walked to an armoire, and I heard a click. She said, 'What I am about to show to you is all I have left of Mary. Swear you won't tell my husband I have it.'

"I swore. Jem, she pulled out of some secret compartment a miniature portrait of a young lady of exquisite freshness and beauty, with pretty teeth and a maidenly blush on her cheeks."

And then Franklin unwrapped the thing inside the handkerchief and held it out in his palm. It was a miniature. He watched me over his spectacles. "As you can see, part of the frame is dented," Franklin said. "The duchess said the duke ground it under his heel when he saw it resting on a velvet bed in her rooms shortly after Lady Mary ran away." Dr. Franklin dropped the miniature into my hand. I didn't look at it.

He continued, "The duchess asked me to take the piece with me to London to have it repaired by a particular jeweler, saying that she would call for it herself when they came back to town for the season. She couldn't take it to the jeweler herself for fear word would get back to the duke, and she couldn't take it to the goldsmith in Newcastle for the same reason. And she couldn't bear that anything should happen to it, because it was the only likeness of Mary she owned."

"Jem," Franklin said quietly, "is this your mother?"

Don't look, I thought, but I tucked my chin anyway. It felt like I looked down twin tunnels at the item in my hand. The miniature showed a girl younger than my mother, with a baby plumpness still rounding her cheeks. I imagined the tiny face smiling, and the curls dancing, and the merry, rare laugh trilling from the slender throat.

"Look what she's wearing round her neck," Franklin said.

The girl in the miniature wore a black and peach cameo pinned to a green velvet ribbon.

The tiny portrait confirmed what I could no longer deny. My mouth went dry. I took a deep breath to force out five simple words that would change my life: "Yes. This is my mother."

"I thought so too," said Franklin. "If I may, then, I'll say out loud what we know, just to put it on the table where we can look at it: Jem, it appears that you are the granddaughter of the First Lord of the Treasury, Thomas Pelham-Holles, the Duke of Newcastle."

Hearing it said aloud made my heart race, yet I couldn't move my limbs. All my life I'd wondered how I would feel if I ever found my family, and now I knew: I felt like one of those helpless women in Bedlam who won't eat and so are tied down and forced to swallow something they don't want.

"What will you do?" Franklin asked.

"I don't know."

"If you claim your mother's family, you could inherit money and position," Franklin said. "You could be a peer. You could rejoin your true family, meet your grandparents. You could take your rightful place in society."

"My mother ran away from her rightful place in society."

"Every stick has two ends, Jem. You might like living as a peer."

"What if I didn't like it? Would they let me come home?" He didn't answer. I said, "I thought not. If I claim my mother's family, I shall lose all of you. They will expect me to live the way they do."

"But, Jem, surely your grandparents deserve to know their only grandchild. If I were in their position, I know I should wish it, no matter who the child's other parent was."

"They could have known me from birth if the duke hadn't hounded my mother out of his life. No." I put the miniature on the table and pushed it toward him. "I won't be their granddaughter. The duke declared to all the world that my mother was dead, so how could he claim me without revealing his lie? The duchess knows the truth, but how could she claim me without his finding out? No, I'm an orphan, and an orphan I shall remain."

Franklin carefully wrapped the miniature and put it into his pocket. "You are not an orphan, Jem, not any longer. You must tell Dr. Abernathy. You cannot keep this secret from him."

"You promised to let me tell him whatever you learned about me."

He pressed his lips together.

"Dr. Franklin, you promised."

He sighed. "So I did. But do not leave it too long, Jem. He must be told, and soon."

"I shall tell him after my birthday," I said, and meant it, but I didn't know how soon after my birthday I'd have enough courage to share this thunderous news.

CHAPTER 10

OCTOBER 1759

Where Angels Fear to Tread

Cold rains in October hinted that winter was on its way. As the weather worsened, I kept looking for the right time to tell Dr. Abernathy who I was, but the right time never came. Did I feel guilty about keeping mum? Yes, but I feared what would happen when Dr. Abernathy found out I had grandparents, especially considering who they were. I'd promised Dr. Franklin I would inform the doctor after my birthday, but I hadn't said specifically *how soon* after. It was stupid of me to think I could put it off forever.

Of the patients we saw at Bedlam, Alice Chalmers remained, along with Mad Penny of the blue eye, but Emily Staunton had decided last spring that she'd rather give in to her husband than punish him any more by staying at Bedlam Hospital, particularly since she was the one enduring the punishment rather more than he. She pulled on her dress over her breeches just in time for our weekly visit. Dr. Abernathy reported to her husband that she was meek, compliant, and docile, which wasn't and perhaps never would be entirely true, but the sour husband came the next day to carry his wife back to their home. We still visited Alice every Tuesday.

In the third week of October as we drove back to Cavendish Square from Bedlam, I suggested we stop at Margery's shop so the doctor could see how nice it looked now that Margery and I had cleaned it out.

"Not a good idea, Jem," the doctor said.

"Why not?"

"I should like to get Giselle home out of the rain."

"Just for ten minutes," I said.

"Frankly, I still haven't decided whether to thank Mrs. Jamison for cleaning the parlor or rebuke her for doing it without my permission."

"Do you plan to spend the rest of your life trying to decide?"

He glanced down at me. "Someone has become quite impertinent since she became a twelve-year-old." The doctor had forgotten my birthday in September until Margery's letter arrived at our house along with a little sachet she'd made for me. He kept bringing up the date, almost as though he wanted to iron it into his memory.

"Sir," I said, "my birthday was a month ago, though my birthday hasn't got anything to do with stopping to see Margery—but might we count visiting her as a gift?"

"I don't recall anyone taking special note of my birthday."

"People can't take note of something unless they know about it."

"Exactly my point about your birthday," he said when we came to the road that led to the shop. Giselle began to turn, but the doctor reined her back as though to go home.

"*Please*, sir, can we go to the shop? You haven't been there since Mr. Galt died."

"I suppose I should inspect it now that you spend a day a week there." He sighed. "Very well, we can stop." The doctor drove round to the back door and let me out, saying, "Tell Mrs. Jamison I shall come in after I blanket Giselle."

I knocked our secret knock, three raps, then two, then three again. I heard the door unbolt, and Margery pulled me in. She said, quick and low, "Stay here. I'll go out and lock the front door."

"What's wrong?" She put her finger to her lips and hurried out.

Bewildered, I held open the back door for the doctor.

"What is it?" Dr. Abernathy said, looking at my face.

"I don't know. Margery told me to hide."

She came in then, and her mouth smiled at the doctor though her eyes didn't. She said, "Ah, Dr. Abernathy, what a pleasant surprise. I hope you were pleased to regain the use of your parlor. Jem and I were glad to do something to make you happy." She put the kettle on. She dumped tea in her pot without even measuring.

"Yes, well, about that—"

Margery shoved her mortar and pestle to the middle of the table and sat the doctor down. "It was a good job all around. Jem learned something about cleaning; I enjoyed the exercise; you are enjoying the result. Everyone benefitted don't you think?" She pleated and unpleated her apron as she talked, rolling over objections he hadn't even voiced like a well-tarred ship rolls over water, but she talked quickly as though she were nervous. I watched her face, for whenever Margery's freckles stood out, I knew something had alarmed her. Today they looked like flakes of cinnamon bark floating in a bowl of cream.

She clattered cups and saucers as she set them out and frowned as she laid out the rest of the tea things. Finally the doctor asked, "Mrs. Jamison, is something troubling you?"

Margery poured hot water into her teapot. She laid her hands flat on the table and said, "I had a visitor two afternoons past. Someone we hoped had gone for good."

She looked at me. My heart sank. "Not—Patch?" I said.

"The very same," she said. "At first, I pretended I'd forgotten that he'd inquired after your mother all that while ago, but Patch hadn't forgotten me. He asked me when the apothecary might return, and I told him the apothecary had died in April. 'Then who is in charge here?' he asked. When I told him it was me, he looked at me as though I was something he'd scraped off his shoe." She poured out my tea and dropped in sugar and milk, then poured for the doctor. "Milk or sugar?"

"Neither. Thank you. Just to be clear: Patch and Duncan are one and the same? This is the person who tried to kidnap Jem?"

She passed the doctor his tea. "Aye. Jem and I call him Patch on account of his eye."

"And he was in this shop two days ago?" Already, I knew what he was thinking.

Margery did, too. "Before you rush out, let me finish, if you please." The doctor raised his eyebrows. "So Patch says to me, 'What a shame to lose so wise a master' and other insincere rot. But the thing that frighted me is he said he'd come to thank Mr. Galt for sending him to Chelsea last fall, because he'd found exactly what he was looking for."

I choked on my tea. "Mr. Galt sent Patch to the physick garden? Why?"

Margery shrugged. "Who knows? P'raps Henry didn't have the herbs he wanted. No doubt Patch gave him a story of some sort, and Henry couldn't see the man's eyepatch or his evil heart. That was our Henry, to the bone, always wanting to help somebody."

"Why didn't Henry send the man to another apothecary or to the apothecaries' hall?" Dr. Abernathy asked.

Margery shrugged. "P'raps Patch said he wanted something special."

I thought of the giant gray snake I'd imagined slithering in the woodland garden in Chelsea, which I'd put down to my reaction to the *Datura*. I said, quietly, "I wonder what day Patch went to Chelsea."

"I know exactly what day he went, and I know that he stole plants. Do you recall the poison garden was broke into and half the valerian rooted up?"

My stomach shriveled in on itself. My knees felt so weak I knew I daren't try to stand. I looked at Dr. Abernathy, who frowned at Margery as though she'd done something wrong.

Margery saw the look, and she snapped, "Don't you dare to look at me like that, doctor. I didn't know Henry had sent Patch to Chelsea any more than you did." She turned back to me, her voice low and tense. "Patch said he saw me walking the Chelsea paths arm in arm with a boy he was most anxious to contact—it had to have been you, for I haven't been there with any other boy. I said I hadn't been to Chelsea since the winter, and I couldn't recall any boy.

"Patch glares at me, and he says, 'I saw you. I saw the boy. Together.'

"So then I says, 'Oh, I think there was a boy. I recall helping Mr. Miller with a patron who'd been overcome by the plants, in December I think, could that be the chap you mean?' and he flashed into a fit like he'd swallowed fire. He left without even wishing me a good day." She swallowed and looked at me. "But he is tracking you, Jem, in smaller and smaller circles, and I am beside myself. You dare not come here any more." Giselle whinnied.

"I absolutely agree," the doctor said.

"Not again," I said. "How does he always find me?" My tea tasted like ditch water.

"I wish I knew. You should go now," Margery said, glancing toward her front door, "in case he comes back," so the doctor and I scuttled like rats out the back door into the downpour. Margery stood in the doorway. "I'll write, Jem," she called out. Rain sluiced between us.

The doctor was thoughtful as we drove back to Cavendish Square. Rain beat down. When we finally got home, the doctor hung the tack and put away the trap and poured a measure of oats for Giselle while I brushed her. Her warm, loving heart beat strongly against my hand. I'd asked the doctor why he took care of the horse by himself, and he'd said he liked doing it himself and asked asked why should he hire a groom since he knew how to do it, and now I did too. Today, I was glad to do something normal after the tale Margery had just told. Grooming Giselle also gave me time to gather my courage.

When we'd bedded Giselle down properly, we went inside, lit the lamps and began to rummage in the larder. While we got out our supper, Dr. Abernathy said, "I wonder why this Patch person is still looking for you. He certainly is persistent."

It was past time for me to tell him the truth. I'd promised Franklin. But the courage I thought I'd summoned in the stable melted, so I stammered. "I-I think I know who Patch could be."

The doctor lifted down plates and cups. "Who?"

"Let's sit first." We loaded our plates with the food Mrs. Pierce had left for us: a loaf of bread, a platter of cooked chicken, a dish of apples in sugar, and a lump of cheese.

The doctor poured us each a glass of cider. He said, "Well? Who is Patch?"

I took a deep breath to steady myself. "It is a long story, sir." I started with Dr. Franklin's fairytale about the runaway lovers. When I mentioned the miniature, Dr. Abernathy began to focus less on his dinner and more on my face. He chewed slower and slower.

When I repeated Dr. Franklin's statement about my being the granddaughter of the Duke of Newcastle, Dr. Abernathy set down his fork. He hardly blinked. I finished by saying, "But don't worry, sir, I've decided not to go to them. I want to stay with you."

"A moment," he said. He put up his hand. It shook just a bit. "Let me take this in. Franklin thinks your grandfather is Thomas Pelham-Holles, Duke of Newcastle, who heads the House of Lords, has been a leading Whig for thirty years, who conducts negotiations with foreign governments." His gaze held me as though I were an insect he meant to attach to a board. "You tell me you are kin to this distinguished gentleman whose wife apparently has paid a man to find you. And you disdain even to meet them? What insanity is that?"

"But, sir, I—"

He threw down his napkin and knocked over his chair as he surged to his feet. "How could Franklin not tell me?"

"I made him promise to let me do it."

"*You are a child!* Have you any idea what sort of trouble I would be in if this were discovered? I could be charged with kidnapping." He paced the length of the dining table and paced back. He stood looking down on me like the wrath of God. He said, "Conducting a social experiment with a friendless orphan is one thing, but conducting an experiment with the granddaughter of a duke is—" He shook his head. He righted his chair and sat in it. "Jem, are you sure? Is Franklin sure?"

Why hadn't I told him earlier? I set down my fork. "My Mum's cameo upstairs is the same one Lady Mary was wearing in a miniature Franklin got this summer from the duchess. She asked him to have it repaired." It took all my courage to meet his eyes. "Yes, we're sure."

Black eyes underscored with gray shadows showed stark in his white face. "How could you not tell me the instant you learned of this? On your first morning here, you spoke up about how a boy would use a privy, yet you didn't speak up when you knew you'd found your *grandparents*? I thought we'd agreed to be honest with one another after you also neglected to tell me about the money your mother put by for you."

"I have been honest. I-I just hadn't told you about my grandparents *yet*. I didn't want to vex you since I have no intention of claiming these people."

His mouth dropped open. I heard him breathing. "*These people* are your grandparents, you stubborn chit, and one of them is the most important man in England except for the king. You, a mere girl and a minor besides, have no right to dismiss a man like that." He stared past me at the painting on the wall, but he didn't seem to see it. "Whatever shall I do?"

There was a knock at the door. The doctor didn't move, so I rose. When I opened the door, there stood Margery, her face shining in the fog like a little sun.

I took hold of her hand as if it were a lifeline, and pulled. She stumbled in out of the mist, and a little gray curl of fog followed her partway into the house.

"Don't tug so, Jem, I'm glad to come in. It was still raining when I left the shop, so I couldn't get a hackney straightaway. I thought I might as well start walking as stand waiting, so I started and got here before I knew it," she said. "Where is the doctor? I hope I'm not interrupting your supper."

"Not at all, Mrs. Jamison." The doctor walked in and took her cloak. "We're quite finished. In fact, I'm glad you're here. Now I don't have to drive all the way back to Aldgate to find out why you kept Jem's secret from me."

"What secret?" Her smile faded. "You don't look well, Dr. Abernathy."

"I've had a shock."

"Whatever is it, Doctor dear?" His head jerked up at the endearment. If he'd been a dog, he'd have snarled. "Good heavens, you're white as a ghost."

I said, "Sir, we should get Margery to a fire. She's shivering."

The doctor said, "We should indeed. Won't you come into the parlor, Mrs. Jamison? You know the way already, I think."

"Thank you," she said. We followed him. She mouthed "What?" at me, and I shook my head. I seated Margery in my chair by the fire and pulled in a footstool for myself. The doctor went directly to the sideboard and poured himself a brandy.

"To what do we owe this unexpected pleasure, given that we left you at the shop not two hours past?" Dr. Abernathy said. He added, "Would you care for a brandy?"

"Thank you. I'll have a drop, if I may," Margery said. "I've gotten chilled on the way over here." He clattered the decanter against her glass as he poured. He thrust her drink into her hands and thumped himself into his chair to glower at us both. His glare prodded me into speech.

"Do you know, Margery, we use this room all the time now, don't we, sir?" I said.

"Yes, Mrs. Jamison. Again, thank you for intervening in my bachelor life. It is pleasant to have a place to relax in the evening and talk about the day's cases with Jem, although apparently we don't tell one another everything." He reached over to grasp a poker and stir up the fire. Margery frowned. "So, Mrs. Jamison," the doctor said, "Have you come to confess?"

"Confess what?" She looked at me. I bit my lip. I'd kept her in the dark, too. First, I'd kept my mother's money a secret from everybody, then I hadn't told Mr. Galt who I was, and now, my parentage had shocked the doctor and was about to shock Margery too. What was wrong with me?

"In a moment," Dr. Abernathy said. "What have you come to say?"

Margery's eyebrows went up. She said, "Well, then, I'll be quick about it, since I seem to have walked into a tempest. Patch—Mr. Duncan—came to the shop today not an hour after you left. He walked in like a dog trying to decide whether to bark or bite."

"He didn't harm you?" said the doctor, his knuckles whitening as he gripped the poker.

"No. But he wanted to. He looked at all my jars on the shelves. He looked behind the counter. He sneered at Henry's half-skull—you know, Jem, the one we set up high to look out over the shop? Then he *whacks* his cane on the counter and says, 'Madam, you have deceived me.'

"'I beg your pardon?' says I.

"'You led me to believe you didn't know the boy I saw you walking with in Chelsea this winter, but Mr. Miller at the physick garden told me yesterday you and the boy seemed very well acquainted, that you whispered with one another whilst he opened his seed boxes. You arrived together, you stood together at the window. He said it was clear you knew one another well.'

"And here, Jem, he points his cane right at my face! I wanted to bite it. So I says right back at him, slapping away his cane, 'And what of it? A woman may keep her own counsel, I think.'

"He says, 'The keeping of her own counsel is not what I object to, madam. I object to the lie. It creates suspicion.' And he took a few steps along my shelves, running the tip of his cane right up to the jars. I feared he might break them a-purpose, and what could I do? I didn't know whether his name is really Duncan or Beelzebub, so how could I have him arrested if he did any damage? I was afraid I'd have to club him with my root."

"Beg pardon, Mrs. Jamison," the doctor interrupted. "You'd have to do what?"

"Club him. I keep a good, thick root under the counter that I got from my gran. I polished it myself. It fits my hand most splendid. Doctor, are you ill again?"

"No, Mrs. Jamison. Carry on."

"So, anyway, I says to him, 'Sir, I'm sure I don't know what you mean. When you stopped before, you asked about the apothecary, and I told you he was dead.

Then you asked about a boy at Chelsea, and I told you I'd helped such a boy. Where is the lie?'

"So then Patch says to me, 'Your speech is improved since the very first time I stopped here more than a year ago and left a message for the lady who lived upstairs. How curious.'

"He had me for a moment, but then I says, 'Sir, visitors to London are thick as flies, and it's certain you're a visitor—where did you say you were from?'

"And he says, all high and mighty, 'I didn't say.'

"'Spain, maybe?' says I.

"'Don't be an idiot. Can't you tell I'm English? I'm from the North.' There, I'd got some information, Jem! So then I says, 'Sometimes I pretend to be thick when I want to get rid of a customer who's taking up too much of my time or wants me to diagnose their great granny's first cousin what lives up in Glasgow.'"

The doctor's mouth twitched toward a smile, the first I'd seen since dinner. "I understand perfectly what you mean," he said. "About people wanting a diagnosis for a friend of a friend, I mean."

Margery's shoulders eased a bit when she saw the smile. She said, "And so I told him I pretended to be a bumpkin that day because I needed him to go. I was busy."

"Clever, Margery," I said.

"Illuminating," the doctor said. "Pretending to be something you're not, I mean." His eyes caught mine over the rim of his glass, so I shifted my eyes back to Margery.

"Then what?" I said.

"Well, he unpuffed himself and lowered his cane, but I didn't like the black glittery look in his eye. He says to me, 'Madam, my curiosity is not idle. I seek the boy who lived above this shop—a boy you clearly are acquainted with, despite your denials—for a very important reason. His name is Jem. Where does he live?'

"I says, 'I haven't seen him since Chelsea,' lying in my teeth. 'The boy was just a lad Mr. Galt knew, not me. If I spoke to him a great deal, well, I only meant to be kind to him, is all. I like to talk.'" She laid an arm protectively around my shoulders. "Nobody I know would be the rat against his own, especially not to somebody like Patch."

I raised my own eyebrows at the doctor, thinking, *See? People keep secrets for a reason.*

Margery continued, "It wasn't his eye patch I didn't like. I've seen many a maimed man in my life, and I pity them with all my heart, but I treat them as men just the same. What made my hand itch for my club was the way he prowled about and trailed the end of his cane along my shelves and the way his one black eye peered at me. He felt *wrong* to me. The hair on my arms rose up—Jem, if you'd been there, p'raps your Sight could've given a clue as to who or what he is."

The doctor's frown returned. "If Jem had been there, she mightn't be here now. And you mightn't either, Mrs. Jamison. It sounds to me as though the man would stop at nothing to bag his quarry—and, Jem, I thought you said you'd shut up your Sight in a cave or something."

"I did!" I said. "I haven't flown since the peregrine. But…it doesn't stay hidden. It still flares up no matter what I do." I hadn't told him about my dizzy spell at Franklin's, either. *Now is not the time*, I thought. I continued, "I never know when it'll happen. I have been trying, sir, truly I have, but it is hard to keep a constant focus when my head hurts."

"Are you taking the powder I gave you?" Margery asked.

"Double doses," I said.

Margery said, "I begin to wonder if the cause of your headaches is something outside yourself."

"Like what?" I said.

"I'll write to Granny and ask."

"What headaches?" Dr. Abernathy interrupted.

Margery said, "Jem, you didn't tell him?"

"I didn't want to worry you," I said to the doctor.

"And so you kept that a secret as well."

Margery looked from one of us to the other. "I beg your pardon—you two had best let me finish before your resume your quarrel, as I've a long way to walk home again."

"I wouldn't think of letting you walk alone to Aldgate in this weather at this hour," the doctor said. "I'll hire a hackney to take you home. If you were Jem, of course, I shouldn't worry. Jem has no trouble going her own way all alone in the dark."

The air in the room felt thick as paint.

Margery's eyebrows met in confusion, as she still didn't know why the doctor was angry, but she nodded her thanks. "Anyway," she said, "Patch left a letter." She pulled a sheet of folded paper out of her pocket. "He said the letter was written to the lady upstairs that died, but if I saw the boy again, he must have it. I said it wasn't likely I would see the boy again, as Mr. Galt was gone now and I wouldn't be needing a driver again."

"Mrs. Jamison, forgive me, but it is too late to lie," the doctor said. "Patch knows Jem is connected to Mrs. Connolly. He knows you are acquainted with both of them."

"How?" Margery said.

"Simple: you worked downstairs when they lived upstairs. Patch has spoken with you and knows your character. He knows you would not mind your own business." Margery's mouth flew open. "That sounded rude, Mrs. Jamison, I apologize," he said, his cheeks flushing. "I only meant that anyone who speaks with you for five minutes can tell you are interested in other people." Margery flushed bright red. Her eyes flew up to the doctor's face then down to the letter in her hand.

I sat on the edge of my stool. "The letter is for my mother, Margery? What does it say?"

"Dunno, love. It's not addressed to me." She offered the letter to me.

"May I see it first?" said the doctor. He looked at the wax. "There is no seal on this wax," he said. "It is just plain wax dripped on. Most people press their seal to a letter." The doctor took a fruit knife from the table beside him, warmed it near the fire, then slipped the knife under the blob of wax.

"Well, I never," Margery said. "How do you know how to do that?"

"When I was a boy, for a time, I intercepted my father's messages. What?" He looked up from the delicate business. "Oh." He sighed. "Yes, it was wrong. My mother made that abundantly clear when she discovered what I was doing. I was anxious to please Father, for I felt every inch the useless third son. I began intercepting his mail to get some idea what he was always off doing, hoping I might distinguish myself in conversation with him. Indeed, my father found me wise beyond my years soon after I started reading his mail."

He glanced at the letter. "Here, Jem, I've got it open. Take care until the wax is hard again. It's a simple matter to re-seal it without anyone's being the wiser."

"Why would we re-seal it?" I asked.

"So Mrs. Jamison can return it to Patch unopened." I frowned. "If she returns it unopened, he may assume it could not be delivered because the person to whom it is addressed could not be found."

"Oh." I looked down at the paper in my hands and then at my selfless friends. *Time to show these two that I trust them,* I thought. *High time.* "I'll read it out loud."

CHAPTER 11

OCTOBER 1759

Letter from Two Strangers

Margery and the doctor sat back to listen as I read.

To Lady Mary Anne Pelham-Holles from His Grace, the Duke of Newcastle

Claremont House, 21 July 1759

Daughter,

"*What?*" Margery turned to the doctor with her mouth open, and he nodded. Margery said to me, "Mary Anne Connolly, your mother, was the daughter of the Duke of Newcastle?"

"We think so."

"Good heavens." Margery downed a hearty swallow of brandy, and it made her cough, but she pressed her hand to her breast and waved at me to go ahead. I read on.

I pray this letter finds you, though it has been thirteen years since you left, and your mother has petitioned the Almighty uncounted nights since then for your return. Mistakes took you from us all those years ago, your mistakes but also mine. I should have guided you more carefully in your youth so as to have avoided the entire unfortunate incident. Since you have been gone, your mother has become the most genial and charming hostess in London, but your absence pains her still, and she bids me now rectify the matter by finding you.

I refused similar requests in the past, for it is a hard thing to ask forgiveness from someone when I am the person who has been wronged. Nor will it be a simple matter to resurrect from the dead a daughter whose funeral was conducted by the Bishop himself. But the business must be managed for your mother's sake. As my wife, she is required to play the hostess, but she exhausts herself disguising her broken heart from our guests. Our memories of what happened at Clumber House make the place seem disagreeable, although there is not a thing wrong with the property. We spend very little time there. Your mother sits alone for her afternoon tea instead of enjoying it with you and your child by her side. Or, worse, she sits with ladies who do have grandchildren and insist on sharing every little detail about them, which your mother finds most distressing. In short, your absence can be borne no longer.

Please show mercy to your mother and send her word that you still grace the earth. Or, if you are so inclined, visit. Bring your child or children—our grandchildren. Your mother says I am also to invite your husband. It is hard for me to see him as a man, rather than a dog without honor who disgraced you when he dared raise his eyes to look into your face. You may reach us at Newcastle House in London or at Claremont in Surrey.

Your mother begs me to remember that youthful pas-
sions are strong for men and women both. She wishes to write a
line now.'"

The handwriting changed from the duke's bold masculine hand to a fine
rounded script. The ink blots also disappeared.

My Sweet Mary: There is so much to say and so
much hope in my heart that this letter will find you that I
scarcely know what to write. So I shall just say what is upper-
most in my heart: Do come home! I have hoped every day for
the last thirteen years to see a carriage driving in to Claremont
House and you emerging. In that hope, I have retained your
lady's maid all these years. Susan airs one of your gowns every
day. They might not fit you any longer, but Mrs. Bainbridge's
daughter has taken on a great deal of her mother's dressmak-
ing clients and could certainly remake your frocks to suit. Or
we could buy all new! Your spaniel Jack died five years ago,
but his bloodline continues, and it would be a simple matter to
acquire another dog.

I must beg you, Mary, if you come, could you bring
the child? He must be twelve years of age by now, nearly a
young man grown. Or perhaps your child is a girl? I should so
love to sit with a granddaughter. I am not sure why your father
has changed his mind about inviting you home. He may see
his mortality better now than he could all those years ago and
wish to settle the order of inheritance. Or perhaps, like me, he

has begun to feel the tender affections of a grandfather and has
no grandchild on which to lavish them. Whatever his reason, I
rejoice that he wants to see you. I have never stopped wanting
it. I have never stopped looking for you, but every time my man
Duncan gets close, he loses you again—

I faltered and glanced at Margery, whose lips were parted. "Patch is *her* man," Margery said. My eyes darted to the doctor, who listened with his eyes closed and the bridge of his nose pinched between his thumb and forefinger. I cleared my throat and resumed reading.

—my man Duncan gets close, he loses you again.
I hope you still have the cameo we gave to you with our love
engraved on it. Please come and see us. Please. I would share
more, but your father reaches for the pen.

"The handwriting is different again," I said, "so this is the duke."

Your mother asked you to visit, but you may not wish
to come. Time and distance create a gulf that can be nearly im-
possible to bridge. But a letter, Mary—can you not send just a
letter? Tell us you are well. Ease your mother's heart. We wish
to help you and your child if you will allow it. Today I am 66
years old. I do not know how much more time God has granted
to me. If you retain any tenderness for the lady who bore you,
send word that you live to ease her heart.

Your Father

"The poor man," Margery said.

"He's not a poor man," I said. "It's his own fault."

"Stop talking like a spoilt child," the doctor sighed. "That you are being uncharitable toward the duke and duchess is the most charitable thing I can say about *you* at this moment." He let go his nose and opened his eyes. "Are you a saint who's never made mistakes?"

"His mistakes killed my family." I didn't care that my voice came out bitterly cold, but I was not blameless, either, having invited into our room the sick boy who gave the putrid sore throat to James, so I added, less coldly, "But you're right. What I don't understand is why they want me back, all of a sudden, after all this time."

"Technically, they want your mother. They don't know about you, particularly. They don't even know if you are a girl or a boy." The irony of his remark was not lost on any of us. He cleared his throat. "It is perfectly natural that they want to see your mother and to meet you."

"Dr. Abernathy, you sound like you're catching cold," Margery said, peering at his face. He stepped away from his chair and blew his nose. Margery turned to me. Her smile didn't reach her eyes. Her voice came out forced and cheery, like the one she'd used on Mr. Galt when he was ill, "Isn't it nice to learn you have family after all, Jem?"

"No. I already have a family. You."

The doctor swung round. "It isn't the same—"

"You're right," I said. I took in a deep breath. "Sir, you took me in when I had nowhere else to go. You have been more like a father than a master. You've taught me medicine. You, Margery, you've loved me like a sister and mother both." I waved the letter. "I don't even know these people."

"Blood relations come first in the eyes of the law," the doctor said.

"I don't care about the law!" I cried. "If I am forced to go to them, I know exactly what my life will become. Last Christmas, sir, your sister and the duchess spent hours a day changing their clothes. The duchess was like a dog with a bone trying to work out if I was worthy to sit at table with the rest of you. Is that the kind of person you want me to be?"

"No, Jem," he said quietly, seating himself back in his chair, "but you don't know that's what would happen."

"It would," I said. "Look at Emily Staunton. She wore breeches and got sent to Bedlam for it. Sir, you made an experiment of me. You wanted to know whether I could learn like a man. Haven't I done well?"

"You've done splendidly," the doctor said gruffly.

"Then why send me to a place I'm not suited for?"

"I wouldn't send you anywhere," he said, "but it is not my decision to make. If the duke finds you, the law will compel you to go to him."

"That's another thing," I said. "Patch knew a year ago Mum was dead, he said so when he tried to kidnap me. But this letter is dated July. Eight months later. Why didn't he tell them where to find me? This letter says the duke and duchess want to see my mother. But the duchess told Dr. Franklin in June that the duke wouldn't let her even remember their child—"

"Dr. Franklin knows of this?" Margery interrupted. The doctor sighed again.

"Yes he does," I answered. "He's the one who figured it out, and I wish I hadn't let him do it."

"Too late now," the doctor said.

"Sir, this letter sounds as though they think Mum is alive. Why didn't Patch tell them she isn't?" I waved the letter. "And why does the duke suddenly want to see Mum now? He held her funeral. How does he expect to bring her back to life in everybody's eyes? And why did Patch give this letter to you, Margery?"

"Patch knew Mrs. Jamison would contact you," Dr. Abernathy said. He turned to Margery. "He may even have expected you to open the letter."

"But I don't read other people's letters," Margery said. "Besides, even if Patch expected me to read the letter and find out Jem's identity, what did he expect me to do about it?"

Dr. Abernathy looked at her with something like pity in his eyes.

"Mrs. Jamison, a woman less noble than you would know exactly what to do if she learned the Duke of Newcastle had an unacknowledged heir." We waited. He sighed. "He expected you to blackmail the duke, or at the very least seek a reward for finding his granddaughter. Either way, he expects *you* to contact the duke."

"But why?" Margery said. "Why doesn't Patch tell them about Jem himself? Why doesn't he tell them where to find her?"

Dr. Abernathy walked over to add coal to the fire. "I can't answer that, but I have a theory about why the duke and duchess want to see their daughter after all this time," he said. "They have no other children. Both are getting on in years. In the absence of an heir in direct line of descent, the duke's entire estate will go to the nearest male relative. It could be that the duke doesn't want the heir apparent to get his property, for whatever reason, so he's hit upon you, the long-lost grandchild, as a way to cut out the current heir."

"Do you want me to go live with strangers for a reason like that?" I said, feeling so dismayed by the thought of it that tears jabbed behind my eyelids like tiny knives.

As the doctor wiped coal dust off his fingers, he said, "Of course I don't. But think, Jem: as a peer, you could have many more advantages than I could ever give you. You could learn social graces and make a proper match when it came time for you to marry. You would want for nothing."

"That isn't true," I choked. "I should want very much for your companionship, and Margery's, and Dr. Franklin's. I should want the satisfaction I feel when we work together." The tears spilled. "They wouldn't let me study with either of you any more."

"Probably not," the doctor said, "but there would be compensations. You can't assume your life would be worse if you lived with your grandparents."

"In Jem's defense," Margery interjected, patting my knee, "Newcastle is certain he knows what's best for the country. I read the newspapers. I'll wager he's certain about a woman's proper place too. Jem's right: he'd make her be a girl again. He'd stop her learning with us."

Dr. Abernathy said, "Mrs. Jamison, may I remind you that the duke expressed regret for his part in the estrangement from his daughter—"

I felt as though I would burst. "The fact is, we don't know what would happen!" I shouted. "But it's very likely the duke and duchess would not allow me to be just—myself."

"Oh, Jem, women never are let to be just themselves," Margery said.

"That's rubbish, Margery," I said. "*You* are your own self. You've run your own business all these years. Have you felt the absence of a man?"

Margery puffed out cheeks gone suddenly red. She looked at her hands, and said, "Not in my business, Jem, no."

"You see?" I said to the doctor, who'd dashed over to pour himself another brandy.

"Jem, the law could compel you to the duke," the doctor said, turning to face us. "You're a minor, and a minor female at that. A passion for freedom and a talent for medicine notwithstanding, the fact is the law can make you go." He added quietly, "And I could not do a thing to prevent their taking you away from us." He fixed his eyes on me, and they were black and sad. "For once, I am at a loss. I don't know what to do."

"Nor I," Margery said. She looked up at him, tears shimmering in her eyes. I felt something spark from her to him and back again. What was *that?* My mind leapt after the spark like a kitten chasing a string, and—slam!—I went slant, and the room and Margery and the doctor looked different, as if I'd stepped behind a window with colored glass. *Another dizzy spell?* I scrabbled to turn back but couldn't see where to go. So I flashed a prayer: *Keep me safe.*

In the past when I'd tilted this way, I'd known that I was about to see without using my eyes or feel without using my hands, that whatever was coming would be something out of the ordinary. I'd seen Mum's spirit twice. I'd felt Alice's muscles in her withered arm at Bedlam, the queer, sluggish tar in Herr Handel's blood, and the cancer in Mr. Craker, the poor man with the terrible bed sores. I'd tasted blood and bone when I visited the lions in the Tower and linked with Giselle, felt my arm sizzle under Patch's hand and gotten sick on spinning images at Dr. Franklin's—all due to the Second Sight I'd tried to control ever since I'd come back from my flight with my peregrine.

But tonight I'd been too distracted and upset to keep a tight rein on my Sight. Now it bore me toward that little spark into Margery like a boat on a fast current. But, somehow—because I'd scrabbled to hang on at the last minute? because I'd prayed?—I stayed behind as well. So I kept a hand on the tiller, as it were, even as part of me followed the spark *inside* Margery and part of me stayed *outside*. Only it wasn't my friends' physical self I saw, exactly, it was—it felt like—it seemed as though I could see their feelings. And both of them glowed the same pink-orange as the spark that danced in Margery's heart. Queer as it felt to be in three places at once, queer as it felt to *see* feelings, I felt happy and free, as I'd felt flying with my peregrine.

Margery's spark yearned toward the doctor, but when, enchanted, I followed it toward him, I lost Sight of Margery and couldn't see into Dr. Abernathy. I hung suspended between the two of them, losing my sense of them both, their pink light fading, and then I snapped completely back into my mind. I didn't feel dizzy as I'd felt after flying for three days with the peregrine, but I did feel heavy and—curbed. That feeling I remembered. Even so, even as I readjusted to my body, I rejoiced I'd managed a short flight all by myself. For what else could it have been?

"Jem, have you thought of something?" Margery asked. "What are you smiling about?" She put a gentle hand on my arm. "Did you fly? Did you…See something?"

"What, you flew again? Now?" The doctor dashed back to his chair. "Where did you go?"

"Nowhere." I tried to find words to explain what I'd seen. "I stayed here. But I saw a spark in you, Margery, and a spark in the doctor—"

The hand on my arm squeezed, and Margery shook her head, just slightly—

"—and I was able to bring myself back, all on my own," I finished. *Does she know the two of them are the same color?*

"Why would you go *now?*" Dr. Abernathy asked. His glow was nearly receded into his skin. "Jem, I'm speaking to you."

"I-I didn't mean to go, sir. But when I felt myself going, I-I think I made an anchor."

"And pulled yourself back!" Margery said. She gathered me in. "I'm so proud of you."

"I'm vexed," the doctor said. He reached over to snatch the letter from my hand. He fluttered it at the two of us. "In the midst of all *this,* we must worry about *that* too." He sat down heavily and glared at the letter. Margery let me go and folded her hands in her lap. After a moment, the doctor scooted to the edge of his chair with a gasp. "Dear God."

"What is it?" Margery said. "Is there a postscript?"

"How do we know the duke and duchess wrote this letter?" he said.

Margery frowned. "What do you mean?"

"I have never seen the duke's handwriting, nor has Jem, I daresay. Have you? I thought not. We haven't considered the possibility that Patch wrote this letter himself."

Margery paled. "Surely not. The details are so personal."

Dr. Abernathy scanned the letter. "Jem, you told me Franklin found out some of these same details from a man in a tavern. Patch could have done the same."

"But why would Patch forge a letter?" Margery asked. "Why would he want Jem to think her grandparents want to meet her if they don't?" The coal shifted in the grate, then—

"We have been stupid," Dr. Abernathy said, "incredibly stupid. It shakes me to my boots to realize how careless we have been." He turned to me. "If Patch wrote this letter, it may be intended as bait."

"Bait?" Margery said.

"Think of it: an orphan learns she has doting grandparents who clearly want to forgive and forget, grandparents who clearly can provide a home and position and wealth—what orphan could resist that?"

"I could," I said, perceiving that I'd come all the way back to myself and was lashed down tight, clear-headed with no hint of floating or queasiness. Neither the doctor nor Margery glowed in the slightest. How had I gotten back to normal so quickly? The shock of hearing the doctor's alarming theory? *Interesting*, I thought, *perhaps a shock fastens me down quicker than just waiting to settle.*

Dr. Abernathy rubbed his eyes with his fingers, something he did whenever he was under strain. "Patch doesn't know you're happy here. He didn't tell your grandparents he'd found you, so he expects you to go to them as soon as you read this letter. Yet if you go to them on your own, he doesn't collect a reward for bringing you to them. Which means something matters to him more than money. Which means—"

"—which means he may plan to take her as soon as she shows her face," Margery gasped.

"But why does Patch want me?" I said. "I'm nobody."

"I don't know." The doctor said. "But any number of ugly possibilities occur to me." He paced to the window to look out into the night. He muttered, "But what if the letter *is* real?"

"If it's real, we don't know why the *duke* wants me," I said. "If Patch forged the letter, we don't know why *he* wants me."

"What can we do?" Margery said.

"I have an idea," I said. "Let me show the letter to Dr. Franklin. He saves all his letters. He probably has one from the duchess, and maybe one from the duke, too. If he does, we can compare the handwriting and see whether the duke and duchess really wrote this letter. There, that's a start."

Dr. Abernathy said, "What do you think, Mrs. Jamison?"

"I think it's a grand idea to compare the handwriting."

"Then we'll go to Franklin tomorrow," the doctor said, "but we cannot let down our guard for a moment regarding Patch or Duncan or whoever the Devil he is until we know the truth."

The doctor helped Margery on with her cloak, offered her his arm, and walked her out to find a hackney. I trudged up the stairs to get ready for bed. I felt clear-minded but tired, so I fumbled with my laces and buttons. I took Mum's cameo out of its box and clutched it to my heart.

I lay in bed with my finger pressed to the cameo's tiny profile. "Why didn't you go back to them after Da died?" I whispered. "Am I supposed to stay away from them too?"

* * *

Rain plastered our hair to our heads. Dr. Franklin and I struggled to stand in the storm that buffeted us. Above our heads, a kite tore holes in the clouds.

"You've already done this experiment!" I yelled over the shrieking wind. "But you tied the string to the church spire. You didn't hang on to it. It's wet. If lightning strikes, I'll be hurt."

"No, don't let go. We must know!" he shouted back. "We must know, know, know."

"Know what?" I held the kite string with Franklin behind me urging, "Higher! Higher still! You almost have it!"

The wind took my poor, battered kite up so high we saw it only when lightning lit the sky around it, and even then it appeared as a tiny dot. I felt it more than saw it as it tugged like a living thing.

"Higher!"

I let out more string, but the slack flapped in the wind. Impossibly, the kite had caught on the clouds. "It's stuck, sir!" I said.

"Haul it in," Franklin ordered.

I tugged. I ran back and forth until I felt a little give in the line, and then I pulled steadily. The kite came hard. I wound the excess string on my hand. The rain and hail stopped; the wind faltered, too. It was so dark that I could hardly see my hand on the string, but still the kite came.

When I saw I had more string twisted round my hand than I thought I'd played out, I looked up to see if I could see the kite yet.

What I saw stunned me: there was no kite. I'd been pulling down the sky itself.

It lowered above me, dark and churning, full of power and malice. Red lightning sizzled mere feet above my head. I cried out. I peeled the string off my hand and flung it.

But the sky didn't fly back where it belonged. It kept coming. A thundercloud wrapped round my arms. Franklin was gone. I was trapped.

"Dr. Franklin, help me!" I screamed. "Get me out of this."

His voice sounded in my mind, "This shouting does not become you. Do be quiet until we learn what we need to learn."

I wanted to please him, but the cloud squeezed me so hard I couldn't breathe.

* * *

When I opened my eyes, gasping, I found my blanket wrapped around my middle several times and my head pounding so hard I had to catch my breath before I could unwrap it. I ate a handful of headache powder, without even adding it to water.

CHAPTER 12

OCTOBER 1759

Hunted, Driven, Cornered

The next morning, when Giselle nudged me as I harnessed her to the trap, I pressed my cheek to her shoulder, breathed in the clean, horsey scent of her, and told her not to worry. But I worried. The duke's letter sat in my pocket like a packet of gunpowder. This morning, the doctor and I would go to Craven Street; this morning, I would know whether the duke and duchess—or Patch himself—had written the letter Patch had left with Margery.

I drove Giselle round to the front of the house to wait for the doctor. Just as we stopped, a man walked to the front door. Mrs. Pierce answered the bell and let the man in. I felt both reprieved and annoyed: if this man had come to fetch the doctor, we might have to put off our errand for another day. Unfortunately, I knew by now that dismissing Patch from my mind would not dismiss me from his.

The door opened and the doctor came out carrying his bag. He called, "Jem, I've been called to a client."

"Shall I go with you?"

"No. I want you to complete our errand. Can you walk?"

"Of course." I jumped out. The doctor and messenger climbed in. "Shall I come and meet you when I've finished?" I asked.

"No. Come straight home regardless of what you discover." The set of his eyes showed he already was thinking about his patient. He and the messenger climbed in, the doctor clicked up Giselle, and away they went. Mrs. Pierce watched out the window, so before she could order me indoors to empty chamber pots, I set off at a trot toward Craven Street.

All the way there, I worried. By the end of the day, I would know whether it was my grandparents or Patch who'd written the letter. That my grandparents might want me made sense, but nothing about me was worth Patch's going to all this trouble to steal me.

At Craven Street, a maid sent me upstairs to knock on Dr. Franklin's door. "What is it?" he called.

"It's Jem, sir. Dr. Abernathy sent me with a question."

He opened the door, his waistcoat unbuttoned and his hair uncombed. "Are you well, sir?" I asked.

"I am physically fit but emotionally shipwrecked," he said as he buttoned and smoothed and patted.

"What's happened?"

"William is—William has—William has gotten himself into a difficulty." Dr. Franklin's mouth pinched and a furrow ran between his brows. I had never seen Dr. Franklin so distressed, not even when he first got word the Penns wouldn't see him. What on earth had William done?

"Can I help?"

"I doubt it. I cannot help him, so I don't see how you can." He looked up. "That was rude. Forgive me. I am angry and disappointed with my son." He pushed aside papers on his writing table, and we sat. He drummed his fingers. "Well? What can I do for you?"

"You recall the miniature."

"Of course I do. What of it?" *Goodness, he's in a temper.*

I pulled out the letter. "Well, this is from the lady that gave it to you. Her husband wrote, too. I want to know if the letter is genuine."

He took the letter from my hand. "This is from Newcastle?"

"Supposedly, it's from both of them. They both wrote lines in it."

"That is something they do—they share paper and switch off like a pair of jugglers."

"Oh." That was dispiriting. "Have you any letters from them so we can compare the handwriting?"

"Didn't this have a seal?"

"No. It was closed with plain wax."

"Hm. The duke is most particular about his correspondence. I can't imagine him not sealing a letter. How did you come by it?"

"A man brought it to Mrs. Jamison's apothecary shop." I paused. Keeping secrets had not gone well for me so far. "I told you the duchess hired a man to find my mother and me. The letter says the duchess's man is named Duncan. We think he and Patch are one and the same."

"Patch, who tried to kidnap you? Good heavens." Franklin opened the letter and began to read.

"Patch tracked me to the shop," I said. "He tracked me to the physick garden in December. He hasn't tracked me to Cavendish Square yet, or to here, but if he does, I don't know what I shall do." Angry tears filled my eyes, but I dashed them away. "It isn't fair. I didn't do anything! I just want to be left alone." I jumped up to look out of the window. Behind me, Franklin read. At last I heard him let out a gust of air, and when I turned, Franklin stood looking down at the letter on the table on it as though it were a charge of gunpowder.

"Well," he said, "this letter lays out the entire affair. I cannot imagine the duke writing down sensitive information like this and then sending it out into the world. Certainly, the duchess's man would have known the truth from the beginning, but this plain wax dripped on without any seal suggests that Patch or even somebody else read the letter before it came to you."

"Oh." I crossed to him. Franklin's earlier pique seemed to have evaporated.

"'Oh' indeed. Anybody in possession of the information in this letter could use it to blackmail Newcastle, unless the duke already planned to reveal the truth to the world. But if he is willing to reveal his lie about your mother's death and burial, that means he is willing to endure scandal and humiliation and worse in order to get his heir back. To get *you* back."

"Oh." *Worse and worse.* "Isn't it possible the duke didn't write it? That's what I came to ask."

Franklin fingered the paper. "The writing paper is heavy and expensive. It would suit the duke's tastes." He fetched out a handsome carved box from his armoire. "But we can look. Let me see…" He rustled the papers in the box. "I was at Clumber House just after the Season ended and before the duke and duchess moved to Claremont House for the opening of Parliament, so there would be a letter dated thereabouts—here!" He lifted out a single page. "This is from the duchess, and—yes, you see here, the duke added a postscript." He brought the letter to the table, and we laid the letters side by side. My heart dropped into my boots.

"The writing paper is the same. Feel it. The handwriting is identical," Dr. Franklin said. "See? The slant of the *l* and *p* is the same in both letters. It is the hand of an energetic person, which the duke certainly is. And look at the hand of the duchess—here, and here. You can see the care she takes to form her words beautifully, as though she believed she might be judged on her penmanship. Nothing is crossed out. She thinks before she writes."

So. The letter was real. Now we knew where we were: I had grandparents who definitely wanted me back. I knew it, Franklin knew it, Patch knew it. Who else knew?

Franklin said, "I take it you told Abernathy everything?" I nodded as I slowly folded up my letter and eased it back into my pocket. "Good." He put a hand on my shoulder. "It's good that he knows, Jem. There is no need for you to carry this burden alone. When will you go to your family?"

"I don't want to go at all."

"But—you belong to them. You may not have a choice."

"My mother said there is always a choice."

"Always? I don't agree. Sometimes, one event ignites another like a fire in a forest. And one can't decide that charred trees should be fresh and green again." He walked to the window, his hands clasped behind his back. "I must confess, it could be useful to me to have an ally in the duke's house."

I stared. "You wouldn't tell?"

Franklin sighed. "Jem, you can't seriously intend to repudiate your family—not to mention their wealth and position—when anyone else would give years of their life to have those things."

I admired Dr. Franklin, but I couldn't ignore that *he* had left his father's house and his friends behind in Boston to strike out on his own, so I said, "You ran away to Philadelphia when you were only five years older than me, you told me so."

He turned. "Five years older than twelve is seventeen, a man grown. I left for a good reason."

"You left because you wanted to make your own choices. That is all I want."

"It is not the same." Franklin said. "I was the son of a merchant, not the grandchild of a lord."

"Would you wish me back with my grandparents if they were poor?"

His eyebrows went up, and he uttered one word: "Touché." But then his face fell into worried lines. "However, apart from your grandparents, I see another difficulty." He crossed back and tapped on the letter. "This fellow—this Patch—has been hunting you for years. He chased a hope of finding you all the way to Cumberland. He came here and found you at the apothecary—with Mrs. Jamison. He tried to kidnap you a year ago—from the shop where Mrs Jamison works. A year after that, just last month in fact, he saw you at the physick garden—with Mrs. Jamison. What can you deduce from these facts?"

My blood went cold. "He wouldn't hurt Margery to find me?"

Franklin waited.

"He won't give up," I said. I felt I was sinking in a mudhole without a bottom.

"There is this to consider as well: Patch has not told the duke where to find you. We don't know why. Yet, if the Duke of Newcastle had any idea where you were, don't you think he would have sent someone to fetch you? If he finds out now that you have been under his nose all this time, he might be pleased—or he might have Patch arrested."

"Good. Lock him in the Tower and throw away the key."

"Newcastle might have Mrs. Jamison arrested for concealing your whereabouts. He might have Abernathy arrested. He might have Franklin arrested, which would please a number of men in government who would enjoy seeing me humiliated. All of us might be ruined."

No. No. NO! "What can I do?" I whispered. I'd sunk to my waist in the imaginary mudhole.

"I think you must go to the duke and duchess yourself."

I jumped up and dashed to the window. Fear and worry and anger boiled up, pushing out hot tears that spilled to my jacket. "No!" I cried. "How can I do it? How can I leave all of you? *I don't want to go!*" I swiped my hand across my face.

Franklin said, "Your response to finding out your wealthy grandparents want you is most perplexing, I must say."

"That isn't the problem," I said. Below, in Craven Street, a woman with a basket on her arm walked toward the Strand. "What bothers me is Mum didn't go back to her parents when Da died, she came to London. Why? She hated laundry! Was she hiding from her parents? If so, why?"

"I can't imagine why your mother chose poverty and toil over the comfort of her parents' home." He cleared his throat. "But if that concerns you so much that you won't go to your grandparents, you clearly must go somewhere else." I opened my mouth, but he held up his hand. "Apart from the mystery of why your mother avoided her parents, something most strange and dangerous is afoot. Patch values you more than he values whatever reward he expects when he delivers you to Newcastle or he would have delivered you already. Patch somehow finds you wherever you go. I must conclude he eventually will track you to me and to the doctor. Why he hasn't yet done so is another mystery.

"I know animal trackers in America, Jem, and they always find their quarry. It is uncanny the way they read the smallest bent twig like the rest of us read a page in a book. Some of them use dogs—"

"Patch doesn't have a dog."

"I am not talking of the four-legged variety. You have forgotten the beggar boy, it seems?"

"Freddie Payne?"

"Yes. You thought him a friend, but he worked for Patch. He has brothers, I think you told me? For everyone's sake, not least of all your own, you should go far away from London until Patch and his dogs—and your grandparents—give up looking for you."

"Where can I go?"

"Talk to the doctor about it. Talk to Mrs. Jamison. I think the wisest course would be to go to Newcastle." He stood. "But since you make a convincing case for caution, I'm afraid I must ask you to leave Craven Street now and to stop coming here." He stepped round the table to put a hand on my shoulder. "It isn't what you think, Jem. It's this: I told you before Christmas that a person on the run needs a bolt-hole that nobody knows about. You, it appears, are now such a person."

When I left Dr. Franklin, I felt like a beetle living in the dirt that wanted only a dark place to hide. I needed to talk to Margery. I walked the Strand to Fleet Street, wending north-northeast toward Margery's shop. I wove in and out of the honeycomb of alleyways, emerging on the alley that led to the back door of the shop. A pot of calendula sat on Margery's hogshead. My mind flitted to one of the early entries I'd penned into Margery's recipe book: *Calendula: birth flower of October. Use on lesions, rashes, burns.* What an odd thing to think about at a time like this. I rapped our special signal on the door: three-two-three.

Margery unbolted the door right away. "Jem, what a surprise! What did Dr. Franklin say?" She shut and bolted the door behind me. "Tell me." I told her that the handwriting in my letter matched the handwriting in Dr. Franklin's letters from the duke and duchess. I told her how badly they wanted me back. I told her Freddie's redheaded brothers probably were helping Patch, that she and Abernathy and Franklin might be in danger, that Franklin thought I should leave London. As I conveyed each difficulty, her face got paler and paler.

When I was done, we both just looked at one another. Margery's eyes were huge, blue agates in her white face. She said, "Well. We wanted to know where we stand, and we certainly know now."

"Oh, Margery, I've brought trouble to your door."

"No, all them others brought it." She sighed. "So, what's next? First, as for Patch coming after me, don't worry: I have my club and…other protections. And Patch hasn't found the doctor or Franklin yet.

"Second, as for the redheads, Dr. Franklin could be right. There's been a redheaded beggar across the street since before you ever came to London, but they seem to change in size now that I think about it. That there begging spot is probably shared out amongst a family of redheads." She bit her lip. "And I hate to say it, but I may know how Patch finds you. If I'm right, it makes all of this worse."

"How can it be worse? Tell me."

She pleated and unpleated her apron. "Well, then…Granny says that people with Sight are…connected. Sometimes. A Sighted person might feel when another one's nearby like a spider feels when something flies into its web."

"*What?* You mean somebody with Sight is helping Patch find me? Who could you mean? I don't know anybody with Sight."

"No, Jem, I mean Patch himself may have Sight."

I teetered on the edge of an abyss. My breath stopped. In a rush, I recalled the handful of times I'd been near Patch. The first time had been two years ago, a month before my birthday, when I'd ducked behind a wall and told myself a story to escape the malice I'd felt flowing toward me from him. I remembered riding home after my first trip to Bedlam and feeling my mind tear itself from my body to float above the street while all the world stood still and a hostile force pulled me down toward him. Then, a year ago, when Patch had hold of my wrist, my skin sizzled under his hand while visions of black clouds and thunder and red lightning drove panic into my mind. Was that Second Sight? Was that—evil—in *me* as well?

"Margery," I whispered. "I've felt him. I thought I'd imagined it. I didn't know he had Sight. But his Sight… it doesn't feel like mine. It feels…like stumbling in the dark and falling into rotted carcass. It feels like a noose tightening around my neck." Was this my destiny, my true nature, the reason everybody in my family was dead? I hadn't felt so alone, so separated from all that was good and decent, since Mum's funeral. I licked my lips. "Margery, does he…is he able to find me because I'm wicked like him?"

She pulled me hard into her arms. "No! Jem, you are not wicked. That isn't it. Never! Patch is of the Dark. He wants something he can never have: to live in the Light." Margery stood. "*You* belong to the Light, and he is attracted to you like a moth to a candle."

"Help me. Hide me."

"I can't. My Sight is gone, I've told you. You have to go my Granny Kestrel, and you have to go now. Before Patch catches up with you. Because if he does, Jem, I fear what he will do if he gets his hands on you again. Dr. Abernathy imagined terrible things, but I can imagine worse."

"What do you mean?"

"I won't tell you, for it I do, you won't stop thinking about it, and then he really *will* find you." She unlocked the back door and peered out. She beckoned, then said, quietly, "You mustn't experiment with flying any more in case Patch is on the lookout for your Sight to go up and show him where you are. You must never go home if you feel you're being followed by one of his redheaded hounds. You must guard body and mind and keep your head down until we can get you away."

"A pack of dogs is hunting me!"

"Aye, you are being hunted slow and careful by an experienced tracker and his hounds. I shall send out a letter to my granny on today's packet and come by this evening. Run along home, now. Be careful."

I trotted home, my mind clenched so tight that houses and carts and people appeared in all shades of gray. I wouldn't have noticed a redhead if I'd seen one.

CHAPTER 13

OCTOBER 1759

Blown to the Four Winds

When Dr. Abernathy came home, he took one look at my face, then steered me into the parlor and closed the drapes. I told him everything.

He said, "This is bad, Jem, very bad indeed. We must face a hard thing now, together. Margery is right. Franklin is right. You must go away for a while, although I agree with Franklin that you should go to the duke on your own and end this." The front doorbell rang. "I hope that's not a patient."

"Margery said she would stop by to speak with you. Shall I answer it?"

"No. What if it's Patch?"

"Would he ring the doorbell?"

"Perhaps not, but hide behind this door all the same." My heart pounded while he went to let in our visitor. I heard a woman's voice, then footsteps, then—

"Jem?" Margery came in. I leapt out from my hiding place. The doctor shut the door behind her. Margery set down a basket and gripped my hands. "I took a cab, love, and then ducked about alleyways in case I was followed."

"That was imprudent at this time of day, Mrs. Jamison," the doctor said.

"I brought my club." The doctor eyed her basket. "Jem, I am beside myself. A carrot-top has been watching my front door ever since you left the shop. I'm certain he was watching for you."

"But I always use the back door."

"It may be they've got somebody watching the back too! It may be Patch is ready to pounce. Regardless, you can't come back to the shop. We have to send you away from London."

"To Cornwall," the doctor said.

"Aye, there," Margery said.

"Come you two. Sit," the doctor said. He poured a brandy for himself and one for Margery, and we all took the places we'd occupied last evening. How quickly things had changed since then!

Margery continued, "Granny Kestrel lives at the edge of Bodmin Moor, a four-hour walk from Fowey harbor. There's not many what goes there. My granny—" She glanced at the doctor—"well, my granny lays down protection around her house. Patch won't be able to find you there, Jem. He won't be able to *See* you."

Cornwall and Granny Kestrel had been looming on my horizon for months as a place I could visit if I wanted to; now, apparently, it was the only safe place I could go.

"She does the same work you do?" I asked.

"That and more," Margery said. "And she may have an answer for your headaches." Margery said, "Oh, Jem, please smile for me. It's ever so lovely in Cornwall. You can breathe air, sunny sweet air, none of this London stink. Gran's got a cottage full of lovely herbs. She's got a big barn and a goat and chickens and, um, a few other animals as well."

"That would be a change, eh, Jem?" Dr. Abernathy said. "You've been prowling about for three years here in the city among animals who wear clothes; now you can prowl about among animals who wear fur." It was a weak joke, but I smiled for him anyway because he looked as downhearted as I felt.

"Would your granny want me underfoot?" I asked. "I don't know anything about animals or the country. How would I get there? How long would I stay?"

Margery said, "Granny Kestrel will love the company, Jem. She's wanted you to come for ages, I've told you. And as far as not knowing anything—well! You didn't know anything three short years ago, and look at you now! You could cure simple things right now for anybody in the world with just the medicines you've learnt from me." She thumped the doctor's arm and leaned forward.

"And this fine man has taught you more than I shall ever know about doctoring. You've learnt how to get about in the greatest city in the world. You know French and Latin. You can read and write."

"I didn't learn all that in three years."

"No, but you shaped and sharpened old skills and laid them over with new ones, like you're a painting, Jem, that keeps getting deeper and better every day."

"Mrs. Jamison, what a lovely sentiment," the doctor said. "You're a healer and a poet." He looked at Margery with true affection.

Margery blushed to the roots of her hair. She said, "Well, Jem, what do you think?"

Margery's granny could teach me to use the Sight instead of burying it away until I lost it, which was an approach I'd begun to question. Journeying to Cornwall would prevent my friends from getting into trouble about me. It would keep me out of Patch's hands. It would prevent my being taken to my grandparents and finding out firsthand why my mother rejected them. Granny Kestrel might have a cure for my headaches as well. In short, it would give me time to think.

"Yes," I said, "I'll go."

And so we made plans for me to leave London. The doctor arranged my travel. My connection to my friends would be by post. Our letters would be carried back and forth from cottage to town by way of Granny Kestrel's fisherman son, Margery's Uncle Lanyon, who looked after his mother as best he could, given that he was out every day fishing and she was at the edge of the moor. It would do Lanyon good to carry the post to his mother, Margery said, for his visits would make a nice change for the two of us. The village of Bodmin was only an hour's walk to the west if I wanted a change of scenery.

We told Franklin I was going to the country for an extended holiday, and he suggested that we continue my lessons via post. I would send a letter with questions and observations about what I read or what I saw on the moor, and he would respond. He suggested we carry on a game of chess by mail as well, with each of us keeping a board close by and faithfully reproducing one anoth-er's moves until we'd completed a game.

Franklin suggested I record my observations in the country and share them, things such as meteorological oddities or unusual birds or insects or animals or plants. "This self-teaching, Jem, will require you to be observant," he said. "If you see a strange insect, rather than brush by it to complete whatever task sent you out of doors, stop, look and listen to it. Careful observation is central if one wishes to learn." The idea of watching an insect crawl on a leaf held no charm for me, but I didn't say that to Franklin.

The doctor and Margery decided that, while traveling by coach, I should use the doctor's surname instead of my own. Jem Abernathy would board a stage-coach for Southampton near Tyburn so as to avoid the port of London and anybody who might be watching it. I'd take ship from Southampton to Fowey, and wait at a tavern called the Mermaid. Granny would call for me there and take me to her cottage, where I would stay until it was safe for me to come home. How we would determine whether it was safe, none of us could say.

These arrangements fell into place so quickly that only two days after we'd decided on Cornwall, I was all packed. In the morning, I would board the dawn coach for Southampton, eighty miles away, which I expected to reach by late afternoon. I felt excited and uneasy. I had just the one valise, packed full with Margery's help. I'd included a fat journal with blank pages so I could keep records for Dr. Franklin and keep a record of my education in the country, like Robinson Crusoe did on his island. Dr. Abernathy thought I should draw pic-tures of what I saw, so he gave me some pencils and quills and ink. I'd packed a change of clothes, a warm jacket, seeds from Phillip Miller at the Chelsea Physick Garden in some of the little sacks I'd given to Margery for Christmas, and the book Dr. Franklin had sent over for our long-distance lessons, *The Fem-inine Monarchie, Or the Historie of Bees* by Charles Butler. I brought my old copy of Burton and a wee chess board for my long-distance games with Dr. Franklin. As my final task, I'd fetched out some small gold coins I kept hidden in my room; these, I'd sewed into the hem of my coat.

The night before I left, Margery came by with two meat pasties for my journey. She said Granny Kestrel would meet me at a tavern called the Mermaid. "How will she know I've arrived?" I asked.

"She has Sight, Jem, don't forget. Trust me, she'll be there."

"I wish you were coming along," I said.

"So do I, love. But I don't dare to leave suddenly at the same time as you disappear. It would look suspicious if anybody's watching the shop, and then it would just be a quick question here and there, and suddenly my mum's telling a stranger at her door I've gone to visit my old granny in Cornwall. But everybody knows I go to Gran at the summer solstice for herbs, and that's just eight months away."

"Eight months is forever."

She pulled me in for a tight, long hug. "I know, it's terrible long! But by then, who knows? We may have sent Patch and his boys packing. The duke and duchess might have given up finding you. You may be able to come home to London with me in eight months." She added, "And I shall be praying that Granny can help you with your Sight."

Before Margery left us that evening, I handed over the recipe book I'd made for her. (I'd had to re-copy it, for the first was poorly done.) I'd organized it in the manner of Dr. Johnson's dictionary, listing the complaint or sickness in alphabetical order on the left and recipes for appropriate medicines on the right.

Margery got tears in her eyes. "Jem, it's ever so elegant and professional. Your drawings are from life, I swear."

"I didn't draw every plant, just the unusual ones."

"And I have my Culpeper for the others. Oh, and your handwriting is so nicely done. What a good idea, to put it in alphabetical order. Some might not agree with the expanses of blank paper, but I think it makes the whole easier to read, and it leaves me space to add notes as I go along. Oh, Jem, it is absolutely the best present anyone ever gave me. I shall treasure it always. And I'll be seeing you again before you know it!"

Before she left, she prayed with me. She reminded me to keep my Sight damped down until I'd got to her gran's. The doctor walked her out to catch a hackney. I missed her already.

* * *

In the morning, the doctor took me in his trap to the inn on Tyburn Road, not far from our house, where Margery and I had gone after our parlor-cleaning and where the coach always stopped. I climbed out to say goodbye to Giselle, to tell her I loved her and would miss her. Her affection seeped through my fingertips into my heart, easing my sorrow a little. My coach came far sooner than I wanted it to. The driver loaded my valise and went inside the inn to call for any other riders going to Southampton.

"Up you go," the doctor said. I boarded and sat by the window. The doctor stood just outside. He wore a trembly smile, jumpy at the corners of his mouth, his eyes bright. His face looked like it didn't know what expression to wear. "Well, Jem," he said, "you're off on a great adventure."

"I'm sorry to leave you alone without any help."

"I don't deny it will be strange to get on without you now that I've got used to you."

"You won't replace me?"

"No one could replace you, Jem." He cleared his throat and said, "You must write me a letter now and again. I shall wish to know how you are getting on, that you are continuing your education, that you are well."

"You'll write back?" A hard lump in my throat made my voice croak.

"Mrs. Jamison and I will write as regularly as we may."

"Thank you," I said.

The driver came out and hauled himself up to his place. The horses pranced a bit and jingled their harnesses. It was time to go.

The doctor reached up to clasp my hand. "Take care, Jem. Take very good care of yourself. You must come back soon. We'll let you know when the time is right," he said, meaning when Patch was gone. His quivery lips tried but could not shape a smile. The door opened, and the coach jostled as other travelers boarded it. But I had eyes only for Dr. Abernathy.

I grasped his hand tightly between both of mine. "Goodbye, sir," I said. "Thank you." I pressed a kiss to the back of his hand, and I saw, through my own blurred vision, tears in Dr. Abernathy's eyes!

"I don't want to go," I said. Now, my tears dripped on to our clasped hands.

The doctor pulled my head close to press a kiss to my forehead. "Nonsense, my boy," he said, "You'll have great times in the country, and you'll be back before you know it."

The driver called down to the doctor, "To one side, sir, if you please. We need to be away." When the doctor stepped back, the driver whipped up the horses, saying "Hi, there!" I stuck my head out the window for a last look at Dr. Abernathy, who stood with a hand raised in farewell.

When I pulled my head in, I couldn't talk around the lump in my throat, so I just looked at the other passengers: a stout older gentleman with spectacles, wearing his own bristly gray hair instead of a wig, and reading a Bible, and a plain woman in an ill-fitting brown dress, with a fussy child who persisted in trying to take something out of the basket the woman held on her knees. She shoved away his hand without seeming even to see it. I looked back out of the window as we clattered away from the perpetual smoke of the city and the city gave way to the country. Shadows of clouds rolled over sheep and cows browsing in pastures.

We jounced along, changing horses four times between London and Southampton. Each change took less than five minutes, although in Basingstoke, we stopped a little longer to have a bite to eat. The tang from the brewery in the town center flavored our dinner with malted barley.

The driver regularly drove this road, so he knew when to walk his horses (not often) and when to have us get out and walk up hills or around hazards like the standing water we came upon at a low spot in the road that came halfway up the coach's wheels.

The water had pooled when a cold autumn rain fell on soaked fields that could hold no more. The bristly gentleman looked up from his Bible when he felt the rain on his face, then he pulled shut the leather window covering, thereby blocking both the rain and his reading light. He reached over to pull the window covering next to the woman with the child. Then he said to me, "Well, boy? Close your window. It's raining."

"I like it open. For the air," I said. The smell inside the coach was a stew of unwashed bodies, sausages, tooth decay, and soiled trousers—the child, no doubt.

"You'll get wet and catch your death," the mother said.

"I'll be careful," I said.

She pulled her child closer and wrapped him in a fold of her cloak, and made a moue at the gentleman. "It's cold," the gentleman insisted.

I pulled the leather flap toward me but didn't tie it so I could stick my nose out the bottom. The gentleman began a conversation with the woman regarding the weather, her history and family—all that tiresome small talk strangers make with one another.

Even though I'd bumped over London cobblestones the last three years, I wasn't prepared for a country ride in a coach. Some turnpike trusts had improved the road in some sections, but, overall, the ride was so rough that the view jounced up and down in its square of window as though we were at sea in a storm.

The bristly gentleman got out at Winchester, but the woman and child stayed on. Unfortunately, the jouncing made the child ill, and he threw up in his mother's basket, thereby ruining whatever was inside that he so desperately had wanted earlier in the journey. When the boy vomited, the woman shrieked, the driver stopped the horses to find out the trouble, and the end result was that the driver let me come up beside him for the last bit of the trip. It was cold out in the wind, but the driver let me stick my legs under his robe while he spun tales of when he was a young driver—"Held up by Robert Darby hisself on this very road!"—and as we got closer to the coast, I smelled the first hints of sea air on the evening breeze.

CHAPTER 14

END OF OCTOBER 1759

Something in the Water

On my first journey aboard a ship, I'd traveled from Sunderland to London aboard a collier called the *Sea Princess*. It had taken twelve days for me and Mum and Jamie to get to London. This, my second journey, aboard the coastal trader *Mary Ellen* sailing from Southampton to Fowey, would take only four or five days barring any storms or other trouble.

When I boarded the *Mary Ellen* with my valise, a skinny man with an earnest face checked my papers and said to a sailor walking past with a coil of rope over his shoulder, "You, Merrick!"

"Aye, Mr. Hollis?" said a red-cheeked sailor in a short jacket, bright red neckerchief, and wide trousers of the kind they call petticoat breeches. Brown curls escaped out the bottom of a cap looked like it had been daubed with tar.

"Take Master Connolly below. Put him across from me and tie down his duffle."

"Aye, sir. Come, boy," Merrick said. "Where're ye bound for, Master Connolly, if I may be so bold?"

"Fowey."

"Y' won't see Falmouth, then. Now there's a town." We climbed down into a dim space lit by a lantern and by the fading daylight that spilled down the hatch. Merrick stopped at two hammocks hanging well above my head. "Pick one." I swatted a hammock, and he said, "Go on, try it out."

"How do I get up there?"

"Pull down on the edge and sling a leg over, then roll. Us'll show ye." He rolled into the hammock as easy as a dog beside a fire rolls over to warm his other side. "Try t' get in. I'll stow your bag." While he tied my valise to two iron eyes screwed into the ribs of the ship, I put in a leg and rolled—all the way out the other side. Helping me up, Merrick said, "Y' all right, Master Connolly?" He dusted off the seat of my breeches.

"Fine. Call me Jem."

"Jem it is. Y're too lively gettin' in," Merrick said. "Do more like this." He demonstrated; I tried again and managed to wedge myself into the hammock with my arms stuck tight to my sides like a moth in a cocoon. "Now y're snugged up nice and tight," Merrick said.

"Wot ye got there, Merrick?" Another sailor with a full beard shuffled up.

"Passenger, Barmy. Name of Jem. Bound for Fowey." Barmy canted his head like a dog listening to a strange sound. "Shake hands, Barm," Merrick prompted. Barmy offered his hand. I tugged an arm loose and placed my hand in his huge paw. When Barmy smiled, I saw he was missing two front teeth. "Let go, Barm," Merrick said.

A queer *thump-shuffle, thump-shuffle* announced the arrival of somebody else, a man gripping the handle of a kettle in one hand and a rattling bag in the other. He shoved along a basket using his left leg, a peg carved from wood. I'd seen cripples struggling just to walk in London, so I was impressed that he carried so many things on a rocking ship.

"Merrick and Barmy!" the man barked. "There's the lads! 'Ere, take this up."

"Aye, Cookie," Merrick said. "That's dinner, Jem. Out, and be quick about it, or there won't be nothin' left." I kept a grip on the edge of the hammock as I rolled out, and a good thing too or I'd have landed on my bum again. "See? Y're getting the hang of it. Come on. Barmy, take the bag. Don't spill it."

"You, boy," Cookie said, "take up this basket o' bread." We clambered topside with our burdens followed by Cookie who grunted and panted behind me. Shortly after we appeared, the ship's bell dinged twice. "Stand by me, boy," Cookie said. "One piece of bread per man. They'll try for more on account of it's soft bread from town, but don't you give it to 'em."

"I won't, sir. What is your name, if you please? I'm Jem."

"They calls me Cookie. When'd Cap'n bring ye aboard?"

"I arrived today."

"Oh, 'arrived' did ye? Ain't we fine? Why ain't ye sleepin' in Cap'n's cabin?"

"Mr. Hollis told me to sleep across from him." By then, a dozen sailors had lined up for their dinner, with Mr. Hollis first in line.

"Cookie, why is this boy serving the dinner?" Mr. Hollis said. "He's a passenger."

"Passenger! Why didn't y' say so, boy?"

"I, er…I don't mind helping, Mr. Hollis. May I?"

"Aye, Master Connolly, if you wish."

Cookie dished up a big bowl of whatever steamed in the kettle. "Put that there big piece o' bread on top o' the scouse, Jem," he said. "Aye, that's the one." Cookie handed the bowl and bread to Hollis. "Tell Cap'n Foster I put butter and jam on 'is bread." Hollis bore away the Captain's dinner. We served up the rest of the meal. The men inspected each other's servings and seemed satisfied that all were equal. Cookie scraped the kettle clean for the last serving—mine.

While we ate and the sun set, a clergyman of some kind boarded. After Mr. Hollis checked his papers, he said, "Mr. Murlin, dinner is served and nothing left. Perhaps you could dine in town?"

"I think not, Mr. Hollis," the clergyman said. "'Tis best for me to travel by sea on an empty stomach. Is there a bucket below?" Mr. Hollis gave him a look.

"Aye, amidships," Hollis said. "You'll sleep next to this boy. Merrick, show him." Merrick handed me his empty bowl and hurried to take Mr. Murlin's valise. They climbed down. I helped Cookie gather the bowls and spoons, carry them down to the galley, and rinse them in a bucket of water.

"I'm goin' back up, Jem," Cookie said when we finished. "The men'll be wantin' t' smoke."

"Sir?"

"No open fire be allowed on deck 'cept I bring it, but the men like t' smoke a pipe afore the first watch." He dropped a hot coal into a covered tankard and hooked a pair of tongs on his apron. Mr. Murlin had climbed halfway up the ladder when we reached it, so at the top, he reached down to give Cookie a hand. As soon as Cookie appeared on deck, a knot of sailors crowded round to light their pipes off his coal.

Mr. Murlin, pale and perspiring, walked to stand near the rail, so I joined him. "I'm sorry you're ill, sir," I said. "I'm Jem Connolly."

"How do you do, Master Connolly?" He leaned over the rail and retched. "Excuse me. Sea travel does not agree with me, but it is faster than walking, and I am pressed to get to Falmouth."

When I asked why he journeyed to Falmouth, Mr. Murlin said he would debark in Falmouth and travel up the River Fal to St. Stephen to visit his mother, who'd taken sick, then hold a prayer meeting in the open air.

"You're a Methodist, then?" I said. The Methodists initially had been persecuted, as had the Quakers, but now the Anglican church tolerated both sects, although Dr. Abernathy said most Anglicans preferred that God stay in Heaven and leave the Earth to them. So it seemed to me that my Da was right when he'd told me, long ago, that it was the body of believers that made up the Church and that a person didn't have to be Anglican or Catholic or anything else, so long as he believed. At any rate, the flavor of Mr. Murlin's Christianity didn't make any difference to me.

"I hope you do not despise our sect," Mr. Murlin said. "We have been a blessing in Cornwall."

"I don't despise your sect in the least," I said. "In fact, I shall pray for you. If I were at home, I could mix you a drink of ginger that would settle your stomach."

"You, mix medicine? Why, what are you?" Mr. Murlin spat over the side.

"I work with an herbalist in London."

"And why has he sent you so far from home?"

"I'm to study with another herbalist north of Fowey."

Mr. Murlin said, "On Bodmin Moor? Judging by your smile, you haven't seen it yet. I've walked the moor many a time on my way from Liskeard to Camelford. Forests edge the moor, but once you leave the trees behind, the moor is a huge, desolate place. Solid granite sits just under a thin skin of earth and heather. Hardly any trees grow. Very few houses stand on it to break up the monotony of hill after hill. And then there are the towers of stone."

"Towers of stone?"

"Heathen places. Standing stones ring the tops of some of the hills. I give the standing stones a wide berth. More than once, I have seen light flickering among the stones, and I fear a coven of witches practices some evil ritual there."

"Dr. Abernathy says there's no such things as witches."

Mr. Murlin frowned. "Whoever Dr. Abernathy is, he clearly believes that faith is secondary to science. Our great founder, Mr. Wesley, says that to disbelieve in witches is to disbelieve in the Bible. Exodus 22:18 says, 'Thou shalt not suffer a witch to live.' The Bible would not say such a thing without reason."

What should I say to that? Science *did* come first with Dr. Abernathy, but he'd said to me when he'd decided to take me on as his apprentice, "why did God give us a brain if not to use it?" He believed it was our God-given duty to never stop learning, to discard old ideas if they were proved wrong. Learning was why he'd sent me to Cornwall in the first place.

Just then, something splashed a short distance from the ship. The sun had set, and the sky had gone a deep, pure blue. Faint stars sparkled. Out in the Channel, not far from the *Mary Ellen*, a large silver body leapt out of the water and splashed again. "Was that a fish?" I said.

"Dolphin," Mr. Murlin said. "It's a fish that breathes air, I'm told. The Catholics say dolphins carry saved souls to Christ."

"Do they?"

"Certainly not! If that were true, how could those who live inland have any hope of heaven? Everyone would have to make his way to the sea when he died!"

Merrick joined us. "Are them dolphins? Jem, did ye know dolphins're good luck? They bring fair weather and good winds."

"You should trust in your Heavenly Father for safety at sea rather than a fish," Mr. Murlin told him. Merrick shrugged. A bell rang. "It's eight thirty, Master Connolly. We should try to sleep and leave these sailors to their duties."

While Mr. Murlin climbed down ahead of me, Merrick whispered, "Preachers're bad luck, Jem. Try t' steer clear of 'im." Louder, he said, "I'll keep a lookout for the dolphins for ye."

Below, we clambered into our hammocks. "Good night, Master Connolly," Mr. Murlin said.

"Good night, Mr. Murlin." I wanted to roll to my side, but I was afraid I might fall out again, so I laid still and tried to sleep. It was hard, for the watch dinged off every half hour. Above me, sailor's feet thumped back and forth. Some twenty feet across from me, Mr. Hollis snored. The dank air smelled of sour water in the bilge, mold from the things in constant wet in the bow, and the men who slept there, for whom bathing was an impossibility.

When eight bells rang and the watch changed, half the crew climbed down to sleep while the other half, including Mr. Hollis, climbed up. Mr. Murlin awoke, groaning, and vomited into his bucket. The smell made me queasy. "I'll take it up for you, Mr. Murlin," I whispered. "I can't sleep anyway."

"Thank you. I haven't anything at all left in my stomach. I hope I can sleep now."

The crew that had just got off watch talked quietly as they settled into the hammocks that the other half of the crew had just vacated. I climbed to the deck. At the top of the ladder, Barmy picked apart a piece of rope. When he saw me, he said, "You ain't s'posed t' be up 'ere."

"Mr. Murlin was ill." I held out my bucket.

"No, you go below. Only us can be 'ere on watch. Merrick, tell 'im."

"It's all right, Barmy," Merrick said from behind me. He took my bucket and dumped it over the side, then poured in water from the scuttlebutt to rinse it.

"There y' are, Jem, good as new."

"He can be up here?" Barmy said.

"Aye, Barmy. Mr. Hollis don't mind." Barmy nodded, but he watched me like a rabbit watches a predator.

"I'll stay out of the way, Barmy. Merrick, I can't sleep. I hoped to see the dolphins again."

"Stand by the port rail and look out to sea," Merrick said.

I took the bucket back to Mr. Murlin before I found a place to stand beside the rail that faced the open ocean. The waves chopped the moonlight into slices of silver. Far out in the Channel, a glowing golden spark must have been another ship that, like the *Mary Ellen*, kept a lit lantern on her stern so other ships could see her at night. The brisk breeze blew the stench of belowdecks out of my nostrils, but also made me glad I wore a good wool coat.

"Ahoy, Master Connolly," Mr. Hollis said. "Can't sleep?" He carried a spool of twine from which dangled a wedge of wood.

"Mr. Murlin was ill, so I emptied his bucket. Merrick said I might stay on deck and take the air."

He laughed, "Aye, air is a rare commodity belowdecks. Since you're here, perhaps you'd like to help me measure our speed."

"Of course! What must I do."

"Come." We walked to the stern. Mr. Hollis carefully set down his spool and handed me the piece of wood. He said, "Feel them knots on the twine? Each knot is eight fathoms from the next—that be just over forty-seven feet for a landsman. When I nod, you toss the wood over the stern. Pay out the line, but don't tug. Let the wood float and the knots slip through your fingers. See?"

"How does that tell us how fast we're going?"

"Because I have a thirty-second hourglass, here, which I shall turn over the moment the wood touches the water. After thirty seconds, we'll haul in the wood and see how many knots you've paid out. And that will tell us how fast we're going in knots. Ready?" He nodded, I tossed, the wood landed, the hourglass turned, and I paid out the line carefully, making sure it didn't catch on the rail. When the hourglass ran out, Mr. Hollis grabbed the line. I hauled in the weighted chip whilst Mr. Hollis counted. "Five knots. A fine speed."

"Five miles per hour?"

"Five knots. A mile on land is a bit longer'n a mile at sea, but that's close. A man on land can walk three miles in an hour, so we're sailing nearly twice as fast as a man could walk."

As he rewound the twine, I asked, "Why do you measure speed in knots?"

"'Tis impossible to measure anything by looking at moving water. No stationary point. But that wood chip's weighted so it stands up and don't move in the time it takes to measure our speed. As for why, once we know how fast we're going and how many miles we are from port, we'll know how much longer it'll be." He pocketed his little hourglass. "Master Connolly, you may stay on deck as long as you wish, but I suggest you try to sleep."

Merrick intercepted me before I reached the hatch. "I saw ye takin' the measure with Mr. Hollis. How fast're we goin'? Seems like five knots."

"Exactly right, Merrick. Good night."

He put a hand on my arm. "Master Connolly, afore ye go below, I wonder if y'd help me find Barmy? When it's cold and we're sailin' easy, 'e tends t' find an out-of-the-way spot t' wrap up and get warm, but then 'e falls asleep. Cap'n Foster whips men what sleeps on watch."

"Whips them? Why?"

"'E does it for discipline. Sailors ain't allowed t' sleep on watch or we could run aground or worse." He leaned in to whisper, "Problem is, Cap'n's already whipped Barmy twice, but 'e falls asleep anyroad. Cap'n says next time 'e'll make Barmy ride the gray mare."

"Do what?"

Merrick pointed up. "Make 'im climb up and sit up on the upper topsail yard for the rest of the watch. Barmy's afeard to climb since 'e fell."

"Fell? From up there?"

"Two year ago, me an' Barmy sailed on a wool ship to the Colonies. A storm come up sudden like they do. Barmy got sent aloft to reef the topsail, only the ship bucked when he reached for a line and 'e fell on 'is 'ead and ain't been the same since." He prodded a roll of canvas with his foot. "Barmy got put off the ship when we sailed home again, so I left too. Cap'n Foster took us on for the coast trade. Anyroad, I don't think Barmy'd climb. I don't think 'e could do it. An' then Cap'n'd put 'im off, an' then Barmy'd get pressed, an' 'e'd never last in the navy. Never. No, it's the *Mary Ellen* or fishing maybe. We'll stay s' long as we can."

"Does the Captain know about Barmy?"

"Aye. But Barmy's real good for haulin' out cargo. Can run a pulley line all by hisself what usually takes three men." He pointed. We found Barmy in the stern wrapped up in a piece of canvas behind a barrel. "Barmy, up, man, and about your business," Merrick hissed. " 'Tis morning soon, and Cap'n'll be up and about." Barmy shucked off the canvas and stumbled to his feet. "Go forward and find summat t' do." Barmy obeyed.

Merrick sighed. "Dawn's comin'. Do you go below, Jem, and wake Mr. Murlin."

Over the next two days, we fell into a routine. The *Mary Ellen* kept "dog-watches" so the same men would not have to be on the deck the same hours throughout a trip along the coast. The watch from four to eight in the evening was divided into two half watches, one from four to six and the second from six to eight. (I had boarded during the first dog watch and Mr. Murlin had boarded during the second.) The dog watches came at twilight when the day's work was done, and before the night watches began, so everybody was on deck during the dog-watches. Captain Foster walked the Channel side of the quarter deck, all alone, while Mr. Hollis walked the coast side. After dinner, the sailors lit their pipes off Cookie's coal, and everybody relaxed on deck and smoked or sang or told stories.

We breakfasted at seven bells (seven-thirty in the morning), usually on porridge, the whole crew together. After breakfast, Mr. Hollis set the watches, so half the crew would stay on duty for four hours and half would be off. Whoever he handed his half-hour glass to was supposed to ring the ship's bell every half hour in a pattern of pairs for easier counting, with any odd bells at the end of the sequence. This was why the bells rang all night and all day.

If a man was on watch, he kept busy. Men climbed the rigging to tighten lines, reefed or furled sails. If they weren't aloft, they tarred, greased, oiled, varnished, or painted anything exposed to sea water, which meant everything. They overhauled, replaced and repaired ropes, or changed blocks if they were chafing. If they weren't doing any of those things, or weren't given a task by the deck officer, they picked oakum, which meant they sat in one spot unraveling bits of old rope to be used in making new or to plug any small leaks that sprung in the hull. Nobody liked the job except Barmy, who seemed to find peace in the simple task.

When a sailor wasn't on watch, he might catch up on his sleep or mend his clothing, but most played at dice or cards or told stories. Some carved bits of wood or ivory. Some practiced tying knots. Merrick drew pictures. These activities took place belowdecks in the bow, where the sailors also slept. Each sailor's bed was a simple hammock hung from the ceiling, like mine, all in a row with less than a foot between one hammock and the next. The bow was not a wholesome place. The bow breasted the waves, so the sea hit it the hardest. Sails and rope jumbled up among the seamen's chests in the space below the hammocks. There was no fresh air and no escape from the damp. So I spent as much time as possible on deck.

At noon every day, Captain Foster took the reckoning off the sun directly overhead and retreated to his cabin to write in his log book. When we got near to one of our ports of call—Bournemouth, Poole, Weymouth—Mr. Hollis gave the order to reef the sails, and he sent someone aloft to spy out a good place to tie up so we could offload some of the tallow or iron or hemp we'd got from the East India ship in Southampton. Cookie went ashore at Poole for fresh butter and eggs. He bought a side of beef at Bournemouth from which he made sea pie. One day we ate Spotted Dog, a sort of moist cake with currants cooked in something that looked like a shirt sleeve. We had grog or water to drink. I always took water, and Merrick always took grog because, he said, "After a while at sea, the water gets slimy and things starts swimming in it. A bit o' rum makes the water go down easier." I looked at my cup. "Oh, that there water is good and fresh," Merrick said. "We have fresh on Cap'n Foster's ship, on account of we sail into port t' offload every day or two, but y' won't find no sailor who won't take rum it it's offered."

After dinner and the dog watches, Mr. Hollis and I checked our speed, a sailor was assigned to the wheel, and the galley was shut up.

A night and part of a day from Fowey, I settled in to my little hammock for my last sleep aboard the *Mary Ellen*.

* * *

Buoyed by waves that tasted of the chalk of this northern land, we followed the singing ship. Few ships sang, but this one we heard across many leagues. We followed the vibrations into water that became ever colder. But we swam into it, gladly, to find the singer. Our memory keepers knew old songs from warmer waters when men who sang in our language sailed southern seas. We swam oceans, bore young, generation after generation, listening for the lost music. Sometimes we heard it, we found the singer, we shared. Four suns past, we'd heard it again. So we came. Louder and louder as we got closer and closer, the music vibrated like the song of a whale moaning his loneliness to the deep. We pushed into shallower water. Between the rocky bottom and the glowing surface, we swam circles and listened, then surfaced in moonlight.

At the rail of a ship stood the source of the music, a human pulsing Light that we felt like our own beating hearts. We swam to the side of the ship where the human stood looking out to sea. We sang greetings. She did not respond.

Louder, then. Some of us leapt out of the water, dancing joy. We sang all the songs

we knew, but she did not sing back, although she pulsed Light, and in the Light
we felt land birds that had known her. Falcon.Pigeon. How lonely she was. Why
wouldn't she hear us?

Then Something like oil seeped from the ship. Our brothers that dove over and
over for the girl felt it first. When the Something reached them, it burned. Did the
girl know the burning thing rode her ship? We swam out to sea and let the Something
chase us, but when we circled wide, we left it on the surface, hoping it could not find
its way back to the ship that carried the girl.

* * *

I opened my eyes. My swaying hammock rocked me as though I were a
dolphin sunning on the waves. Music I'd dreamed sounded familiar final notes
in my mind. I felt peaceful and happy, bemused by my dream of dolphins. I
climbed up on deck to see if they still swam beside the *Mary Ellen*. The breeze
blew cold. Mist shrouded the shore, making it look like a land in a dream. The
sun pinked the eastern sky. No dolphin shapes tumbled in play beside the ship.

I sat near the rail with my journal and a pencil and drew the dolphins I'd
dreamed: blocky bodies flowing into strong tails, long noses above smiling
mouths. I drew one alone, then three, then a pod of them breasting the waves
that mimicked their shape. I drew them playing in the water, leapfrogging over
one another. I drew them as lords over a fantastic land where only strong swim-
mers could go.

"What you got there, Jem?" Merrick joined me at the rail. "Let me see. Why,
them're dolphins, as real as can be. Where's this?"

"The bottom of the ocean. The dolphins' kingdom. I dreamed about it."

"If that there is Davy Jones's locker, it's a sight nicer'n I ever thought of."

"Have you seen the dolphins this morning?"

"No, but if y' dreamed about 'em, it means they're looking out for you." His
eyes swept the stern. "Blast."

"What's wrong?"

"Barmy's s'posed t' be on watch at the stern. He ain't there. If 'e's sleepin' again…Come on." Merrick headed for the stern, but before we'd gone three steps, Captain Foster emerged from his cabin and walked aft, turning his head this way and that, apparently looking for whoever was supposed to be on watch. We ran to intercept—but we were too late.

Captain Foster shouted, "You, there! Barmy! Up and on your feet, you lazy, worthless son of a gun!" He kicked once, twice, thrice. "Up, I say!" Barmy hauled himself to his feet. The heads of the crew on watch all turned toward the commotion, just as Merrick and I reached the angry captain.

"Cap'n Foster, beggin' your pardon, sir," Merrick said. "I was on watch all night, same as Barmy. I swear I saw 'im on 'is feet not five minutes past. I'm certain 'im weren't asleep long."

"No one sleeps on watch, Merrick. Not one wink." By this time, Mr. Hollis had run to us all the way from the bow. "And where were you, Mr. Hollis, when this good-for-nothing was asleep?"

"Sir, I took a turn on deck at four bells and all was well, so I went forward to speak with the helmsman."

"See, Cap'n? He weren't asleep long," Merrick said.

"He is not allowed to sleep at all!" Captain Foster growled. Barmy hung his head like a scolded dog. "You have been warned before, Barmy. Up you go. Top yard. Stay for the rest of the watch." Barmy looked up. He swallowed. Merrick tried to smile encouragement. Barmy fisted a line in his hands and began to climb. He climbed three feet, then stopped and began to cry. "Go on or it's the whip!" Captain Foster shouted. "On the double, or you'll stay there over the next watch too." Barmy pulled himself up another couple of feet but then wrapped both arms around the mast, howling and sobbing.

"'E can't do it," Merrick said. "Cap'n, you know 'e fell."

"A sailor afraid to climb," Captain Foster said. "If he were in the navy, he'd be keelhauled. Come down, Barmy." Barmy slid down the mast, his hands squeaking on the polished wood. Weeping, he stood at the foot of the mast, his breast heaving as he fought for breath after his fright. "Can't stay awake on duty and can't climb. What kind of sailor are you? No sailor at all!"

"M-Merrick, I almost fell again. I almost did," Barmy slumped to his knees, sobbing.

"Mr. Hollis, prepare him," said Captain Foster. "Stand aside, Merrick."

"Whip me instead," Merrick blurted. "Whip me instead o' him. 'E can't bear it, not right now."

"You would take his punishment?" Captain Foster said. "It's fifty lashes."

The sun was full up. Merrick eyed the knotted rope in the captain's hand and then Barmy, dissolved in sorrow. "Aye, sir," Merrick said. "'Elp 'im," he directed two sailors, who pulled Barmy to his feet. Merrick removed his shirt and wrapped his arms around the mast Barmy had just slid down. Mr. Hollis tied his hands.

Captain Foster said, "Barmy, sleeping on watch is a grievous offense. You have committed it three times now. The punishment is fifty lashes. Your friend has chosen to take your punishment for you, more fool he. Perhaps seeing Merrick suffer will cure you of your laziness. Mr. Hollis, if you would keep the count?" Captain Foster stepped back, spread his legs into a wider stance, raised the rope. The sailors held their breath. The lash whistled down and *thwacked!* on Merrick's bare back. He flinched. A fat red welt rose where the knot had struck.

"One," said Mr. Hollis.

Five more times, the knot came down. Each time, Merrick's body jerked. Sweat and tears ran down Merrick's face. Barmy reached for Merrick, but the two sailors held him back. The whipping continued. *Stupidity*, I thought. *Madness. Senseless cruelty.*

"Seven," Mr. Hollis said.

My heart pounded. My ears hummed. Every time the knotted rope landed, I flinched. It could not be borne. It must not be borne. *End it, then.*

"Eleven."

I leaped forward and grabbed Captain Foster's raised arm, shouting, "Stop!" and felt all that I was burst like a cannonball against the captain's raised arm.

And *everything* stopped: the sailors watching, Barmy's weeping, even the waves rolling past the Mary Ellen. Everything was still as a painting except for me. The initial physical shock of my hand absorbing the force of Captain Foster's downward swing drove me back toward Merrick. But then, where I gripped the captain's arm, my hand began to burn as though the arm were a hot coal. I tried to let go. I couldn't.

I gasped when I saw that where my hand touched Captain Foster's skin, my fingers didn't grasp human flesh but were sunk to the knuckles in black ooze. Except for its temperature, the ooze felt like the cold, tarry stuff I'd waded through long ago on Bonfire Night when I'd somehow lost Margery in the crowd. Margery had said that the icy ooze might be the veil that separates the spirit world from ours. She hadn't liked that it had touched me.

Today, the ooze under my fingers sizzled, like when Patch had grabbed me the day of the Lord Mayor's Show. Patch's grip had conjured nightmare pictures in my mind of black clouds over a tossing sea, of thunder and red lightning. I'd felt seasick and polluted. Today, I saw no pictures, only the frozen world around me, but I felt something…hungry roiling just under Captain Foster's skin.

My eyes flickered back to Captain Foster's face—and he moved! "So here you are," he said. "We've been looking for you." The hungry thing in him swarmed to where my hand gripped his arm. It flowed into my hand and crept up my arm. Captain Foster's eyes brimmed with—oil? I began to panic. My arm burned to the elbow, but I couldn't open my hand.

Desperate, I began to pray, *Go away, go away.* The oil sludged toward my heart. *Please.*

Faintly at first, then louder, music sounded in my ears. Light wove into the music. Happy memories flooded my mind. I remembered my Da's arms around me. Laughing with Margery. Mr. Galt's ropy arms hugging me in forgiveness.

My mother. Jamie's giggling. All the good I'd ever known I remembered now, and the shining music took it and pushed at the flowing ooze.

The sludge stopped. It retreated. I kept pushing memories and music and light against it, like dolphins herding fish, faster and faster, until the ooze flowed out of my hand all the way back into Captain Foster, with me behind pushing so hard I found myself looking through Captain Foster's eyes down at my own face. *Enough!* I thought, and ebbed back into myself. Captain Foster stood, frozen once again. *Stay there.*

I blinked. The world woke up. I trembled. *What had I done? How had I done it?*

"Back, Master Connolly," Mr. Hollis said. He hauled me away from Captain Foster.

"Jem, leave it!" Merrick panted.

"The count was eleven, sir," Mr. Hollis said.

Captain Foster looked at the rope in his hand. "That's enough," he said.

"Sir?" said Mr. Hollis. The sailors stared.

Captain Foster strode to the rail and flung his rope into the sea. The men gasped. "Untie him. Cookie, bring up breakfast." Nobody moved for a moment. Their eyes skittered from Captain Foster to Merrick to me—and then stayed on me.

"Back to work on the double, I say!" Captain Foster barked, and the men came out of their trance. When Mr. Hollis let me go, I grabbed a line to prevent myself falling down. Merrick comforted Barmy. The men busied themselves while they waited for breakfast. I stood alone, feeling every glance that fell on me like something crawling across my face in the middle of the night.

At breakfast, the men peered at me over the edges of their bowls. Nobody invited me to sit with them. Barmy and Merrick made a place for me.

I whispered, "Why are they looking at me?"

"Nobody here never saw Cap'n back down, so they think y're some kind o' wizard," Merrick said. "'Tis good y're leavin' today."

"I just asked him to stop," I mumbled.

"We all asked him lots o' things lots o' times, but Cap'n does as he pleases, make no mistake," Merrick said. "And the way 'e throwed 'is rope overboard?" Merrick shook his head. "That whip was 'is best friend. No, Jem, y' did summat more'n askin'. That's what's got the others jittery. Best ye stay below until we get to Fowey." I left my bowl with Cookie, who wouldn't take it from my hand but watched me place it in the bucket. All eyes watched me descend the ladder.

Mr. Murlin, who never took breakfast, said from his hammock, "What was all the commotion on deck?"

"A man fell asleep on watch, so the Captain gave him a whipping."

"I've seen such punishments before. Sea justice is brutal. But sometimes chastisement of the flesh serves as chastisement of the spirit. How many lashes? Fifty, I suppose."

"Eleven."

"For sleeping on watch? What an odd number. I'm surprised."

"Captain Foster had a change of heart," I said, and bent over my notebook to finish my dolphin picture as a parting gift for Merrick. But drawing the dolphins was just a task to complete now, it didn't feel peaceful, because my fingers still burned cold from having touched the thing inside Captain Foster.

CHAPTER 15

END OF OCTOBER 1759

A Nasty Dinner and a Strange Dessert

Near sunset, we docked at Fowey. I bade farewell to Mr. Murlin, who got off to stretch his legs. Mr. Hollis directed the offloading of iron, but the sailors gave me a wide berth when I climbed the ladder to depart, all except Merrick. I'd folded up my dolphin drawing, and when I pressed it into his hand, taking care that nobody else saw me do it, I whispered, "Dolphins, for luck."

"Thank ye, Jem," he said, slipping it into his shirt. "I'll look at it private-like later." I waved at Barmy, who simply watched me go. I had a bit of trouble at first walking on the dock and then on the street as my legs had become accustomed to the pitching of the ship, but I found the Mermaid Tavern where I was to meet Granny Kestrel. She lived north of Fowey, so I hoped she'd already arrived in town and I wouldn't have long to wait. Would we walk home yet tonight? How long would I stay with her? Was she anything like Margery?

Inside the Mermaid, the last light of day shone weakly through a very dirty leaded-glass window. A small fire smoked more than burned, for the breeze blew brisk from the sea. Two men sat at the bar nursing beers. One of them reminded me of a weasel with his slim body and snaggly teeth. The other was a redhead. The barman saw me come in and called, "Hallo, young gent. What's your business?"

"I'm just off the *Mary Ellen* out of Southampton. I'm to meet someone here."

"Who?"

"Kestrel Penhaligon of Bodmin Moor."

He stopped wiping the bar. "You mean Granny Penhaligon?"

"Do you know her? Is she here?"

"No, she ain't. Well, come up, lad, and sit. Did they feed you on the ship?"

"Not dinner, no."

He smiled. "I got fresh scrowlers already cooked." He set before me a plate of cold fish, tough on the edges. He set down a bottle of cloudy vinegar. "Beer?"

"No, thank you." He poured me a glass of beer anyway. As there was nothing else and I was hungry, I nibbled my fish and sipped the beer. My nose wrinkled.

Ten minutes later, the fish was gone, but not the beer. "Drink up," the bartender said.

"I don't care for it, thank you."

"Oh, you don't care for it." He said to the two men, "It's mother's milk here, ain't it? Granny Kestrel herself drinks it all day long, so you'd best get used to it." He grinned. "Have another swallow."

I tried another swallow to please him. The barman and the two men watched. I set down the glass and pushed it toward the barman. If this was all Granny Kestrel drank, I would suck dew off the grass. The barman said, "Are you sure Granny was to meet you here?"

"Aye, sir. I was to wait at the Mermaid for her to come and fetch me."

"What you coming to see her for?"

"Just a visit. I'm to help her...farm," I improvised.

He leaned back and crossed his arms. "Is that so? I hadn't heard she'd took up farming." Dr. Abernathy advised against telling lies, and this was why: one lie led to another and before you knew it, you were lost in a forest and no way out. Before I could think of an answer, the bartender asked, "And who're you to Granny?"

"I'm acquainted with her granddaughter."

"Which one? Margery?"

"Aye, her." I didn't tell him Margery had married and changed her name to Jamison, for it seemed prudent to keep my cards close to my chest, as it were, especially as the beer had left me a bit muddle-headed.

"It may be Granny Penhaligon were delayed coming down from the hills, or she may've fallen and broke her head," the bartender said.

"I hope not, sir," I said. The weasel-eyed customer raised his finger for two more glasses of beer.

The bartender said, "You'd best go along to Lanyon Penhaligon, that's her son what should be back in from fishing by now. Ask him after his mother. His is the last cottage going nor-east along the shore road. Looks out on the harbor. Green shutters."

"I think I should wait here for her."

"What if she's there waitin'? Best pay up and go find her," the barman said. "You owe one and six."

Mum had paid Mr. Galt one and six in rent for a whole month above his shop, but maybe that was the going rate in Fowey for a nasty dinner. Reluctantly, I took coins from my pocket and set them on the bar. The weasel and the redhead watched. The barman scooped up the coins, cleared away my dishes and wiped my place. Clearly, I was supposed to go. I took up my valise. I would have preferred to wait inside, but I decided to stand near the front door for a while in case Granny Kestrel came for me.

"Tom Ennis, y're a shame to the memory of your father," said a voice from the direction of the fireplace. A shadow rose from a stone shelf set low like a bench. It was a woman, her head and shoulders wrapped in a black shawl. I hadn't seen her when I'd arrived. Who was she? Why did the barman startle as though she were a ghost?

"Mother Penhaligon!" the barman said. "Where'd you come from?"

"Through the door like everybody else, I expect," she said. "You cheated the boy."

"Well, he's et and drunk and must pay for it." This apparition was Margery's grandmother, the lady with whom I was to stay? Why hadn't she called to me the moment I'd entered the Mermaid?

"Aye, he et and drunk, I saw it all," the woman said in a voice that sounded like a tomcat with a bird stuck in his throat. She edged closer to us where the faint firelight couldn't reach, so she seemed like a talking shadow. "I saw him drink a few sips of your foul brew and a small plate of fish cooked hours ago, and I saw you charge him enough to feed a family for a week."

The barman's face shone with sweat. He seemed to have shrunk since she'd appeared. "Mother Penhaligon, I were only playin' with the lad," he said. "See? Here's his money back again." He pulled my coins out of his pocket and slapped them on the bar.

"What would you charge these two for what you gave this boy?" she asked.

He glanced at the two men, who seemed transfixed by this exchange, and said, "Five pennies apiece."

"That fish weren't fresh, and he told you he didn't want the beer. Jem, give him three pennies and take back the rest," she said, and I thought, *yes, she does know who I am.* I fumbled threepence from the coins on the bar, pushed them toward the barman, and scooped up the rest of my one and six. "And now you're square, Tom Ennis, except for the black mark on your heart for tryin' t' cheat a stranger and a child and a friend o' mine."

By now, she'd reached my side, and I saw that her eyes were a clear, light gray. Her nose curved down at the tip. White hair escaped from under her shawl, flying up in unseen currents of air as though it had a life of its own. She was taller than me but not by much. She pressed a strong hand on my shoulder and said, "Come, then. We'll go." We walked to the door.

The barman called, "Granny, 'twere only in fun. I'd not cheat the lad. Surely you know that. I'd'na planned to keep his money."

"I know you're good at heart, Tom Ennis," she said, "But I know evil lounges close and never stops luring you t' do wrong. 'Tis not the Devil that wants you, Tom. 'Tis an older Darkness." She pointed a skinny finger at his face. "Harry the Darkness from you, Tom Ennis. You must harry it from your life and soul or it will come and live inside you, and then there will be terrors for you and yours to the end of your days." I swallowed. Her words made me think of the ooze I'd escaped earlier in the day.

The barman paled. I saw it even in the dim light. The heads of the other two customers swiveled from the barman to us and back again. The barman said, "I heed you, Mother Penhaligon, I won't forget."

"Blessings on you, Tom Ennis if y' keep your word," she said.

We walked out of the Mermaid into the street. Clouds scudded across the moon. The handful of cottages and shops that made up the town shone golden squares of light onto the street. We walked north in the direction the barman had said Lanyon Penhaligon lived.

"So you're my Margery's friend Jem, the one what flew without a tether," she said.

"I am. Were you sleeping by the fire when I went into the inn?"

"No, I were awake the whole time," she said. "I knew 'twas you when you walked in."

Why didn't you say anything? I thought. "Tom Ennis's the barman, see, what tried t' cheat ye," Granny continued. "Tom's a good lad, but the Dark hovers over Tom and always has." She talked about "the Dark" like Margery did—as though it were a living thing.

We walked past the last house in the village, one with shutters that might have been green in daylight.

"That there's my boy's place," she said, but we didn't stop. We continued down the road with only the moon to light our way. Shadowy shapes huddled beside the road. Boulders, I hoped—after all, it was All Hallows' Eve.

"What do you mean, the Dark wants Tom?" I asked. "What Dark?" I gave her my arm to hold on to.

She said, "There is day and night. Good and Evil. Sun and shadow. Everything has two halves. The other half of Dark is Light, and that's where your Sight comes from."

"So…Light and Dark don't get along?"

"Y' need both t' *see* both, only the Dark ain't content t' just be. It always wants more. The Dark wants Tom Ennis. Since Tom were a boy, I've See'd it malingerin' near him, trying t' catch him up. I've felt it close these last months, but it being so far to come to town, and me so busy, I let it go longer 'n I should."

"Let what go?"

"Why, savin' Tom, o' course," Granny said. "See, for Tom I'm sort of the clapper of a bell. I speak, and it sounds inside his head. I've rung for Tom Ennis these many years. My voice keeps the Dark away from Tom for a time, because he needs t' be told t' depart from evil and do good. I thought the Dark might try t' slither in close to Tom tonight."

What is she talking about? I thought. *Does Margery know her gran thinks she's a bell?*

"But what *is* the Dark?"

"Have y' seen animals beat and purses stole? That's the Dark. Have y' seen good people struck down by sickness? That's the Dark. Have y' had dreams so bad you're scairt to death but can't wake up? That's the Dark. Some Dark is needed so's we know there's Light. But the Dark always grasps after more'n it's got a right to. It wants the Sight in Tom."

"The…that barman has Sight, like me?"

"As a lad, Tom had a great well of Sight. I never saw so much in a child, especially in a boy."

"What happened? Did he hide his Sight in a box until it went away, like Margery?"

"No, Tom's mam were Church of England. She beat him every time he told a vision. She thought the Sight were the Devil tryin' t' steal away her boy, so Tom learnt the Sight was bad. He turned away, so now he's always facin' the Dark." She shook her head. "The mother meant well, but Second Sight comes from the Light. Tom's mam got it exactly wrong. Such a loss."

I tried and failed to imagine being beaten for something I'd been born with. I said, "But why does the…Dark…come for Tom, if his Sight is gone?"

"It ain't gone, it's sleepin'. But Tom can't use it hisself, just like my Margery.

The Dark feels it there. It thinks to tap into Tom an' gobble up his Light."

"Gobble up his Light?" *So even if I hadn't come, I'd be in danger.* "The Dark is…alive?"

"The Dark an' the Light ain't alive like you an' me, with hearts and blood, but they're ever'where in everything," Granny said. She suddenly stopped and lifted her head like a dog who'd caught a sound or a scent. "Come, now, Jem. We'll dip into this copse. Hurry." She led me into a small thicket and bade me crouch down. Springy moss gave way under our feet, and I heard small things skittering away from us over last year's dead leaves. "Quiet, now," she whispered. "Cover your mouth with your sleeve so they can't see your breath."

We sat breathing quietly but not moving. Two figures trotted past us on the road, the weasel and the redhead who'd watched me count out money at the Mermaid and had overheard Granny scolding Tom Ennis. Granny Kestrel laid her left hand on my arm and lifted her right forefinger to her lips. The men stopped on a rise in the road and looked in all directions. Then they walked back our way!

Granny Kestrel took up a handful of moss and moved her lips over it, like she were saying a prayer. She sprinkled some on me and some on herself and again motioned me to be quiet. She replaced her hand on my arm. She closed her eyes. I kept mine open. I felt like a rabbit waiting for a dog to pounce.

Red said, "Where've they got to?"

"Maybe they stopped in the son's cottage," Weasel said.

"Maybe the old witch flew away with the boy." Red's voice quavered.

"Maybe I should break your face for bein' stupid."

"Why? Where'd they go, then?" Red whined. "There's no sign of 'em. The barman said they'd be on this road. Where are they?"

"Hiding," said Weasel. He walked toward the thicket. His black eyes glinted in the moonlight. Granny Kestrel didn't move a muscle. The man pushed aside a branch that actually brushed the top of my hat. I bunched my muscles to run, but I couldn't move.

Red called from the road, "Robbie, come on then. We've lost 'em. I don't like it out here. 'Tis All Hallows'. Better luck next time."

"Oh, poor little lad's afraid of ghosts," Weasel taunted. He peered past our hiding spot, then hissed and returned to the road. The two of them groused and grumbled back toward town, but Granny Kestrel kept her hand on my arm until they were just two shadows. Then she nodded. I helped her back to the road.

It was impossible that the robber hadn't seen us. He'd nearly stepped on me.

"What just happened?" I said.

"Keep your voice down. Sound travels farther at night."

"Sorry," I whispered.

She said, "Them two wanted your money."

"I know that. Why didn't they see us?"

"We hid," she said.

"Robbie's foot was a hand-span away from me."

"We hid well." She smiled and kept walking away from Fowey.

The hairs rose on the back of my neck. What had she done so the robbers didn't see us? I remembered my own desperate prayer when Patch had me trapped in the apothecary shop: *Don't see me.* I remembered praying *Go away* at the thing inside Captain Foster. I didn't yet understand exactly what the Sight was or how it worked, but now I suspected I'd come to the right person to find out.

With wonder in my heart, I followed Granny's black shape when she left the road and began walking a narrow path that paralleled the River Fowey at a little distance. Trees and brush grew along the river, and after an hour, we entered a little wood. I heard rushing water off in the dark. "That's the Fowey," Granny Kestrel said. "Dungarth, the King of Cornwall, drowned in it a thousand years ago. We'll be walking a while. My cottage is in a copse two hours north of Lostwithiel, alongside Callywith Stream."

"How far is Lostwithiel?"

"Two hours."

"You walked four hours to come and get me?"

"How else would y' find your way?"

Walking kept me warm, but I was sorry I'd packed so much in my valise. I kept switching arms, but finally I said, "Granny Kestrel, might we rest for just a moment?"

She stopped. "Not used to walkin'?"

"I walk all the time. But I don't carry a valise all the time." I set it down.

She reached for it. "I can take it for a while."

"No, I wouldn't dream of asking you to carry it. I just want to rest my hand." I flexed my fingers and rolled my shoulders. Above us, the sky was so thick with stars it looked like somebody had flicked silver paint on black paper. "I haven't seen stars so bright since I was little," I said.

"Do y' know your constellations?"

I pointed. "I know the Plough and the North Star."

After I'd rested exactly enough, Granny said, "Ready?" She reached down to pick up my valise. I protested, and she said she'd hand it back when she got tired, but we arrived at her cottage before that happened. By then, it smelled late, like when Dr. Abernathy and I watched over a restless patient until he finally went to sleep a couple of hours before sunrise.

Inside her cottage, Granny Kestrel set down the valise, flexed her hand, stirred up her fire, added what looked like a brick, lit a candle, and regarded me with her silver-gray eyes.

"Y're tired," she said, "and I as well. Your bed's up there." She pointed up a ladder to a loft, where I saw the edge of a straw tick. "Margery sleeps up there when she comes. The necessary's outside. Use it now if y' need to. Are y' hungry? No? Then we'll talk in the morning, aye?"

She padded to a bed in an alcove beyond the front door and climbed in. "Blow out the candle afore y' go up," she said.

And so I did.

CHAPTER 16

NOVEMBER 1759

The Back End of Beyond

On All Saints' Day, I noticed the wind before I opened my eyes, heard it wheezing in the cracks and whistling under the eaves. Daylight from below lit the slanted roof over my head. I heard shuffling footsteps and the clatter of crockery. I smelled smoke. Granny Kestrel must be up.

Something rapped on the foot of the ladder. "Get up, then," Granny called. "The day's broke."

I sat up. A little heat funneled through the hole in the floor that opened to the downstairs, leaving most of the loft cold. I dressed quickly and descended the ladder. "Good morning, Mistress Penhaligon," I said. "What are you burning? It doesn't smell like coal, or wood either." I backed up to the fire to warm myself.

"Good morning to you," she said. "Call me Granny Kestrel or just Granny. I'm burnin' turf, peat, you know, cut on the moor and dried." She padded to a dark corner of the room.

"Can I help you with the breakfast?"

She turned. "Aye, put these bowls on the table. We'll sit by the fire. Pour the tea, would you? There's mugs on the mantel." I got down the mugs and poured the tea from a large pot. I sipped. It was very strong.

"Do you have any sugar? For the tea?"

"Honey only," she said, sawing off two slabs of bread. "In a pot on the table." I couldn't see a spoon. A sharp rap at the other end of the table was Granny Kestrel setting down a spoon. "Hungry?" she asked, ladling porridge into the bowls.

"Very."

"Sit, then. Eat." I sat facing the fire. Granny placed a slab of bread beside each bowl and sat. She dipped a spoon into her bowl and slurped. "Well? Did y' need something?"

"Nothing. Thank you." She hadn't added salt when she cooked the porridge, but I didn't complain. I examined the room as I ate. The fireplace dominated the cottage. The stone chimney took up a third of the eastern wall, with the door beside it. In the north wall, a small window set high up let in enough light to show a bed, some shelving, and a handful of pegs that held clothing.

Across from the front door a larger window with mullioned glass let in the morning sun, which shone down on a large basin and a few pots and pans. A stack of baskets sat just behind the ladder to the loft. Herbs and strips of onions and other dried things hung from the ceiling. A mortar and pestle on the table cheered me because it reminded me of Margery. Remembering Margery gave me the courage to say, "Er...Granny, may I ask you a question?"

"Ask away."

"Last night when the robbers came, you said some words and threw moss on me. Is that why they didn't see us? How did you do that?"

"That's two questions."

I blinked. "One question, then: why didn't the robber find us last night when he was close enough for me to touch?"

"Better. Try always t' be exact in what you say, as a stray word can go off and do damage."

She made it sound like a word and a squib were the same thing, but I wanted an answer so I just said, "Yes, Granny."

"As to the robber, I asked him not t' find us. I asked him not t' see us."

Exactly what I'd done myself twice now, when Patch had me cornered at the shop and when Captain Foster's shadow slithered up my arm. Excited, I said, "Did Margery tell you I asked Patch not to see me and he didn't?"

"She did."

"On the ship coming here, it happened again." She waited. "The captain of the ship was whipping a man, and I put out my hand to stop him, but as soon as I touched his arm, something oozed out of the captain's arm into my hand and up my arm. It burned, and it felt…hungry. The captain said, 'We've been looking for you,' so I was afraid. I prayed for it to go away."

Granny Kestrel's mouth thinned. She set down her spoon. "Which hand? Can you show me?" I held out my hand. She looked closely at my palm and ran soft fingertips over my wrist. "'Tis gone now, I think." She looked into my eyes. "Y' told it t' go away, an' it did. Ain't that right?"

She does *know*. *She* can *help me*. I said, "Yes! I prayed…Light came, and we pushed it out. Music helped us push. We pushed so hard I was inside the captain looking down at my own face."

"What music?" I hadn't noticed last night the tiny green streaks that radiated from her pupils, all the way round her silver irises.

"I dreamed I was a dolphin, and all of us sang to a girl on a ship. It was their music that helped push the captain out."

She lightly enfolded my hand between both of hers. She asked, "Who was the girl?"

"I didn't see her face, but the dolphins…felt her. They came a long way from a warmer place when they heard her in the water. She was a…a kind of light to them." Granny held my hand lightly, like a nest holds an egg. I said, "The girl felt…the dolphins felt…that land birds had been with her." Granny's eyes glowed. And I knew. "Granny," I whispered, "It wasn't a dream, was it."

"No, Jem. 'Twere another vision, I think."

"So now I swim with fish, too?" I pulled my hand free and stood. "I fly and I swim and I have no control over any of it!" I paced to the fireplace.

"That's why you come here, Jem. T' learn how t' manage your Sight." I turned to face her. She regarded me from across the table. "Listen now: you've had no trainin', yet you knew t' push against the captain on that ship. You knew to call for help. All alone, with nobody t' show you how." She carried our empty bowls to a basin and splashed hot water from the kettle over them. "Y' may be the kind what comes along once a lifetime. Maybe that's why this Patch wants you so bad."

"Patch wants to take me to my grandparents." I frowned. "Doesn't he?"

"He's been chasin' you ten years, Margery said, and he had you once, and he could've had you many more times I'll wager, but he can't keep ahold of you. This captain had you too, and he couldn't keep ahold of you neither. Both of 'em are Dark, Jem. Dark is the enemy o' Light. The Dark an' the Light is both everywhere. Those with Light're like a candle to a moth, or a lighthouse to a ship."

"B-but…why does the Dark want me?"

"It wants to suck out your Light, every scrap, an' leave you high an' dry."

That's what Margery meant when she said she Patch would do something terrible to me. Shocking! "Would that…*kill* me?"

"Your body would live, but y' wouldn't have no more Light, not even so much as is locked up in my Margery. You'd be dead to the world."

"Everything would be gray and dull, all the time, like when I blocked my Sight?"

She put her hands on my shoulders. "Aye."

"I wouldn't have visions any more? I'd be like everybody else?" *Would that be so bad?*

"Jem, you're not like nobody else. You're who God wanted you t' be. Don't let the Dark take that from you. Don't deny your gift."

"But—"

"—please, Jem, give it a chance. I'll keep y' safe until y' learn how t' live with it or decide for certain to give it up for aye." She carried our tea mugs to the basin. "But now 'tis late. The beasts're waitin'." She poured hot water into a bucket, tossed in a rag, and started for the door. "Can y' bring the porridge pot? And that empty bucket there, aye, that one."

She walked ahead of me to a small barn made of stones. The bucket of hot water in her hand sent up clouds of steam. Before we went in, Granny Kestrel said, "This here's my milking parlor an' hospital, both."

"Wait, Granny, please: if I blocked off my Sight like Margery did, could the Dark still find me?"

"All in good time, Jem. 'Tis their turn now." She smiled. "Calm yourself. They'll feel y' all slurried up." I snapped my mouth shut. She opened the door. To the right was an area strung with lengths of twine like the drying lines in Margery's shop. A goat in a little pen bleated when she saw us. "Morning, Snowy," Granny called.

Chickens and smaller goats and rabbits in the other half of the barn had lifted their heads as soon as we'd opened the door, and other eyes gleamed, and straw rustled with movement in dim corners. When the others heard Granny greet the goat, some moved toward us, while others stayed where they were. Everybody watched Granny with their shiny eyes. "What do they want?" I said. The animals stopped moving when I spoke.

"Breakfast."

"Are they...pets?"

"They're friends, mostly, but some of 'em are patients." She put a hand on my arm to lead me in. "Hello, my dears," she said, "I've brought someone t' meet you. Keep a hand on me, Jem." She moved into a roiling sea of fur and feathers. Her hands patted and scratched and stroked. "I'm a sort of Pied Piper to the animals hereabouts," Granny said as every head shoved in to claim its share of attention. "Oho! One at a time. Y' see, Jem, when I find somebody with a hurt leg or paw or somebody who's been orphaned or poisoned, I bring him here and tend him 'til he's better."

Cold noses snuffled my hands. Mouths nibbled my clothing. A score of souls churned around me. Their little lives and their little hearts pressed so close I felt I couldn't breathe. I retreated to the door, and as soon as I let go of Granny, the furry and feathered backs flowed around to her far side.

"They don't like me," I said.

"They don't know you yet. You can milk the goat whilst I tend the rest."

"I don't know how to milk a goat."

"Well, y' can't stand there wringin' your hands whilst I do all the work! Come, I'll show you. You lot stay back now. Jem, bring that bucket o' warm water." The animals parted like the Red Sea, and Granny led me to the nanny, who rubbed her head on her mistress's leg. "Good Mornin', Snowy." Granny placed my hand on the goat's neck. "This here is Jem. She's goin' t' milk you. Get down here and watch, Jem."

I knelt in the straw. Granny sat on a stool. She wrung out the rag in the bucket of warm water and washed each teat. Then she said, "Put your thumb and forefinger in a circle like this, see, at the top of the teat. Don't squeeze too hard. Then stroke the rest of your fingers along the teat, like this. Don't pull, just think about what a baby goat does—his mouth would be up here at the top and his tongue would stroke along, see? Try it."

"Will milk come out?"

"I surely hope so. Here—milk into this bucket." She left the stool and brought the porridge kettle around by Snowy's head. I sat and faced the goat's flank. I was afraid to touch her. What if I fell into her like I did with the pigeon? Could Granny pray me home like Margery did? But if Snowy were like other domesticated animals that kept themselves aloof from humans, I needn't worry.

I placed my hand on Snowy's coarse hair and felt her breath go in and out, felt her heart pumping and her easy-going temperament. I left out my air, relieved. Snowy wasn't interested in me. She was interested in getting milked. She was interested in our leftover porridge.

I placed my forefinger and thumb on the soft teat and stroked—and milk squirted into the bucket. "I did it!" I said.

"Aye, so y' did," Granny said. "Keep goin'. You'll know she's emptied out when her udder's looser and the teats are floppy. Then rub her udder real gentle to get out the last of it." Granny held the porridge pot for Snowy, whose tail wagged. "Go on, Jem! The best time t' milk a goat is when her mouth's happy."

I focused on the goat. Granny set down the porridge pot and stepped away to tend to her menagerie.

I heard the crunch of her steps in straw and her voice consoling and praising. I peeked over my shoulder. "Good morning to you, sir," Granny said to a deer with a bit of cloth tied to its leg. "And how's your leg today?" Was the leg broken? Cut? How had the deer gotten here? There was no way Granny Kestrel could have carried that heavy, huge animal in her arms. Even if the deer had limped all the way to the barn and lain down waiting for Granny to wrap its leg, how did it know to come here in the first place?

The roiling mass of fur and horns and paws on the other side of the barn behaved…oddly. In the Lamesley woods long ago, I'd learned that nature's way was for animals to live and play with their own kind. I'd learned that nature was arranged so one creature was food for another—cats ate birds, birds ate insects, insects ate plants. But nature's rules seemed to be in abeyance here. A nest of rabbit orphans ate from Granny's fingers rather than rustling off to hide when she knelt beside their nest. A chicken sat atop the deer grooming its coat.

"Finished over there?" Granny said.

"Not yet," I turned back to my job. When the goat was empty and the bucket full, I watched Granny. I said quietly, "They certainly like you." The orphaned baby rabbits turned their little shiny black eyes toward me to blink, then turned back when Granny soothed them.

"Aye, they do like their old granny."

"Do these animals get along because they're sick?"

He head bobbed up. "No, a-course not," she said. "When a creature's hurt, he's most afraid and most liable to lash out and hurt whatever's near. He thinks maybe the thing that's near is what's hurtin' him. Even if they ain't hurt, animals tends t' stay with their own kind." She stood and went to the hen boxes. She began to gather eggs.

"But this lot is getting along. This is a peculiar family you have in your barn."

She laughed. "I s'pose it is. But y're right, they are family. They know I love 'em. They know they mustn't harm one another in this barn. They know they can run free under the sky quicker if they worry about healin' instead of huntin' or matin' or anything else they think about when they're out bein' themselves."

"They get along because they know you love them? Do you…*think* love at them and that's how they know?"

"Aye, that's how they know." She placed four eggs gently in her basket, then, with a fifth egg in her hand, turned toward the far corner of her hospital. "I suppose y' learnt that too on your own."

"Dr. Abernathy has a horse—Giselle—who hears me when she wants to."

She laughed. "That's a horse for you—stop, Jem, stay back a bit. I've the badger t' see to next, and I don't know if he'll let y' come too close. Don't talk." She went soft and easy, humming, to a nest that held a creature about the size of a fat lapdog. It had a striped head shaped a bit like a pig's. When it hissed, I saw fangs extending past its lower lip.

"Come now, my grand brock," Granny said, " 'tis only me. Won't y' let me see to you?" The badger's claws were an inch long and looked like curved daggers, but the creature allowed Granny to lift his paw and gently unwrap his bandage. The injury showed healing pink flesh. "Poor grand brock," she said, "y' won't get back the hair on that scar. Let it remind you t' smell for iron always, and if you smell it, go another way." The badger kept its eye on me but gently gnawed on Granny's knuckle. "I thank y' for that," she said. "I believe you can go away home day after tomorrow." The badger laid his head on her knee and let her scratch behind his ears, just like a cat. She fed him the egg and bits of fruit out of her pocket and I don't know what else, because I kept waiting for those sharp teeth to chomp down on those soft fingers.

But Granny got up from the badger with all her digits intact. I whispered, "Why didn't he bite you? He's a wild badger, isn't he?"

"Aye, he's wild."

"How can you make a wild badger behave himself when he's just ten feet from a nest of baby rabbits? How can you say 'Be good' and he does it?"

"He feels what I want for him, and he wants it too, so he does what I say. It's feelin's from my heart he hears. Here, let me show you." She lifted a coil of twine from a nail. "Take this end," she said. She stretched the twine taut between us, retreating to a dark corner of the barn so she was just a black shape shrouded in shadow. "Turn your head so's you can't see me at all. Now, feel this?"

"I feel a vibration."

"Good. I'll change it now. Keep turned away." The vibration I felt next was stronger.

"All right. I felt the difference."

I heard her feet moving toward me in the straw. "You can turn back now."

She stood in the light, and I saw that she had the end of the twine in her mouth. "What are you doing?" I said. She spat out the twine and wound it up.

"Which vibration was angrier?" she asked.

"Angrier?—why, the second. Were you chewing on the rope?"

"Aye. Did y' see it?"

"No. The second time, the rope *felt* different."

She put her hand on my shoulder. "That's how I talk to the animals. I feel peace and calm in my heart for 'em. I push my love and care for 'em out of my heart and along my arms and out the ends o' my fingers."

"They feel what you're thinking. Like Giselle, the horse. I know she feels me thinking."

She nodded. "An animal flees from a hunter because the hunter has no love for it. The hunter's thoughts're full o' killing. The hunter carries thoughts o' death wrapped round him like a cloak. Animals feel that.

"In days long ago, people called out t' animals in the Old Language. They asked the animals if one of 'em would come so's the hunter might feed and clothe his family. An animal would come and give itself, usually one that had borne its own young and knew what it was t' care for offspring."

"Animals *chose* to die?"

"Aye. In them days, people took only what they needed and left gifts in thanks: choice grass, fruits the animals couldn't reach. But the animals could tell if a hunter didn't truly have a need and was after profit instead, and they would not come. So men made traps to capture 'em by stealth, and weapons t' shoot 'em from far away. The ancient pact betwixt man and beast were broken. Hunters still eat animals, but I don't. I believe my patients'd feel their brothers' blood knitted into my bones. No point in scarin' 'em when I'm tryin' t' doctor 'em."

She took up the bucket of milk. The animals watched us. "We'll come back in a bit," she said to them. "Stay warm. Help each other. Come along, Jem."

Already, just a couple of hours into my first day with Granny, I felt better about having come. I felt like a neglected plant in a dark corner that had been brought to a bright window and watered. If my usual headache hadn't come pounding while we were in the barn, I would have felt quite cheerful.

A few feet from the door of the cottage, Granny stopped. "Wait." She put a hand on my shoulder and turned her head to the east. "Somethin's there." She closed her eyes. "It's—in the clouds, miles and miles away." She turned to me. "Do you feel it?"

My head throbbed. I needed my headache powder. "Is it…the Dark? What should I do?"

Granny moved to stand between me and the eastern sky. Her hand hovered before my face, then she looked at my chest. "You're wearin' a necklace. Can I see it?"

"It's my mother's cameo." I pulled it out. Granny touched it. She frowned.

"Take it off."

"But why?"

"Off. Now. Put it in my hand." Confused, I obeyed. She peered at the cameo as though it were a drowsing snake. "You say your ma give it to you?" I nodded. "And do y' wear it all the time?"

"Most of the time. It reminds me of her."

"It does more'n that, Jem, I'm sorry to say. This cameo is magicked."

"There's no such thing as magic," I said.

She narrowed her eyes. "You flew with birds, and y' saw your mother's fetch as she lay dyin', and you've felt the Dark crawlin' up your own arm." My face got hot. "'Magic' ain't a word used much in London, I s'pose—my Margery writes about clever men what make up new machines and easier ways t' do work, but she never wrote about magic until she started writin' about you—but you need t' know the true name of somethin' if y' hope t' understand it, aye?"

Of course she calls it 'magic,' I thought. Of course Second Sight would seem like magic to a person who lives out here and hasn't been educated. But the earth revolves around the sun. Gravity makes things fall. Variolation prevents smallpox. There must *be a reasonable explanation for this phenomenon. If I pay attention and experiment, I shall figure out what it is.* "You're right," I said.

Granny pressed her lips together. Then she touched the tiny portrait of my mother and closed her eyes. "What's in this is old. Very faint. 'Twas long ago that someone put a Call in it."

"A Call?"

"A Call leads a Sighted person to whoever wears the necklace, especially if there's a link. You're linked to this by blood, because it was your mother's."

"But—what?" *Pay attention.* "How does it work?" I asked.

"Somebody put in somethin' that's a part of him. A lock o' hair. A fingernail. A bit of spit or maybe blood. That bit Calls to the rest of him."

Newton's law of gravity: bodies are pulled toward one another because of gravity, and the strength of their attraction is greater if they are close together and lesser if they are far apart. What if a "Call" were a part of that law Newton simply hadn't discovered?

Excited to have worked out something that made sense, I said, "You think somebody put his fingernail inside my mother's cameo, and that he's 'calling' to it right this minute?"

"Aye. We need t' clean it." She set the milk beside the door and covered it with a cloth. Inside the cottage, she removed the eggs from her basket and lined them up on the mantel. "Come along to the brook. We need to beg some twigs off an alder tree."

"Can I take my headache powder first?"

"Aye, go ahead, but I don't want this anywhere near you again 'til it's clean. We'll put it in my Blind Box, and it'll go to sleep." She dropped the cameo into a wooden box on the mantel and shut the lid.

"The cameo will go to sleep."

"Aye. I scratched runes on this here box and prayed over 'em. I marked this cottage too, and more besides. I did all in case the Dark found you here. 'Tis all meant t' protect you."

"Thank you."

"You're welcome. Now go up and come right back." I dashed up the ladder to my valise, pulled out my bag of headache powder, and dumped a healthy bite into my mouth. I climbed back down and drank some water from Granny's dipper, my eyes on her Blind Box.

When I stepped back outside, Granny stood with her face turned up to the sun. She said, "Better?" I nodded. "Good. Come along, then, we mustn't delay. Whoever made the Call's already had a night t' seek you out." She followed a path between the trees toward the sound of rushing water.

CHAPTER 17

NOVEMBER 1759

Clear Mind, Bright Eye

"Who are you talking about?" I asked. "Who's had a night to seek me out?"

"Whoever put the Call inside that neck bob. A Call is—" She began again. "See here: say I want to keep track of…oh, a goat, say. Snowy. I snip off a bit o' my hair or a paring of fingernail. I wrap it up. I put it around Snowy's neck. Then if she wanders off and don't come when I call, I think about that bit of hair or fingernail. *Like* seeks *like*—I try to let ever'thing else fall away and just see that bit o' hair or fingernail back attached t' me again. And once I find that bit o' me, I link to it—I see it back on me—then I back up my mind to feel where I am, and that's how I know where the silly goat's got to."

"So…you *send* your mind away from your body?"

"Aye."

"You can control it?"

"Yes."

"That's what I need to learn!" I said. "I need to learn how to keep my mind with me so it *doesn't* go. That's why the doctor gave me leave to come here. I flew with birds—my mind flew—only I didn't send myself like that. I just went."

"Margery told me. 'Tis strange y' flew like that without no trainin'," Granny said. "Your Sight must be deep and wide for you t' be able t' do that." She stopped on the path. "But though that's what I suspect, Jem, I touch you and feel your Sight hummin' under the skin, but 'tis blocked like a great river swishin' and growlin' behind a dam. And yet, y' said the dolphins swum a long way because they heard you. 'Tis a puzzle."

"Margery told me how to block my Sight."

"Aye, my Lanyon wrote my answer to Margery the same day he read me her letter about you flyin' off with a pigeon. But if y're blocked, how did the dolphins hear you?"

"Could I be…leaking?"

"Leakin' Sight? You'd have to be overflowin' to be leakin', and if you're overflowin'—well, the sooner you're trained, the better." Granny shook her head. "Still—it may be if you're leakin' Light, that's how the peregrine found you. Three days. 'Tis a wonder you come back from that at all. I never heard of nobody flyin' so long. Somebody or something must be protectin' you. I've only heard of one other goin' away for so long, an' he didn't come back."

"Who was it?"

"He was my brother," Granny said, and left the path to take a more direct line toward the sound of rushing water. "Charlie. He was small. He'd go off into the woods, following an animal t' see how it went. He'd look up at a bird and whistle at it, and the bird would whistle back. He was always starin' off into space like he saw somethin' grand. We'd look an' not see nothin'."

I used to follow animals back home in Lamesley, I thought. Had I seen something grand, too? All I could remember was feeling happy when an animal let me be with it. *Had my Sight taken hold of me, even then?* "Can you tell me…what happened with Charlie?" I asked.

"One day, we couldn't find him," Granny sighed. "We searched ever'where. Then I felt him, far off, and I took Ma's hand, and we went out on the moor. We found him in a cave, starin' out with glory in his eyes. We brung him home, but Ma couldn't get him t' eat. He just smiled and kept sayin' 'I want to go. I'm tryin' t' fly away with you,' and by and by he died."

"Oh, Granny, how terrible." A lump swelled in my throat. "I lost a brother too."

"I think what Charlie saw was so much better'n even us, he wanted to go more'n he wanted to stay."

I swallowed. "What do you think he saw?" I said quietly.

She stopped walking and said, "Light, I think, but it weren't enough for him t' see it, he wanted t' *be* it."

"He wanted to *be* Light?"

She began to walk again. "When we die, Light is where we're s'posed t' go."

"You mean Heaven?"

"Heaven is a name for it."

"I'm sorry about your brother."

"Aye, 'twas terrible sad for Ma. When I was a mother myself, I told my sons if they saw Light and felt the need t' go, they must tell me. When John—that's my eldest—brought Margery's ma here, he told her about Charlie. So when little Margery started t' go off with the mice, her mum said they must move to London so's they wouldn't lose Margery like we lost Charlie."

If Margery hadn't prayed so hard, it might have been me that never came back. I now knew for certain that coming to Cornwall had been the right thing to do.

Granny stopped walking at the foot of a tall tree. "We need twigs only," Granny said. "Don't take anything thicker'n a mouse's tail." She laid her hands on the tree's trunk and said, "Thank you for knowin' so long ago we'd have need of you today. We shan't gather more'n a couple handfuls."

"Granny, are you...talking to the tree?"

"It's got no ears, but I told you this mornin', 'tis the intent that matters. You don't s'pose I'd just take without askin' or thankin' first? Come here and lay your hand next to mine."

"My mother talked to a duck," I blurted. Granny waited. "She...thought what she wanted to say and then she quacked." I felt my face heat again.

"So, this ain't strange to you. Come, lay your hand here and thank the alder for sharin'."

I *wanted* to fully participate in whatever this was, but when I did as she asked and said, "Thank you for your twigs," I felt a bit silly.

"Y' don't b'lieve what you're sayin', Jem. Find the heart o' the tree, then say it again." She waited.

Find the heart of the tree? Granny watched. I said, "I feel silly talking to a tree."

"This here's a living thing tryin' t' thrive just like you. It's willin' t' help a creature it owes nothing to."

"What if I find the heart of the tree and...it takes me?"

"Like the peregrine? It won't. I'll tether you." She put a hand on my shoulder.

In for a penny, in for a pound, I thought, but I didn't feel as lighthearted as those words. I laid my hand on the gray, sun-warmed bark. I looked up at the opened cones and the handful of leaves that still hung at the ends of branches, noting the buds that would open in the spring. I let myself seek the heart of the tree, and as I did, I felt the sap seeping up the trunk under my hand, and my own blood slowing to pump at the same creeping rate, and then Granny's hand gripped tighter, and I quickly said, "Thank you," before Granny lifted my hand from the tree. I stepped back, panting and chilled.

"That was quick," Granny murmured. She blew out some air and added, "It may be you've somewhat trained yourself without knowin' it. You'll need t' take care what y' touch, Jem." She handed me the basket. "Let's gather twigs. Be careful as you go not t' step on the baby alders scattered all underneath here." When we'd collected a little bed of twigs in the bottom of the basket, she laid her hand on the tree trunk and said, "Thank you, friend." She didn't ask me to touch the tree again.

Granny led the way through winter sunlight filtering through bare tree branches. Birds flitted from branch to branch. Granny was quiet. I'd got my breath back and tried to start a conversation. "What's that smell in the air?"

Granny spoke over her shoulder. "I think what y' smell is clean air. London stinks of coal. And dung. And rot. My Margery says people dump chamber pots right out the window. 'Tis a wonder people in London don't choke t' death in the streets and add to the stink."

She was right; what my nose detected was a not-smell, like fresh snow.

Granny said, "Margery said you two got acquainted when y' moved in above Galt's shop."

"Yes. When my da died in the mine, Mum and me and Jamie moved to London."

"You had no family t' go to?"

"Da's family was in Ireland. I never met Mum's family."

"Both sides're alive, then, y' just don't live with 'em?"

"I—" *She doesn't need to know about Newcastle and all that. Not yet.* "That's right. And have you always lived here, Granny?"

"When I were young, we lived in town. My father fished, like Lanyon."

"Why did you move way out here?"

"My da passed when I were nine. One mornin' the sky was red as blood. Ma begged Da not to go out, for, as they say, 'red sky in the morning, sailors take warning,' but he said he must bring in somethin'. He promised t' keep watch on the sky."

"What happened?"

"A storm blew in, black clouds tussling and rolling like giants wrestlin'. Ma fretted all morning. Rain pounded down all the wheat, and the sky turned green, and the wind blew from the nor'west, screamin' around the house. Ma pushed me and Charlie under the table—that very table in my cottage—and come in behind us. Ma said the wind wanted her."

"The wind wanted your mother?"

"Ma and Da were bound t' each other, and the Dark wanted him," she said. "The Dark rode the wind that day."

Who or what *were* Margery's people? Granny's mother believed the wind was in service to the Dark. Granny herself spoke to animals as though they understood and to trees as though they heard her. Granny seemed to walk through life as though everything were...*animated.*

Is it? I wondered. My heart thudded. If everything were alive, how could I take even one step out of doors? Did it hurt the grass when we walked on it?

If Granny taught me how to use my Sight, would I, too, feel every soul that touched mine? The briefest brush with Granny's animals had made me feel like I were drowning; if I were completely open to the Sight, wouldn't I feel smothered if the *mind* of everything I met crashed into me?

I don't think I'm strong enough for this, I thought, feeling something like relief, followed by shame. I said, "So you came here after that?"

"My granny said I would live here all my life. She saw the future."

"People with Sight see the future too?" My mouth fell open.

"Some do."

"How do you know your grandmother saw the future?"

Granny stopped again and turned. "Because I'm livin' today what she foretold. She dreamed an old woman livin' in this place—that's me—and the woman lived with a Light in a bottle—that's you." I frowned. The "prophecy" seemed vague.

"She couldn't have meant a lantern?" I asked.

"My granny didn't say 'lantern,' she said 'Light,' an' she meant the same Light as my brother went t' be with." She laid a hand on my shoulder. "Somebody like you." She continued, "Jem, y're all slurried up again. Take a breath. In. Out. Easy. Tell me: do y' believe in God?"

"Of course," I said.

"Why? Where's your proof o' God?"

"I…well, look at all this! Trees and grass and animals didn't just happen."

"So your proof o' God is the things God made?" Her steady gaze held mine. "Did y' ever see God with your own two eyes?"

"No, I didn't." Granny's setting out a chain of logic calmed me. "Granny, I think I know what you're trying to say."

"You believe in a God you never saw on account of the things you b'lieve God made," she said. "That's faith, Jem. Don't the Bible say if y' have faith as big as a mustard seed, y' can tell a tree t' move an' it will?" I blinked. "Aye, I know my Bible. You been seein' odd things your whole life."

"You are saying that my Seeing things proves Sight exists. I don't doubt it, Granny." I paused. "I just don't know if I'm strong enough for…all this."

"You are. Jem, *you* seein' things is proof *you are s'posed t' see 'em.*" I stopped walking. "D' you think God made a mistake when He made you?"

"No," I said, "God doesn't make mistakes." I hadn't thought of it that way. Before I'd come to Cornwall, I'd viewed myself as an oddity, as somebody broken who needed repair. A freak. When Granny asked if God made mistakes and I'd answered "no," logic and faith had fused. I was forced to accept that I'd been fashioned deliberately, different from others, to be sure, but meant to be just as I was. I, Jessamyn Marietta Connolly, was *supposed* to be born with a gift—all right, born with magic—and like a healer or a natural philosopher, I was supposed to use my gift.

I still felt afraid. It would take time for me to master a gift I'd discovered ranged wider and deeper than I'd suspected. Once I learned how far it went, it would take time for me to work out why I'd been born with Second Sight. I would have to learn how to live all over again.

"I feel you thinkin' back there, Jem," Granny said. The roof of the cottage came into view. "Tell me."

"I haven't even been here a full day, and already I've learned a great deal." *There's an understatement.*

"The day Lanyon read Margery's first letter t' me about you, I knew you had t' come here one day. Ever'body needs a teacher, Jem. I been prayin' and prayin' for you t' come soon." She opened the cottage door. "Now, then, we've work t' do." Inside the cottage, Granny Kestrel arranged some of the alder twigs in the bottom of a big cooking pot and made a little circle on the table with of the rest of them. She took Mum's cameo out of the Blind Box.

I said, "You said you made this years ago? Why do you call it a Blind Box? What do the marks mean, those carved all around?"

Granny said, "This rune means *sleep*. This one means *quiet*, and this one means *lock*. So when I put somethin' inside, whatever it is goes t' sleep." She placed the cameo inside the circle of alder twigs and fetched a small knife. "There's somethin' inside this neck bob that must come out. I may dent it when I take it apart."

"Isn't there another way?" I reached for the cameo.

Granny blocked my hand. "Don't touch it!"

"Granny, please don't ruin it! That cameo was my mother's."

She set down the knife. "Jem, y' must listen: I think whatever's inside the cameo is what lets Patch find you so easy. I'll put it back together after, all right?" She took up the knife again and waited. I nodded. She began pry at the back of the cameo. She said, "What I can't make out is how somebody got a Call inside. Did your mother have ties to somebody with Sight?" She eased the point of her knife between the bezel and the cameo itself.

"Mum had Sight herself when she was young," I said. "I told you about her talking to a duck. But her mother said the Sight was a family curse. She told Mum to pray it away."

"So 'tis likely your grandmother's Sight were blocked as well. She must have had the Call put in here by somebody else so's she could always find your mother."

"But—if that were true, my grandmother would have found Mum a long time ago."

Granny wiggled the knifepoint all around the edge of the bezel. "Unless your granny's hunter *did* find your Mum but didn't tell your granny. Maybe the hunter's got reasons of his own t' go a-hunting." Once again, my mouth fell open: *Granny had reached the same conclusion we'd reached in London.* If Granny were right about something being inside the cameo, then the duchess not only had hired Patch to find me, but she'd also given him the means to do it. I watched Granny working her knife. What if something of *him* were inside? Panic made my heart pound, as though the cameo might spit fire as soon as she'd opened it.

Granny said, "Tell me about your Sight. Tell me what you've seen. Tell all y'

remember. Margery's told me some, but I want t' hear it all so's I know why this
Call made for your mother is workin' on you, too."

I took a deep breath and began. I told Granny about Mum's soul splitting
off from her body the night Da was trapped in the mine, and about feeling Da
down behind tumbled rocks. I told Granny about the caged lions at the Tower
of London trading places with me and making me vomit. I told her about the
tar in Herr Handel's blood, and the man with liver cancer, and about seeing my
mother's fetch the morning she died, and about the jumbling pictures that laid
me out the day Dr. Franklin visited. "And you already know about the dolphins
and Captain Foster," I said.

"You saw your mam before she crossed over?"

"I—yes."

"And had y' seen such a thing before?"

"No."

"My ma did. Long ago, in that storm that took my da, Ma saw him that
same way. He come to her as he was goin' down because he had t' untwine his
soul from hers so the part of her tangled up with him didn't go over t' the other
side. He didn't want her alone in this world without all of herself all together,
see? Maybe you was bonded to your Mum, too." Her knife slipped under the
cameo and eased it up. "Ah, there it comes. Just as I thought—look here."

I peeked over her shoulder: there lay a curl of dark hair. Granny said, "That
there is a Call."

Gooseflesh prickled along my arms. "It looks like my mother's hair."

"Does it? Hm. 'Tis hard t' tell with hair. Could be anybody's, but if this is
your mother's, then the person callin' must have a bit of your mum's hair too,
an' that's why he keeps findin' you when you're wearin' the cameo, only it ain't a
clear Call. First, because it ain't your hair. Second, if you've took this off, he'd've
lost Sight o' you."

I gasped. I'd hidden the cameo in Franklin's workroom just after Mum and
Jamie had died, and it had stayed there until I'd had the opportunity to fetch

it. After that, I hadn't worn it until I'd found a new ribbon. Just lately, Franklin had held on to the cameo for weeks until he'd had it cleaned. And, I suddenly realized, my headaches had come and gone depending on *when I wore the cameo.*

Granny took up the curl in her fingers. "Now who would have some of your mother's hair t' Call t' this bit?"

She knows more about this than you do. I said, "Patch. My grandmother hired him. She could have put Mum's curl in the cameo and given another curl to him."

Granny shrugged. "That's it, then." Did the duchess have any idea what she'd done by giving Patch a bit of Mum's hair? Of course she did. She'd wanted to be able to find Mum, no matter what, but did she know the Call also would find me? Did she know he'd already done so? I felt I'd been punched in the stomach.

Granny had put two and two together as well, but she went farther. She said, "Well, your grandmother an' you ain't met yet, so they may not be workin' together no more. Patch may be leadin' her a dance. That ain't safe for him, on account of promises is made when a Call is crafted. Unless the Dark is shorin' up Patch's magic, an' that's a worry." Granny laid the curl in the pot of alder twigs and got a brand from the fire. "Before I burn this, I want you t' tell me it's what you want. That you don't want your grandmother t' find you."

"I don't." If the Duchess of Newcastle had given Patch power over me, I never wanted to meet her, even if she didn't do it on purpose. People with no mastery over the Sight should not be mucking about with it.

You've been doing that very thing in London, Jem Connolly, ever since your peregrine. Admit it. You yourself may be the reason Patch has found you. My face flamed, but Granny didn't appear to notice, so intent was she on her work.

"So be it," Granny said. She lit the twigs, and when the flames reached the Call, it flared up, filling the air above the table with the smell of burned hair. "Now for the rest of it," Granny said.

She made to drop the bezel upside-down on the smoldering alder twigs, but

I cried, "Don't burn it up!"

"It won't melt. It's gold. Gold needs a hotter fire t' melt. But we must let it sit in the smoke while I pray. Be quiet now." She dropped in the bezel, and said, "Let this bond be broken. Let this link to the Dark be burnt away in blessed alder." She turned over the bezel with the point of her knife. "Let the dead be dead and the living be free." She used the knife to lift the bezel out and lay it inside the alder-twig circle. "When it cools, y' can rub off the black," she told me. Then she picked up the cameo itself.

"Please don't put my mother in the fire," I begged.

"This here is stone and ivory. It won't crack if we don't let it sit. But it must be cleaned too." She raked the unburned ends of the twigs over the coals and blew gently until they'd caught fire, dropped in the cameo, and prayed again. She flipped over the stone-and-ivory token just as she'd done with the bezel, then placed it inside the alder circle. The two pieces of Mum's cameo lay on the table like two black eyes.

"I hate this," I whispered.

"Your mother's piece'll be better'n new once it's cleaned and put back together, because the Dark won't be able t' use it t' find you." She picked up the cameo pieces. "Here—clean off the char with a bit of rag. I've vinegar in that crock. When y're done, I'll put it back together." She carried the pan of alder ash to the door.

"Where are you going?"

"The ashes must go in the stream so the Call's washed away to sea."

Later, when I'd rubbed the carbon off, Granny Kestrel put Mum's cameo back together. The bezel wasn't quite smooth any more, and the specks of blue paint in the cameo's eyes were burned away. And yet…and yet I didn't have another headache all the rest of the time I lived with Granny Kestrel on the moor.

CHAPTER 18

DECEMBER 1759

A Letter from Home

My first six weeks at the edge of Bodmin Moor spanned the turning of autumn to winter. Granny Kestrel taught me how to look in sheltered places among the trees for overwintering herbs and plants. Granny cooked no meat, and it took my body a few days to adjust to a plant diet.

I have said that every Christmas since I'd left Lamesley showed the changes in my life. Christmas with Kestrel Penhaligon marked another big change. London bustled at Christmas. Confectioners' windows displayed holiday treats, bakers' windows featured Christmas loaves, peddlers in the streets and markets sold trinkets nobody needed but everybody liked to get anyway. Granny's cottage stood alone, the nearest confectioner and baker an hour's walk west to Bodmin. For Granny, December 25 didn't mean plum pudding and rounds of visiting. It wasn't even the most interesting day in December.

But we did gather holly in the woods. (Granny asked for and got permission from the holly, which she called holmbush.) I sorted holly branches while Granny placed it where she wanted it. As she laid a branch of the fresh-smelling and cheery holly, Granny said, "Lanyon will come today."

I'd wondered when I would meet Granny's son. "Will he spend Christmas with us?"

"No, he spends it in town with his family."

"Oh. Are we going back to town with Lanyon for Christmas?" I asked, picking off leaves that were chewed or spotted.

"No. It's four hours to town, and I've the animals t' tend. Besides, Lanyon's wife has her own ways."

"So it will be just you and me, here, for the holiday?"

Granny Kestrel smiled. "No, the girls'll come."

"Girls?" I scooped a double handful of faulty leaves to toss into the fire. "Granny, I can burn these, can't I?"

"Aye, go ahead. The holly'll be glad t' be rid o' that lot. The girls are two friends o' mine what always comes for solstice."

"You mean Christmas?"

"I mean solstice, Jem. Winter solstice is the changin' over of the year from dark to light, and it comes first. Christmas is Jesus' birthday, when folks celebrate the comin' of the Light. I celebrate both." She arranged holly on the mantel.

"I didn't know a person could celebrate solstice. I thought it was just a date on the calendar, once in winter and once in summer."

"I celebrate it. Margery does too. She comes for summer solstice."

"I know. I can hardly wait. How do we celebrate it?"

"First we bring in holly, like we did today. 'Tis nice to have a bit of green indoors, aye? It reminds us we'll soon be able t' plant. On solstice night, I put a pot o' soup in the coals and walk to the Trippet Stones."

"The...what?"

"A stone circle. 'Tis a walk north of an hour or so, t' the foot o' Hawk's Tor. Once we get there, you'll see how the circle lines up perfect with Rough Tor and the Ploughman's belt buckle, the brightest star in the sky."

I paused. *Mr. Murlin said bad things happen in the stone circles.* Twirling a branch between my fingers, I said, "Er...Granny...I met a Methodist preacher on the *Mary Ellen* who walks on the moor to get from Liskeard to Camelford. He said the stone circles on the moor are heathen places. He said witches use them."

Granny cocked her head to examine the mantel. "I never saw no witches at the stones Jem, not in all the years I been goin'."

"Well...why do you go all that way in the dark? Why not celebrate here?"

"We can't celebrate in a house. The sun needs t' see our fire inside the circle. We tell stories and sing so the sun hears us, so as t' coax the sun t' bring back summer. Then the sun comes up, and it peeks over the tallest stone and slices through our fire to t'other side of the circle. And when the circle's cut in half, we come back here and have some soup. And pretty soon, summer comes."

My eyebrows went up. I said, "Granny, you do know summer comes regardless of anything you do?"

"Oh?"

"Of course! After the third week of December, the earth moves closer to the sun. That's why warm weather comes back. Copernicus figured it out three hundred years ago. Sir Isaac Newton proved it. Getting closer to the sun is what brings us summer."

Granny crossed her arms over her chest. "Jem, y' spoke your piece there just like a Master at Oxford. But a few candles lit on the longest night o' the year can't go amiss, aye? After all, a person gets a year older whether his birthday's noted or no, but 'tis pleasant to mark the day."

"Yes, but—"

"Jem, we mark holidays for the joy of it. Look at Christmas. It don't change a thing to celebrate Jesus' birthday, but we do it every year. Solstice is the same." She stood back to look at her arrangement on the mantel. "Besides, Second Sight come from Light, and that's another reason t' celebrate the sun comin' back. And maybe goin' up to the tor'll give you a vision of what y're s'posed t' do about your Sight."

"Do?"

She took up a branch of holly and looked for an unadorned spot. "Y're willin', but y're smart enough t' know that your magic'll take you down a lonesome path. Not ever'body uses the gifts they're given. I know y're scairt. Flyin' with birds and seein' sickness and tradin' places with beasts are fearful things. Many who See such things close their eyes so they never See 'em again. You wouldn't be the first t' refuse a gift, especially a gift that brings so much risk." She placed more greenery. "But I hope y' accept it."

"If I do, everything will change."

"It's different for ever'body," she said. "I can't say how it'll be for you. I do know y' can always give it back, like any gift." She lifted the last sprig of holly, then said, "Oh, look here." She held out the holly. Affixed to the underside of a leaf was a fuzzy brown lozenge two inches long. I hadn't noticed the cocoon on my own.

"See this?" Granny said. "Can y' tell what's inside this cocoon?"

"A moth."

"What made the cocoon?"

"A caterpillar."

"Why ain't there a caterpillar in the cocoon?"

"Because a caterpillar changes into a moth."

"How does a worm that crawls in the dirt turn into a creature that flies in the air?" She didn't wait for an answer. "This small creature's whole life is built on magic. 'Tis as normal for him as breathin'."

I looked into her level gaze and sighed. "You're saying I would get used to my Sight."

"Just as I have." Abruptly, she raised her head. "Lanyon's here. Come, let's see if he's brought my grandsons this time!" Granny took the cocoon outside and placed it between the cottage and the turf rick before trotting round the cottage straight toward a man holding the lead of a black pony. The man reached out a hand and pulled in Granny for a one-armed hug. "Come meet my Lanyon, Jem," Granny called with a smile that didn't quite reach her eyes, for Lanyon had come alone. "Jem, this is my son, Lanyon Penhaligon. Lanyon, this here's Jem Connolly, a friend o' Margery's who come out on All Hallows' Eve."

"Tom at the Mermaid asked me t' greet you, Jem, and he sends his respects t' you, Ma," Lanyon said.

"How do you do, Mr. Penhaligon," I said, "I've met your brother in London. Margery invited us for Christmas."

"Lanyon, if y' please. My, I haven't seen John since Margery was this high," Lanyon said. "I should go up to London one of these days."

"If Elaine don't like you t' come out here, she sure won't let you go t' London," Granny said. She and Lanyon exchanged a look I couldn't quite interpret. "Come, let's unload Jasper so y' can tell me about the boys." We carried everything into the house, and Granny said, "Jem, would you take Jasper to the barn for a bite of oats?"

Jasper and Snowy seemed glad to see one another, but on the way back to the cottage, I heard raised voices. Lanyon was saying, "Ma, I've tried, more times'n I can tell you. She won't allow it."

"Lanyon, 'tis a shame to deny them two what's rightfully theirs, and deny me seein' my own flesh and blood."

"Elaine's like a singed cat every time I load up to come here," Lanyon said. "She won't let the boys come near you."

I cleared my throat loudly and went in. The air in the cottage was thicker than London fog, and Granny's face was flushed. "Is everything all right?" I asked.

"Well enough," Granny said. "See there, Jem, there's a letter from Margery on the table."

Finally! I picked up my letter, and despite the tension between Granny and her son, I felt like dancing. Granny said, "Go on up and read it in case she's asked you somethin' you can answer in that novel y've been writin' to her."

My face warmed, but I didn't stop smiling. I said, "It's not a novel, it's just a long letter."

"Well, go and have a read anyway, so's me and Lanyon can have a gab."

I carried my treasure up to the loft and opened it. Margery wrote,

> *Dearest Jem,*
>
> *We miss you ever so. Dr. Abernathy turns up at the shop more often than he ever did, looking for you, I suppose,*

though we both know he won't find you hiding under the bed.
Our other visitor has not shown his face of late. How are your
studies coming along? Dr. A. wishes me to remind you to be
on your best behavior. Dr. Franklin and Mr. Miller send their
regards, and Mr. Miller sends also seeds of calendula, which he
says makes a pretty flower and a good poultice for infection.

Below, Granny said loudly, "How can y' let her say such things to 'em about your own mother?"

"Ma, I know," Lanyon said. "I tell 'em different when she goes out. Ma, please don't cry."

Should I go down? I listened. "Granny, do you need me?" I called.

"No. Bide a while more," Lanyon called. I frowned.

"I'm fine, Jem, bide a while longer," Granny said.

Lanyon's wife doesn't like Granny, I thought. *Why not?* I listened for more trouble from below. Nothing. Uneasy, I returned to my letter.

I hope Gran is well and that you two are getting
along. Dr. A. was invited to his sister's for Christmas and he
means to go, but we had our own little holiday early so we could
write to you. I hope you enjoy celebrating solstice. Try to think
of a story to tell in the circle, for that's part of the fun of it.
Jem, here is the doctor again.

So the doctor was coming oftener to see Margery at the shop. That meant they were spending time together. They'd written this letter together. They'd even had a little Christmas together. *Very good.*

Dr. Abernathy had written,

Jem, I hope you are well. I hope you are doing all

*you can to learn as much as you possibly can from Mistress
Penhaligon, so you can come home. It is devilish hard to
manage with you gone. I don't wish to appear selfish or helpless,
as though a grown man who got along perfectly well without
you can't do so any longer, but the fact is I miss you, even your
incessant questions. I miss your cleaning my instruments, for
now I have to do it myself, as Mrs. Pierce refuses to touch them.
She insists she is afraid she might damage them, but I suspect
her complaint has more to do with aversion to work outside her
sphere.*

*Franklin asks me to inform you that on November
the twenty-second, the Royal Navy delivered a resounding
defeat to the French along the coast of France at Quiberon
Bay. They'd thought to invade England, but Admiral Hawke
attacked their fleet in a gale. The French lost all but two ships.
Admiral Hawke's victory means no more supply ships to
Canada, which Franklin particularly wanted me to mention.
He says this will hasten the end of the war. May God grant it
be so. Mrs. Jamison reaches for the pen, but she must wait for
one last word from me: Do be so kind as to get on with your
learning so you can come home.*

There was just one more sentence from Margery, and it made my heart hop like a rabbit.

*I usually come to visit my gran the third week of
June, which I plan to do this year. The doctor and I hope you*

will have learnt enough by then to come home with me.

With our love and best regards,

Margery

I decided to make a calendar to mark off the days until I saw her.

I took out my quill and ink to add a postscript to my own fat letter to Margery.

Margery, I shall count the days until you come!

Dr. Abernathy, please tell Dr. Franklin that I am delighted the war is done, but I hope that doesn't mean he is done with London, for I have no wish to see him sail all the way home and be gone from us forever.

Granny has taught me how to milk Snowy, and I have learned how to cook food in a hearth over a peat fire. She says she will teach me how to gather herbs in the spring. Margery, your Uncle Lanyon is here at this very minute and will be going back to town soon, so the last thing I must tell is about my mother's cameo, which I wore a great deal, as you know. It had a Call in it, a curl of Mum's hair. Granny said P. has one to match and that's how he found me. We burned the hair in alder twigs. Granny agreed I might be leaking Sight, so I must learn to manage that as well as my flying. I cannot say how long it will take for me to learn, but I miss you both every day and pray for you every night.

With more affection than could fit in a letter, I remain,

Your own Jem

From below I heard a thump. Somebody bringing in turves of dried peat. I called out, "May I come down?"

"Aye, come," Granny said.

I put my letter inside my waistcoat, for Granny might want to add a message to Margery, tucked my bottle of ink in one pocket and my sealing wax in the other, and descended the ladder with my quill in my teeth. I turned round to see Lanyon stacking turves. Granny, her eyes a bit red around the rims, watched. They seemed farther apart than the space between them.

"Er, Granny, did you want me to tell Margery anything?" I asked, my voice plopping into the silence.

"Did you tell Margery about the Call?"

"I did."

"Then seal it up," Granny said, so I did. Despite the tension in the room, Granny and I sliced bread to go with Lanyon's butter, and we cooked the fish he'd brought. The Penhaligons carried on a polite exchange for my sake, but I sensed a whole other wordless conversation going on between the two of them. After the meal, when Granny watched Lanyon go out to fetch Jasper, I didn't know what to say, so I put a light hand on her shoulder. Her hand crept up and covered mine.

Granny said, "Help me gather some things to send with him." Granny fetched out a big chunk of goat's cheese and put all our fresh eggs in a basket. Lanyon tied all the packages to Jasper, and then Granny handed him a bag of pine cones we'd gathered for her grandsons. "Tell 'em to toss these one at a time in the fire and see the pretty colors," Granny said.

Lanyon thanked her, added them to the load, then turned. He and Granny stood looking at one another.

"Son, I know she's waitin' and y' must go," Granny said. "Blessings on you, Lanyon, my boy, and on my grandsons and on Elaine and her family too. Forgive my sharp words. 'Tis wrong of me t' scold that way. Jem, give him your letter so's he can mail it in town."

Lanyon slid my letter in his coat and tipped his hat to me. "A pleasure, Jem. Take care of Ma, aye?" He wrapped his arms around his mother and rested his chin on the top of her head. "I wish things was different, Ma. I wish y' could come to us for Christmas."

"So do I, son. Maybe one day Elaine'll change her mind. Maybe I will."

Lanyon smiled with one side of his mouth as he eased his mother to arm's length and said, "Ma, y' are what y' are, an' so is she, an' I love y' both. So." He kissed her forehead and set off. We watched until Lanyon and Jasper vanished below a little rise. Granny shrunk some once he was out of sight.

"He's a good person," I said, "but he's more serious than his brother."

"That's partly because Lanyon's Elaine is wound tight as a spool."

"She doesn't like you." I looked at my toes. "Why not? If you don't mind my asking."

She sighed, "Elaine and some others in Fowey, mostly her people, thinks I'm a witch."

Witch. The word snagged between us like the outline of tree branches in the sky above her head. This improbable notion had been niggling at my mind ever since she'd muttered over moss, since I'd seen her fingers scratching behind the ears of a wild badger, since I'd watched her toss my mother's cameo into a pile of burning twigs and heard her plans for us to spend solstice inside the standing stones. Despite my education and the doctor's skepticism and my studies in science, a deep-down part of me had been thinking *witch* ever since she'd uttered the word *magic*.

When I was little, the words *witch* and *magic* would have belonged between the covers of Mum's books for me to take out and play with and put away again. But now I knew magic was knitted into my blood and bones. It belonged to me. Granny even had said that if I turned my back on magic, I wouldn't *be* me.

But how would my life change if I embraced it? What doors would open? What people would come into my life? What dangers? Would accepting my magic turn me into… a *witch*?

"And…are you? A witch?" The barn, the trees, the cottage, the sky, me—all of us leaned in to hear her answer.

"Me? No! I s'pose there's some like me what thinks they're witches—and maybe they are, I dunno—but that ain't what I am."

She is not a witch; I am not a witch. I let out my breath and followed her back into the cottage. We washed dishes and tended the animals, all our usual evening tasks. The whole time, I pondered: if Granny Kestrel wasn't a witch, what was she? I had been gathering information for two months, but I still had no idea what to make of Granny Kestrel, or, for that matter, what to make of myself.

CHAPTER 19

DECEMBER 1759

The Longest Night of the Year

"When will we leave for Hawk's Tor?" I asked, the day before the solstice.

Granny chopped onions and carrots whilst I sorted beans for a pot of soup that would cook all the while we were celebrating solstice inside the Trippet Stones with Granny's friends.

"We'll go after midnight and meet the girls there," she said. "We'll tell stories and watch the sun come up, then come back here for soup. They'll go home after breakfast."

"Where do they live?"

"Elowen and Dolly live together east of here, near Kilmar Tor. Dolly keeps bees, and Elowen makes candles and soap and such."

"Oh, they're sisters? How old are they?"

"They're close like sisters," Granny said, dumping her vegetables into the pot. "As to their age, I ain't certain. Thirty? Forty? Dolly's older, but Elowen acts older."

Once I'd added my beans, Granny poured in water to the top and placed the pot in the coals. She packed a basket with bundles of herbs and holly, and four little bells tied to circles of twine. She hauled out a chunk of partly charred wood about as big as my forearm.

"Why Granny, is that a Yule log?"

"'Tis a mot, aye, saved from last year. We'll save somethin' for next year from this year's fire. The girls'll bring Dolly's honey mead. Now *that* is a treat."

After we tended the animals that evening, Granny said, "So: To bed. Sleep in your breeks, as we'll be leavin' in the wee, dark hours for the tor."

* * *

I awoke to thumps on the ladder and the smell of beans and onions cooking.

"Jem, up with you. Time t' go," Granny called softly. I pulled on my boots and descended. "Quiet, now," she said, "we don't want t' wake the beasts or they'll think it's mornin' and time for the day t' start." She picked up her basket and said, "I've tied the Yule log to some other sticks. I hope y' can carry 'em all?"

I rested the bundle on my shoulders and said, "I'll try."

We walked into a cold wind blowing from the north. Our walk was easy, across mostly level ground, and we'd been walking not even an hour when Granny pointed to a glow dead ahead and said, "There they are." To my right, a faint glimmer far off suggested somebody else was out on the moor. A flicker to the northeast might have been a star peeking over the top of Brown Willy, but it could have been a third fire.

"Do other people come out for solstice?" I asked.

"Some, but there's more in summer." The fire that was our destination burned on flat ground. When we got close to the circle, the firelight lapped the toes of the giant stones standing all around, with a block of stars above each one hidden by their heads. The circle looked to be some hundred feet wide, as best I could tell. Granny and I stepped inside the circle, rounding one of a handful of collapsed stones stretched out like fallen warriors. Hawk's Tor rose beyond the circle.

Granny called to two cloaked figures standing beside a small fire, "Greet-ings, sisters, 'tis me." Four enormous candles flickered in the shelter of four big boulders at each of the compass directions. I didn't know how old the standing stones were, but they *felt* settled. They felt *patient*. Granny set down her basket. I gladly set down my bundle and rubbed my shoulder.

"Who's this?" said the taller of the two figures. She and the other one came closer. Both were younger than Granny. One was tall, and the other was Granny's size but plumper. Granny Kestrel said, "Jem here's come all the way from London. Jem, this is Elowen"—the taller woman nodded—"and this is Dolly"—the little one nodded.

"How do you do?" I stuck out my hand.

Elowen took my hand but just held it. She said, "Hello and welcome. Why, Kestrel, she's asleep."

"Not so, Elowen," Granny said. "This girl heard her da speakin' t' her from underground afore he died. She saw her mother's fetch as she died." Dolly moved to the other side of me. Granny added, "Jem here flew with a falcon for three days."

"Three days?" Dolly put a hand on my shoulder. "Oh, my," she said, then lifted her hand. To Granny, she said, "Why, she's full up to the top!"

"Aye, I know," Granny said. "She's been with me since All Hallows'. She ain't all the way awake yet, El, but 'twon't be long, I'm thinkin'."

"Has she got a mark?" Elowen asked.

Granny said, "No, Elowen Bloedden, she ain't marked, neither, but all are welcome at solstice." Granny put her arm around my shoulders. "Especially Jem, for here's one more thing: she come to me with a Call round her neck." Dolly gasped. Elowen's teeth clicked as she closed her mouth. Granny continued, "'Twas old, and not even made for her, but the Caller was usin' it t' find her anyhow."

Dolly said, "El, she had a Call!"

Elowen came closer and said to me, "May I?" She placed her hands on my head and closed her eyes. A shock of cold wind—a wind with intent, like the one Granny said had come for her Mum—blasted through my mind. I heard Elowen's intake of breath. "My," she said. "Kestrel, 'tis…'tis like nothin' I ever saw. Like a lake in a cave. You can't see it at all unless you're lookin' for it. Dolly's hovering hand landed again, and she *hmmmed*.

I felt uncomfortable. Very. I'd just walked an hour in the dark carrying a load of wood, and now two strangers were, well, trespassing. I didn't like having wind inside my head, which appeared to have dislodged something up there that now tickled like a moth.

Granny slid between me and the girls saying, "El, Dolly, all in good time. Here, put your bells on. Jem, here's yours. Dolly, help me with the fire. El, show her the Crown."

"Come," Elowen said. She turned me to face west; I eased away to make a little space between us. Stars pin-pricked the black sky, shining very bright because the moon was new. "What stars d' you know?"

"I know the Plough. Granny told me about the star on the Ploughman's belt."

"Find it." I pointed. "Now then, look to the left: see that curve o' dim stars next t' the Ploughman?"

"Yes."

"That's Caer Arianrhod, the Crown, where 'tis told the Oak King stays until tonight. 'Tis where the Holly King goes to get his strength back after sunrise. Them two kings've been fighting since time began."

"Tell the story, El," Dolly called. We turned. The Yule log smoldered in the fire.

"I'm t' be first? Right," Elowen said. "Come, Jem, let's sit by the fire." We turned the soles of our shoes to the fire, and Elowen said (in a storytelling voice that reminded me of Mum's), "In days of old, 'twas summer year-round. Two brothers wanted t' rule the world, the Oak King and the Holly King. They agreed t' take turns. The Oak King ruled first. He grew mighty trees that covered the land. In the shadows beneath those trees, the Holly King huddled. He couldn't take his turn in the sun, for the oak was larger and stronger and refused t' let his brother have a turn.

"After a thousand years, the Holly King was done with waitin'. He begged a boon o' the Moon. 'Help me defeat my brother lest I die,' he said. The Moon called on the north wind t' help her save the Holly King.

"Now, the north wind loved the Moon, for she turned the ice and snow in his kingdom to silver but never melted 'em away. And so, from the frozen north, the wind begun to blow. It blew day after day, nipping the leaves of the Oak King. They died and fell, and the Oak King stood bare. At last the Holly King could feel the sun on his leaves, and he grew big and strong and thought t' himself, 'Finally, it's my turn.'

"But the Oak King was beloved of the Sun, so *he* prayed. The Sun burned as hard as he could until the Oak King warmed enough to sprout buds an' leaves, and the Holly King was stuck in the shadows once again. So he prayed to the Moon, and she and the north wind froze the earth again.

"Tonight, at solstice, the Oak King'll defeat the Holly King, who'll go t' Caer Arianrhod. The Oak King'll grow strong in the warming days. But at summer solstice, the Holly King'll defeat the Oak King, and *he'll* go off t' Caer Arianrhod. Each brother reigns half the year, for the earth needs both t' keep in balance: the Holly King brings rest and harvest, the Oak King brings sun and growth."

It was a wonderful story made magic by the dark at our backs and the fire at our feet and Caer Arianrhod itself glowing overhead. I wasn't sure if I was supposed to say anything, so I just smiled. Then Granny and Dolly rang their bells, so I did too.

"I've a story about balance as well," Dolly said. "The balance of dance."

"A bee story?" Elowen guessed.

"Aye, a bee story," Dolly said. "So? I listened to you, El." Elowen grunted. Dolly continued, "It happened this summer, but I think we need a bit o' mead first. Jem, you're our guest; you go first." She handed me a little stone bottle. I sipped. The mead did not taste like honey, but it left the fragrance of honey in my mouth. I passed the bottle to Granny. Dolly said, "So: the time was summer. The place was home. I was at my hives mindin' the bees when a worker come back t' the hive. The other bees come to see what she'd learnt, and she danced until the lot of them were hummin' and flingin' themselves up, eager to go see what she'd found. But she kept dancin'. I wondered why she kept on even though the others already knew where she wanted 'em t' go."

"Dolly, I'm sorry to interrupt," I said, "but are you saying bees talk by dancing?"

"O' course they do," Dolly said, "what a funny question, Jem. So finally she stopped, and ever'body lifted up in a cloud and flew west. I wondered what on earth was over there, so I followed. I lost the cloud, o' course, but I followed the stragglers 'til I topped a little rise—and what do you think I saw?

"A meadow with trees at the edge that had holly at their feet, holly bushes as far as I could see, flowering o' course, as this was June. The hollies was awash in bees, so many bees on each holly it looked like a line o' nuns in golden robes marching along. Out in the meadow, where there was sun all day, poppies and catmint and wild roses were s' thick 'twas like they was planted special for the bees. Why the sheep an' ponies thereabouts hadn't gobbled every flower, I can't say. I harvested some of the honey made from all them flowers, and I made this mead from it."

"So, Dolly, we're drinking your story right now," I said, ringing my bell.

Dolly beamed. "Aye, Jem, we are."

"A sweet story, Dolly," Granny Kestrel said and rang her bell. "My story was told to me by my husband, Dylan, about the long-ago time in his homeland of Wales when giants and humans lived in peace side by side.

"Long ago, the King of Ireland, Matholwch, wanted to take to wife the most beautiful girl in Wales, Branwen daughter of Llyr, King of all the Britons. He asked Branwen's brother, Bendigeidfran the Giant for her hand, and sailed across the Irish Sea to fetch her. But Branwen's half-brother, Efnisien, was not asked about the marriage. In a fit of rage, he attacked the horses of Matholwch." Dolly gasped. "Efnisien cut off the horse's lips and ears and eyebrows to the bone. He cut off their tails to the spine. This great crime ruined the noble horses, who had done nothing whatever to earn such cruelty.

"Matholwch demanded the death of Efnisien as payment for this evil, but Bendigeidfran could not kill his half-brother, so he offered t' replace every horse. He offered a silver rod as thick as Matholwch's little finger and a gold plate as big as Matholwch's face. Even all this was not enough.

"So Bendigeidfran offered a magic cauldron to Matholwch. If one of Matholwch's men ever was hurt, or even killed, Matholwch could throw the man into the cauldron and bring him back to life. Finally, that was enough. Matholwch sailed home with Branwen, but he never forgave Branwen for the horses, even though she was as blameless as the beasts.

"The insult ate away at the Irish king's heart. After Branwen birthed a son, Matholwch banished her to the kitchens where the butcher beat her every day. Branwen got word to Bendigeidfran that her husband had turned cruel, so Bendgeidfran gathered an army to free her. Bendigeidfran's fleet sailed to Ireland with Bendigeidfran walking alongside them as there was no ship big enough to carry him.

"Matholwch's men were watching the coast one day when they saw a wonder: trees walking on the sea alongside a mountain with a tall ridge and a lake at each side of the ridge, all moving toward Ireland against the wind. Matholwch had Branwen dragged before him, and he asked, 'What are those trees on the sea?'

'The masts of Welsh ships,' said Branwen.

'What is the mountain alongside the ships?'

'That is Bendigeidfran, my brother. There isn't a ship big enough to contain him.'

'What is the ridge and the lake on either side of the ridge?'

'They are Bendigeidfran's two eyes on either side of his nose.'

"Matholwch gathered his men and retreated to the other side of the River Shannon. They destroyed the bridge across the Shannon, but Bendigeidfran lay across the river so his men could give chase to Matholowch. A terrible war killed thousands of men on both sides. Efnisien, whose cruelty began it all, broke his own heart to pieces inside the magic cauldron, destroying it. Bendigeidfran was struck in the foot with a poisonous spear. He ordered his men to behead him when he died, and to bury his head on the White Hill in London, facing France, so he might watch over England forever. The Tower of London was built over his head, and the ravens stand guard over it and England to this very day."

"What happened to Branwen?" I asked.

"When the war was over and her son and husband and brothers all were dead, Branwen, most blameless of all, fell to her knees, crying, 'Oh, Mother, have mercy one me! Woe that I was born! Two fair islands are laid waste because of me,' and she died then and there on banks of the River Alaw, and her grave is still there." The firelight played on our sober faces. I felt surprised that any story told by Granny would include cruelty to beasts.

"I don't want to ring, Kestrel," Dolly sniffed, "your story is too sad."

"But there's a lesson in it, Dolly," Elowen said. "Be careful where y' lay blame, and be careful where y' place your trust."

I wished I'd learned the first half of that lesson when I was younger. I hoped I'd learned the second half by now. Elowen rang her bell, and then Dolly and I rang ours.

Dolly said, "I don't s'pose you have a story, Jem?"

I was glad Margery had advised me to make up a story. It had been a long time since I'd told stories to the Freddie Payne outside the apothecary shop, for Dr. Abernathy and Dr. Franklin were more interested in fact than in once-up-on-a-time. But I loved it.

"Once upon a time," I began, "before God made man, all the animals on earth had legs, for God knew they all needed to be able to go from place to place, and He didn't think one animal should have to carry another. True, some animals rode others—lice, for instance, still ride a host all their lives. But even lice have legs."

"Fish don't," Dolly said.

I said, "Fish have fins. Birds have wings. The point is, all creatures had a way to move. Even worms push all their insides all to one end and pull up the rest."

"They do, but they don't much care for it," Dolly said, "especially after dinner."

Granny whispered, "Dolly speaks to crawlers and fliers like I speak to my beasts."

"In return for movement," I went on, "God said that when He had need of their help, the animals must help, for God was still shaping the world, putting in the finishing touches. God said"—I pitched my voice low—"'So, if I need to move a mountain, you elephants must help me move it. If I need to change the course of a river, you fish must fan the sand in the channel.'"

"Why would God need any help?" Dolly asked.

"Because work is work, Dolly," Elowen said, "and why not use the help if it's there?"

"God wanted them to be *willing* to help," I said. "So one day God was making a new tree. He decided to try something new. The new tree would be fat on the bottom and skinny on the top. God needed to see what kind of leaves would look best, so He gathered long, wavy leaves from the willow and leaves shaped like a hand from the maple and leaves shaped like a foot from the oak. The birds helped God gather leaves, but once God had many kinds of leaves, He needed someone to hold them up to the branches of the new tree. He picked the snake, for the snake tended to disappear whenever he saw God's shadow stretched over the land. God was keen to test him.

"In those days, the snake had a hundred legs just like a centipede. God asked the snake to climb into the new tree and hold up a hundred of each kind of leaf so God could stand back and decide which would look best.

"But even though God Himself summoned the snake, he came very slowly. The snake said he'd stubbed all his hundreds of toes. God made them better. The snake said he was sore from running after his breakfast. God healed his muscles. The snake said he was afraid to be way up high in a tree. God promised to catch him if he fell. The snake had no more excuses, so he climbed the tree. God gave the snake leaves to hold up, but after only two kinds of leaves, the snake was bored. He wrapped himself round a limb and went to sleep. The leaves fell to the ground. God had stepped *way* back to look, so when the leaves fell, God thought the snake had fallen. God ran back to the tree, But when He got there, He found the snake asleep.

"God thundered at the snake, 'I asked a service of thee! Couldst thou not help with a small thing such as this after all I have done for thee?'

"The snake's eyes flew open. He said, 'Ma*ss*ter, I am *sss*orry. I grew weary trying to hang on *ss*so far above the ground.'"

"*Sss*," Dolly giggled, "that's good." Elowen batted Dolly's arm.

"God chastised the snake, saying, 'Never again will I ask thee to climb a tree for me, for never again wilt thou have legs to do it,' whereupon God lifted the snake out of the tree and ran his hand along the snake's body. Each of the snake's hundred legs broke off and slithered away. 'They shall grow up to be like thee,' God said, 'creatures without legs, as a reminder to all that *what God wills must be.*'

"That is why, when God made men, the snake sneaked into the Garden of Eden and wound his way into the branches of the Tree to tempt Adam and Eve."

The fire burned. Nobody said anything.

"The end," I said.

Nobody rang her bell. I was afraid I'd told it badly, for I'd made it up just the day before and hadn't practiced. Finally Dolly said, "What kind o' leaves did God choose in the end?"

"For the new tree? Er, needles," I decided, "because God could stick on needles without the snake's help. The tree God was making that day was the evergreen."

"That ain't a story I heard before," Granny said.

"I don't suppose you did," I laughed. "I made it up." The women stared at me over the fire. I explained, "Margery said in her letter I should make up a story to tell for solstice."

"Jem, y' never made that up!" Dolly said. "Why, that's…that was…"

"A storymaker, are you?" Elowen said. "Kestrel y' didn't say that."

"I didn't know, El," Granny said.

"Have I done something wrong? I—" I looked at the faces around the fire. "Nobody rang a bell."

All three grabbed up their bells and rang like mad. Elowen said, "We're all agog because we haven't had a storymaker in our circle for—how long, Kestrel?"

Granny said, "I remember an old, old man who come to this circle when I were a girl. Old Aerwith was his name, an' he always had a bagful o' new stories to tell."

"Old Aerwith used t' come t' the fair in town an' tell stories for pennies, remember El?" Dolly said. "He'd spread a red blanket and sit on a milking stool in the middle. If you was big, y' had to stand up around the blanket, but if you was little, y' could sit on the blanket at his feet."

"It sounds lovely," I said. "Is that a second story, Granny? The one about Old Aerwith?"

"No, I've told of Old Aerwith because storymakin's a gift," Granny said. "Most times when people opens their mouths, a story comes out, but most stories is either lived or borrowed. A person who can pull words out o' the air and spin 'em into somethin' that never was until they spoke, why—"

"It's magic," Dolly said.

"Maybe that's your gift, Jem," Elowen said. "She must be opened, Kestrel."

"P'raps Jem's storymakin's her Light tryin' t' break through," Granny said. "See, Jem, the Light shines different in all of us. Dolly here shines for little creatures, bees and worms and such. El can See with her hands. She's somethin' of a healer, too. And I See the future a bit, like my granny, and you know I have a heart for beasts."

Elowen said to me, "When y' first come, I put my hands on your head. Y' didn't like it."

I mumbled, "We'd just met. I felt like a horse at market."

"What I Saw in you was—I never felt nothin' like it. I couldn't see what color your Light was neither, which also never happened. I thought maybe you had Dark threaded through you like a drain of milk swirlin' in a mug of tea."

I swallowed. "And…do I?"

"No," Granny said, "Jem, I been seein' y' all these weeks like stained glass sooted over with smoke." Elowen nodded.

"What does that mean?" I asked.

Granny said, "'Tis queer you've got a rainbow inside, for most folks is only one color. But you, you may have every kind of Sight there is." Dolly gasped. Granny continued, "You've a heart for beasts, a hand for healin', eyes that See the future, the gift of storymakin'. And maybe other gifts. Somebody with all that comes along once a hundred years."

"Two hundred," Elowen said. "More."

Granny nodded. "If that's what y' are, Jem, I hope and pray you choose t' live in the Light. I pray I'm enough of a teacher."

Elowen stood and looked east. The sky had lightened, and the stars had dimmed. "We must sing, Kestrel," she said, "It's time. The sun's about to break." Granny tossed her herbs and holly on the fire, then turned to me and said, "Will y' join the circle, Jem?" I glanced east. Bands of pink and orange glowed on the horizon. The Oak King was coming. The women pushed themselves to their feet and joined hands. Granny held her hand out to me.

Was this my moment, already? Was it now I must decide between being normal and being—like them?

CHAPTER 20

DECEMBER 1759

There Are More Things in Heaven and Earth Than Are Dreamt Of

Take Granny's hand or turn away? Accept as my fate something that couldn't be proved? Open my heart to danger—or to my destiny? The women waited; the fire flickered; the sun was about to rise. *What should I do?*

I thought back to singing down a mineshaft to my da, smelling smoke and feeling him down in the darkness. I thought of the stars in Mum's eyes the last time I saw her. I thought of Patch's hand on my arm sizzling up my insides. I recalled Giselle's easy affection, and the singing of dolphins, and once again felt myself hurtling from a wide blue sky toward a pigeon's back—

And I knew what to do. Not from reading or hearing about it, but from seeing and feeling and living things other people would never know. It was granted to me, not to others. This gift, if gift it was, was mine. I looked at Granny's hand and at Dolly's and Elowen's. They watched my face. The sun was almost up. I looked into Granny's gray eyes, shining like silver.

"'Tis your choice," she said.

Yes, I thought, *it is*, and I placed my hand in hers. I reached over to take Dolly's hand, completing the circle. *So be it.* Granny squeezed my hand.

The women began to hum a single, low note that echoed back from the circle of stones. Gradually, the humming changed from something I heard with my ears to something that thrummed along my veins and beat along with my heart. It throbbed at the ends of my fingers. The hum around me and in me seemed to enclose all of us inside a dome of sound. Then Elowen sang in a sweet contralto,

> Mother Moon, thy glory beams
> Round us all in silver streams.
> We now await, O mother dear,
> Wisdom from you to appear.

Granny Kestrel sang next in her husky voice,

> Mother Earth, with you we stand
> Linked by love to all the land.
> Serving you is our desire
> Touch us now with Wisdom's fire.

Dolly sang in a soprano high and clear like a piper playing to his sheep,

> Summer sunshine, passing fair,
> Bringing life in summer air,
> Grant us now one boon, we pray,
> Guide us to thy will today.

"Now you," Granny Kestrel nudged me.

"I don't know the song," I said.

"Look in your heart," she said.

I tried. I felt the humming round our circle like a steady stream of water. I felt the energy of the other three through our linked hands. I felt a surging power just beyond us, our circle a tiny loop through which it sent a push of— what? Energy?

Whatever it was ran from person to person through our clasped hands. I closed my eyes and tried to see this thing that poured through us, but in trying to see how it flowed, I lost sense of my connection to the others. I flittered like a sunbeam to a shining river rushing through a dark land. I flew over the water like a bird. In the distance, I saw a tableau: all three women stood shoulder to shoulder beside a small figure, toward whom I arrowed, and touched, and... became. Each woman had a hand on *me*, then, and all four of us stood beside a shimmering waterfall as vast and tall and wide as the sky, thundering as it fell into a silver river. We reached our hand toward the waterfall.

I both watched this tableau and lived it; it was like when I'd flown with my peregrine not as *I* and *she* but as *us*. I looked up and around; the waterfall provided the only source of light in a black expanse that had no borders, no horizons, no boundaries. We four stood like ants at the edge of it—standing on nothing that I could feel or see. I should have been afraid—I would have been afraid—but the women beside me shielded my touch on the great, glowing waterfall with their strength. We anchored one another to the shore like tree roots. Together, we were strong. What bonded us? What kept us from pitching off the bank?

What was this great fall of light? The source of my Sight? Was this—this magnificence—was this what I had been born with, what I had feared, what I could tap into? It seemed too vast for one person to manage. How could I ever cope with anything like this?

As I trembled, as I thought to pull away my hand, as my knees weakened, I felt something like warm honey wrapping round my legs, my arms, my heart, pouring into me strength, and courage, and a sense of the rightness of my being here, now.

Anyone who's felt the Light knows it; if the Light has called someone, if the Light is inside, that person belongs to the Light. It is a part of him and he of it. It can't be taught or acquired or learned. It simply is or is not. The person can choose to See it or not.

This is the first truth I understood in the Light. I understood it because it already was in me and because my friends held me steady long enough to understand. How was it possible I might have missed it? How could I have ever wanted to turn my face away from it?

The Light flowed into me where I touched it. It filled my heart. It flowed all along my limbs and into my throat. I opened my mouth, and the song that came out was of me and of the Light:

> Loving Mother, we who stand
> Seek a blessing: guide our hand,
> Show the way that we must grow,
> Show the road that we must go.

There was more. I sang:

> Keep the Dark ones far away
> Hide us from them, this we pray
> To See our path is our desire:
> Show your plan by light of fire.

Our Yule fire leapt up! I felt surprise in the others. The figures in my mind turned from the waterfall of Light to the real fire, and the flickering flames replaced the rippling silver waters, and I opened my own eyes and saw real faces once again. The firelight danced in their eyes, and I looked into the flames as well.

I can't say what the others saw when they looked into our fire, but I saw places I knew I'd never been—

I saw distant mountains from atop a horse with great trees rising above me;

I saw a man's shadowy face, twisted in pain, and my hands tending him by firelight;

I saw a manicured lawn through a rain-spattered window;

I saw flames rising from a building and gunpowder smoke and men running;

I saw a girl child laughing in a sunny meadow on a cliff, the light turning her hair to gold and a great lake in the distance spread out like a sea—

"Wait!" I called to the girl, but when I spoke, she faded, and all I saw was our fire sending a column of smoke up into the sky above Bodmin Moor. Morning had broken, and the sun shone over the tallest stone in the east. It laid a golden path through our smoldering fire to the other side of the circle, cutting the top of the tor like a sword, exactly in half. *Balance.*

We four looked at one another. Had they seen what I'd seen? Only one thing seemed appropriate for me to say. "Thank you, all of you," I said. "Bless you f-for being with me. For letting me touch…that…" I shook my head. "Was that the Light?" Elowen nodded. Dolly smiled a tiny smile. It felt to me as though the Light that had bonded us beside the waterfall still linked us here and now. It was in us and of us. We were connected.

Granny reached out for the end of a log, wiggled it out, knocked off the red coals, and carried it off a ways to cool to be next year's Yule log. It sent up a plume of smoke like the incense burned in church at Easter. Granny came back and put our bells back into her basket. Then we sat.

Elowen said, "She has strength."

"I could hardly hang on!" Dolly added, flexing her hands.

"Y' did fine, Dolly," Granny Kestrel said. "But, El's right, Jem. I've never felt the like. Never seen the Light lookin' like a waterfall. If that's what y' have, well—" She spread the coals out.

"Jem, y're linked with the Light, now," Dolly said. "Y' must learn how to hold it without spillin' lest it overfill and make you mad."

Elowen said, "Don't scare her, Dolly." She turned to me. "'Tis like anything else new. You'll adjust, and y' won't even remember a time before y' felt the Light in you." Elowen turned back to Granny. "But p'raps she might come to me and Dolly when she's learnt all she can from you?"

"That'll be her choice, El," Granny said. "But it's a good idea."

"To think, she had all that in her, all this time, and didn't even know it," Dolly said. "Jem, y're a rare one, for absolute certain, not to've gone stark, staring—"

Elowen jabbed her.

"Or run off like my Charlie," Granny said. "It felt t' me like we was keepin' Jem from fallin' into the Light, but I think Jem held herself back just as hard."

"I froze like a rabbit!" Dolly said.

"Jem, maybe y' kept all that behind a dam because y've been holdin' yourself in this world so long all by yourself," Granny said. She breathed deep. "This is a solstice I'll never forget." She stood. "Well, who's for some soup?"

We brushed ourselves off and threw dirt on the coals, and walked back to the cottage to tend the animals and fill our bellies with Granny's bean soup, just as though it were a normal day and I hadn't just turned into somebody else.

CHAPTER 21

CHRISTMAS 1760

Keeping an Open Mind

On Christmas Eve, Granny and I made special treats for the animals, "for Jesus was born in a stable, amongst the best company of all," Granny said. For a gift, she gave me a stick, about the thickness of my little finger, as long as my hand, and smooth as satin.

"This isn't just a stick, is it," I said.

"It's a trainin' stick."

"How does it work?" It fitted perfectly into my palm.

"Let me tell you things in order, aye? You've decided t' accept your gift, good. But the Sight can't be took on an' then ignored. You must learn t' live with it."

"All right. How do you and Elowen and Dolly live with it?"

"Livin' with Sight ain't a burden, but y' need t' fold your life around it. Let it be the heart of you. I live out here all alone, but I ain't alone. The Light—it fills you. You're never alone when y' live in the Light."

"So the Light is animate? Like the Dark?"

"Somewhat, but the Dark's like a fire y' got to watch lest it go astray an' do harm. The Light's like—like the sun. It fills you. My own son can't visit 'less he gets leave from his wife, but my heart is full, always. Elowen and Dolly—neither ever married at all, and ain't likely to, but El's family is the scores o' people she's doctored. Dolly's children're every creeping thing she sees. I'd like t' hope y' might have Light and love, both, like I did."

I wasn't all that keen about marriage and children, but I kept quiet. "You talk about Light and Sight like they're the same thing. Are they?"

"Light is—" She cast her eyes around the room and picked up an extra-large acorn we'd found in the woods. "Light is whatever's inside this acorn that makes it sprout and grow into a tree. Light is what tells geese when t' go south and when t' come home. Light is your heart beating. Light is the love I push out my hand in the barn."

"So...Light is Life? Love?"

"Aye. Here." She half-filled a mug with water, dropped in a pinch of salt, and stirred. "Taste that." I sipped. "What do y' taste?"

"Salt."

"Could you take the salt out o' the water?"

"If I evaporated the water, yes."

Granny sighed. "Leave science alone for now. Could y' separate the two and have both whole again, just as they were before I stirred in the salt?"

"No."

"That's Light," Granny said. "There's a Bible verse I always liked that talks of 'the substance of things hoped for, the evidence of things not seen.' That's Light too."

"So the Light is God."

She put her hands on her hips. "What's God, Jem?"

"God is..." I cast back in my memory for the quotation. "'There is but one living and true God, everlasting, without body, parts, or passions; of infinite power, wisdom, and goodness; the Maker, and Preserver of all things both visible and invisible.'"

"You learnt that in church. What do *you* say? Is God big? Small? Kind? Wrathful?"

"All of those," I said. "Are you trying to confuse me?"

"No. I'm tryin' t' show it ain't easy t' talk about God. 'Tis easy t' use God's name without thinkin' about it. Like God told Isaiah, 'For my thoughts are not your thoughts, neither are your ways my ways.'"

"Granny, I don't understand what you're trying to tell me. Salt and geese and acorns—what do you mean?"

"There be plenty o' things we won't never understand all the way," she said. "The Light is one of 'em. The Light showed like a big lake in your vision: y' might dip your toes in that lake without bein' able t' see t' other side, but that don't mean the other side ain't there."

"You saw that big lake too?"

"Aye, but it weren't my vision. It were yours. And it was give to you by your Sight. The Light's there whether y'see it or not, but Sight lets some people see it."

"Who was that girl?"

Her eyebrows went up. "I didn't See a girl. Only the lake. Did y' See yourself with the girl, like you was older?"

I sighed. "I don't think so."

"You should write down visions in that book o' yours."

"I will." I waved my stick. "Can you tell me why you gave me a stick for Christmas?"

"I'll show you. The stick helps aim your mind so the Light knows your need. Let's try it. First, feel it all over. Know the shape and grain and size until y' know the stick like the back o' your hand. Know it by heart."

"Done."

"Oho, y' know it that fast?"

"I know the stick," I insisted.

"Put it down on the table and turn your back, then." I did so. I heard a tiny clatter. Granny must have picked up the stick. "Turn back," she said, and I obeyed.

"Did you hide the stick?" I asked.

"Why don't y' look for it?"

I looked on top of and under the table, for I hadn't heard her walk away. She hadn't had time to hide the stick anywhere else in the cottage. "It's in your pocket," I said.

"No, it ain't."

"In your hair."

"No, see?" She shook down her hair.

"Is it in the Blind Box on the mantel?"

"No."

"Well, it couldn't just disappear," I said. Granny Kestrel just looked at me. I slapped my hands on the table. "All right, I give up: where's the stick?"

"'Tis on the table just to the right of your hand." I looked down—at my stick.

"How did you do that?" I breathed.

"Pick up the stick." I did so.

"You didn't answer my question," I said.

"Yes I am. See the stick. Feel it. *Know* it."

I closed my eyes. I felt the stick. *It's a blasted stick.*

"Anger ain't helpful," Granny said. "We'd best stop."

"No, wait," I said, "let me try again." I concentrated. Instead of just using my senses, though, I let my mind hover over the stick like I'd hovered over that long-ago pigeon's eye on Margery's back step. As with the pigeon, I moved closer and closer to the stick until I felt a lurch and—fell. Visions of the stick as an acorn and as a sapling and as forest giant flashed by in a twinkling. I saw storms of rain. I bore up under heavy snow and felt parched in summer heat. I felt the burning slash of a lightning strike. I felt smoothing and blessing and human sweat and *effort* poured into it over generations.

"Jem," Granny said. I opened my eyes. I saw the stick in my hand.

"I know the stick," I said, and this time it was truer than I'd ever imagined.

"Well done, Jem, and your first time too," Granny breathed.

"It feels like I just lived sixty years in a minute."

"But y' aimed your mind like I told you."

"It's hard."

"Oh, aye, it ages a body. Why, I'm only twenty." I blinked, and she laughed. "I'm teasin' you. Sorry. But, Jem, think: ain't there lots o' things that're hard at first that gets easier as y' get used to 'em? With practice, 'tis like closin' and openin' a door.

"You'll learn t' See what you want the other person t' see—truly *See* it. Elowen says when she lays on her hands on somebody and goes in, it's like goin' into a cave with a candle. She holds up that candle to the cave wall and sees what she needs t' see right there."

"She reads minds?"

"Not exactly. She feels…oh, trouble, or hurt, or whatever needs fixin' and tries t' fix it."

"I wasn't touching Patch when I said 'Don't see me' at Mr. Galt's shop."

"When Patch and you was in the shop alone, you was thinkin' harder'n him. He was angry an' couldn't think. Like before with the stick—when you was angry, y' couldn't think. Why, there's animals in the forest what blend in with wherever they're hidin', and y' don't see 'em even if your standin' right next to 'em. They live in the Light, so when they have need of it, it's there, just like air. People don't live in the Light. We doubt. That's why y' must *train* your mind not t' get in the way." She pointed at the chair. "Think of Margery sittin' right there in that chair smilin' at us. See her? See her hair, her dress? See the way she sort of sprawls in the chair?"

When Granny described someone I missed so much, I could see her as clearly as though she really were sitting there, smiling. "Yes, I can see her."

"If y' practice, you'll be able t' open an' close the door as easy as that. But y' must practice. Only not right now." She took a small package from the mantel and handed it to me, saying, "Y' don't really think I'd give y' nothin' for Christmas but a stick?" She smiled.

"Oh, thank you Granny. I didn't expect anything. I have something for you in the loft."

"No, you sit. I'll have mine later. Open it."

I untied the ribbon and unfolded the cloth. There lay a knitted cap with very long bits on the side like a hound's ears. Granny said, "I noticed your hat didn't cover your ears." I tried it on; the cap had two knitted ties at the ends of the ears, and the whole of it was lined in something soft.

"Granny, it's a grand cap. I love it. Thank you."

"I made it at night whilst you was sleepin'," she said. "I shoulda made mittens too. Next year."

As sudden as blinking, my pleasure in her gift wilted. I slipped off the cap. "Do you really think I'll be here next Christmas?" I said softly.

"Oh—well, no, it ain't likely," Granny said, "but I can send a package t' London, I think?"

For Christmas Eve supper, we had a lovely bread pudding with dried fruit, eggs, and milk. Granny made fish chowder. But my mind kept circling back to her remark about my being on the moor next Christmas. The idea churned in my belly, and I chewed my pudding and slurped my chowder and stared at the fire, all hunched over in a lump.

But when I glanced at Granny, so calm and kind—and all alone for who knows how many Christmas Eves, never mind how full of Light she claimed to be—I felt ashamed. I had no right to feel sorry for myself. None.

So, after supper, I gave Granny her present: a drawing I'd made of Margery. Then I pulled on my new cap and said, "Let's sing every song we can think of." We started with "As I Sat On a Sunny Bank," to the tune of "I Saw Three Ships," and I smiled and sang and pretended this was the very best Christmas I'd ever had.

CHAPTER 22

SPRING AND SUMMER 1760

A New Member of the Family

Winter thickened the clouds and briskened the westerly winds. It rained or misted every second or third day, and a handful of days brought snow that stayed on the ground, which Snowy disliked despite her name. As the weeks passed and spring came on, I worked with my stick and on other exercises Granny said would strengthen my mind. She taught me, for example, to mine my memories. Granny said, "Start with somethin' y' saw or heard long ago. Or tasted. When I think of Ma's splits spread with her redcurrant jam, I can hear her 'n' see her like she's right here."

I started with my own mother, for I'd expected to remember every little detail about her but already had forgotten too much. The way it worked, Granny said, is that I should write down something I remembered—pink carnations in the rain, for example—and then write whatever else that picture made me think of or see or hear.

Remembering the past carved little runnels in my mind, which made my thinking more pliable, more flexible, more elastic. At first I started with familiar things: I wrote "sewing" and listed everything I could remember, like hemming Polly Stevenson's old dress and stitching up a cut on a cadaver under Dr. Abernathy's direction.

Then I went further back. I tried to remember my life back in Lamesley. I wrote down "Nan Knowles" and recorded everything I could recall about her hands and her voice and the way she managed everything for Mum when Da died. I wrote down the smell of the steam off our tea and the sound of the rain pouring off the roof the day we decided to come to London. Every memory sparked another, and I began to see my life laid out like stepping stones in a garden, one thing leading to the next, which bolstered Granny's claim that things fell out as they were meant, for my Sight had been there all along. Memory truly became a way to understand my gift.

Granny taught me to imagine a door between the hidey-hole in my mind (my cave) and my everyday life. "A door's got a knob you can open and close whenever y'like," she said. "And you can lock it, too." Imagining a door helped me feel I had control over when and where my Sight surfaced. I wouldn't fly again unless I wanted to, which was a great relief.

We practiced talking without talking. Granny said she'd turned her ankle badly once and had conveyed the word *Come* to Elowen across the long miles between them. Elowen had heard her and arrived later that day. The way Granny talked without talking was to focus on her breathing, think her message at me, and imagine me hearing her. Granny would pick up a spoon or a bowl or some little thing and hide it behind her back, *think* at me what it was, and ask me to guess. Or she'd hide something and picture where it was. We tried getting one another to do something physical, like *pat your head* or *lift your foot*. Sometimes I conveyed my message, but other times Granny would say, "I've no idear what I'm s'posed t' do, Jem, y're all muddled on account of y're laughin'." Learning what was possible filled me with awe. Weeks passed.

When the prevailing wind changed to the northeast, Granny said it was time to move our studies outside. She taught me how to forage wild plants that taste their best in spring, so we picked and ate brooklime and watercress, chickweed and goosegrass, nettle shoots, the first leaves of the cuckoo flower and the sow thistle. I hadn't eaten such things before. We gathered different plants at different times: by the light of the new or full moon, at midnight or at dawn, when the wind blew from the land to the sea or the sea to the land. Granny declared there was a perfect time for doing everything, and although the part of me that had been trained by Dr. Abernathy and Dr. Franklin could find no logic in her methods, my new self took in what she taught without quibble—after all,

Dr. Abernathy had taught me things I initially doubted but tried anyway, so why not take in Granny's lessons too?

Granny pointed out little signs of spring from day to day—a plant poking up new leaves, squirrels and birds building nests—and, slowly, the rhythms of the moor seeped into my heart.

Everything here was different from London. I awoke to sunlight and birdsong rather than to cart wheels over cobblestones. I ate eggs and goat cheese rather than whatever the doctor and I could scrounge at home or buy in smoky, noisy taverns. I spent my days fetching water or processing plants or exercising my mind rather than sterilizing instruments, winding bandages, analyzing cases, or dashing down the streets on emergency runs for the doctor. Instead of documenting physician calls in my book or recording recipes, I drew pictures of plants or wrote down my memories. The moor was peaceful. The moor let me think.

Summer came in buzzing and humming and fluttering. Green, growing things perfumed the air. Our winter patients had long gone, so Granny decided on a particularly fine day that we should muck out the barn so it was clean for whoever came in with summer injuries. We already had a raven in residence, who Granny suspected had eaten something bad, but he was on the mend. He watched us rake out the old straw, which Granny placed around our young cabbage plants. "Keeps 'em warm," she said. Then she turned her head to the south and said, "Lanyon?"

I heard the jingle of harness and saw Lanyon and Jasper topping the rise—with a passenger next to him in the cart.

"Margery!" I dropped my rake and ran. Margery jumped down almost before Jasper could stop, and we threw our arms around one another.

"Phew, Jem, what have you been about?" she said. "You smell like a barn."

"You smell like camphor," I said.

"Must be the elencampe I brought for Gran," she said, and we grinned at one another while Granny Kestrel caught up and Lanyon climbed down.

"What a nice surprise," Granny said. "Margery, I didn't look for you for another week."

Margery wrapped her arms around her grandmother. "I know, Gran, but it's already warm and close in London, and I wanted to be here with you two in the air! I wrote Lanyon to say I'd come early this year. Oh—and we've another surprise for you." She walked to the back of the cart. "Come on, you two, come and meet your granny." She reached into the cart and lifted out two small boys.

Granny's hand flew to her mouth. She blinked tears from her eyes. "Oh, Lanyon," she said in a husky voice, "can it be? How'd y' manage it with Elaine?"

"It weren't me, Ma, it were Margery," he said. "She gave Elaine a bottle of perfume John concocted special just for her, and some lace and other things from the city, and Elaine were *that* pleased. So when Margery asked if she could take the boys for the day, Elaine let her."

"So Elaine don't know you've brung 'em here?" Granny said.

Margery and Lanyon exchanged a look, and Margery said, "Well, no, but we didn't say we *wouldn't* come here. Besides, when we bring 'em back with rosy cheeks and filled up with fresh air, she won't mind so much."

"I doubt that," Granny said, but she knelt in the dirt and held out her hands. "Come boys, won't you come and meet your own granny?" The boys looked up at their father, who nodded, and they walked slowly to their grandmother.

Lanyon said, "Ma, the taller one is Alan, and the other is Kenan."

"Alan, how d' you do?" Granny said. "And Kenan, how d' you do? Would you like t' see a big raven? He's sick, but we're makin' him all better."

"Are you making him better with black magic?" Alan asked.

Granny glanced at Lanyon and said, "Not a bit. I'm makin' him better by feedin' him medicine and bein' nice t' him, just as your mother does when you're sick."

Alan looked at Kenan and said, "As long as there's no magic, I'd like t' see the raven. Can we, Da?"

"Aye, go with your granny. We'll unload the cart, Ma."

With a boy clinging to each hand, Granny walked to the barn. I heard her telling the story of the raven: "Why, the poor thing fell clean out o' the sky, he were that sick, so me an' Jem started in t' nurse him." They disappeared inside the barn.

Margery's eyes brimmed with tears but she smiled. "Oh, Uncle Lanyon," she said, "that there was worth every bit of trouble I had getting here, to see her hand-in-hand with Alan and Kenan." She wiped away her tears. "And, Jem, look at you! Why, you're a foot taller than you were last fall." I shook my head, but, honestly, hearing Margery's silly exaggerations after such a long time grew my heart big enough to fill my chest. I kept the door to my Sight closed, for just then I felt like flying, and there were plenty of birds about.

Margery put a hand on my shoulder and peered into my eyes. "You feel different, Jem," she said, "more…gathered in, like. It's good you came here." She pulled me in for another hug and whispered, "I've news to tell later, when it's just us." She let me go and started for the cart. "Shall we unload, Uncle? Let's you and I take the big chest and Jem can start on the rest?"

The smaller parcels contained food from town. "We'll open the chest later," Margery said when we finished, "but now let's go find Gran and the boys." We walked to the barnyard, where Snowy nuzzled oats from the boys' hands. "She likes it!" Kenan said.

"Oh, aye, oats is her favorite thing," Granny said. "She turns oats into milk."

Alan wiped his hand on his breeches. "How does she do that?"

"Cows an' goats an' sheep and so forth bear young and make milk inside," Granny answered. "Don't y' drink milk, Alan?" He shrugged. "Kenan, you?"

"I do, Granny." Kenan giggled as Snowy lipped his hands.

Lanyon said, "Alan, it ain't witchcraft for Grannys's goat t' make milk! 'Tis just the way of things on a farm. Why, Mrs. Rundle down from us milks a cow."

Alan moved closer to his father. "Witches keep animals t' do their bidding, Ma says."

"And I've said there ain't no witches," Lanyon said, "but there are folks that

God gives special skills to, so's he don't have to keep coming down all the time t' fix whatever's wrong."

"Perfectly sensible," Margery said, swooping in to pick up little Kenan. "I know two boys who have been very good the whole way out here, and I wonder if they might like to try making some bread and jam disappear?"

"Yes, Aunt Margery!" Kenan said, and so we went in and prepared the tea while Lanyon unhitched Jasper. Granny's hands wrapped around her mug like tree roots wrapped around a rock, and her eyes drank in the sight of her grandsons like seeing them was all she'd ever want again.

After tea, Lanyon said, "Come, boys, I promised you we'd look for frogs. Shall we go?" The boys leapt to their feet, crumbs tumbling from their shirts to the floor. Lanyon said quietly to his mother, "I'll make sure the boys don't hurt 'em, Ma."

"Let's all go, shall we?" Margery said, and so I put the dishes to soak and Granny grabbed up a basket for watercress. Lanyon and the boys hunted for frogs in the reeds of a little pond of still water the stream had carved out. Granny and Margery took off their shoes and stockings and hiked up their skirts and waded in to harvest cress. I wandered upstream, not looking for anything in particular, but feeling a pull in that direction. I stopped when I saw a pile of snow on the streambank. I walked closer and saw that it was a large bird, a pelican.

What are you doing here? I thought. *You're supposed to be near the sea, not in a wood.* The pelican watched me. When I took a step closer, it startled, and I noticed its wing hanging at an awkward angle. Was it broken? Could I carry the bird to the barn? Would it let me?

Then I thought, *Can I…love you?* Before I tried, I focused on Granny, imagined her hearing me, and sent a single word: *Come.* Then I sat down.

I'd imagined green hills for Giselle back home, so now I imagined sun sparkling on the sea and waves washing up on the beach and fishing boats and how the Earth looked from above. I'd seen all these things with my own eyes. I tried to think gently, for I remembered how the lions in the Tower of London had forced their pictures on me. I felt peace and calm in my heart, imagined it flowing out of my heart and along my arms and out the ends of my fingers and into my throat. "Hello," I said.

The pelican stretched its neck toward me. I kept the love flowing and kept the flying picture in my head, and the pelican took a step toward me.

But then my mind lurched. I felt myself sliding along the path I'd made between us, falling into the pelican as I'd fallen into the pigeon and Captain Foster. I tried to stop. I spun, tumbled, turned, saw myself tensed on the bank, eyes wide-open—a dizzying reflection of a reflection—the view changing, passing back and forth. The pelican's heart thumped faster and faster, my heart pounded, panic rushed like blood between us. We tried to fly, but moving stabbed a searing, agonizing pain along the path between us deep into my shoulder. Pushing against the pain increased it—I screamed, I grunted, I snapped my bill—we couldn't separate. My legs fired up to run; our shoulder burned. We struggled, felt terror sparking along the link between us.

Heard the snap of a twig.

Something warm soothed our pain. It eased between us and pushed us apart. I felt myself flowing back to my own body, felt the damp of the streambank through the seat of my pants. The pelican drew in its good wing and watched something downstream with its beak open, panting. I turned to look—at Granny Kestel walked toward us easy and slow. She sent the steady warmth that took our pain and eased us apart.

I focused on my breathing, waiting for my heartbeat to return to normal. When I felt calmer, Granny ebbed away from me and sent all of her healing into the pelican. I turned back to the bird but didn't reach for him again. Instead, I touched Granny. I tried to ride her lightly, for I wanted to learn what I should have done. She sent out a tendril of warmth rather than her whole self. This little golden strand followed the path I'd made, but soon flowed to the bird's chest, for it wasn't his wing that was broken. One of two bones that formed a solid strut between his shoulder and his keel had dislodged from its ledge on the keel, tearing ligaments and pressing on the pelican's heart.

Granny thought, *My touch is good.* She laid the lightest of hands on his back and twined round his ligaments and pulled his pain—into herself. How could she bear it? Then she pushed ever so gently on his chest and slid the displaced bone back onto its ledge.

Next Granny thought, *Come for healing. Come if you would fly again.*

The pelican gingerly folded both wings close to his body, closed his eyes, and waited.

"Gently now," said Granny, and she lifted that huge bird as though he were a bundle of sticks. Pelican are not small creatures. I'd seen them from the deck of the *Mary Ellen.* A pelican is as big as a turkey with a wingspread that could cover Giselle from nose to tail. I don't know how Granny lifted that bird so easily, but I suppose I shouldn't have been surprised to see her do it. I followed her back to the barn.

Margery and Lanyon had kept the boys back whilst Granny and I tended the pelican, but the boys had seen the big white bird in their Granny's arms. We settled the pelican into a small cage made of sticks to restrict his movement while he healed. Granny said, "'Tis up to him now." Outside the barn, the boys' high voices queried their father about Granny and the bird. We emerged and all headed for the cottage, where Margery already had tea brewed. Margery poured, and I sank to a bench, done in. The boys attached themselves to their grandmother.

"Can we pet the pelkin?" Kenan asked.

"No, love, he ain't got a bit o' sprall left in him," Granny said. "He fell fast asleep after me an' Jem wrapped his wing."

"Did he bite you?" Kenan asked.

"No, he was glad for the help," Granny said, "an' the longer he sleeps, the quicker he'll mend. Now, then, would you two like t' take home somethin' special from the moor?"

"What, Granny Kestrel?" Alan asked, and Granny Kestrel's eyes shone when he called her by her name for the first time.

"I've some pretty stones over in yon box, and you can each pick out one t' keep, would y' like that? Margery, fetch it down, please."

Alan bit his lip. "I hope the rocks ain't magic," he said. "Ma wouldn't like that."

"No, love, they's just rocks. Maybe they have some love in 'em, would that be all right with your ma, y' think?" Alan shook his head. "Just a plain rock for you, then, neither love nor magic inside, cross my heart." Margery dragged the boys to a patch of sunlight to look at Granny's rocks.

Granny and I sipped our tea and caught our breath. Lanyon said quietly, "Ma, they're bound t' tell Elaine what happened."

"Helping creatures is what I do, and Elaine knows that," said Granny. "Is it so bad for them two t' see their granny bein' kind to a wild creature?"

"No," he said. "But—"

"—'twill be all right, Lanyon," Granny said. "The boys've seen me for themselves, an' now they both know 'tis all right for 'em t' make their own judgments."

When it was time to go, Lanyon hitched Jasper to the cart. The boys wanted to see if the pelican was awake, but Granny said he would sleep for a long time, and would they give her a kiss goodbye instead? They did it, and Alan decided he wanted love in his rock after all, so Granny kissed the rock, and then Margery needed a kiss, and I needed my hand shaken, and so the Penhaligon men climbed into their cart later than they'd expected to, although the longer days meant they'd be home before dark. Granny and Margery and I helped the boys into the cart and loaded in a package of cheese and a basket of eggs.

"Tell Elaine I'll bring her back something lovely from the moor," Margery called. "I don't know what, but it'll be a nice surprise."

We waved until the little cart dropped out of sight, but this time Granny didn't droop when her loved ones disappeared.

CHAPTER 23

JUNE 1760

Of Love and Honey and Pelicans

Once back inside the cottage, however, we both drooped. Granny said we must "have a zog"—a nap. "We spent ourselves today and must get our strength back," Granny said. "Margery'll make a big dinner for us." I was glad to obey, for my body still thrummed. Before I went up to the loft, Granny laid her hand on my forehead and prayed a blessing. She said, "Y' never faltered when that pelican called, Jem, and y' stayed with him as long as y' could. I'm proud o' you. But y' need more trainin'. Y' must keep yourself separate from a creature's pain."

"Granny," I said, "what did you do with his pain? I felt you take it in."

"I put it in a box."

"Like the Blind Box?"

"No, it's a box"—she pointed to her head—"up here. I'll open the lid an' feel it a little at a time."

"*You're holding all that pain* now? But, Granny, it was awful."

"Well, Jem, 'twas a bad injury, though not a break, I'm glad t' say. Breaks're hard t' heal from, an' this pelican was on a long journey when he got blowed off course. Don't worry. His pain's not s' bad a little at a time. 'Tis bein' doused by pain all at once over an' over for a long time that's distressin'. That poor bird."

"How long before his pain is emptied out of your box?"

"Oh, 'twill be empty by solstice, for certain. I'll let some of it out now when I lie down."

"Can you teach me how to put pain in a box?"

"Later. You've a great deal t' learn before I teach you how t' go in for a healin'. Up you go to the loft, now, and rest. The first time y' go in on purpose is some drainin'.'"

Which was like saying the ocean has a few gallons of water in it. I'd been buffeted like a toy by the Tower lions and carried like a bit of fluff by the birds. I'd connected somewhat with Giselle, but we'd never truly melded. Today, putting my thoughts into my bloodstream and my speech, opening a channel from my deepest mind to my face and lips and throat, was different. Today the pelican and I had been like wax and wick, burning together to make one Light— only our shared pain had burned so fiercely that I still felt like I was flickering.

I must have slept, for when I opened my eyes, it was twilight. Margery shook my shoulder. She said, softly, "Better?"

"Yes. Thank you. I'm so hungry!"

"As I expected. I made a nice big dinner for you two. Come down and eat."

Granny and I bolted our fish, bread, and greens. After a bit, when my hunger eased, I said to Granny, "When I flew with the birds, I was inside their mind. Why did it feel different today with the pelican?"

"With the others, you didn't try t' go, so you wasn't trying t' hold back, y' just went all in. Today, you was tryin' t' do two different things, go in t' see the damage an' stay out t' fix it. 'Tis dangerous to hold nothin' back from a creature what's hurt."

"You sent in just a wisp of Sight. You felt warm."

"That's right."

"You saved us both."

"Margery, did y' tell her about the peregrine and the raven?"

Margery set down her fork. "Not yet, Granny."

"What raven?" I said. "The one in the barn?"

"No, Jem," Margery said. "The one that tried to take your food a year and a half ago. When you flew with the peregrine."

"The one that chased me back to the city? What about him?"

Granny's eyes gleamed. Margery held her breath. "That raven were me, Jem," Granny said. She clasped her hands together in her lap. *Impossible!*

"But we…you didn't even know me then. How did you know to come? Why did you chase me?"

"I chased you because y' wouldn't leave that bird. D' you recall peelin' away from the falcon? That were me, Jem, splittin' you two apart just like I split you away from the pelican today."

Stunned, I said, "But…how did you know I was flying with a falcon? How did you find us?"

Margery said, "Because of me, Jem. When the doctor and I were nursing you those three days, and I frantic we'd lose you, Granny felt it. She's always been able to sense when I'm stirred up because of my mark. Shall I clear away?"

"Mark?" I asked.

"Thank you, Margery," Granny said. "Jem shines, that's how I found her," Granny said. "I felt you comin' on the ship, Jem, before I even got Margery's letter sayin' you was on your way. When you got here, all unknowin' about anything and wearin' a Call but brimmin' over and fightin' with all your might t' keep your Light to yourself, well, I was glad t' get you inside my wards, I can tell you." Finished with her task, Margery returned to the table.

"Wards?" I said.

"Wards're marks I pray over," Granny said. "They protect whatever's inside 'em."

Margery said, "Please, Granny and Jem—I can't wait one more minute to show you what I've brought you from London!" Margery's chest contained tea, books, India ink, paper, quills, a mirror, brush, and comb set from the doctor, another bottle of her da's perfume, a bundle of copies of *The Chronicle*, and a length of lightweight tan wool. She laid out everything on the table, grinning happily as Granny and I exclaimed over our new riches.

"What's the cloth for?" I asked.

"The doctor thought you might be getting a mite threadbare," Margery said, "and we thought Brian's things might be too small now. So we thought 'twould be wise to make new clothes for you whilst I'm here. It's another reason I came early."

"There's quite of lot of fabric," I said.

Margery answered, "We-e-ll, yes, that's because the doctor sent enough in case you wanted a dress this time."

"Me? Why would he think that?"

"He—" Margery blushed. "That is—I, well, I thought p'raps you might be, er, growing a bit of a chest by now and might be thinking differently about wearing breeches."

"Not enough to want a dress," I said, "but I wouldn't mind a carrying bag with a strap that goes over my shoulder so my hands are free when we go out to gather our dinner. Could we make one of those?"

Before bed, whilst Margery told Granny about her other grandchildren in London, I settled near the hearth with my journal to record everything that had happened with the pelican. After today, I knew for certain that my emotions affected my Sight. That was why Granny insisted on my focusing before I tried to do anything. So, I focused on putting the entire event into words.

Linking with the pelican was the most honest connection I'd experienced with another living creature. Half the time, we humans don't mean what we say: "You look lovely," and "This won't hurt." But with animals, a person can't lie. They sense what you most deeply feel and think. They know what's under the masks we wear to fool other people. Animals have their own kind of Sight.

A dog's sense of smell is a wonder. In a footprint we don't even see, a dog knows what species of animal made the track, how big the animal is—even whether it's sick. A cat chasing a mouse puts human hunters to shame: she can hear mice dreaming in the walls. A horse might refuse to cross a bridge, despite the whip, and a minute later the bridge might tumble into the torrent—the horse felt danger in the air. Animals are netted to nature with cords of the strongest manila, while a mere handful of silk threads links normal humans to the natural world.

Some rare people know animals as they know us. Granny never said so, but

I believe she lived alone at the edge of the moor because when humans were cruel to animals, she felt it like a knife in her heart.

All these things I wrote down, much as I wanted to visit with Margery. I had to: more and more, writing helped me make sense of my Sight.

The next morning, I felt less spread out, though my vision was altered: the trees and animals and Granny herself looked the same as always straight on, but when I turned my head, out of the corner of my eye, their outlines glowed in different colors. This was not unpleasant, but it was strange. Margery got our breakfast while Granny and I looked after our birds, the goat, and Granny's chickens. Granny said, "They feel y' comin', Jem, now your door's open. But you've got more'n they can hold. Block it a bit. Margery says you know how." She opened the barn door then, shining daylight on animals so glad the day had broken that I felt their joy like I felt the sun on my hair and the Earth under my feet.

With Margery, we had a third voice to join our conversation, a third mind concocting opinions and observations and jokes, a third set of hands to help with the chores. In the evenings, we three sat by the fire, which we lit mostly for the light. We'd light Elowen's candles too, as Granny Kestrel liked to knit and Margery and I were sewing new breeches for me. As I have said many a time, sewing is not my strong suit. Still, I preferred the torture of a needle to any joy I might have had outside of Margery's company.

"Jem, I've something to tell you," Margery said one evening.

"Ouch!" I said, sticking my finger in my mouth.

"Did you stick yourself again?" Margery asked.

"I po' m'sel' alla tine," I said around my finger.

"You'll get the hang of it," Margery said. She dropped her sewing to her lap. "Jem, I've something to tell you about the doctor. It's good," she said when she saw my face. "Well, I-I guess I shall just out and say it: the doctor and I have been keeping company these last months."

About time, I thought.

Margery said, "It started when Mrs. Pierce wouldn't clean his tools. He wrote that to you. So I told him to bring them by and we could clean them together at the shop. Vinegar is nothing to me compared to all the other smelly things I work with. So he did. We got it done in a trice. He's started coming by at the end of every day."

"Has he?" I said, surprised. If Dr. Abernathy made a point of going to Aldersgate every day, he most definitely thought a great deal of Margery.

"Aye, and one day, he said, all serious—you know how he gets—'Mrs. Jamison, I hope it's not too short notice, but I have tickets to a comic opera at Covent Garden for a week from today, and I wonder if you would care to go?' Well, after I picked up my jaw from the floor, I said I should love to go. You know me and plays, Jem."

"What play was it?"

"It was called *A Jovial Crew, or the Merry Beggars*. It was all about four rich young people who decide to try the life of a beggar, all in disguise, of course. It was rather a silly play, but the music was nice.

"I thought that would be the end of it, but when Vauxhall Gardens opened in May, he had us rowed across the river one evening. Oh, Jem, the flowers smelled divine! And there was music, and ladies and gentlemen strolling about in silks of every color. John gave an order for a light supper when we arrived, and when we sat at a table to dine, somebody blew a whistle—and lamp lighters came from every corner with lit cotton-wool fuses. But somehow all the lamps were linked, so the flame sparked from one lamp to another. Thousands of lamps throughout the gardens turned on, it seemed, in an instant!"

"I'd like t' see that," Granny said.

"It was astonishing," Margery said. "We strolled after dinner and saw huge paintings and an orchestra raised up on a stage above our heads, and there were strolling musicians, and we sang songs." Her eyes glowed, remembering. "Later on, men and women sneaked off into the bushes, and Dr. Abernathy said he didn't believe they were inspecting the foliage." Granny barked and Margery blushed. Margery finished, "So we went home. But we've been seeing one another quite a bit outside of a basin of vinegar. He's—he's quite an interesting person."

"Indeed," I said. I waited for more, but Margery let her hands fall to her lap.

"We get on well." Margery sighed. "I thought you'd like to know. That's all." She picked up her sewing and bent to it, but then tossed it to the table. I blinked. "No, that's not all. Jem, I can't see how you've tolerated the man so long. He drives me mad!" She stood up and paced to the door.

"B-but you just said you got on well," I said.

Margery spun back to the table. "We do, but he's the perfect gentleman!"

"That is a terrible thing in a man," Granny Kestrel said. I giggled.

"Please, you two." Margery thumped herself back down on the bench. "What I mean is sometimes a girl wants a kiss, is all."

"Margery!" I said.

She blushed. "I think of him all day long," she said. "I mark the hours until he comes in the evening. I've even grown to like the smell of vinegar because it reminds me of him." My eyebrows went up. "All right, I still don't like vinegar. But you know what I mean."

"Why, Margery Penhaligon Jamison—y're in love with him, Granny said.

Margery's head spun to face Granny, her mouth a perfect *O* and her eyes so wide open the white showed all around. "Goodness gracious, Granny," Margery said. Then she looked at me. "Oh, my stars—it's true. I do love him. I love John Abernathy. Oh."

"That's wonderful," I said. "He's sour and you're sweet. It's perfect."

"But I—really, Jem?" Margery said. "You think so?"

"I really do."

"But what if he doesn't love me?"

"Well, it's been a long time since my man come walkin' off the moor," Granny said, "but I'm thinkin' things ain't changed so much. A man wants a warm heart. A steady hand. Kindness. A good mind. So, Margery, just keep bein' yourself, and he'll come around." She pursed her lips. "I *could* make a love charm, if you like."

"A charm like in a story?" I said.

Granny shrugged. "Just herbs tied together with a prayer."

"I've a pot of lavender in the shop already," Margery said.

"Try ginger," Granny said. "And, er, maybe add a sprinkle of horse-heal when the two of you have tea."

Margery's face shone like glory, and she reminded me of a big, cheery pot of flowers. I let myself imagine a happy, new life in London with the three of us living together in the same house. If only Granny could come back with me. Then everything would be perfect.

CHAPTER 24

JUNE 1760

Doors and Doorknobs

The morning before the summer solstice, Margery asked, "Granny, does Jem have a mark yet?"

"Not yet."

"You said something before about a mark. What is it?" I asked Margery.

"Well, you poke holes in a shape on your skin and put ink in the holes, and it makes a mark that don't wash off that shows you belong to the Light."

"Are you talking about marks like natives wear?" I said. I'd seen pictures in *The Chronicle* of native men inked from head to toe. "Why would I want a mark?"

"Once y' wake up, the Dark finds you easier," Granny said. "Some with Sight don't have a mark, like Tom Ennis, the barkeep. That's why I have t' keep after him. You don't need a mark, but it's sort of ward that protects you. It braces up your link to the Light, like you touchin' your Mum's cameo brung her closer. For some, it warms when somebody with Sight is nearby." She put fresh leaves in the teapot. "I've a mark. Margery has one."

"Margery, what's yours?" I said.

"Only a tiny little daisy, Jem, you can hardly see it. 'Tis on my rib, just here."

Rivers of Light and talking to pelicans and love charms—and now inked marks. My altered perspective was certainly bringing new things into my life.

"Where's your mark, Granny?" I asked.

Granny lifted the hair at the nape of her neck. "See the wavy line, just at the hairline? It's s'posed t' be the Fowey. When I were a girl, my grandmother marked me. She said it'd keep me safe but wouldn't cause no trouble t' me in town because my hair would hide it."

"Why would a mark cause trouble in town?" I asked.

Granny said, "Elaine an' her family ain't the only ones afraid of witches. It used t' be any mark on a body was proof o' witchcraft, even a mole or a scar." She saw my frown and said, "Jem, I've said we ain't witches. My granny was what we are: a person with Second Sight."

"Your mother had Sight too."

Granny nodded. "Aye. Blood passes it along."

"I got it from my mother, then?"

"And maybe your father too. Connolly is one o' the four tribes of Tara, descended from kings. 'Tis said Second Sight kept 'em on the throne 'til one of 'em turned Dark." *Da had Sight, then*, I marveled. *That's why I always knew where to find him.*

When I thought about coming home with a permanent mark on my body, though, I said, "Margery, I don't think the doctor would like me to be marked."

"I think the doctor would like anything that keeps you safe," Margery said.

"Jem, like ever'thing else, it's your choice," Granny said. "But now y're Awake, an' newly so. Y' need help t' keep back those that would steal your Light."

"The ones who serve the Dark. Who would suck me dry." She nodded. "You told me before if that happened, it might kill me, but if I had a mark it couldn't? If I had a mark and that happened, could I...find the Light again?"

"I never seen anybody sucked dry," Granny said, "but it seems t' me once a candle's burnt up, it's done, aye?" Margery pressed her lips together. "But I can't say. The ones who steal Light was called *magi* in the old days," Granny said, "or witches, I s'pose, or wizards, but the names don't matter. The names're wrong anyways."

"And a mark protects you from someone like that?"

Granny said, "They can still steal your Light, but y' won't die from it."

"Does getting a mark hurt?"

Granny said, "O' course, it hurts! It's a needle! Do you want t' think about it?"

Yes. "No. If you think I need a mark, I want one."

"I'm like you," Granny said, "better water under the bridge than worry about a flood."

"I'll get the willow bark," Margery said.

"Make it strong. Where d' you want it, Jem?"

Someplace I can easily touch. "Right hip," I answered.

"What picture?"

"A pelican," I decided. "I'll draw one, shall I?" I got paper and pen and drew the outline, scarcely an inch wide, of a pelican with his beak open and wings spread. Whilst I drew, Margery set the willow bark to steep. She sterilized a long needle in a candle flame. Granny heated some India ink and dropped in comfrey, and then she pricked her finger and added a drop of blood.

"Wait, Granny," I said, appalled. "Why did you put blood in the ink?"

"T' help you when we're parted." She looked up from the bowl. "Don't y' want it?"

"Blood? No! It's ghoulish."

"Christ shed his blood for all the world."

"He shed it. He didn't ask his disciples to wear it."

Margery said, "Jem, the blood bolsters your bond with Granny—remember, 'like seeks like.' Remember how Granny flew with the raven to save you from the peregrine? Part of why she knew to come is that her blood is in my mark." Margery paused. "Usually only family offers blood."

"You don't have t' take it, Jem," Granny said, "But I'd surely like t' give you the bond."

It was touching, the way they spoke of offering blood as a kindness, though the idea of being marked with blood still made me uneasy. Except...at one time the doctor's dissections in the cellar had seemed gruesome too, but now I understand the human body because I'd learned it at his side. Everything Granny had said to this point had turned out to be true. So I stopped arguing.

"Do it," I said, and steeled myself.

Margery shaved my bare hip so not even the finest hair could hinder the marking, and then she wiped the area with a cloth dipped in whiskey. Granny dipped the needle into India ink and stuck it into my hip. "Ow!" I said. "How long will this take?"

"Two hours if y' wiggle, one hour if y' don't," Granny said.

It took all morning. Granny poked and daubed, poked and daubed. When the mark was done, Granny smeared on a layer of honey and wrapped it, and I pulled up my breeches and drank down the dregs of the pot of willow bark tea. My hip *hurt.* "The healin' takes a while," Granny said. "Keep it clean. Keep honey on it. When the redness goes down, it's healin', and when it shows proud-flesh that starts t' peel off, it's done."

"I'll toss this rag in the fire," I said.

"No, leave it," Granny said, putting it in her Blind Box. "It's got your blood on it. I'll take care of it later." For the rest of the day, Granny had me making cheese. As I stirred thistle rennet into goat's milk over the fire, I had time to mull over having put a permanent mark on my hip. What if someone saw it? Well, if someone did, that would mean we were on an altogether different footing, which was unlikely to happen any time soon, although Margery seemed so happy about the doctor I wondered if I'd been over-hasty in rejecting marriage.

The morning of solstice, we took care of the animals and packed our basket and made Granny's soup, but my hip was red and tender. I felt over-warm. Margery made a cool compress of the calendula we'd harvested and said to Granny, "I don't like the look of this. P'raps Jem and I should stay here." Granny came over to examine it.

"No, Margery, go," I said. "I'll lie down with a compress while you're gone— and I can have breakfast all ready when you come back."

"Are you certain?" Margery said. "I'd hoped to celebrate solstice with you."

"Margery, let her rest," Granny said. "We'll know now if she needs us."

So that's what they did. Margery changed out my compress before we went to sleep. She said in my ear just before they left the cottage, "I made fresh willow bark tea, Jem. It's on the table. Drink a cup if the hip starts to pain you. We'll be back at sunrise."

"Mm," I said and went back to sleep.

I awoke some time later. *Why is it cold?* I thought. *It's June.* I opened my eyes. I couldn't see firelight reflected on the ceiling. I put out my hand; I couldn't see that either. *The fire's gone out.* I felt my way to the ladder and descended, still fumbling in total blackness.

My hip burned. I pressed my hand to it, and suddenly saw the outlines of Granny's furniture and fireplace. The fire was not out, but it wanted feeding. I limped over to toss on a turve, but when I lifted my hand from my hip to pick up a turve, total darkness fell like a blanket over my head. *What on earth?*

The black must be another bad dream. I hadn't had one since we'd cleansed Mum's cameo, but I remembered how I usually got out of a bad dream: I woke up.

I put my hand on my hip so I could see to add a turve to the fire. *I'll make breakfast and have a bite*, I thought. I dumped oats and water in a pot and placed it on the fire. I sat close, shivering and wondering whether I'd caught a fever from having the mark done.

The fire warmed me. It chased back the shadows. I reached for the teapot to pour Margery's willow bark tea into my mug—and saw something dark behind the loft ladder where we'd stowed Margery's chest. The fire played off everything in that part of the cottage except the black thing that sat on the lid of the chest. Was it a trick of the light? Of the fever? "What *is* that?" I murmured.

When I spoke, the black thing boiled bigger with a *whoosh* like a gust of storm wind pushing through a window just before you shut it against the rain. But there was no wind, no storm blowing in; the night was fair. *Maybe the black thing is something Granny left behind to guard me.* Except it didn't feel like Granny. It felt cold-hot, like gripping a handful of snow. It felt wrong.

"Go away," I said. I'd meant to shout, but I hardly made a sound. But as soon my voice sounded, the black cloud made a noise like a roomful of people sifting gravel and muttering. The cloud swelled until it filled Granny's tiny kitchen under the loft.

Then a black tongue of the stuff slid along the floor toward me like spilled water. I watched it spread in my direction. "Stop!" I said—and the pool of black shot straight to me.

I jumped up on the bench. The black spurted up, and before I could jump down, it flowed up my leg and side and twisted round my arm like a shiny glove. I couldn't brush it off.

It squeezed *under* my skin. It burned. In the firelight, my veins showed black and pulsing. Like a leech, the black sucked—life, it felt like—from me and sent it down the tarry tongue to the black thing that had filled Granny's kitchen. The thing boiled bigger.

I screamed. I teetered on the bench and fell on my hip. The tongue broke off and reared above me like a bear. I backed to the door, felt for the handle with my good hand, and pushed it open. I ran toward the tor. In my heart I called *Granny!*

Through the night I ran, every lunge scraping my bandage across the little pelican on my hip. Once, I stumbled and fell and knocked the air out of me. I lay gasping. I glanced behind me and saw a hole in the sky where there was nothing—no stars, no cottage, no moon, only something like the black opening of a cave blotting out all the world and bearing down on me.

I heaved myself to my feet and ran toward the tor again, exhausted and breathing hard like I was trying to run on smooth ice. A distant light had to be the solstice fire flickering between the standing stones. Suddenly, I ran into something soft that stumbled back. I fell into softness and soothing hands. A voice cried, "I have her. Circle! Sing!"

Margery. It's Margery. She held me close. Elowen and Dolly and Granny took hands and faced out and started humming. I tried to breathe. Margery prayed over me, "Heavenly Father, protect us. Mother, preserve us." The sound of her prayers sliced through the roaring in my ears. My left arm, the one the black cloud had suckled, hung at my side like a piece of wood. I couldn't wrap it round Margery.

Granny and Elowen and Dolly sang to the night in one voice:

> Bar this Sending from our Sight
> Back to Darkness—Rise, O Light!
> Do not let it plague this place
> Do not let it see this face.

Again I heard wind, like a cyclone this time, like a fall of rock.

The great river of Light flooded into me. Silver drops from the waterfall danced to my wooden elbow and trickled to my wooden hand like tiny beads.

The humming stopped. Each of my friends had a hand on me. The sky lightened, the black was gone, and my arm tingled back to life, all pins and needles.

Margery said, "Jem? Jem, are you all right?"

"I think so."

"Where did *that* come from, I'd like t' know?" Granny said. "How'd it get past my wards?"

"It was black as sin," Dolly said. "If you two hadn't been with me, I couldn't've stood against it."

"It was as Dark a Sending as I've ever felt," Elowen said. "It were a ravenin' lion, Kestrel."

"I know," Granny said. "Let's get Jem home."

"That's where that thing came from," I said. "From the cottage. It was in the kitchen."

"Impossible," Granny said. "Something's wrong at home, then." We started walking.

"Did you sing it gone?" I asked.

"We did," Granny said. "It weren't the song we were expectin' t' sing, but it did the job."

"Granny, I'm sorry," I mumbled. "Bad things find me everywhere I go."

"It ain't your fault," Granny said. "There's somethin' Dark that wants you real bad. This was a Sending."

"That black thing?" I asked.

Granny said, "It's like a Call, only the Caller don't come hisself. He uses his own blood t' open a door for the Dark."

"My arm tingles," I said.

"That's good," Elowen said, "for it was drainin' you. If it hurts now, well, that means y' got your arm back before—"

"And only a bit the worse for wear," Margery said.

"I would rather cut *off* my arm than see that black thing again," I said.

"Don't say that," Margery said. "If you feel that way, the Dark'll have won."

We reached the cottage as the sky turned pink. Dolly hurried to the fire to rescue the burned porridge. Elowen stood in the middle of the cottage, her hands out, slowly turning. She stopped when she faced the ladder. "That's where I first saw it," I told her, "behind the ladder above Margery's chest."

Elowen stepped to the chest. She said, "Margery, did y' bring something from town that wasn't yours?"

"Well, I gener'ly don't bring cloth, but I brought a big piece this time. What's left of it's in the chest. And I brought a cake to share out this morning for solstice. It was supposed to be a surprise."

"Are the cloth and the cake in the chest?" Elowen asked.

"Aye," Margery said, "I'll show you." She got up and fetched out the cloth.

Elowen said, "Dolly, help me," and the two of them ran their hands over every inch of fabric. When they got to the end, Dolly shook her head. Then they placed a cloth-wrapped bundle on the table, peeling back the layers to reveal a little round cake with a red marchpane flower on top. Elowen looked at it. Then she held her hands close to it as though she were warming her hands at a fire. Her face paled. She said, "This is it. This is how the Sending found her."

"My cake?" Margery squeaked. "But how? It never left me. It was the last thing I bought and packed before I hired a cart to take me to the docks. 'Tis impossible anybody tampered with it."

"Where'd y' buy the cake?" Granny asked.

"Why, across the street at the confectioner that's been there forever—Jem, you know the place." Margery turned to Elowen. "Are you sure it's the cake?"

"'Tis this flower on top," Elowen said. "'Tis made with blood."

"No," Dolly breathed.

Granny reached out a finger to touch the flower. Her mouth turned down. "Burn it."

"We need alder," Elowen said.

"I don't want it in here," Granny said. "Can you bring it, El? Dolly, fetch a basket to gather alder. We'll burn the cake beside the stream. Margery, stay here with Jem."

Dolly grabbed a basket, Granny grabbed a brand from the fire, and Elowen carried the cake as though it were a keg of gunpowder. The three of them, lit by the flame at the end of Granny's stick, drifted into the woods toward the alder grove. When they were gone, Margery set the table and put on water for tea. She scraped the porridge that wasn't burnt into five bowls and poured water over the burnt porridge in the bottom of the pot to soak. She sliced bread and said, "Can y' make toast, Jem?" and so I speared a slice of bread and held it close to the fire. "I s'pose I'd best go milk Snowy," she said.

Hadn't Granny said Margery was to stay with me? But my friends had banished the Sending with their songs and prayers. I knew I should be safe, but it still seemed like it took ages for Margery to do the milking. I kept one eye on the ladder to the loft all the while I made the toast. She still wasn't back by the time I finished, so I made the tea.

When Margery finally came back with a bucket of milk, she said, "Jem, I've thought and thought, and I can't work out when anybody could have got into my chest. I'm sorry, so, so very sorry I brought this trouble to you." She sank down beside me, all worn out and hunched over, and it was *my* turn to provide comfort.

"You didn't know," I said. "If I'd bought you a cake, I wouldn't have known either. And Granny didn't See anything wrong in the chest. Here, let me pour you some tea." Voices outside announced the return of Granny and Elowen and Dolly. They came in smelling faintly of burned sugar. We all sat down to nibble our smoky porridge.

"I don't understand it," Margery said. "I bought that cake off a man I've known for twenty years and not one *hint* he was Dark."

"Maybe he ain't," Granny said. "Is there somebody else who could've tampered with the cake?"

"The confectioner's got a new 'prentice that started the middle of November, but he doesn't seem like someone who—" Margery dropped her spoon into her bowl, and her face turned white. "Oh. Oh my. Oh, Jem, I'm a fool. The 'prentice wears a cap, but the hair on the back of his neck is red. Your Freddie Payne was a redhead, and he had redheaded brothers besides." She sank her head in her hands. "I wondered why the 'prentice ran in back whenever I came in. I thought he might be a thick relative the confectioner's was helping to get a leg up."

"You think the 'prentice is working for Patch?" I said.

"I'd lay money on it," Margery said. "I should have noticed him straightaway. Oh, I've been so selfish to be thinking about the doctor all the time. I shouldn't have been so careless." Her eyes filled with tears.

"Margery, there's not a selfish bone in your body," I said. "You aren't the problem. The problem is Patch." I'd felt more than one emotion in the last twenty-four hours, but the one that roared in when I saw Margery crying was anger. This hunt for me had gone too far. It had driven me away from home and upset Margery and now had shoved into Granny's life. *Enough!*

Elowen said, "I s'pose Margery asked the confectioner to keep an eye on her place"—Margery nodded—"so when the 'prentice knew Margery was going away, he told his true master, the one y' call Patch. Why, he likely danced a jig when he learned that Margery ordered up a cake with marchpane."

"And Patch made the flower for the top," Granny said.

"I sent you all this way to get away from him, and now he's found you anyway," Margery wailed.

"It's not your fault!" I said. And then I stiffened: *What if Margery marries the doctor, and the Dark finds me at his house? How could I protect them, all by myself?*

Granny said, "All the same, Jem, I think y' should go home with Elowen and Dolly, just for a few days. Me and Margery'll stand guard here. See if the Dark comes back. I don't think it will, for we've sung it away and its doorknob is burnt. But it don't hurt t' be cautious."

"What if it follows me?" I asked.

"It can't," Elowen said. "The door opens only where the knob is, and the knob's burnt in alder. 'Tis possible the Sending showed whoever made the flower the inside o' Kestrel's cottage, but the moor's a big place and there's many a cottage on it."

"So I could be on a moor in Scotland or Wales or China," I said. "Patch and his Sending might never find me here again," I said. "Must I really go?"

"I want you t' go, Jem," Granny said, "better t' be safe than sorry. It took all four of us t' drive away that Sending last night. If it does come back, I want you gone." I opened my mouth, but she said, "I ain't sure I can fight it off alone, Jem, and you're new to all o' this. And your mark's not even healed enough t' help you focus an' help me. But if I set a few extra wards, 'twill be enough, I think."

"We'd be glad t' have you," Elowen said.

"I'll be taking off honey soon, and you can meet my bees!" Dolly said.

"Please go, Jem," Margery said, "I couldn't bear it if something else happened to you because of me."

Margery's appeal decided me. After breakfast, I hauled my swollen hip and prickly arm and angry heart to Dolly's and Elowen's little home across the moor.

* * *

Neither Elowen nor I talked much on our walk to their cottage, but Dolly went on and on about her bees. "The little ones are workers—those are the girls—and the big ones are drones. Boys. There's one very large bee that a silly traveling player said is the emperor of the hive, but I know the big one is a queen."

"I've a book about bees you would like very much, Dolly," I said. "How did you know the big bee is a girl?"

"She told me so."

Of course she did, I thought. After a while, I confess, I began to respond, whenever she stopped talking, with "My goodness" or "That's interesting," until she said, "Jem, I asked Elowen if we'd have you sleep in the barn or with one of us."

"Sorry, Dolly," I said, "My mind is a bit woolly today."

"With a fresh mark not healed and Light sucked out of you by a Sending, I'm not surprised," Elowen said.

They put me in Dolly's bed, and she and Elowen slept together. In the morning, Dolly asked me to help her clean all her mead barrels. Then she took me out to meet her bees, which were in their summer glory harvesting nectar and storing it up for the long winter. The bees landed on Dolly, humming their love for her. Dolly had given me a funny hat to wear with fine silk cloth tacked all round the brim, and she'd said, "The hat's because I told 'em not to sting you, but some of 'em might forget."

I wished I could Send the whole hive after Patch in London.

Dolly and I carried the buckets of honeycomb back to the cottage to strain out the honey and set the combs aside for later. We added water to the honey in Dolly's big kettle, and then boiled and skimmed and strained all day. Adding raisins meant mashing and juicing and pulping, then more cooking and straining, before it all went into a clean barrel and Dolly covered the opening in the cask with cloth. "We'll take off the cloth and stop it up before Michelmas and let it sit for a year," Dolly said. "Won't it be jolly to drink your own mead, Jem?"

"Yes," I said, forcing a smile, because if I were beside a fire inside the Trippet Stones a year from now drinking this mead, I wouldn't have gone home with Margery a few days from now.

After the honey harvest and mead-making, Elowen had enough wax to make candles, which she could sell in Liskeard. I decided I might as well learn that too, but whilst we were putting the beeswax combs into a pot, Elowen said, "Oh, look, there's Kestrel's crow. Dolly, fetch a crust of bread."

"Granny doesn't keep a crow," I said.

"He comes when she needs to send a message," Elowen said. When the crow landed, Elowen offered the crust. The crow hopped over and let Elowen remove a white strip of cloth from his leg, then he launched himself into a tree to enjoy his reward.

"That's a message from Granny?" I said. "I thought you might take the message directly from the crow's brain."

"That would be a feat," Elowen said, opening the white strip of cloth. "It says 'Margery London 3 days. Dark gone. Come home.' Margery must have written this."

"Granny just uses colors," Dolly explained. "Green means 'come for fun' with a number telling us how many days until we should come. Blue means 'help' and we go over to do something she can't do by herself. Red means somebody's hurt and she needs us to help her pray. If the red has an *X*, it means *she's* hurt so we go without delay." She added, "We haven't got a red *X* in years. Don't worry."

"This message means I can go back to Granny's right now?" I asked. *Before Margery goes home!*

Dolly checked the angle of the sun and said, "It'll be dark before you get there."

"She's right," Elowen said, "and I'd like to send some honey and beeswax candles for Margery to take back to London. Go in the morning."

"Can you get them together now, please? I'd like to leave straightaway."

Elowen and Dolly looked at one another. *That was unforgivably rude, Jem Connolly*, I thought. "Forgive me," I said, "you two have been most gracious. It's just that Margery is leaving two days after tomorrow, and I may be going home with her. I need to say goodbye to Granny and pack."

Elowen said, "Don't fret, we understand. I don't s'pose you'll meet any robbers out on the moor."

Dolly said, "But, El, what if she runs into a bear?"

"There hasn't been a bear on the moor in a hundred years," Elowen said.

"What if she meets a piskie?"

"She'll wear her coat inside-out so they can't lead her astray."

"I'll be fine," I said. "Truly. I'm not afraid."

"No. You're not faint-hearted," Elowen said, "and that's half the battle anyway." They put their gifts in a basket, and I hugged them both.

"Thank you, Dolly and El." I swallowed. "I don't know if I shall see you again."

"P'raps not," Elowen said, "but we've stood t'gether in the Light, so we'll always be in your heart." I started walking back to Granny's cottage in late afternoon (wearing my coat inside-out), and I was still walking after the sun set.

The moon ducked in and out of clouds, making it darker than I'd expected. My nerves began to play tricks on my eyes; I would see out of the corner of my eye a shadow creeping close and spin to face it, only to find—nothing at all. By and by, I saw a tiny light bobbing in the distance and recognized the gait of the walker—it was Granny herself coming to meet me. I ran. I hugged her, hard, smelling herbs and wool and peat-smoke. "My, y're a sight for sore eyes!" she said. "Margery's been worried."

"I'm so glad to see you," I said. "We got your message." She picked up her lantern.

We started walking, the shadows no longer looming and the night no longer as great a concern to me as the answer to the question that had been on my mind the whole time we were apart. "Granny, do you think I'm ready to go home with Margery?"

We squished a few more steps while she pondered, then she said, "'Tis your choice, Jem, but we don't know if the confectioner's 'prentice still lurks across from Margery's shop. And I ain't sure—now, think it through before y' answer—I ain't sure y're ready t' live with Sight on your own just yet." *Had she read my mind?* "What d' you think?," she continued. "Could y' face down the Dark all alone? Could y' shutter your Light without thinkin' about it, like blinkin' your eyes? Like this?" She shuttered the lantern abruptly. The night loomed large around us. I desperately wanted to say yes, but—

"Not yet," I said.

She opened the lantern. "That's what I thought as well. You've more t' learn from me and Elowen and Dolly, I think. And y' just got your mark. Y' must learn t' use that too. None of it's easy or quick, but it might ease your mind t' hear that whilst you was gone, me and Margery made poppets t' fool Patch."

"Poppets? You mean little dolls? What…why?"

"Dolls, aye. We know the Dark is helpin' him, an' we know he uses magic. There's no magic stronger'n blood magic. When you got your mark, you bled some on a rag. While you was gone, me and Margery made three dolls smaller'n sparrows an' sewed a bit o' that rag inside each one. We cut up your old breeches and dressed the dolls, then Margery drew on your face and we prayed over 'em. Me and the raven flew t' Falmouth and hid a doll in the crow's nest of a big seagoin' ship. The next day, I turned loose the pelican with another one—"

"—I wanted to see him off!"

"'Tis better he left now," she grinned, "for he was on his way t' Africa. He'll leave the doll on a mountain he flies over near a desert down that way. Margery'll take the last doll when she goes an' hide it on her own ship."

"Are you saying Patch will think one of those dolls is me?"

"I'm sayin' if he should try t' Seek you, them three dolls might call to him. They might throw him off your scent, maybe long enough so's you could grow strong enough t' fend him off. Mind, though, spells don't last forever."

Relieved laughter bubbled. "So Patch might think I've gone to Africa?"

"Or Spain. Or India, maybe." I giggled, astonished, wondering what Franklin would make of *this*. What did *I* make of it? Blood magic sounded an awful lot like witchcraft, which Granny scoffed at—

Granny said, "'Tain't much, Jem, but add them dolls to your mark, an' my wards, an' how strong you are already. All y' need is time."

The rest of the way home, because Granny made me feel safe, I felt easier under the stars despite not fully understanding how the Sight worked, despite not quite having as much faith in Granny's dolls as she did, and despite knowing Margery would go home and I wouldn't. I told Granny about the bees and Dolly's mead. "We'll have toast and honey for supper," Granny said, "and tomorrow, we'll go to the Fowey where the salmon is runnin'. We won't take many, mind," she went on, "for they're goin' upriver t' raise a family."

Margery didn't cry when I told her after supper I felt I must stay with Granny a while longer, she just gathered me in for a cuddle and said to take all the time I needed.

The next day, we took a big net to the confluence of Granny's stream and the River Fowey and seined out some fat salmon to fillet and dry for the winter, which Granny did not like to do. But she harvested fish every year anyway so she could feed her patients over the winter.

I felt a great deal of sympathy for the big fish who could see where they wanted to go and smell where they wanted to go but couldn't get there, stopped by barriers they could not get around.

CHAPTER 25

JULY 1760 TO SEPTEMBER 1761

A Fledgling Gets Tumbled Out of Her Nest

On her last day, Margery took a long walk by herself. I'd asked to go along, but Granny bade me stay behind and wrap herbs for Margery to take home to the shop. When Margery was out of earshot, Granny said, "She goes out alone t' gather in birds and sky and moor, and she buries 'em deep in her heart t' last the whole year. 'Tis hard for a girl like Margery t' live in a city."

"Why doesn't she come here to live?"

"Her family's in London. Her man was there. Her business is there." She tucked another bundle into the chest and added, "But I think Margery ain't entirely sad t' be goin' home this year, for the biggest draw of all, now, is your doctor." She rolled a layer of fresh herbs in damp muslin. "Jem, I know y're disappointed not t' be goin' home with Margery. But I hope y' know I'm glad t' have you, and glad t' teach you. It won't be forever. I don't see you spendin' the rest of your life on the moor."

"Where do you see me?"

"America," she said. "That's where you belong."

It was the last thing I expected to hear. "America? Surely not. What about London?"

Granny said, "London's not for you. You're s'posed to cross the ocean. Your path is over there." She turned her face to the west window and closed her eyes. "There's love for you there. Danger. The Light's there for you, too. Y' must go to America, Jem."

I frowned. Just as when Mrs. Stevenson and the others decided I should be apprenticed, somebody other than me was deciding my destiny, or so it seemed.

Granny looked at me. "Y' don't want it?" I shook my head. "But I feel you there, Jem! Don't you feel it too? I See a line from you here t' you there. I feel y' bloomin' near a great lake, so great y' can't see the other side—maybe that lake we saw at solstice." She smiled. "I See you in the Light there, on that lake, with children of your own who'll have children too, and on and on in a line stretchin' from you t' the end of time." She opened her eyes and took my hand. "Oh, Jem, 'tis grand t' know my own Jem'll bring Light so far away and keep it burnin' for so long."

I said, "What if I don't go? What if I stay in England?"

"Stay?" She peered into my face, then closed her eyes. She seemed to be scenting the air like a hound trying to catch a whiff of the fox. She frowned and turned back to her herbs.

"What's wrong?" She began to wrap another bundle without answering.

"Granny, what did you see?"

"I saw nothing." She let her hands still. "When I followed your paths any-where but across the sea, they just stopped, some longish but some short."

"What does that mean?"

"I could be wrong," she mumbled. "'Tain't certain at all, none of it."

"*What does it mean?* Tell me. Please."

She sighed. "Sometimes not seein' a path means there ain't one," she said. "If y' don't go where you're s'posed t' go, your life could end with yourself. No love, no babies, no bloomin' in the New World. No Light, no Sight. You could wink out like a star, Jem. And it'd be a terrible waste, for you and for others down the years who won't have the Light t' guide them, because your babies' babies never brung Light into their lives."

We finished bundling the herbs in silence. I turned over Granny's prophecy.

I'd known from the moment I'd seen the Great Waterfall that the Light shimmered through everything that was alive, everything that was good. I knew that learning to properly use my Sight would take the rest of my life. I knew that accepting my destiny set me against the Dark and everything it touched.

Battling the Dark would be and must be a part of my destiny.

But surely my life could be more than a constant struggle against the Dark. Why couldn't I have medicine and science and a life in London with Margery and Dr. Abernathy? Why did living in the Light require that I go all the way to America, three thousand miles away from everybody and everything I loved?

I didn't tell Margery about America when I said goodbye to her the next morning, because saying goodbye was hard enough all by itself. Margery's doll was safely stowed in her valise, ready to pull out and hide when she boarded her ship. Once she'd climbed up and sat next to Lanyon, Margery said, "It's not forever, Jem. Learn all you can before winter, and write to me, and we'll try to get you home by your birthday in September."

* * *

But something completely unexpected happened to me as the days passed: the longer I stayed, the longer I wanted to stay.

I learned to link with animals without tumbling into them and exhausting myself trying to get out again. I made a pain box, but I didn't like putting an animal's hurt into it knowing I should have to feel it myself bit by bit, although it certainly made me more sympathetic to our patients. Granny and I worked outside and did our chores during the day and took turns reading aloud out of the bee book and my Burton and sometimes out of Granny's Bible in the evening after our work was done. (She liked the books of Proverbs and Psalms.) We played chess; once she learned, I mostly lost. Granny and I orbited one another. We became the kind of friends for whom a sigh and a smile convey a whole conversation.

So I wasn't ready to leave her by my birthday. I wasn't ready to go home in October when a letter came from Franklin whilst he was touring Wales. He asked if I thought we might resume our lessons before winter, but I wrote back, "No, sir, probably not" and told him about the latest additions to Granny's menagerie.

We had a letter from Margery saying that when she went to take out her doll, she found a stick wrapped up instead in one of Kenan's stockings. "The scamp swapped it out," Granny said. "Oh, my, I hope Elaine don't see it. I must tell Lanyon t' look for it. It shouldn't be in their house if Patch goes seekin' it." The doll didn't turn up. Granny said the dolls were a precaution not a guarantee, but she didn't like knowing my blood was on the loose somewhere, nor that Kenan might have hidden it in his own house. She told Lanyon he must find the little doll, and he promised to keep a lookout for it. When it didn't turn up, Granny sent me to Fowey to set wards of protection around Lanyon's house, warning me not to let Elaine catch me doing it. I said I wasn't certain I should be trusted with such an important task, but Granny said, "If not now, when, Jem? When the Dark comes after you all alone? Go and do it. Have faith." So I went, and I prayed, and Granny told me when I came home that I'd done well.

The more time I spent with Granny, the more I wanted. Ever since I'd lost Henry Galt, I'd been aware that every day with an older person I loved was precious. There would be so much time—years and years—I would never spend with Granny once I left her.

The weeks passed. Winter came. The first flakes of wet snow fell on the tor, and the water in the falls froze on the edges that ran close to the frosty land. Then, in a heartbeat it seemed, the buds on the trees swelled and burst into a fine green lace.

We got a letter from Margery in May that surprised me. And also didn't. She said she was not coming for solstice this year because, she wrote,

> *Dr. Abernathy and I are to be married in September,*
> *and I have ever so much to get done before then. The greatest*
> *gift we hope for is that you will come home and see us wed, as it*
> *is because of you that we are the happiest couple that ever lived.*
> *If you cannot come, we shall come out to you as soon as ever we*

may.

I doubted they'd come all the way to Cornwall *ever* given the way they both were kept so busy with their own affairs. Then—

"Granny!" I said, "Why don't we both go to London to see Margery married? You could see John and your other grandchildren! Wouldn't that be grand?"

"Who would milk Snowy? Who would care for any patients that might turn up?"

"Elowen and Dolly could milk and gather the eggs, and we haven't any patients now."

"Jem, I'd like t' go, for Margery's sake. I ain't seen my John since Margery were little, nor her two brothers, nor any of the others born after John moved to London. But I've no love for boats, nor no love for cities, neither," Granny said. "And what should I do in London? Bein' in a city muddles me. Too much hurry-skurry. No, I'd best stay here. But you'd never forgive yourself if y' didn't see our Margery wed to your doctor."

"I know," I said, but September was weeks away, so I made no plans to leave. Dr. Franklin and I continued to correspond, and eventually Granny began adding to my letters. Franklin enjoyed her postscripts. He said Granny's writing reminded him of Mrs. Franklin, who, I knew, also relied on creative spelling.

One evening about a fortnight before my third summer solstice on the moor, Granny sat knitting and I sat writing letters by the light of one of Elowen's candles. Margery's last letter had been full of her wedding—her dress, her flowers, the food—so I responded that it all sounded lovely and perfect and that I planned to attend. I wrote that I expected to stay home afterward, if that would be acceptable to the new tenant in Cavendish Square. It was as subtle a query as I could manage. I did fret about how I would fit in to this new life of theirs. Without a doubt, the doctor's house would be more jolly with Margery in it, and both of them would welcome me, but who and what would I be to them, exactly? Would I make their life…awkward, as someone they couldn't easily explain?

Whilst I wrote my second letter, this one to Dr. Franklin, a particularly
large moth fluttered in through the window of the cottage, and landed on the
table nearest the fire. Granny said, "Aye, warm your wings, my fine fellow, but
don't go no closer, not on your life." The moth opened his dusty black wings as
though to expose the greatest surface to the warmth of the fire, or perhaps to
show off the tan bands running along the top and bottom of a span nearly five
inches across. His red and black and tan abdomen throbbed below a furry black
thorax. When he bent his leg to rub the scales and spines of his abdomen, he
hissed like a tea kettle.

"What's his name?" I asked.

"I don't know. Ask Dr. Franklin." She crooned to the insect, "Go on, then,
and find a lady friend," and the moth flew away.

"Granny, did he hear you?"

"No, Jem, 'twas a coincidence, truly. He went where he was meant to go all
on his own." And she pottered over to her fire and stirred it up, her message to
me delivered whether or not she meant to send one: I, too, must go where I was
meant to go. But surely I didn't have to go yet.

Dr. Franklin's reply to my letter reminded me that he was a devotee of
insects along with all his other enthusiasms, which I should have guessed
when he sent the bee book along with me to Cornwall. Franklin was the best
of teachers: he encouraged with praise, corrected with humor, instructed with
humility and charm. Whenever Granny and I sent or got one of his letters, we
felt like members of an elite club with only three members. Dr. Franklin's insect
letter said,

> *Your observation of the moth, so carefully and thor-*
> *oughly recorded, suggests to me that it is a privet hawk moth,*
> *a native of England. In America, we also have a large moth.*
> *She is called the luna moth, for she comes out by the light of the*

moon.

Each of her wings is the size of a man's hand, and each wing has a tail like the tail of a kite. Her antennae are like tracings of frost on a window. She is all over a pale green, with eye spots on her wings. She is altogether a lovely creature, rare and beautiful. Perhaps she is an American cousin to the one you saw?

How much insects' lives intersect with ours! Consider the silkworm, the lac insect, the locust. Lowly insects all, but how they have changed man's fortunes! The silkworm enriches the East and clothes our ladies, the lac insect gives us shellac for our furniture and our violins, and locusts cause famine all over the world, sending untold thousands to their deaths before their time. Consider what is lost to humanity when one person starves to death, taking with him all his descendants, and all because of an insect!

"You've the right of it, Dr. Franklin." Granny said, "Yet you yourself're needed at home."

"Is he? How do you know? Did you See something?"

"No, but I can put two an' two t'gether. Mrs. Franklin's run his home an' business for four years now. Doin' ever'thing wears a body out."

"You do everything."

"Aye, but I've no people to fuss and fret about. People is what takes the toll. Me, I live on the moor because here is where I'm s'posed to be." She fixed her silver eyes on mine. I held Dr. Franklin's letter between us, like a shield I suppose, against what Granny had laid out in plain sight: it was time for me to go.

Still, I kept telling myself *one more day.*

I ended up tasting, after all, the mead I'd helped Dolly make the previous year. Summer bloomed and faded. The Holly King triumphed. The first of September came and went.

Granny hadn't mentioned my going back to London since we'd seen the privet hawk moth, and I'd let one day blend into the next without making any move to pack my things. But as we gathered lamb's ears, damp with dew, one morning when we woke and the air was cool, I said, "I wonder what Margery is doing right now."

"Likely she's sewin' her weddin' dress," Granny said. "I'm glad y' brought up Margery, Jem, for there's something I've been meanin' t' talk with you about."

I curled my fingers into my palm to warm them. "What is it?"

"I've enjoyed my time with you, p'raps more'n I had a right to. And p'raps I've encouraged you t' stay by not makin' y' go. But it's gettin' late. 'Tis time for you t' go home."

My heartbeat pulsed in my ears. When I could talk around the sudden sensation that my mouth had filled with sawdust, I said, "But I still have so much to learn."

"We learn as long as we live, I hope. Don't let that hold you back. Don't y' feel the pull across the water?"

I didn't. I'd spent nearly two years with Granny Kestrel learning to read the sky, learning to find and harvest herbs, learning to tend hurt creatures. I'd learned to channel my Sight without its burning me up. And still I felt like a first-year student in a dame school. I wasn't ready to leave.

"What's in America that's so important?"

She set down her gathering basket. She went to sit on a tree that looked to have fallen down before Eve ate the apple. Granny patted the space beside her, so I sat down too. A wren sang; a woodpecker hammered out his dinner; a squirrel scolded us from a tree. The September day's noontime warmth couldn't quite dispel the cool in the woods. Granny Kestrel took my hand.

"Jem, if I could tell what's in America, I would. I would tell you exactly where it is, chapter and verse. But the Sight don't work like that for me, not over time and distance. The kind of Seein' that's been on my heart for you these last weeks, well, 'tis not exact. Seein' the future is like a river takin' in a storm of rain: most of the water goes down the deepest valley followin' the best path; there's only a few places where it flows different. I See the direction you're s'posed t' go Jem, not why or where to. But I do know y' must ride the flood."

"How can I go? How can I leave you here alone?" I said. "It breaks my heart to think of you sitting here poking up the fire by yourself with nobody to talk to but the beasts in the barn."

"They're fine company," she said.

"But they're not the same as a person."

"Aye, that's true," she answered. "But there's a path each of us is meant t' walk, Jem, and we must walk it. Most people can't see where they're s'posed t' go. They stumble along blind. It's just pride t' be able t' see what others can't and close your eyes to it on purpose. And you tossed out your pride long ago, I think." She let go of my hand and stood. She said, "Y' must be in America before winter. See Margery marry your doctor, an' then get on a ship without delay."

And that was that.

So I wrote Margery I would be home the week before the wedding. It was a messy letter, dotted with blots and tears.

CHAPTER 26

SEPTEMBER 1761

A Welcome-home Robbery

The day before I was to begin my journey back to London, I placed a full bottle of ink atop a stack of paper on Granny's fireplace mantel and showed her how to make a quill pen—our last shared task. I soaked my best feather overnight, then stuck it in a pot full of sand I'd heated in the fire. When the sand cooled, the point of the quill had hardened, and I showed her what cuts to make and how to bend the tip to make an even split. When she joked, "Now, 'tis I who'll have t' start keepin' a journal," I forced myself to smile, because leaving her weighed on my heart.

When I carried my valise down the ladder, Granny handed me a small packet wrapped in linen and tied with twine. "'Tis for your birthday, Jem. 'Tis seed: wild pear, lady's mantle. Some other things y' might not find in the New World. They'll keep a long while. Take 'em along on the crossing. And when y' plant 'em there and they grow, they might remind you of your old friend Kestrel Penhaligon."

The lump in my throat choked me. This sage in a faded linen dress had more wisdom in her little finger than there was in all the fine gentlemen of the Royal Society, for they believed that research and evidence led to truth, but Granny knew "There are more things in heaven and earth than are dreamt of," as Hamlet says to Horatio. How could I leave her? How could I say goodbye to this loving, patient woman who'd helped me understand who I was and what I was meant to be?

Imagining myself never seeing her again was like a death. My eyes filled. "There will never be day in my life when I don't bless your name," I said. "You've given me the world. You've given me myself." She folded her arms around me.

"I didn't give nothin' you didn't already have. I just helped y' See it."

Our mutual devotion made a kind of humming all around us. Down in the barn, the goat baaed. In the woods, a woodpecker stopped drumming.

"They can hear us," Granny laughed. I stowed her packet of seeds safe at the bottom of my valise.

Besides the paper and ink, I gave her my bee book (which I asked her to share with Dolly), along with the Burton that had been my mother's. I had so little to give compared to what she'd given me. All I had left to give was the gold I'd brought with me so very long ago. Still, in the world of men, gold is useful. So I took out all but enough coins for my journey. I laid the gold in her palm. "It's only money," I said, "but you can buy what you need in Fowey or even Plymouth without having to wait for Margery or Lanyon to bring it. You can buy things for the animals." When I smiled, tears squeezed out of my eyes. "You can pay the postage when I write you a letter."

"An' I'll write back." She tucked the money in her pocket. "Thank you, Jem. I'll take it for them, then, and so's I can keep in touch."

We spent our last evening together talking quietly and watching the stars prick through the deep blue sky at twilight. We made a small fire between the cottage and Hawk's tor. We listened as the night creatures bestirred themselves, and we sent waves of peace toward them so our fire didn't alarm them.

The earth turned. Sparks from our fire drifted to heaven. The sky became a veil of black velvet sprinkled with diamonds. We saw shooting stars and made wishes, but I grieved that my most urgent wish wouldn't come true. We had peace. We had time. Until tomorrow.

* * *

It is a sweet thing to hear the birds greet the dawn, but on my last morning with Granny, their songs sounded mournful. After breakfast, Granny and I stepped outside. My valise stood beside the turf rick, but I didn't move to pick it up. Granny Kestrel said, "Y' must go, no lookin' back and no dawdlin'. Hide your mother's cameo under your cravat so nobody Dark gets hold of it. Go back t' London. Give my love to Margery an' her doctor, but don't stay. Your destiny's across the sea."

"In America. I know."

"Go there before winter. Be brave, my heart. Be strong and true. Remember the power of a loving heart." She pressed her lips to my forehead and, without another word, stepped into her cottage and shut the door. The abrupt action shocked me. Then I realized: *She did it to make it easier for me to go.*

And so I did.

I decided to walk to Plymouth rather than to Fowey, as the weather was pleasant and, to be honest, I had a great deal on my mind. Besides leaving Granny and going back to my old life, now I would be managing my Sight on my own. I needed practice. By the time I got to the path along the coast, I'd decided to practice shuttering and unshuttering my Sight. I sent it ahead, and only once did I step off the path to avoid somebody who felt sour. I booked passage in Plymouth on a ship bound for London, which landed just two days later, due to a favorable southwesterly in the channel. It's likely I'd have enjoyed the journey, maybe even seen dolphins again, if I hadn't been so downhearted about leaving Granny behind.

We docked below London Bridge on the nineteenth, two days after my birthday. More than half the ancient houses on the bridge had been removed, and I wondered where the pin- and needle-makers had got to, the ones who used to live and work there. Even the Great Stone Gate was being demolished. Now, Westminster Bridge would have to bear the traffic of London, indeed, of all the world—for, of course, all roads lead to London.

But as I walked west, I saw workers building another bridge at Blackfriars that looked to be as tall as the Tower of London. Granny might have liked seeing the new bridge, as it was a man-made miracle rather than the natural miracles she saw every day on the moor, although she wouldn't have liked all the rush and hurry of the city.

People swarmed like ants. Women carried buckets and baskets in their arms and on their heads or were followed by servants doing the carrying for them; men heaved lines on the wharf, pushed carts in the street, clutched leather satchels and folios. Everywhere was bustle and stink and coal smoke. London hadn't changed.

But I had. I'd gone to Cornwall to hide and come back not needing to. I'd left London not understanding my gift and had come back prizing it. My body had changed, too. My breasts had sprouted on the moor, so Granny showed me how to wrap them. I'd grown taller, so my breeches and coat were too small now. I looked like a ragamuffin.

Once I reached St. Paul's, I circled around the alleys to Margery's shadowed back step with its handful of shade-loving plants in pots. The big hogshead still sat beside the apothecary's back door, with a very big potted plant on top. I skipped up the step, reached for the knob, and took in air to sing out—and heard the doctor's voice saying, "Jem will be our daughter. Why, we're nearly her parents already. We've mothered her and fathered her more than her own parents had a chance to do. We've one more Sunday of having our banns read out, and that's tomorrow, and after that we marry. Why can't we introduce Jem as our own daughter immediately afterward?"

Daughter. I'd wondered how I would fit in to their new life as soon as I'd read Margery's letter announcing the marriage, but I hadn't considered this. *Daughter.* That they wanted me as their own thrilled, but surely they didn't want to turn me into a girl again? Possible: I already was two years past the age of consent. Margery had wanted to sew a dress for me, not another pair of breeches. It would be awkward for them if they adopted Jem and a year or two later trotted him out for dinner wearing a dress.

I can't be their daughter anyway, I thought, *I have to go to America.* I was fourteen years old, no longer a child, and I had to be gone before winter, Granny had said. I had to convince Margery and the doctor to let me go. I had to convince myself that leaving was the right thing to do.

I had to think.

Tucking my valise beside the hogshead, I crept quietly away from the door and headed toward the cathedral. I would step inside St. Paul's and pray for guidance.

It hadn't taken me long to revert to my city way of walking, which was to fix on my destination and let my inner compass guide me. I walked in the general direction of St. Paul's and pondered. I strode down Old Bailey, skirted a collision between two handcarts along Amen Corner, and passed Stationer's Hall in Ave Mary Lane. St. Paul's dome with its circling pigeons rose into the sky not two blocks away. I walked past booksellers and cloth merchants, then cut through an alley, kicking at rubbish. Suddenly a hand clapped over my mouth and another shoved my arm behind me in a painful grip that wrenched my shoulder.

I kicked back at my assailant. I felt my heel connect with a shin. "Aww!" he yelped. He pushed me face-first into a stone wall, and I just had time to turn my head to save my nose being broken. My attacker ground my cheek into the wall with a hand to the back of my head. Then I felt the point of a knife at the base of my skull. "Quiet! Hold still!" he said. "One quick shove right 'ere and y're done for." I stopped struggling. I'd heard that voice before. Where? "Oi wants that coin Oi 'ear jingling in y're pockets. Give it over."

I fumbled in my coat pocket for the coins. I handed them awkwardly behind me and felt them scooped out of my hand. I shook with anger, so upset I didn't even think of using my Sight to defend myself.

"Where's the rest of it?"

"That's all I have."

"This 'ere's not 'ardly enough to make it worth the breath t' rob you. Take off y're coat."

"It's my only coat!"

"Off." He ground my face into the stone to emphasize his request. A crack in the stone scraped skin off my cheekbone. I cried out and bit down on grit. The knifepoint slit my cravat, and it slipped to the ground. My mother's cameo fell with it. I struggled out of the coat, praying he wouldn't see the cameo.

"Wot's this?" he said. A hand picked up the cameo. If I hadn't feared the knife, I'd have turned and fought him for the cameo tooth and nail, because by now I'd recalled the voice: it belonged to Freddie Payne's younger brother, the one who'd inherited Freddie's begging spot at the confectioner's across from Margery's shop, the mean one who'd told me to bugger off when I'd tried to make friends. His blade pressed to my neck proved he'd gone from mean to dangerous. I dared not let on I knew his name.

"Give that back! That's mine!"

"Not no more, it ain't," he said. "Now turn y're face t' other way when Oi go. Oi promise, if y' take a look, it'll be yer last? Understand?"

"Yes." I turned my head toward the back wall of the alley. Tears burned my scraped face.

Then my assailant leaned in close, and his sour breath seeped into my nose like poison. He said, "Oi knows wot you are." My heart stopped. "Mind, now: move and Oi'll skewer ya." Footsteps dashed away.

Blood dripped down my face and neck. After a minute at most, I turned my head to look. The world of men rushed by at the head of the alley indifferent or oblivious to my trouble.

I darted to the street and looked both ways, but nobody was hurrying faster than anybody else. I lifted my hand to my cheek and pulled it away blobbed with red. My cheek burned. My neck bled where the knife had nicked me. But the very worst was I'd lost Mum's cameo, after all our trouble to cleanse it, after all I'd done to keep it safe.

I walked back to Margery's, tears running down my face. Passersby noticed my bloody face, but nobody offered to help me; in fact, more than one person crossed to the other side of the street. *Welcome home*, I thought.

My hand shook when I turned the knob of the shop's back door. This time, I spoke up: "Margery?"

Margery sang out from the front room, "Jem, is that you? We found your valise half an hour ago but—my stars! Dear heaven, whatever's happened? John!" she called, "Come quick! It's Jem. She's hurt!" She began to pat my body down. "Where else are you hurt?"

"Nowhere. Just my head."

Dr. Abernathy hurried in. When he saw the blood, his eyes became two bits of coal in a mound of snow. He barked, "Basin of warm water. Cloth. Skin salve, if you've got some fresh, the one we use on rashes." Margery scrambled to fetch the things.

The doctor sat me on the chair at Margery's table full of medicine-making tools. He examined the injuries. "Where are your clothes? What happened? Thank you, Margery." He began to gently bathe my cuts. The water smelled of cloves, calendula, and myrrh, all soothing herbs, but the warm water stung nevertheless.

I said, "I just got home. I was on my way back here. I came to the back door and put down my valise." I flinched.

"Sorry," said the doctor.

"Why didn't you come in?" Margery asked. The doctor rinsed the cloth and kept gently patting away the dirt. The herbs eased the pain as the water turned pink.

I said, "I heard the two of you talking about making me your daughter."

"Well, what of it?" Dr. Abernathy said.

"I went away to think about it. I don't think it's a good idea."

Margery took my hand. "Why ever not?" Her beautiful eyes sparkled with tears. *How can I go to America and leave her behind?* I thought.

The doctor said, "What nonsense! You already *are* our daughter, for all intents and purposes." *And how can I leave him?* The doctor continued, "Carry on. What happened next?"

"I left the valise to nip in for a quick prayer at St. Paul's. On my way, somebody grabbed me and shoved me into an alley and pushed my face into a stone wall. He held a knife to the back of my head and threatened to push it in if I didn't give him my money and my clothes."

"Dear God," Margery said. The doctor swabbed the back of my neck.

"I gave him my jacket and—Margery, he got Mum's cameo."

"So it's gone." Margery's eyes bored into mine. She knew what that meant.

"Did you recognize the fellow, Jem?" the doctor asked. "Could you point him out if you saw him again?"

"I didn't see his face. But the voice sounded like Freddie Payne's brother, Margery. The one you thought might be apprentice to the confectioner across the street."

"The 'prentice? No!" she said. "I've had my eye on him ever since I got back from Granny's. I'll run over and see if he's there." She flew out.

The doctor said, "Margery told me everything. Tilt your head back," he said. He mashed lamb's ears and placed them on my lacerations.

Margery dashed in. "The confectioner said the little red-headed beggar that works this street barged into his shop less than an hour ago and whispered something to the 'prentice, and the 'prentice tore off his apron and ran."

"How did they know I was back? I didn't come near the front of the shop," I said. Margery shook her head. She tossed the pink water out the back door. The doctor dried his hands, frowning. "The robber said something to me," I said.

"What?" Margery said, and in a move as natural as breathing, she placed a hand on the doctor's shoulder. He turned slightly toward her, attuned to her; they were a team, as perfect a match as ever was made. No matter what the future held for me, these two would face it together. The sight of them side by side showed me I needn't fret about going to the other wide of the world, at least not on their account. They strengthened one another. So now, the only obstacle between me and America was my own reluctance to leave them behind.

"Jem, what did he say?" the doctor asked.

"Just before the robber left, he leaned in and whispered 'I know what you are.' What do you think he meant? He knows I'm a girl? He knows my grandfather is the duke? He knows I have Sight?"

The doctor's black brows descended. Margery's lips pressed together. They looked at me and then at one another. Margery said, "If the 'prentice is Patch's man, Patch'll have told him there's money to be made if they catch you, and Patch may have bragged about who's paying out. The 'prentice's older brother knows you're a girl, and he might've said. Patch maybe found out you're a girl when he magicked my cake. I wouldn't think he'd tell the 'prentice you've got Sight, for that might scare the fool away."

Margery's rosy, cheerful face had gone white enough to show her freckles. The doctor's fingers drummed the table. More than anything, their worried faces made it clear as rain that I had only one choice. Only one thing would keep all of us safe.

Enough. It's time to end this. "I shall go away," I announced. "I shall go to America."

"Are you mad?" the doctor said. "That's far too drastic a solution."

"Granny Kestrel feels my destiny is there."

"She does?" Margery said.

The doctor frowned. "Destiny? We're not living in a Greek tragedy! This is the eighteenth century. We make our own destinies. I understand the appeal of putting an ocean between yourself and your problems, but America is very different from London. America is a wilderness with a sprinkle of cities on the edge. The people are savages—and half of them are transports from our prisons. Bodmin Moor is more civilized than America."

I said, "Dr. Franklin is an American. He can't be the only civilized man in the Colonies."

"You're only fourteen years old," Margery said. "That's too young. And we just got you back!"

"America is weeks away from Patch and anybody else who hunts me. Who would cross an ocean to bring me back?" *Maybe Granny is wrong*, I thought. *If they forbid me to go, I'll stay.*

The doctor pressed his lips together.

Please tell me I can't go.

The doctor sighed. "I see you've got the bit in your teeth." To Margery he said, "We both know her. She won't change her mind." Margery bowed her head and slipped her hand into his.

"I shall look at shipping schedules," Dr. Abernathy sighed.

And just like that, my dithering was done.

CHAPTER 27

SEPTEMBER 1761

A Coronation, a Wedding, and a Basket of Apples

Dr. Franklin got home from a month in Holland just in time for the coronation of George III and Queen Charlotte. He sent a message saying he wanted to see me, but not until the coronation was over as he planned to attend. Margery and Dr. Abernathy decided I should keep out of sight, which was bitter to me, as nobody in all of London could talk about anything but Coronation Day. I wanted to see it. Margery did as well, for she'd admired our new king from the time he was a prince. She pretended—for my sake, I think—that she didn't care to go now that he was married. Naturally, the doctor wanted no part of the crowds. So we stayed home.

As it turned out, though, we got a detailed report of the event from Franklin, who knew we hadn't attended. He wrote several descriptions of the coronation for his friends around the globe; we were delighted that one of them came to us. He wrote that he'd stood for part of the six-hour service until someone recognized him and gave him a chair, and he saw when King George bared his head to partake of Holy Communion and a gem fell out of the crown, which some viewed as an ill omen. When the Archbishop of Canterbury began his sermon, some of the hungrier people in attendance decided to sneak food from the picnic baskets they'd brought, so the sound of clattering cutlery and clinking glasses punctuated the Archbishop's sermon, which Franklin found rude.

Unfortunately, Franklin hadn't been invited to the banquet afterwards, as it was hard for an American to get a place when every person in the land wanted to be there. But when those who were invited to dine removed to Westminster Hall, Dr. Franklin took a spot in the galleries above the floor, the better to enjoy every moment of the spectacle. He'd brought along a basket of apples from America, which he lowered to a table below, festooned with a little label: "Fresh from Philadelphia!" When Franklin hauled the basket back up, it contained a roasted chicken and a bottle of wine in exchange for his apples! Franklin sent a message the next day inviting me to Craven Street, but the doctor went in my stead to explain our plan to send me to America.

Two days after the coronation, the doctor said, "I've investigated shipping schedules as I promised." He pulled out a piece of paper. "Now is not the best time of year to sail the Atlantic, but the *Red Queen* bound for America leaves London on Saturday, the third of October. If you must go, you should be on it. That's only nine days from now. Three days after our wedding."

Nine days. Only nine days left at home. I want more! "All right," I said.

"It should land four to six weeks after it sails, which puts your landing sometime in November. North American winters begin thereabouts, and Franklin says it would behoove you to be settled before then. You don't want to cross the Atlantic in winter." He looked at me over the top of his paper. "Well, Jem? Do you still want to go?"

No. Never. "Yes, sir," I said, my heart pounding. "Please book passage for me."

"As I expected," he said. "Dr. Franklin wants you to carry baggage to his wife in Philadelphia and keep her company until he's tidied up his affairs. He expects to sail for America himself next summer."

"Oh! I'm to stay with Mrs. Franklin?"

"He hopes to find you still there when he goes home. He is writing letters of introduction for you as a way to meet important people in Philadelphia."

Dr. Abernathy cleared his throat. "We think it best that you travel as Jem but change into a dress once you arrive in Philadelphia. Franklin believes it would be too difficult to maintain your present charade in Mrs. Franklin's household."

So I must be a girl again. Well, Granny had foretold I would have children in America, which required my being female. I sighed. "It was kind of you to arrange it," I said, relieved to know I had a place to land when I threw myself into the void, as well as an entrée to American society. I looked forward to meeting the woman Dr. Franklin both missed and lived happily without. I began to assemble in my mind a list of things it would be prudent to bring on a long journey.

But I had to steel myself to take my leave from the people I loved most in all the world—maybe forever. Why, oh why, must I always and forever be telling somebody goodbye?

* * *

The night before the wedding, we tossed all Margery's chipped dishes outside the shop's back door so she could step over them for good luck the next day. In the morning, very early, Dr. Abernathy sent me to Margery's with her groom present—a pair of pearl earrings. I found her mother and sisters helping her to dress. Mrs. Penhaligon, distracted by her duties, didn't seem to remember me as Jenna, the poor girl she'd invited for Christmas three years before. Nessa and Tressa smiled, but they didn't remark on my breeches. Maybe Margery had told them who I was. The bride sent me back to the groom with a yellow silk shirt she'd made for Dr. Abernathy to wear under his new coat of blue brocade. She gave me a rose to pin to his coat.

Dr. Abernathy and I drove to St. Mary Abbot's in the trap. A curved swag of flowers over the door reflected the roofline. Philip Miller, curator of the Chelsea Physick Garden, had made it along with a wreath for Margery's hair, which I had yet to see.

Richard Campbell, the doctor's brother-in-law, walked Dr. Abernathy through the gate and up the church steps whilst I tied Giselle to a post near the pillory. She was glad to be out in the air, though she turned her head away from smell blowing over from the butcher's across the street. At the top of the steps, the doctor sent in his brother-in-law and beckoned me forward. Inside the church, violins played a sweet duet.

Dr. Abernathy put his arm round my shoulders and took me to one side. Sunlight flooded the flowerbeds, turning yellow and orange asters into glowing lights set off by deep green grass. He said, "Well, this is it. Everything is changing, isn't it?" He turned me to face him and said, "And all the changes are due to you, Jem. Margery and I never would have become more than acquaintances if it weren't for you. And Margery is—I love her with all my heart. Jem, I owe you a debt I never can repay."

"I owe you my life, so I call it even."

"Done," he said. The church bells rang. Margery's brother Artie dashed through the door. "Dr. Abernathy, Da says to hurry up and go in before he changes his mind about givin' away the bride," so I followed Artie to his family's pew, and Dr. Abernathy walked to the front of the church and turned to watch for Margery.

The church wasn't crowded. Margery's whole family, including Lanyon and Elaine, along with Alan and Kenan, sat near the front along with the Campbells. A handful of Margery's regular customers and the doctor's colleagues had come. Of course, Franklin attended. He and Phillip Miller had their heads together, probably discussing plants.

The violins struck up a new tune. We all stood and turned.

Margery appeared at the back of the church, looking so lovely she took my breath away. She wore a bright blue silk gown with white lace trim. She'd pinned her red curls to the top of her head, where Mr. Miller's wreath of myrtle and pink roses encircled them. The doctor's pearl earrings and a small bouquet of flowers in a basket simply gilded the lily; it was Margery who made it all beautiful. She radiated light.

Seeing my friend looking so happy made me wonder if I would ever glow like that, for the same reason. Might I marry one day, as Granny foresaw? When I'd met Emily Staunton at Bedlam, imprisoned there by her husband not because she was mad but because she'd disobeyed him, I'd decided I wanted no part of marriage. Seeing the doctor's casebook drawings of a birth gone wrong convinced me I didn't want to risk childbirth. But Granny had Seen that I would marry; today, Margery's happiness made marriage seem, well, not unappealing. Margery saw me, smiled, took her father's arm, and walked with head high down the aisle to the doctor.

By eleven o'clock, it was done. They were wed. I had the honor of driving the newlyweds to Dr. Abernathy's sister's house in Chelsea for the reception. The Campbell boys as lords of the manor invited me to see the duck pond, which I'd missed seeing at Christmas. Janet Campbell deputized me to go along to keep her boys from soiling their clothes, which I agreed to attempt, despite thinking (knowing her boys) that she might as easily ask the sun to cease rising in the east.

Just as our expedition was about to embark, Lanyon Penhaligon walked up with Alan and Kenan in tow. "Can y' take two more?" he asked. "These two're lookin' for some air, I think."

"Jem!" Kenan wrapped his little arms around my waist. "Is the pelkin all better?"

"Yes, he's gone home. The more the merrier," I said to Lanyon. The Penhaligons and Campbells introduced themselves as boys do by showing one another their recent injuries. While they got acquainted, I asked Lanyon, "How is Granny?"

"Well, very well. She'd took in a starvin' pony about t' foal last time I visited. She sends her love."

"I miss her. Send my love back."

Brian, the second-oldest Campbell boy, called, "Ready, Jem?"

Lanyon called out, "A moment, if y' please." He lowered his voice. "Jem, I couldn't've brung Elaine an' the boys here without you." I frowned, puzzled. "Elaine's been wantin' t' see London since before we were wed. Ma give me money t' bring her, and Elaine's been havin' the time of her life. Ma said she got the money from you." I glanced into the room where the guests had gathered and caught sight of Margery introducing Dr. Abernathy to Elaine Penhaligon, who made a deep curtsey to the doctor.

"It was Granny's money to do with as she liked," I said, smiling at the doctor's reaction to Elaine's extravagant display. "I'm not surprised Granny used it to make Elaine happy."

"Come on, Jem, I can't hold 'em!" called the eldest Campbell boy, John, as Richard, the second-youngest, slipped out of his grasp. I would have a riot on my hands at any minute.

"Jem, one more thing," Lanyon said. "Elaine don't know Ma give me money t' come here. I said I earned it cartin' things here an' there."

"Which is somewhat true."

"Aye, but don't tell Elaine where I got it. And she saw you settin' wards when you come to visit us in town, so you're tainted as far as Elaine's concerned. Word to the wise."

"I'll watch for her, Lanyon," I said. The boys already had started for the duck pond without me. "I'd best get along." I trotted to catch up, lifting the littlest Campbell boy, Trafford, for a pick-a-back ride. Once arrived at the pond, I succeeded somewhat in keeping six boys from soiling their clothing, but Trafford's shoes got sucked off his feet by the mud at the edge of the pond and his stockings suffered for it. Nevertheless, they returned to their nanny in better humor for having got some fresh air and exercise, and she took them and the other children up to the nursery for their dinner.

At dinner, I was seated between two of Margery's sisters, Nessa and Tressa, who were sizing up the eligible bachelors in attendance. We feasted on white soup, sirloin of beef, pigeons, halibut, new potatoes with butter, syllabub, coffee and chocolate, and plum cake with almonds, citrus, and spices, and Bride's pie. Tressa asked me to share my seagoing adventures, so I obliged. Toward the end of dinner, Nessa, the elder, said, "Jem, Margery is taking me on as her helper now that you're off to the Colonies."

"Is she?"

"Yes, though I wonder if I'm suited to working in a shop. Da's been teaching me about scents alongside Dylan and Alfred, which I like fine. Jory's the one who should be going to work with Margery, but Da wants me to go."

"Because he wants you to meet someone," Tressa said sweetly to her sister.

"What about you?" Nessa snapped, and then she forked up the glass ring out of her piece of Bride's pie. "Look here! P'raps I'll meet someone after all."

Eyeing her sister's prize, Tressa said, "Da's trying to persuade Margery to sell his perfumes out of her shop."

"That would be—interesting," I said.

So much had changed in so short a time. In three days, I would board my ship to America. How much time would pass before I sailed home again? What if I never did? Granny had Seen me building a life in the Colonies, which meant I had only a few precious hours left with Margery and the doctor for who knew how long—perhaps forever. That thought was too big for me to think about.

After dinner, the company withdrew to a hall for dancing. The married ladies surrounded Margery. They danced her round and round until she danced off her bridal wreath. Then, laughing, she bundled up her curls in a white lace matron's cap as tradition required. Once she'd got her matron's cap on her head, the doctor claimed her. For me, this ritual underscored two things: one, that their marriage would be happy; and two, that I wouldn't be here to see it. A lump swelled in my throat. Rather than discourage them with my long face, I stepped out to a portico that ran along a row of tall windows just outside the hall. The afternoon was fine, and the moon waxed faintly visible in the sky despite the sun's not having set yet.

"So, Jem Connolly," said a woman's voice, "I've been looking for you." I turned. Elaine Penhaligon clutched the ends of her shawl, her eyes like chips of ice.

"Nice to see you again, Mrs. Penhaligon," I said, offering my hand. "Alan and

Kenan have gotten so big." She took the tips of my fingers briefly, then let go.

"Aye, they have. I'm glad t' catch you alone. I've somethin' on my mind."

"Oh? What's that?"

"Why'd you come all the way t' Cornwall?"

I blinked. "I—well, Margery said her Granny would like help with her animals and so forth. And Granny enjoyed having company." I hadn't thought how my lengthy visit might look to someone who didn't know I'd gone both to hide and to learn magic, but now, thanks to Lanyon's warning, I knew Elaine had worked out the second reason.

"I don't believe you," Elaine said. "I saw you makin' marks and mumblin over 'em when you come to my house." She slid a hand into her pocket and pulled out something. "I found my Kenan playin' with this after Margery went home the last time. I wanted t' toss it in the fire, only I were afraid t' do it in case it were witched t' harm my boy." She opened her hand. A doll the size of a sparrow laid in her palm, dressed in breeches with a tiny face drawn on. The face had green eyes. "This is you." My eyes locked with hers. Elaine demanded, "Why'd you give this to my Kenan?"

"I didn't. Granny Kestrel and Margery said they'd made a doll while I was over by Liskeard visiting Granny's friends, but I had no hand in making that doll. What's wrong with it?"

"It's witched," she hissed, "and I know it! You take this, right now"—she pressed the doll into my hand and crunched my fingers over it—"and you take the spell off. And leave my boys alone."

"Mrs. Penhaligon, I didn't put a spell on this," I said. The doll felt as warm as a little bird in my hand from having ridden in her pocket.

"Take it off!" Elaine said. She dug her nails into my arm, her voice desperate and her eyes glittering with angry tears. "Do it now."

I stammered, "I c-can pray over it." I wrenched my arm free, closed my eyes, and placed my other hand over the doll. "Heavenly Father, I pray your blessing on this doll. Cleanse it of...of evil. Shower your love and protection on this woman and her family, and give them a safe journey back to their home. Amen."

I opened my eyes. Elaine wrung her hands, her eyes on the thing in my hand, which felt warmer. "Do you want it back?" I asked.

"No!" she said. "Kenan's forgot it by now. I took it off him soon's I saw it and hid it under my Bible, but I didn't dare burn it up without havin' the curse took off it."

I sighed. "Why didn't you take it to your vicar to, er, bless?"

She snorted. "People already whisper about Kestrel. Y' think I want t' remind the vicar my boys're tainted with her blood? Y' think I want people t' rise up against me an' Lanyon, burn our house down, or march upriver and hang Kestrel, even though 'tis no less than she deserves?"

Anger roared to life in my heart. I thrust the doll into my pocket and left my hand on it because I itched to slap her. "Hang her? You can't be serious. The very last thing on earth she deserves is harm at the hands of stupid people," I hissed. "Granny works miracles of healing in her barn. How is it possible you haven't figured out that Granny's gift is of God?" Elaine sneered. I persisted, "Tell me: in your Bible, isn't it Jesus who does the healing?" The doll felt warmer. "Saint Matthew says, 'Every good tree bears good fruit.' Think about what she does!

"And speaking of the Bible," I continued, "we read it together, Granny and I." Elaine's eyes narrowed. "Granny likes the Psalms, although her favorite verse is the one about faith being the substance of things hoped for."

The skeptical look on her face faded a tiny bit. She murmured, "'The evidence of things not seen,'" she said. "That's my favorite as well."

"That's the one. She loves animals and plants, all good things God made. She writes back and forth about them with Dr. Benjamin Franklin himself."

Elaine's face tightened again. "Kestrel don't know Dr. Franklin."

"Ask him yourself. He's inside."

She lifted her chin. "I might do so."

"Good." I should have left it alone, but I might not see Elaine again, so I added, "Forgive my frankness, but to deny Alan and Kenan their grandmother is cruel. It drives a wedge between you and Lanyon." In my mind, I gathered into a tight ball my memories of Granny's hands, her eyes, her love—and I threw that ball at Elaine, and perhaps it was too much all at once, because Elaine gasped.

"There y' are, wife." Lanyon stepped onto the portico. "I come to beg a dance of you." Elaine slid her hand around his elbow and turned up her face, squinting as though to bring him into focus. Lanyon said, "Is everything well out here?"

"Lovely," I said. "We were just getting reacquainted." Lanyon looked from me to his wife.

"I was thinkin' next time we come, p'raps Mother Kestrel can come with us," Elaine said, and then slapped a hand over her mouth as though she'd spoken a curse.

Lanyon blinked. His eyes shifted from Elaine to me and back again. "Er, she likely wouldn't come as she's beasts t' tend, and y' know she's as faithful as though God himself give her the job." Elaine blinked. Lanyon added, "Wife, y're well?"

"Aye, Husband, daydreamin' is all," Elaine said eyeing me, "Let's go in."

I exhaled. Maybe Elaine would still argue next time Lanyon wanted to take the boys to visit Granny Kestrel. But maybe she wouldn't. Regardless, my immediate problem was the doll in my pocket: it burned like a coal. I took it out and wrapped it in my handkerchief and went in search of Margery to ask how I should dispose of it.

I found Margery fanning herself and chatting with her mother. "Jem, there you are!" Margery said. "I wondered where you'd got to."

"I was talking with Lanyon's Elaine," I said. Margery's face sobered a bit.

"Sweet girl, Elaine," said Mrs. Penhaligon.

"Very." Margery and I exchanged a look. Margery's da, smelling like one of his perfumes, came up to claim his wife for a dance, so before anybody else claimed Margery, I blurted, "Margery, Elaine found that doll Kenan took out of your bag last year."

"Good heavens!"

"She brought it all the way here so I could take the curse off it."

"It's not cursed."

"I know that, but I prayed over it anyway, and now it's burning a hole in my pocket."

"What?"

"It's *hot*! It's so hot I wanted to toss it into the duck pond, but I thought I'd better ask you first. Why is it so hot? What should I do with it?"

"Give it to me." She hid it in a fold of her dress. "It's hot because it's found its way back to you. The blood wants to come home. You can't keep it."

"Can I burn it?"

"Never," she whispered, glancing around to make sure nobody overheard. "You never give your blood to the fire, Jem. It's something to do with a fragrance going up, like in the Bible with sacrifices and such. When blood burns, the Dark smells it easier, like a dog walking by a butcher's. Not that the Dark has got a nose, exactly, but—"

"But Granny burned that flower that was on your cake."

"She burned it in alder. That's different."

"Can I throw the doll in the river?"

"No. The water would wash away the blood, and the magic with it. Besides, there's no telling where the current would take it. The doll must be placed somewhere on purpose, like the raven put one on the ship and Granny sent one with the pelican to put on that mountain."

"Can I bury this in the woods right now?"

"Jem, sit. You can't hide it on the Campbell's property or anyplace else you might ever go. In fact, *you* can't hide it at all, for then you'd be thinking of it, and that would help the Dark to find it. I must be the one to hide it, but I can't leave my own wedding, and I don't want to keep it and risk losing it again." She thought, then said, "What about this? I hate to ask, Jem, but I don't know what else to do: can you take the doll to the shop? I've a pot of marigolds upstairs near the window sitting on a Blind Box, like Granny's. Put the doll in the box. Patch already has looked for you at the shop a number of times without finding you, so I think he'd dismiss it if he sniffed you out there today before you lock up the doll. Tomorrow, I'll hide the doll." She glanced up at Dr. Abernathy, who now danced with Margery's mother. Margery's mouth relaxed. "Or perhaps the day after tomorrow." She turned back to me. "At any rate, after you leave the shop today, don't go back. I shall hide the doll the very hour I return to the shop, I promise."

"When should I bring the doll to the shop?"

"Now. You'll have to leave the party, I'm afraid." My face fell. "Jem, you cannot keep it on you, you can't throw it away, you can't hide it, and you can't let anybody here see it." She stood. "In fact, come with me. Er, pretend you're crying." She led me into the dining room, which was being cleared by the Campbell's staff. She plucked up a napkin, put her arm around my shoulders, and daubed at my face with the napkin. She guided me into the study where I'd conversed with the Duchess two Christmases before. Margery wrapped the doll in the napkin and said, "It's so odd, Jem. This feels like a bundle of cloth to me, no warmth at all." She handed it back. "Be careful with that." I stuffed it into my pocket.

"Should I drive Giselle to town?" I asked.

"Yes, but I'll have Jory go along just in case. I'll tell the doctor where you went and that you'll be back before sunset. Go tell the stableboy to hitch up the horse." She kissed my forehead and hurried out, and I did as she asked. Whilst the stableboy got Giselle ready, I laid a hand on her back and thought, *Sorry, old girl. We have to go back to town.*

Giselle's shoulder twitched as she conveyed her reply, *Going and coming is life.* Jory wobbled into the stable—clearly, I would be doing the driving—and we clattered away toward London.

CHAPTER 28

SEPTEMBER 30, 1761

Disaster

Bumping along jostled Jory into a more alert frame of mind. "What's Margery forgot now?" he complained. "I was enjoyin' myself."

"You can't expect her to remember everything on her wedding day," I said. "We'll be back by sunset, and you don't even have to leave the trap. I'll just pop into the shop, take care of Margery's business, and then we'll turn around and go back again."

"Why do I have t' go at all? You can drive."

"Because the markets close in an hour or so and the roads will be crowded with everybody coming at us on their way out of the city. Margery doesn't want me alone on the road."

"Fine." We skirted Hyde Park and took Tyburn Road east to Holborn. By the time we smelled Smithfield, the streets, indeed, were crowded with wagons and carts. I drove Giselle to the rear of the shop, and Jory climbed down to unlock the door. "Hurry up," he said, "I want t' get back."

I ran upstairs and deposited the doll in Margery's Blind Box, glad to get it out of my pocket. Margery's room was cluttered with the detritus of her wedding preparations. Although Jory was anxious to get back, I took a few minutes to tidy the room as a last service to Margery. I hung garments and wiped up powder and straightened combs and brushes. Somebody had spilled her pins, so I picked those up as well. I heard a faint *click* from below and the dull thud of heels in the back room.

"All right, Jory," I called, "I'm coming. My, you're impatient!"

I ran down the stairs and pelted into a pair of arms that vised around me. I looked up at…*Patch*! Panic set me to thrashing. Patch said, "Stop. Now."

"What are you doing here? Where's Jory? Let me go!" I shouted. I screamed. A hand clapped over my mouth and he hissed in my ear, "Quiet. If you cry out again, your friend will pay for it. He's only been knocked on the head, but we easily can slit his throat for him. The horse as well."

I stopped struggling, and Patch took his hand away.

"Better. Come along. Quietly."

In the alley, Giselle stood snubbed up tight. Her eyes showed white all around. Jory slumped over, blood on the back of his head.

"We are going to leave here now. If you cause me any trouble, if you try to attract anyone's attention, your apothecary friend, Mrs. Jamison, will suffer for it. It would be as easy as breathing to make sure she never troubles me again, starting with a fire in her shop. Do you want that?" I shook my head. He tightened his grip. He led me to a wagon where the confectioner's apprentice, Freddie Payne's brother, gripped the reins. "Told you I knew what you was," he said. "Gotcha at last, didn't we."

Could I delay them? Would anybody come if I did? "How did you know I was here?"

Freddie's brother, the robber who'd bloodied me and stolen my cameo, snickered. "Me brother Tim likes a nice cozy hogshead to rest in an' earn his livin'. 'Tis better'n beggin' with a crutch and gettin' pinched or walloped." I swiveled my head. *No.* But the huge barrel was a perfect size for a boy. How many days had he waited in that dark, close barrel spying on the shop?

"Quiet, you fool," said Patch. Shoving me into the back of the wagon, he said, as though remarking on the weather, "If you make a noise, Bill will cut your apothecary friend's throat for her. That, I promise." Bill showed a wicked knife that must have been the same one he used on me. Patch threw a moldy tarpaulin over my head.

The wagon jostled as Patch got in. Bill clicked at the horse. We bumped along. I tried to think what to do. I could roll out of the wagon and run. But then Patch would hurt Margery. We clattered toward the smelly Thames. I heard the slap of water. We crossed a bridge—it must have been Westminster—and finally stopped. Had we come to Lambeth? I heard the clink of coins. Patch threw off the tarp. The wagon had pulled up under the shadow of a covered brick arch beside a huge house. "Take that away," Patch ordered, and Bill drove off. I smelled the rot of the Lambeth marshes, the stench of the tanneries.

He unlocked a great wooden door and pushed me inside. We stood in an entryway that smelled dusty and unused. No lingering smells of food or people. No warmth. He pointed at a stairway. "Up," he said.

"You've made a mistake," I said, "I'm n—"

His hand struck so hard and fast my head snapped to the side. I hadn't ever been hit before. The shock of it was as bad as the pain that exploded in my face, for Patch had slapped me just where Bill had shoved my face into the stone wall.

He hissed, "*Do not attempt a lie!* You are Jessamyn Marietta Connolly, formerly of County Durham. Your mother was Mary Anne Pelham-Holles, daughter of the Duke and Duchess of Newcastle. Your father was an Irish dog who died in a cave-in and good riddance."

"Why do you want me?" He pushed me toward the stairs.

"The Duchess of Newcastle wants a grandchild. The Duke of Newcastle detests his nearest relatives and refuses to let them inherit his estate, so he needs an heir of his body. You are the answer for both of them." He pinched the back of my neck between iron fingers and nudged me forward.

We climbed up. My hand on the banister scuffed off rolls of dust. *Whose house is this?* I thought. *Are there servants?*

"I saw the letter," I said. "I don't want to live with them." The fingers squeezed. "Stop it. That hurts." He squeezed harder.

Into my ear he said, "Your wishes are less than nothing to me. Your grandmother has paid me generously for fifteen years to follow any lead she received about your mother. Or you. I am promised two thousand pounds when I deliver you." It was a shocking amount of money. A frugal person could live on that much money for years.

At the top of the stairs, his fingers clamped on my wrist like a manacle. He shoved me into a dark room and turned the key in the lock, pocketing the key. I scuttled away and fell against a bed, sprang up and ran round to the other side of it.

Patch took out a tinderbox to light a candle and a wood fire that had been laid. "Are you stupid, Jessamyn? Do you think hiding behind a bed can protect you now? Come and sit so we can have a civilized conversation." I didn't move. He looked toward the bed. "If you don't come on your own, I shall drag you by your hair." He smiled and waited. I crept around. When the fire caught, I saw that I was in a bedchamber bigger than Granny's entire cottage. Sheets shrouded the furniture. The merest slices of fading daylight showed between heavy, closed curtains. Patch swung a kettle over the fire.

"Where are we?" I asked.

"This house belongs to someone other than your grandparents, someone who also is interested in you. Unfortunately for you, this person has offered me a thousand pounds more than the duke has to ensure that you are hidden away."

"Who? Hidden where? What for?"

"Hidden until he has need of you. The problem for me is deciding which offer to accept. Do I take you to your grandparents and reap my reward—which certainly will include continued employment as a trusted servant for the rest of my life, if I should desire it, in addition to the money—or do I get rid of you, as this other person wishes, and take the greater reward?"

"Who wants you to get rid of me?"

"My problem is," he said, ignoring my question, "that having you here suggests a third possibility that tempts me."

His tone, his eyes, the way his body held itself poised to strike—all froze me where I stood. Did he mean draining my Sight? Did he mean something—corrupt? I quivered.

"Good. I see you finally understand your situation," he said. "The man who owns this house wants you kept alive. The Asylum for Female Orphans and the Magdalen Hospital are right here in Lambeth. Given your penchant for wearing men's clothing, and his influence, it would be easy to lock you in an asylum. Any one of them would keep you indefinitely, if paid enough. And they would be. Nobody would find you. You would be there for this person to take up when you were old enough."

"Old enough…for what?" Again, he ignored me. He pulled a dust sheet from the bed. He shook out the blankets and pounded the bolsters.

If it were Bedlam, I could contact the doctor—but what if it were one of the others? I said, "If I must choose between the duke and an asylum, I'll take the duke."

He laughed, a sound that slithered up my back. Patch said, "Suddenly you're anxious to meet your grandparents. I shouldn't wonder—I smell your fear all the way over here." I didn't answer.

He poured hot water from the kettle into a teapot and set out cups and saucers, sugar and lemon. That a man who casually talked of tossing me into a madhouse or worse also could assemble a civilized tea made me quiver.

"Oh, sit down, for pity's sake and have some tea," he said. He poured me a cup and said again, "*Sit.*" I sat. He smiled. "Sugar?"

I took the cup he handed to me. It wasn't very hot, and my throat was dry as dust, so I gulped down half of it at one go before I noticed its nasty bitter taste. I set down my cup. He hadn't yet touched his own.

"It's hard for me to decide what to do with you because I am angry. I was so close in Lamesley. Sir Henry's man described your mother perfectly, down to the cameo around her neck." He dug into his waistcoat pocket. "This cameo." He held it up. "When Bill brought it to me four days ago, I knew I was close. Deliciously close."

My fingers twitched to take it out of his hand.

"Oh, no, my dear. This is my proof that you are Mary Anne's daughter." He slipped the cameo back into his waistcoat pocket. "Where was I?"

"You thought you found Mum in Lamesley." His face wavered in the fire-light.

"Ah, yes. Sir Henry's man wrote to me, but before I got the letter, your mother left Lamesley for London. I understand you had a brother born after you?"

"James." *Why did I tell him that? Stop talking!*

"That's the one buried in Chelsea." I didn't say anything because I was sorting out the scents and tastes on my tongue left by the tea. *Valerian. Opium. And—something else. He's drugged my tea.* Patch's cup of tea sat cooling. I knew now he had no intention of drinking it.

"More tea?"

"No." *Please don't let him have given me* Datura.

"Are you tired?" He leaned forward.

"No," I said. *I'm dizzy.* "What about Lamesley?"

"An old crone there sent me on a fool's errand all the way to Cumberland. The trail got colder and colder. I circled back to Lamesley and found the witch."

"You didn't hurt Nan Knowles?" The room gently rocked as though I sat on a boat.

I thought of Nan's soft hands brushing my hair for Da's funeral. Her arms around Mum as she cried. What she'd risked to turn this man away from us. What had he done to her? Suddenly I hated Patch with a hatred so hot my ears pulsed with it.

Patch said, "I didn't kill her." I squinted; he was becoming blurry. "She might be useful later. As a lever, like your apothecary." I exhaled. *Know thy enemy,* Franklin had taught me. *Find out all you can.*

"And then?" I asked. Clearly, Patch liked to talk. He reveled in detailing his genius, his brilliance, his mastery. I needed to learn as much as I could before the drugs in the tea took me. I prompted, "You came to London."

Patch leaned back in his chair. He draped an arm over the back of it, like a bird stretching a wing. He was enjoying this. He'd finally got his hands on

Mary Anne Pelham-Holles—well, a piece of her, *me*—after a decade and a half. He was over the moon that I had no way to escape.

Patch nodded. "I came to London. But still I couldn't find you. I'd just decided to go back to the crone and try again when I heard you."

"Heard me?"

"Heard you. At the Tower. Having a gab with the lions." My thoughts spun round this terrifying confirmation: *he has Sight.*

He laid more wood on the fire. "Haven't you felt me close to you all these years? Every time you use your Sight, it's like someone shouting. It calls to me. I was interested to learn at the Chelsea Physic Garden that drugs make you… louder."

Shock rippled up my backbone, but didn't spread to my limbs, as the drugs had turned my body to jelly. My mind, though, circled round and round the fact that Patch had been aware of me this whole time. My hallucination of a giant snake had been no hallucination at all.

"Then you went quiet," Patch said. "I'd lost you again. I walked circles from the Tower, going wider each time." His fingers strayed to his waistcoat pocket. "I knew you were close. In the spring, you called again, as loud in my mind as if you were shouting. I tracked you to Aldgate. I reached up to you—you saw me, I think."

He bared his teeth. I think he meant to smile.

"But you slipped away. Again. I walked circles from St. Paul's this time. I felt you strongest near the Old Bailey, so I paid street urchins to keep watch along that street. Eventually, one of my spies found a beggar boy who had an interesting story to tell: he'd once known a dark-haired girl and her mother who lived above an apothecary, but both of them went away.

"The beggar's younger brother—Bill, my charioteer, you've met before today, I think—said that some months later, a dark-haired boy began coming regularly to the shop. He thought the boy was having lessons of the apothecary.

"I hired all three of these ginger-haired brothers to patrol the neighborhood. I left a message with the idiot woman in the shop, but she said you were gone." His eye glittered. "You didn't feel gone." He clenched and unclenched his hands. "I continued to pay the redheads, and when they told me that you and the apothecary had gone across to the fair, I followed. But you stuck like a burr to the woman. On Guy Fawkes' Night, I laid a trap. You escaped it."

The tar I thought I'd walked in.

"But then we finally met, you and I. I had you in the palm of my hand. My search was over. I had only to take you to the duchess." His smooth voice turned to a growl, "But you escaped me again. How? Who is helping you?"

"Nobody." My lips could hardly form the word.

"Liar. I felt you all around London until you disappeared entirely. Where were you, this last year? Where was that cottage?" I shut up everything I knew of Granny Kestrel behind a door in my head. I sealed it shut. For all I knew, Patch could read my mind, although now the drugs were taking my mind away even from me.

"You'll tell me everything eventually," he said. "I can wait. You do see why I'm still angry. If there weren't so much money at stake, so many opportunities for me to choose from, I might keep you here. It could prove interesting." He spoke calmly, but his knuckles showed white on the arms of his chair.

He means it. I focused on speaking: "You wouldn't dare."

He bared his teeth. "Do not school me." He leaned over and slapped me again. My ears rang.

"Hit me 'gin an' I hichoo back." It was a lie; I couldn't make a fist. Numb lips made me slur the words.

"What do you think you can do to me?" he sneered. He took me by both arms and shook me so hard I thought my neck might snap. "Well?"

"Tella duke," I mumbled.

"You will do nothing of the kind. You will do nothing unless I tell you to."

How did he hope to make that happen? There was something he wasn't saying.

I felt something pulsing in his hands as they clenched my shoulders, some-thing inside him, something strong and big like the waterfall of Light I'd seen on the tor, but not beautiful. Not appealing. It was a void, a great, hungry emp-tiness. I'd felt it before, swarming up my arms aboard the *Mary Ellen*. Slither-ing into my veins the night of midsummer solstice. *The black cloud in Granny's cottage.*

The Dark. Burning, ravenous, sucking on my life. I wanted to break free but the drugs had hold of me. Patch gripped harder, like a mantis clutching its prey before devouring it head-first. My courage contracted. My vision blurred as well. "Be gone," I whispered. Or tried to whisper. Was Patch able to master the Dark that swamped him? *Could* he call it back? I whimpered, my body refusing to obey my command to break free and run.

His good eye glittered. The Dark swarmed like a cloud of wasps to the limits of his skin, buzzing, angry, hungry. Patch said, "You will never turn your step in any direction without our permission." *Our?* "You are ours to use as we wish. Your Sight is ours."

I tried to talk. "Nn."

He leaned toward me. "Would you like to see why you will do exactly as we say? Why you will never run from us again?"

He reached for the patch over his bad eye. The power of the drugs had taken over to a point where I could do nothing but look. He lifted his patch. If I could have screamed, I would have.

The patch concealed no empty socket or closed lid. No eye made of colored glass. Under the patch lay an eye as well-formed as the good one but, in all oth-er respects, no eye at all. It was solid black throughout, like the eye of a bee: no iris, no white, just shiny blackness, with red lines forking like lightning over the otherwise featureless eyeball, playing over it as though a storm raged in Patch's head and this eye was a window that looked in on it.

I knew anatomy. This was not a human eye. Before that eye, my heart shriv-eled. Swirling in those streaks of red was a great evil that saturated every bit of Patch's body like blood. Neither speech nor action could persuade that evil. Nothing could dislodge it but death.

Patch had kidnapped me for the money, but the Dark wanted something else and didn't intend to let me go until it got what it wanted: my Sight.

This was it, then. The end of Sight. Light. Everything. My heart pounded. My mind screamed.

Help me. Please. Someone help me.

CHAPTER 29

OCTOBER 1, 1761

Secrets on the Wind

Ice formed around my heart. My blood chilled. Resolve stiffened my spine. Not the smallest sliver of Sight would be stolen from me easily. I steeled myself to resist the hot Dark beating against me like storm waves beating against the hull of a ship.

Then—the boiling water ebbed. The Dark subsided. Patch fumbled the covering over his sinister eye, breathing hard. "So you see, Jessamyn, wherever you go, I can find you."

What just happened?

He grimaced. "Time for bed, I think." He lifted me into his arms. The Dark slithered further away, apparently sated for now with the pleasure of possessing me. My body wouldn't obey my order to struggle. Patch placed me on the bed and stood there just looking at me, sweat sheening his face.

I couldn't even move to cover myself. I looked up at him, and I hated him and feared him with all my heart. He mopped his face, laughing. "So fierce!" he said. "Or perhaps you're simply overtired. You've had a long day, what with your friend's wedding. Of course you were there. Who did she marry? Anybody I know? The good doctor, perhaps?"

His questions penetrated the fog in my mind and gave me a minuscule spark of comfort: they proved Patch couldn't read my mind. He hadn't connected Margery with Dr. Abernathy, not for certain. Astonishing stupidity on his part but a blessing for us.

I didn't have to feign sleepiness; the valerian and opium thrummed in my blood as they slowly shut everything down. He must have given me a great deal of it. I closed my eyes.

I felt him watching me. "Jessamyn?" he said. My breathing went deep and smooth.

He pulled the blanket up over me, trailing his hand down my face and arm. Inside, I quaked like a rabbit.

But he left. I heard him unlock the door, take up the tray, and close and lock the door again. Now I could think.

Except I couldn't. Every time I tried to grasp an idea, it fell apart like wet paper. If I wanted to escape, I wouldn't be able to eat or drink anything he gave me in case it were drugged.

My mind floated in fog. Finally, I felt the wakeful part of my mind lie down next to the sleeping part like a kitten lies down beside her mother when she's run herself into exhaustion.

* * *

I was in Cornwall. I had climbed the tor in daylight, but the sky was low and gray. The grasses were brown.

From the top of the tor, I looked out. Nothing, no living thing, moved. Except—

A black dot in the distance sped toward me from the forest south of the moor.

The dot grew larger and larger as it came closer. A raven. Suddenly, it launched itself. It rode the wind that blew into my face, but I watched without fear as it came on. I knew who rode the raven.

The raven blew to the foot of the tor and fluttered up the path and landed, shaking out its feathers and changing before my eyes into Granny Kestrel, her cloak spread like a sail.

"Granny! I'm so glad to see you."

"Shh—no names here. Someone may be listening."

"Someone is. The man who sent the door has got me. I'm locked up somewhere in Lambeth. He knows when I use the Sight. The Dark lives in him. It wants me. He says he'll hurt...someone we both love if I don't do as he says. I don't know what to do."

"Hush, now. Y've the power of the Light. Be calm. We'll work out what t' do." She grasped my hands. Her silvery eyes gleamed. "You've spent Light fightin' off the Dark already, ain't you? I can feel it."

"If this is real and not a dream, I need to know how to get away without bringing harm to your granddaughter. He said he would cut her throat and burn her...home."

"She can't be killed by the Dark, nor can I, nor you. We're marked, all three of us. He could burn her place, but 'tis a risk with no reward."

"So if I can get away, Patch won't be able to hurt her?"

"No names, I told you. A name is like an alarm bell."

"It's not his real name."

"No matter—if y' see his face when y' say it, 'tis the same. Oh. Look." She pointed up.

Clouds boiled in the sky, black clouds that boiled up fast from the northeast. The wind blew up sudden and strong, not the sweet wind that had whisked Granny to me, but a cold gale that tore our breaths right out of our mouths. I clung to one of the standing stones.

"He heard us," Granny said. "He's coming."

"What should I do?" I shouted above the scream of the wind.

"Get away. The worst that could happen for all of us is you losin' your Light. Those you love are somewhat safe if they bear a mark. I'll go to the girls, and we'll see what we can do."

The wind became a gale. I would have blown away if I'd let go of the boulder.

Granny said, "Time to fly" and spread her arms.

The wind filled her cloak, taking Granny into the sky, pushing her toward the sea. Lightning forked all around her. The black cloud opened to swallow her.

"No!" I screamed.

* * *

I woke up. The curtains didn't quite close, and the sun shining between them painted a bright line on the floor that slashed the carpet and split the fireplace into halves. I got up on wobbly legs to peek out, hoping to see a busy street, but the window looked over a copse of trees to the southeast, the direction of Cornwall. Unless the nearest neighbor had extraordinary hearing, nobody would hear if I called for help.

My arm hurt. A spider must have bitten me in the night, for there was a little red dot in the crook of my elbow. I paced the room looking for something I could use as a weapon.

I heard the key in the lock. I lunged for a fireplace poker and backed away.

The door opened. When Patch saw the poker, he said, "Don't be stupid." He walked over to open the curtains. I ran at him with the poker raised. He spun and caught it with one hand, twisting it away and throwing it aside. I turned to run. He grabbed me by my hair, then bent my arm behind me. Pain exploded in my shoulder.

"Now what kind of 'good morning' is that?" Patch said. "Did you have pleasant dreams? I dreamed of a great, ugly bird blown away by a storm." His lips turned up in a contorted smile. "Come have breakfast."

"I don't want any," I said. "Let go, you're hurting me."

"As you wish." Patch released me and lowered himself into a chair, pouring himself a cup of tea and taking up a slice of buttered bread. He saw me watching him. "Nothing in the tea this morning," he said. "I need you awake today."

The tea smelled heavenly. The bread and butter looked fresh. I was thirsty and hungry. I circled the table, rubbing my wrenched shoulder.

"I'll pour you a cup," he said, but when he lifted the pot to pour my tea, I snatched up his cup and bread. "What are you doing?" he said.

"I don't trust you." I took a big bite of the bread.

"Foolish girl. I told you, I need you awake today."

"Why?" I chewed and waited. If I asked the right questions and looked interested or afraid, he might let slip something that I could use to get away.

As long as that thing inside him doesn't wake up.

My courage had flooded back when I'd learned Margery was safe. I hoped my dream about the tor wasn't only a dream.

Patch said, "I need you awake because a dressmaker is coming today." I frowned. "What, did you think I'd take you to the duke and duchess in breeches? Like it or not, you're a peer of the realm. They expect you to be clothed as befits your gender. I gave your waistcoat to a dressmaker ten days ago as soon as Bill brought it to me. She guessed your size from it and began immediately to construct something suitable for you to wear when I take you to your grandparents."

"Did you tell them you'd found me?" Relief flooded me. *He's decided against the asylum and the orphanage—and against keeping me a prisoner or giving me to the Dark.*

"I sent a note that I had good news for them. *You* are the news. I'm taking you there as soon as you're dressed." His good eye locked on my face, while his fingers drifted to stroke his eyepatch. "But I can take you away from them again at any time. Remember that."

We heard the bell. "That must be Mrs. Thomas now." He opened the door, but then he turned. "Do not ask her to help you. It is not in her interest to do so since I've hinted that if her work today is satisfactory, it might lead to bigger things. Money is a powerful incentive. And there are…other considerations." He locked the door behind him. I finished my bread and tea; I had to keep up my strength and watch for a chance to escape. I heard voices below, then someone treading up the stairs.

The key turned in the lock. Patch held the door for a woman in a red cloak. A feathered hat sat atop a row of curls. She looked familiar, but I couldn't place where I'd seen her. *Craven Street?* The woman carried a large bundle wrapped in a sheet. "Put it on the bed," Patch said.

"So this is the girl," the woman said. "She's smaller than I expected. I'll have to adjust the dress so it fits properly."

"As long as it doesn't take too long," Patch said. "We must be off this morning. I'll go fill her bath. I must lock you two in together—you understand."

"Of course."

When he'd gone, the dressmaker said, "If you try to harm me, I shall stab you with my scissors," as though she were remarking on the color of my new gown.

"Why would I do that?"

"Mr. Duncan explained about your fits," she said, "and paid me double to take on the work of making a dress for a girl who can't control herself."

"Are you referring to me?" She unwrapped her bundle. Undergarments and a pair of stays sat atop a mound of brown silk.

"Who else, mademoiselle? He says you are lucid one moment and a tiger the next. But he says you behave yourself if you are afraid." She snapped her shears open and shut. "These are very sharp."

Where had I seen her? The theater? The hospital? "You wouldn't dare to use those on me," I said.

Her mouth stretched in a smile that didn't reach her cold eyes. "I beg you not to try me, mademoiselle. Put this on. I haven't enough time as it is." I peeled off my breeches and shirt and slipped on the shift. I desperately tried to place her face.

"*Vite! Tout suite!*" She snapped her fingers. The gesture irked me, but it knocked loose a memory: this was the woman I'd peeked at so long ago through the crack in the door the day the doctor began his social experiment. The dressmaker I was supposed to have been apprenticed to. Patch had said her name. What was it?

Mrs. Thomas. And I'd seen the back of that red cloak the day Dr. Abernathy diagnosed Henry Galt's consumption.

If the dressmaker knew her identity was not a secret, that she could be found and punished for helping a kidnapper, could I use that to help me get away?

CHAPTER 30

OCTOBER 1, 1761

Full Disclosure

Mrs. Thomas laced me into the stays with both hands but kept the shears in her pocket, taking no chances with the lunatic.

She held the brown silk petticoat so I could step into it. "Hm—not bad," she said. "Put the shoes on." I stepped into shoes of soft calf leather. "Ah, look at that," she said. "Perfect length. Lucky us." She'd made the top of the dress in the style I'd seen on women since I'd come home: a hip-length jacket with a high neckline and a hood. The upper sleeve ended in a flounce at the elbow, with green ribbon trim, and the lower sleeve was tight to the wrist. "Here's where we have a problem," the dressmaker said, tugging at the bodice side seam. "I knew it."

I raised my arm to look. Her hand flew to the pocket with the shears. "Do you think I am the one you have to be afraid of?" I hissed. "Do you know who he is? Who I am? Do you?"

She stuck some pins into her mouth and began to tug at the waist of the jacket. Around the pins, she said, "I know that monsieur has paid me handsomely to make a Brunswick dress for a young lady, and I have done so."

"Did he tell you he kidnapped me from my home?"

"He said you suffer from delusions that you are persecuted."

"I was at home yesterday. He broke in, and he kidnapped me." She looked up for a second, but there was no sympathy in her eyes.

She slipped the jacket off my shoulders and got out needle and thread. "I think you should be quiet now," she said. She began to take in the jacket at the waist.

"Why would anybody bring you to a deserted house for a dress fitting? Did he tell you the reason he hired you to make me a dress is so he can sell me to a rich man?"

"I go where my clients wish me to go. I do not ask questions. I know that if my dress pleases, I can expect business from an important person that monsieur has as yet declined to name."

I tore the jacket from her hands and tossed it to the bed. She brandished the shears. "What makes you believe him? Important people already have dress-makers! Why would they need another? What's to keep him from selling you along with me? What's to keep him from killing you now that he's got what he wanted? What do you really know of him?"

She pocketed the shears and rescued the jacket. "I know more than made-moiselle can imagine," she said. She began to thread her needle.

The key turned in the lock. Patch strolled in like the cock o' the walk. "Your bath is ready." I snatched up my waistcoat and shrugged into it. The doctor was the only man who'd ever seen me partly undressed, during those three days my body lay helpless while my mind rode my peregrine. I wanted the earth to swallow me whole so Patch would stop looking at me in my shift.

"I shall have the jacket finished by the time the young lady has bathed," the dressmaker said.

"We'll drive you back into the city," he said.

"How kind of you." She smiled at him.

"Come along, Jessamyn," he said.

"I don't need help bathing," I said.

"But you need help finding the bath, don't you?" he said.

We left Mrs. Thomas taking in the jacket with tiny, even, quick stitches, as calmly as though she hadn't heard a single argument I'd offered.

Patch gripped my wrist and pulled me all the way down the stairs to a little room off the cold, echoing kitchen, a sort of pantry with just the one door and no windows. Inside was a bath full of steaming water. He pushed me into the room. Linen towels sat on a chair beside a dish of soap.

"Go ahead," he said.

"You can kill me right here if you like," I said, "but I am not taking a bath with you watching."

"Such a prude," he said. "Very well, if only to save myself another argument. We haven't time for one." He shut and locked the door.

I felt like I was being watched, but I bathed anyway, if for no other reason than to scrub his touch from my body. Afterwards, I wrapped one towel around my waist, another around my chest, and a third around my shoulders. I began to finger-comb my hair.

I heard the key in the lock. Patch said, "I don't hear you splashing. I'm coming in."

I stood. My skin gleamed. My hair already had begun to curl. My pink feet crabbed on the cold floor. He didn't say anything, just stared.

My face flamed. I clutched tight to the towel around my shoulders. Nobody but my mother had ever seen me like this. My stomach churned when he said, "You clean up nicely."

I stopped myself slapping his face. He might not be able to use his power against Margery, but he still could poison her, or burn her shop, or anything. I had to pretend I was still afraid of what he might do—and I rather was.

"Your jacket is done," he said. "Time to get dressed and meet your grandparents."

He grabbed my shift in one hand and my wrist in the other and dragged me up the stairs. Behind a screen, Mrs. Thomas put me into the shift and a pair of stockings. She laced me into the stays, then into the Brunswick dress. She fetched out a muslin pinner cap woven with green silk ribbon. She put up my hair, pinned on the little ribboned cap, and pushed me out from behind the screen.

Patch said, "That green is perfect. My compliments, madame." He reached into his waistcoat pocket. "One more thing will finish the outfit." He pulled out my mother's cameo. "I changed out the ribbon. The other wasn't fit to tie around a dog's neck." He circled his forefinger to make me turn my back to him. He tied the cameo around my neck, and then turned me back and smiled down at me. I thought I might vomit. *Of course he's put a Call back into the cameo.* He raised the hood of the Brunswick jacket and pulled down bits of my hair to curl on my forehead and in front of my ears. I wanted to bite his nose off. My fingers strayed to Mum's cameo hanging from its new ribbon. *Could I cleanse it myself? Could I find an alder tree?* While Mrs. Thomas gathered her things, Patch sat me on the bed and slid on my shoes. "Just like Cinderella," he said.

Don't kick him, I ordered myself. "Cinderella got her shoe from a prince," I said, "not a monster. You're mixing up your stories."

He squeezed my ankle and said, "I may not be a prince, Jessamyn, but I am ruler over you." Then he slipped a heavy canvas hood over my entire head, saying, "This will keep you calm, little falcon." He took hold of my arm above the elbow as we descended the stairs. I couldn't see a thing. "We're off to Lincoln's Inn Fields," he said over his shoulder. "Where can we drop you?"

"The Strand at Covent Garden, and thank you," Mrs. Thomas said.

Patch helped me into the carriage. Mrs. Thomas got in behind me on my right. Patch got in on my left. I couldn't leap out either door unless I cleared one of them first. I couldn't get a look at where we were going, but after a short time I heard the shouts of the watermen, so I guessed we'd reached Westminster Bridge. We started across.

Craven Street would come just after Westminster off the Strand. If I could get out, I could run through the alleys to the back door at Craven Street. *If* I could get out.

"Are you looking forward to meeting your grandparents?" Patch asked, perhaps in a show of politeness for Mrs. Thomas.

"I am, yes," I lied. *I can't run from both of them,* I fretted. "Can't you take this hood off? I can't breathe."

"Of course," Patch said. "We've come far enough now." He lifted the hood.

I blinked as my eyes adjusted to sunlight. I looked out Mrs. Thomas's window. Westminster gleamed just over the river.

Gods or Grannies were looking out for me, because when we reached Charing Cross, the driver slowed down. Patch thumped on the roof. "There's trouble ahead," the driver said.

We stopped. Patch growled, "We haven't time for this." He got out to look.

That left just Mrs. Thomas and me in the carriage. This was my chance. I put my hand on her arm. "Mrs. Thomas."

She twitched her arm away, frowning. "How did you know my name?"

"I know who you are, Mrs. Thomas," I said, "so if you don't help me escape, I shall bring charges against you."

Her eyes sharpened. I could see her weighing prison against Patch. Out the window, I could just see the roof of the first house on Craven Street. I'd walked by it a hundred times.

"I can't help you," she finally said. "He'll make me sorry if I do."

"Then *move!*" I said, and shoved her out.

She shrieked. The driver looked around. Bill, all got up like a coachman! I stepped on Mrs. Thomas's stomach. "Sorry!" I said. She grabbed the bottom of my dress, but I tore it free. Patch was making his way back to the carriage. He saw me. I slapped one of the horses' rumps as I ran by so Bill would have to rein them in.

"Stop! You there in the cap—stop!" Patch shouted. I kept running, tearing off the cap as I pelted around and between and through the crowd that had gathered around a downed cow. "*Thief!*" Patch cried. He pointed and began to shove people out of his way.

All of London hates a thief, the ones who are stolen from because of what they lose, the thieves because of the competition. That's why thieving is punished by branding or even hanging. Ahead of me was a dense thicket of bodies and hands and eyes. I ran toward them. *Move aside,* I thought. *Stop him.* "Please let me through," I said.

To my shock and everlasting relief, the crowd parted like the Red Sea and closed behind me. I didn't stop to see how close Patch was. I legged it to the head of Craven Street and dashed around to the back of Mrs. Stevenson's house. My stays dug into my belly like hands around a throat.

Without knocking, I burst into Mrs. Macintyre's kitchen. She spun around from the stove with a spoon in her hand and said, "Here, what's this? Who are you?"

I gasped, "Mrs. Macintyre, it's me, Jenna."

"What on earth—"

"Hide me, please! I'll explain later."

"But—"

"Please! Now!"

She was a Scotswoman, drilled from infancy to protect her own. She pushed me into the pantry and stood in the doorway with her hand on the knob. I heard banging on the front door and Myrtle's feet hurrying downstairs. Mrs. Macintyre said, "Shh, now. Listen." Footsteps approached the pantry. Mrs. Macintyre eased the door shut. I listened.

I heard Myrtle say, "There's a gent outside who wants to know if we've seen a young lady in brown silk hurrying by."

"When?" Mrs. Macintyre said.

"Just now, I think," Myrtle said. "What shall I say?"

"Did you see someone like that?"

"No, I was upstairs fetching Dr. Franklin's tray."

"Well, tell that to the gentleman. Say if a person wanted to duck out of sight, there'd be no better place to do it than the Strand."

Myrtle's feet retreated, and Mrs. Macintyre slipped into the pantry with me. She put her hands on my shoulders. She whispered, "Let me look at ye! Oh, Jenna, you've growed up so lovely! What're ye doin' here? Oh—you're not on the run from the dressmaker? Does she beat ye?"

Oh, dear! As far Mrs. Macintyre knows, I've been a dressmaker's assistant for the last three and a half years. "I am on the run, yes," I said.

"You'd best go back. She c'd blacken your name so's you c'd never do dress-making again."

"I never wanted to make dresses, Mrs. Macintyre, but right now—is Dr. Franklin in?"

"Aye, but he's goin' out presently. What d'ye want with him?"

"I've got to catch him before he goes. It's urgent." I hugged her. "Thank you, Mrs. Macintyre. I'll try to explain it all to you after I talk to Dr. Franklin. Please."

"Well! But—"

I slipped around her and dashed to the servants' stairs and started up. I was halfway up when Mrs. Macintyre stuck her head around the wall and called after me, "I'll be waiting for answers, my girl, and if I don't get 'em, I'll spank 'em out of you with my spoon."

"All right," I hissed down. I dashed down the hall, knocked on Franklin's door, and ducked inside.

"Why, hello," he said. "Who are y—*Jem?*" He looked me up and down. "What on earth are you doing here got up like that? It's very becoming, of course, but surely it defeats your purpose? Did anybody see you?"

"Mrs. Macintyre. She thinks I'm Jenna on the run from the dressmaker. Listen, Dr. Franklin: I just escaped from Patch. He kidnapped me yesterday from the apothecary and planned to deliver me this morning to the duke."

The smile faded from his eyes. "Dear God. I wondered where you'd got to yesterday."

"I escaped his carriage just off Westminster Bridge and ran here. He said he'd hurt Margery! I must get to the doctor and Margery and warn them."

Dr. Franklin went to his door and looked up and down the hall, then closed the door and said quietly, "This is the man who tried to take you before? The duchess's man? Does he know Abernathy or where he lives?"

"I don't think so."

"Is he still about?"

"Mrs. Macintyre sent him to the Strand, but I don't know if he went."

"You can't leave this house. I shall go warn the doctor. Stay here."

"But—"

"Jem, you can and must cooperate. He's sniffing around one of your bolt-holes. It's unlikely he's working alone. Stay in my laboratory. I'll go fetch the doctor. I'm sure he and his bride are still settling in together."

The wedding had been only yesterday, but it seemed a lifetime ago.

Franklin fetched his hat, and I went into his laboratory to wait, but I fretted about the cameo around my neck that might be calling to Patch even now. Patch had tied a hard knot in the ribbon, so I had to cut it off. For lack of something better, I dropped it into a Hessian crucible and popped on the lid. I could try to cleanse it later with alder twigs, but I dared not leave it with Franklin again. For now, all I could do was pray *Don't see me.*

* * *

Three pairs of eyes looked at me, one set peering over spectacles, one from beneath a row of red curls, and the third from under thick eyebrows massed in an angry line. Margery said, "Jem, we've been frantic since Jory came back with a lump on his head. What happened?"

"I'll tell you everything, but first, Mum's cameo is in the laboratory. I have to get rid of it."

"Your cameo! How did you get it back?"

"Patch's man, the confectioner's apprentice, was the one who stole it."

"But if Granny burned the Call in Cornwall, why is the cameo still a problem?"

"Because Patch put in another one. He couldn't wait to tie it around my neck."

"Show me." I led her to the lab and pointed at the crucible. Margery lifted out the cameo and closed her fingers over it. "One good thing about being dead to Sight is that I'm dead to the Dark as well."

"He can't see you, Margery?"

"Not by Sight." We rejoined my doctors and sat on Franklin's settee. "Now, Jem, tell us everything." During my recitation, Margery put her arm around me. When I got to the part about Mrs. Thomas, Dr. Abernathy said, "The *dressmaker* Mrs. Thomas?"

"Yes, the one with the rows of curls across the top of her head."

"Can *she* be involved with this devil? Thank heaven she never met you, or he would look for you at our house." He and Margery exchanged a look. The doctor said, "You're robbed at knifepoint the day you return to town, and now Patch is on to drugs and coercion."

Franklin exhaled. "This is a ridiculous situation. Why don't you just go to Newcastle House on your own and meet your grandparents? You might like them, and once they hear what Patch has done, he would be discharged."

"And then I would be trapped in their house." *How much could we tell him? How much could he believe?* I said, "Sir, it isn't that simple. Patch said someone other than the duchess wants me to disappear into an asylum or the Magdalen Hospital or someplace like that." I turned to Margery and said, "Patch said he would hurt you. He said he would burn down your shop."

Margery laughed! "I've a good, stout club if he comes to the shop. The confectioner gave his 'prentice the boot when I told him the rat robbed you. Mr. Miller won't let Patch into the physick garden any more—and anyway, I don't eat or drink anything I haven't prepared myself or seen prepared, not after that marchpane cake! Besides, Jem, I'm no use to Patch except to threaten you with. If he harmed me, he'd lose his lever, aye? I s'pose he could burn the shop, but what would be the point of it?"

"To punish you for helping me," I said, "just that. We were right about him, Margery. Patch can hear when I use my Sight."

Franklin said, "A moment: how can the man hear you looking at something?"

Abernathy cleared his throat. "Jem, may I?" I nodded. "Jem has a…talent, that helps her attend to our patients. It's one of the reasons I took her on. It's called Second Sight." He cleared his throat. "She can lay hands on someone and feel disease inside him."

"By touch? Can this be true?" Franklin said. "Jem, this must be studied!"

"I have been studying it," I said.

Dr. Abernathy said to Franklin, "Jem's Sight is very like the so-called witch-craft of old. You would think mankind would have got past believing in witches, but if Jem told the average Londoner all the things she can do, they'd burn her at the stake."

"Why, what else can she do?" Franklin asked. He rested his elbows on his knees and looked at me over clasped hands. "In what other ways does your… Sight manifest itself?"

I took a deep breath, praying that the man who played with lightning would believe my incredible story. "I can hear animals thinking. I can see the future, not clearly, but just…pictures. That day I fell at your feet when we were wind-ing bandages, I…I saw great iron birds who laid eggs as they flew, and the eggs exploded when they hit the ground. At solstice, I saw flames and gunpowder smoke and myself tending to someone beside a fire. It seemed like—felt like—a battle."

"You think you saw a war…in the future?" Franklin said.

I shrugged. "Maybe. I saw mountains and a forest from horseback, and then a view of a lake as big as a sea. I don't know where I was, exactly, but Granny saw the lake too. She says it's in America, and I'm supposed to go there."

"Remarkable. What else?"

"When I focus, I can feel…Light everywhere, in everything."

"Light?"

"Not light, as in a candle or the sun. Light, as in whatever allows something to exist in the first place."

"You can't mean…Divine Providence?"

"Maybe. I just call it Light. Its enemy is the Dark. The Dark wants my Sight. That's another reason Patch wants me."

"Patch is…what, he is in league with this 'Dark'? He doesn't want to give you over to your grandparents?"

"He wants both, but I don't know which he wants more."

Franklin leaned back in his chair. "Is that all?"

"No, sir." I paused, looking down at my fingers busily pleating my skirt. "I can fly, too."

Franklin sat, blinking.

Dr. Abernathy said, "These last two years when Jem lived in Cornwall, she was training with Margery's grandmother who is…skilled in this same talent."

"Mrs. Penhaligon?" Franklin said. "Well, well. How intriguing. This talent is called Sight?" We watched his face. "Well," he said, "once I was blind, but now I see." It was a poor joke, for him, but it lightened the moment. A bit.

Franklin cleared his throat. "It sounds to me as though the powers conferred on you by this 'Sight' are the same powers attributed to practitioners of the old religion of the Celtic peoples of this island," Franklin said, "a religion, I confess, I dismissed as fairy tale and legend. More fool I." He stood and paced to the window, then turned with concern in his eyes. "If Patch drained this Sight of yours, as you believe he wants to do, would it kill you?"

"No. But I would be dull, and I couldn't see colors. I couldn't See or Do anything ever again."

"I wish I had known of this from the beginning of our association," Franklin said, "for we could have spent our time together studying this phenomenon." He turned. "Unfortunately, I cannot study you now, because it is clear we must get you out of London as soon as possible." To Dr. Abernathy, he said, "You've booked her passage on the *Red Queen*?"

"She sails in two days."

Franklin clasped his hands behind his back and began a slow pace to and from the window as he talked. "If I may, I should like to lay out the facts so we can look at them. Patch has been paid by the Duchess of Newcastle for fifteen years to find Jem's mother and Jem, and now the duke wants Jem as well."

"Patch sent them a note saying he'd bring me to them today," I said. "If I hadn't jumped out of the carriage, I'd be there now."

"Which works in your favor," Franklin said, "for if Patch doesn't bring you, they will demand to know what happened to you. They may detain him. To continue: Jem, you learned last night that another party wants you hidden away but kept alive for some undisclosed purpose."

"What purpose, I wonder?" the doctor said.

"In order to speculate, I would need to know the identity of this second party," Franklin said. "Who owns a great house in Lambeth that he leaves empty? That is highly unusual for London. At any rate, whatever this mysterious person wants with Jem must be terribly important or he would have paid Patch a great deal more than the duke offered to simply do away with her." He regarded me over his spectacles.

Franklin continued, "I wonder if this unnamed person also is interested in Jem's…special abilities. Flying, foretelling the future, sensing disease, talking with animals—any one of these would be a useful advantage to any number of people. Myself included, to be honest." I wiped my palms on my skirt. Franklin sighed.

"To sum up: In two days, we must get Jem aboard the *Red Queen* without her being seen or heard. Not by Patch, nor his spies, nor the unnamed person from Lambeth, nor anybody who might be working for him. Are we agreed? Good.

"Let us move on to obstacles. Jem, you say when you use your Sight, Patch can hear you?"

"That's what he said. There was a Call in Mum's cameo—a bit of Mum's hair, put there a long time ago. Granny thought Patch had a bit of Mum's hair as well, and that was how he kept finding me, because 'Like seeks like.' I thought the attraction between the two bits of hair might have something to do with Newton's law of planetary motion."

"Good heavens," Franklin said. "Now I really regret having to send you away."

"I know, but Granny says I have to go to America."

"Why?"

"Because there's something there waiting for me, Granny says. She felt it."

"Extraordinary," Franklin said. "What does your cameo have to do with your Sight?"

"Patch can find me when I wear it. He put it on me this morning. He tied a knot in the ribbon."

Franklin said, "But he could have done that so your mother's jewelry was clearly on display for your grandparents to see immediately." All four of us frowned at Margery's fist. "Might I ask a question? If Patch could track you as easily as listening for you, wouldn't he have found you long ago? What if your Sight doesn't call to Patch as loudly as he says? What if he exaggerated to make you feel helpless, Jem? He told you himself he uses spies and bribes."

"Do you think so?" I breathed.

"He couldn't find you over the last two years," Margery said, "and you were training with Granny then. Using your Sight all the time."

I'd wondered about that. "Why couldn't he?"

"Maybe because you were so far away? Or it might be because Granny makes wards and asks the Light to keep her safe," Margery said. "Our marks give some protection as well. Granny, er, used the same ink for my daisy that she used for your pelican. The marks warm just a bit if someone Sighted is close—didn't you notice?"

"No, but my mark is on this side, and that's the pocket the doll was in. That's the only thing that felt warm."

"I would like to suggest that that Patch hears Jem most clearly when she wears that cameo," Franklin said, "that it amplifies her whereabouts, like an ear trumpet magnifies sound."

Dr. Abernathy's jaw dropped. "Franklin, I believe you've hit it! Jem, you don't wear the cameo all the time."

"You hid it under my bureau the day your mother died," Franklin said.

"And then the ribbon fell apart—"

"—and then Franklin had it for weeks while awaiting the jeweler's report."

"—and then I wore it to Cornwall."

Margery said, "Patch felt you leave London, Jem, but Granny removed the Call before he could find you, and that's why he made a Door in that march-pane flower, hoping I'd bring the cake to wherever you were. Which I did. But we've got it now," she raised the fist that had the cameo inside, "and I'm as good as a Blind Box."

"This story would defy belief if I'd heard it from anybody other than you three," Franklin said. He shook his head. "Well, allow me to voice my theory: the evidence suggests Patch can *not* track Jem as easily as he says, which, in turn, suggests that he relies on normal eyesight as well as on…magical Sight."

"But he does have a queer eye," I said. "I saw it last night. It was all black. No white. It had red lightning forking down over the eyeball."

"Did you see this before or after you drank the tainted tea?" Dr. Abernathy asked.

"After." I paused. "Do you think I was hallucinating, like when I saw the snake at the physick garden? Because I think Patch put *Datura* in my tea, along with valerian and opium."

Margery gasped. Her freckles stood out. "Dear heaven, Jem, I've just thought of something. What if you weren't hallucinating at Chelsea? What if the snake was Patch? He said he saw you there with me."

"If that is so, then chemicals must affect your Sight, Jem—which now that I think about it makes perfect sense. Even in normal people, certain substances affect perception. Oh, how I regret not being able to study you!"

"Excuse me," Dr. Abernathy said, "but may I suggest we press on? Jem, you stayed away from the shop for months because we suspected Patch had hired spires, which was a correct assumption. That is still an obstacle, as I don't doubt they still are there, including the one in the barrel beside the back door. No doubt they will watch Margery's every move once she returns. A third obstacle is that anybody between here and Westminster Bridge who saw Jem on the run might gossip about it to anybody who expresses interest, so she can't stay here."

"She can't wear that dress out of here, either," Franklin said.

"Then we all agree Jem must stay hidden until we can get her aboard the *Red Queen*."

Margery jumped up, *giggling*. "I've just got a mad idea. Listen to this."

CHAPTER 31

OCTOBER 1, 1761

Farewell to London

When she'd finished talking, Dr. Abernathy said, "Wife, that is a mad plan. And a brilliant one. Don't you two agree? Franklin, stop laughing."

"Sorry, Abernathy, my imagination whirled me away. Yes, I agree, it's brilliant."

"But you can't hold that cameo in your hand for two days, my love, not if you want to execute a plan like that." Dr. Abernathy kissed the top of Margery's head. "Shall I go fetch the Blind Box from the shop?"

"No. Take the cameo there. Let's not risk having the doll and the cameo both at home. Besides, I'll need them tomorrow when Artie and I go to the shop. But you might go to my Da's house and tell Artie and John what we propose to do. Tell them I'll come over later today. John can drive me and Artie to Claremont House in the morning after we bait the hook."

"I'll go to the bank after I talk to them. Perhaps I'll stop at a ragpicker's in Spitalfields for some sort of traveling dress for Jem to change into when she arrives in Philadelphia."

"Go to a haberdasher instead. Bring Tressa with you. She drives a hard bargain and has an eye for sizes."

"Dr. Abernathy," I said, "you should bring this dress for Artie to try on. Then Tressa can have a look at it as well."

"Good idea," Margery said. "Mum and Alice can alter it this evening if it needs it. Jem, have you anything here to wear?"

"Yes, I left a suit of clothes here last time Dr. Franklin and I swam in the river."

"The first time was also the last, if I recall," Franklin said. "Swimming was not to your taste."

"It wasn't the swimming I didn't care for, it was the Thames."

Franklin fetched out my spare clothes, and he and Dr. Abernathy left the room whilst I tore off the dress and the stays and all the rest and put on my breeches, shirt, and waistcoat. "I can breathe again," I said.

"I hope John and Tressa can find something nice for you to wear in Philadelphia," Margery said, "because Artie will have to wear this tomorrow, including the stays if he's to fit into this jacket. It might not come back looking very nice."

"Mrs. Thomas took it in at the waist. Alice should be able to let it out again. Are you certain Artie will agree to do this?"

"He's my one brother mad for adventure. He's the one always game to go to a play with me—didn't you hear him mimicking birds and animals at the wedding? "

"No, I must have been talking with Elaine on the portico."

"Well, he does people too. He could do you easy, I think."

"Finished in there?" Franklin asked. "Abernathy is anxious to leave, and I have an engagement I'm already late for."

"Yes, all done, sorry," Margery answered.

The men came in. "Here, let's wrap that dress." Franklin took the case from his pillow and handed it to Margery, who rolled up the dress and stuffed it inside. "There you are, Abernathy. Before you go, let me just confirm that I am to precede Margery's brothers to the *Red Queen* early Saturday morning. I assume you will drive me there in your trap?"

"Yes. I'll come early." He turned to Margery. "Wife, I'll see you this evening, I trust?"

"'Tis twenty years 'til then.'"

"And now she's quoting Juliet," he said, but the way they looked at one another—honestly, it warmed my heart and brought tears to my eyes, both. The doctor kissed her check. "My clever wife. I'll see you at home for dinner." He left straightaway.

Franklin said, "Mrs. Abernathy, my compliments. A plan like this is worthy of Robert Rogers himself."

"The commander of the Rangers in America?" Margery blushed. "Surely not, sir."

"Well, let us just say I should hate to oppose a strategist like you in a conflict," Franklin said. "However, I do see a difficulty with your plan. You've thought of everything but the fact that Patch may be able to 'hear' Jem a little, even without the cameo. What if he doesn't follow you and your brother to Claremont House because he isn't fooled? Jem herself might scuttle your plan. It's unfortunate we cannot put her into a Blind Box."

"Can you go into your hidey-hole, Jem?" Margery asked.

"Yes, but I think my Sight leaks."

Margery bit her lip. Franklin got up to pace. Margery's brilliant plan covered every possibility—except for me. How could I be contained for a day and a half? If only there were such a thing as a girl-sized Blind Box.

I gasped. "Margery, I know! Dr. Franklin, may I borrow a quill and paper?" He fetched them out. I scribbled, then held up the paper. "Granny's Blind Box has these marks on it. This rune means sleep, this one means quiet, and this one means lock."

"Yes, mine has the same marks."

"The cameo and the doll are dead to Patch once they're in the box."

"I've said so."

"Then let's make a Blind Box for me."

"How?"

"Make one out of the trunk I'm to hide in to go from Cavendish Square to the wharves. We can carve these runes into the trunk. Once I'm inside, I'll be hidden to any normal person and masked to any Sighted person. You and Artie and John can lead Patch away from the city tomorrow, and I'll stay at home until Saturday morning, when I'll go into my big Blind Box and stay there until the ship is underway."

"Jem, it would be dreadful to be shut up inside a trunk. It would be like being in a coffin."

"It'll only be for part of a day," I said. "I'll scratch Granny's protecting runes at the corners of my room at home so I'm safe all day tomorrow. I've already made them for Lanyon. On Saturday morning, Dylan and Alfred can cart me down to the ship. Dr. Franklin can insist that his own men must place the trunk in Master Abernathy's cabin." I grinned. "You can say sailors would jostle the trunk too much."

"I think I can play the meticulous gentleman without any trouble."

"Let's go home and get started, Jem, for I must be off to speak with Artie."

"One moment." Franklin fetched out a thick packet from his desk. "Jem, here are your letters of introduction. I used the name Jem Connolly only, in case events dictate another change in your gender," he said. "And try writing a letter of introduction for someone without using a pronoun. It's a challenge."

"Thank you."

"You're welcome." He rubbed his hands together. "I always play the statesman. It will be great fun to play the man of action for a change. Off you go. I shall see you the day after tomorrow."

As for me, the only improvement to Margery's plan I could think of was finding out that by some miracle I didn't have to go after all.

* * *

Margery helped me make the marks of protection in my room in Cavendish Square. "Can you do the rest?"

"I think so," I said. "Granny taught me to pray with intention, believing. She told me to think of the Light, to imagine it making a sort of moat all around the place I want protected."

"Good. Have at it. I'd best go teach Artie how to walk like a girl and see that all is well. Now that I think of it, I may stay there tonight. If I'm not home for dinner, that's what I did. Tomorrow about ten o'clock, Artie and John and I will take Da's horse and trap to the shop. Artie and I will have a nice loud whisper on the back step about driving to Claremont House to meet the duke."

"I hope Tim is still hiding in the barrel."

"Well, you got away from Patch, so I imagine he'll double the watch on any place you might go. Patch doesn't know that *we* know about Tim hiding in the barrel. For good measure, Artie and I will go around to the front so 'Jem' can have one last, fond look at the shop before she goes to her grandparents. One of Patch's spies is bound to see us."

"Tell Artie to be sure to leave the hood up on the Brunswick dress."

"Of course. We'll leave for Surrey before eleven on Friday. That ought to give Patch's spies enough time to get word to Patch that you plan to go to Clare-mont House. Even if it takes them a while to find Patch and tell him, it's three hours to drive all the way from London to Esher if we walk the horse, which we will. We'll keep the doll and cameo with us until we get to Claremont, then we'll hide them somewhere on the estate, maybe in the woods if there is one. If Patch does catch us up and finds out it's Artie wearing your dress, well, John wanted to kill the man who bashed Jory on the head. I'll be bringing my club, and Artie carries a dagger in his boot—don't tell Mum."

"I won't, but you three shouldn't try to fight Patch."

"Jem, love, it's three against one. And think about this: nobody fights as fierce as a mother or a friend, and I'm both of those to you and more besides. Anyway, by the time Patch figures out what we we're up to, it'll be too late for him to get back to London and find you, what with your wards splashed all around. No, I'd say our nasty Patch is done for."

She took my shoulders in her hands. "Jem, I know my plan will work. The only bad part of all of this is that I can't be with you every single second of your last day in London. I love you, dearest Jem." She kissed me and hurried out, and I couldn't get myself started for several minutes.

Finally, though, I wiped my eyes. *To work, my girl,* I told myself. I locked the door so Mrs. Pierce couldn't come in. I wasn't certain how she would feel if she saw me praying over runes given that she didn't think a great deal of me in the first place—except in my capacity as general dogsbody.

I stood in one corner over the first mark, gathering up my courage. So much was at stake. I prayed, and I tried to imagine Light setting aglow the mark Margery and I had made.

A hum like I'd heard at solstice began to pulse at the edges of my focus. Did that mean my prayer was taking hold? I tried to see a line of Light flowing from the first mark toward the second at the window. That was when I noticed the humming was louder and the room had grown dimmer. I stopped praying. Instead of the Light, had I somehow called the Dark directly to me? In fear, I glanced at the window.

It was half-covered with bees, their throbbing little bodies thick on the glass. The last place I'd seen so many bees in one place was Dolly's hives. But the bees didn't feel like a threat, so I walked closer and placed my fingertips lightly on the glass.

The sprinkling of bees opposite my fingers flew out and swooped a bee dance. I lightly placed my whole hand on the pane. From every direction, bees on the wing began to converge on the window. They landed, one after the other, until a living, golden blanket draped the entire outside of the window. I closed my eyes and sent out a little sliver of Sight to the bees clustered over the outline of my hand. What came back was the slightest taste and smell of mead. My heart leapt up: these *were* Dolly's bees. Granny must have walked over to Kilmar Tor and asked Dolly to send her bees to protect me.

Gratitude and love flooded my heart at this simple act of sisterhood. Elowen had said, "We'll always be together in the Light," but I hadn't imagined the three of them finding a way to protect me from so far away. Bees never flew far from their hive, but out of love for Dolly, the swarm had come, against their nature, to a city thick with smoke to find someone they'd met only the one time.

Had they flown all the way to London without stopping? Were they hungry? Could I direct them to the flowers in the parks nearby? I placed my hand on the glass again, visualizing the asters, delphiniums, carnations, lilies, and other fall flowers across the street in the park. When I lifted my hand, every single bee on the other side of the glass had gone, leaving behind a hand-shaped piece of blue sky. I put my hand back, and other bees came. I sent them the same pictures. The blanket covering the window lightened a bit, though the bees didn't all go at once.

If the sisters could work such magic all the way from Cornwall, surely I could show enough faith to bring about a smaller miracle. I returned to the first mark of protection and imagined Light flowing from that one to the next, all the way around the room like a shining silver rope.

A knock at the door was followed by Mrs. Pierce calling, "Master Connelly, I've brought a tray." I unlocked the door and reached for the tray, but Mrs. Pierce brushed past me and set it on the table. She said, "Why have you drawn the curtains on such a pretty day, are you ill? Is that why the doctor told me to leave you alone?" Then she saw the bees. "Heaven help us! What are those nasty things doing there? Go away!" She raced over and rapped on the glass. Some of the bees rose up, humming their agitation.

"Don't!" I said. "It's all right. They're just sunning themselves. They're fine."

Mrs. Pierce backed away from the window. "Bees sting," she said to me as though I were an imbecile. "They could get in."

"Mrs. Pierce, I'm sure they'll move on after they've rested. They don't bother me at all."

"I've never seen a swarm on this house in all my life." She twisted her hands together.

To distract her, I said, "Well, they're on the other side of the glass. Here, I'll draw the curtains so you don't have to look at them. You've brought tea and bread. How kind of you."

"The doctor ordered it for you. You don't look sick to me." Her eyes darted to the closed curtain.

"I'm not. I'm leaving for Philadelphia on Saturday. I have to pack."

"I see. Great deal of changes around here lately."

"I'm certain you and Mrs. Abernathy will get along. She's a good person."

"She seems quite…energetic. And she says she likes to cook, which would seem to let me out of a job."

"Hardly! There's a great deal to do in a house this size. Perhaps the doctor will even hire a maid to help you now that he's taken a wife."

"I should hope so. I can't be expected to light the fires and wash the kettles and empty the chamberpots on top of everything else."

"I'll ask him, shall I?

"As you wish," she said. "Well, I must go to the market. I can bring back your dinner, unless Mrs. Abernathy plans to cook?"

"I believe she has been called to her mother's, but she may be home. I can't say. Why don't you carry on as always until you hear differently?" I stuck out my hand. "I guess this is goodbye then, Mrs. Pierce. It has been a pleasure to know you." She took my hand, and I thought I felt a little fizz at my hip when our fingers touched. I dismissed it, for if Mrs. Pierce were Sighted, surely I'd have known before today.

Yet the moment we touched, her eyes fell to our clasped hands and then up to my face. The line between her eyes smoothed somewhat. "Goodbye, then— Jem. Happy voyage." It was the nicest thing she'd ever said to me.

When she was gone, I opened up the curtains again. Enough light came in between the blanket of bees to let me start packing my trunk and my valise. Into the trunk I put my casebook and my rough copy of the medicine book I'd made for Margery, plus quills and ink and paper. Margery had said I'd need thread, needles, a comb and a brush, so I put those in too. I raised Granny's seeds to my nose to enjoy just a whiff of the faraway cottage on the moor before wrapping them in muslin and stowing them inside the trunk. I packed a spare shirt, waistcoat, and breeches. Into my smaller valise I packed a change of stockings, a second shirt, and the journal I'd kept at Granny Kestrel's.

Then I faced the empty trunk that I would ride to my ship. I took up a knife from the tea tray and carved the three runes that made a Blind Box on the bottom panel and the lid. I prayed over them with as much intention as I could muster. They *had* to hide me. I slipped down to the cellar and rummaged until I found nails and wire so I could fasten the trunk shut from the inside. I lined it with my winter cloak.

Just as I finished, I heard the front door open and steps coming up the stairs and down the hall. "Jem?" the doctor called.

"In here. I'm just working on the trunk."

He carried in an armful of clothing, which he dumped on the bed. "Tressa insisted my 'niece' be given a choice, but I persuaded her that my 'niece' didn't care tuppence for dresses."

I fingered the blue wool and then the green-figured linen. "Both, don't you think? Who knows how long I'll be in Philadelphia." At that thought, I swallowed, hard, then turned away so he couldn't see my eyes. "Thank you." I began to fold the dresses.

"I have something else in my room you need to pack." While he was gone, I knuckled the tears from my eyes. When he came back he handed me a stone bottle corked closed. "What's this?" I said.

"Lemon juice with sugar and brandy for the scurvy. I read about it in a treatise several years ago by a Navy doctor from Edinburgh, where I studied. Obscure little paper I'm afraid nobody else read, but the fellow who wrote it described a series of experiments done on a ship with sailors who had the scurvy. I recommend you take a sip of this every day. Just a sip. Make it last." He pulled something out of his pocket and handed it to me. "This is a brush for the teeth. I just got it from Brussels. You scrub your teeth with it."

"Thank you."

"Franklin and I will bring Mrs. Franklin's dishes to the ship tomorrow and tell them we'll bring the rest of Master Abernathy's things just before the ship sails."

"Good."

"Jem? What is it?"

I let my hands rest on the smooth wool skirt in the trunk. "It doesn't seem real that two days from now I'll be sailing away from you and Margery, and Granny as well. That I might not see any of you ever again. Everything I do takes me one step further away. I want to stop time. I want to stop moving altogether."

"Oh, Jem. I know." When he pulled me in to his arms, the lump in my throat felt like it might choke me. I began to sob. "There, there now."

Over the top of my head, he murmured, "Jem, you're going away to a world I've never seen. You'll make a life there among people I've never met. You may return to us one day; you may not. This could be our last conversation."

"I know. I can't bear it."

He continued, "When my wife and son died, I didn't think I had a heart left to break. Then I met you. You began with me like a burr under my saddle, but now you're like an extra arm or a second set of eyes. You've been a professional and a personal blessing to me, Jem, and I don't want you to leave us without hearing directly from me how very much I treasure you—and love you—and how much I shall miss you."

His words sank into my heart like an arrow. Images from my years with the doctor flooded into my mind: a pool of light guiding us on a dark street; his hand on my shoulder bringing comfort when a case was bloody or ugly or sad; his considering frown when he checked my case book as though he fully expected me to follow in his footsteps one day. In two days, I'd be parted from him, perhaps forever. Oh, how desperately I wanted to stop us here, now, freeze us just like this!

I swallowed, hard. "I can never, never repay you for all you've done for me. Never. I shall think of you as a father as long as I live."

He forced his lips into a smile. He cleared his throat and said, "And I shall think of you as a daughter. An extremely eccentric daughter." I blubbered out a laugh. He handed me his handkerchief saying, "You really should carry one of these on your person."

He smiled, and I smiled, and then he suddenly looked blurry again. He pulled me to his heart with both arms, and I wrapped my arms around his waist. True to her word, Margery stayed at her mother's that evening, and the doctor and I dined together in my room, just the two of us, although I didn't dare step outside my wards to help him cobble together our evening meal.

The next day, Dr. Abernathy had rounds in the morning but came home early enough to help me finish packing. He prepared an assortment of basic medicaments—opium, Jesuit bark, powdered willow bark, Vinegar of the Four Thieves—stoppered tightly in jars and wrapped to prevent breakage, as well as a tiny case of surgical needles, along with catgut and silk and a small German scissors.

I added these treasures to my trunk. Then he reached inside his waistcoat. "I brought you some money. You'll need it America. Here." He handed over a jingling pouch. "It's a hundred pounds. You can pay me back when you come home, which I hope you do before your money in Freame & Barclay earns another shilling of interest." I took it, packed it, wept again.

That night, I lay down for my last night in Dr. Abernathy's house, and he lay down for his second night without his new wife at his side.

* * *

In the morning, Dylan and Alfred Penhaligon drove up in a wagon whilst the doctor and I finished breakfast. Dr. Abernathy said, "I'll let them in to load you up, Jem, and go to fetch Dr. Franklin. We'll meet you at the *Red Queen*. In you go." The moment I put both feet into the trunk, the bees, who had vibrated on my window all night, began to flick off the window like blobs of yellow paint. *God speed,* I thought.

I folded myself down, shut the lid, and wired it closed. Dr. Abernathy said, "It's just for a little while, Jem." I heard the doctor's steps leave and then come back, followed by the heavier tread of Dylan and Alfred. They loaded me into the wagon, and we started off. I hoped Margery and Artie would meet us at the wharves before I sailed so I could find out what had happened with Margery's part of the plan.

We rattled along, the rumble of the wheels on the cobblestones shuddering up all four sides of the box in which I rode, but enough sounds penetrated the clatter to let me imagine our entire route: cattle lowed on Holborn on their way to market; the bells at St. Paul's tolled the hour; the shout and thump of sailors loading ships announced when we'd reached the wharves. The wagon, blessedly, stopped, and I heard Dylan shout, "Hy, there, over here."

"Hello, gentlemen, well met." Dr. Abernathy's voice. "Let's get Dr. Franklin's trunk aboard, shall we? He's just over there conversing with the first mate. I wonder where my wife can be? Did she come home to her father's last night?"

"Not that I know of," said one of the Penhaligons.

"Right. Ah, here comes Franklin. All right, then?"

"The mate says we haven't much time," Franklin answered. "They prefer large items go in the hold, but I insisted this trunk must travel in Master Abernathy's cabin. He says the cabin is so small Master Abernathy may have to sleep in it. It took a great deal of self-discipline to maintain my stern expression." He rapped on the trunk. "All well in there, my treasure? I hope my wife finds you as great a source of joy as you have been to me."

"Go along and load the trunk," Dr. Abernathy said, "I'll watch for Margery." I felt myself hoisted into the air as Dylan and Alfred carried me on to the ship.

"Hold a moment, sir. Our lads can take it from here," said a voice I didn't know.

"I was told my men would be allowed to carry the trunk to Master Abernathy's cabin," Franklin said. "Really, I must insist. Where is Captain Peterson? Perhaps he could reassure you."

"Let him pass, Smith, we've spoke," said somebody new, "but we're sho-vin' off soon's the tide starts runnin', Dr. Franklin, so if you and these two ain't ashore by then, you'll be swimmin' home."

"Thank you. We shall be off long before then. Gentlemen?" We moved for-ward.

"Give a tap where your head is, Jem," Dylan muttered, and when I did, he tipped the trunk so I wouldn't smash my head when they lowered it down the hatch. Franklin made a great deal of fuss, admonishing them at every turn, playing his part to the hilt.

They set down the trunk, then shoved it back and forth and up and down until I assumed I'd been properly wedged in place. I heard a thud, then and "Ow! Jem'll be stuck in here for six weeks? I'd go mad, I would."

"Shh," Dylan said. "Where's our Margery, then?"

The trunk creaked as someone sat on the lid. "I don't know," Franklin said. "I'm worried. She should have arrived by now."

"And so she has!" came a woman's voice, and I exhaled. Her voice got louder as she moved closer—she must be commenting about the ship to Dr. Aber-nathy—but the only remark I caught was "dark as a ditch," and then she must have arrived at the doorway to the cabin, for I clearly heard her say, "You three must step out so Artie can swap clothes with Jem, for Dr. A. told the first mate this was the lad going to America."

I heard footsteps shuffle out, and the door close, and Artie's voice saying, "I'll just wriggle out of these an' you wriggle out of yours. I don't think we need t' change shirts, d' you? Hand out your breeches and waistcoat under the lid, and I'll pass mine to you."

"I can't move in here," I said. "Turn your back and we'll trade clothes, and then I'll pop right back in."

"Well, come on out then." I got the trunk unwired and opened the lid. The light, even though we were belowdecks, seemed bright, and the air, even though it stank of fish and tar, smelled fresh and clean.

Artie was already out of his waistcoat. I hurriedly pulled off my own clothes and tossed them at him. "What's in that bag?" I asked.

"That brown silk cocoon of yours," Artie said, "and the stays as well. Margery wouldn't let me burn 'em."

I giggled. "What happened? Tell me!"

"Jem, you should have seen it, it was enough to make a dog laugh," he said, rapping his elbow. "Ow! It's like tryin' t' change clothes in a coffin. Anyhow, Margery made me walk up and down yesterday 'til I'd got your walk down, then this morning, John drove us to the shop.

"Margery and me goes in, and she ties that necklace on and puts the doll in my pocket. Then we go to the back door, and Margery says, loud, 'Well, Jem, here it is. Your last view of the shop. I don't suppose the duke will let you come and see me ever again, oh woe is me.'"

I laughed. "Margery said 'woe is me'? You can turn around, I'm done."

Artie spun around. "Aye, I thought it was a bit much as well, but she were getting into the spirit of it. So anyway, I says, playin' you, 'I fear I shall never see you again. Oh, but how could the Duke of Newcastle be so cruel to me, his very own granddaughter? Let us go together to his house in Surrey. I feel certain once he meets you, he will let us remain friends forever.'"

"Do I really sound like that?"

"Close enough. And then John, my brother, comes around in back with Da's trap. Mind, I've got that brown silk dress on with the hood up, the cameo round my neck, and the doll in my pocket. And the dress is only a little bit too short, but I figure the boy in the barrel won't see that. So we climb up in the trap, and off we go to Surrey.

"And all the time, I'm talkin' like you, and Margery and John are laughin' like fools. And we get on the road to Esher, and no Patch yet, and in the distance on a hill we see Claremont House! And we're wonderin' what to do if we gets all the way there, when we hear horse hooves gallopin' toward us. Margery turns and says, 'By God, it's him! Whip up the horse, John!' so John snaps the whip, and the horse speeds up.

"And this mopus wearing an eyepatch goes sailin' past on a horse all lathered up, and he's laughin' and he shouts, 'I'll announce you to your grandparents!' and he gallops ahead of us and inside the gate at Claremont. So we get to the gate, and we can see a groom takin' his horse and him goin' inside—and we turn around. I tear off the dress, Margery claps a bonnet over her hair, and we take a different road back to town."

I'd been smiling at Artie's recitation since he'd begun; he really was a most marvelous mimic. He'd got Margery and Patch and all the rest just perfect. And what a proper reward for Patch!

I said, "So Patch went in to announce Jem, and Jem didn't turn up. I'll wager he's still standing at attention answering the duke's questions. What did Margery do with the cameo and the doll?"

"She put 'em back in her Blind Box and wrapped 'em up, and I'm to take the parcel to Granny Kestrel to clean soon as you're off. Margery decided she didn't want 'em here in town."

"You're going all the way to Fowey? I wish I were."

"No, you're for a brand new place. As for me, Uncle Lanyon's goin' t' show me the fishin' life to see if I like it."

"Well, if you don't like it, I certainly could see you on the stage here in London."

"Really?" He grinned. "D' you think I'd be let to do it?"

Somebody rapped on the door. "Done in there?" It was Margery. "Artie, shut your gob, we've got to get off the ship. They're ready to shove off."

"Aye, coming," Artie said. "Jem, I never had so much fun in all my life. I'll think about what you said about the stage an' all, but I'll try the fishing first."

Before he left, I clasped his hand. "Goodbye, Art, and thank you." I stepped into the trunk, but Margery stuck in her head and said, "I have to go, but let me just give you a quick hug and a kiss, and remind you that you must write as often as you can."

"I will."

Franklin called out from behind her, "Don't forget to put on a dress for my wife."

Dr. Abernathy squeezed in beside Margery. "Jem, I said all I wanted to say to you at home, yet I feel I'd rather say goodbye a thousand times more rather than let you go." Margery took his hand. "Write to us. Write us every little thing. We'll meet again one day soon, I know it."

"Goodbye. I love you both with all my heart."

Out in the passage, an unfamiliar voice said, "Here now, who're all you? You three ain't s'posed t' be here." Margery gestured *down* with her hand, so down I went and wired myself in. "And you two as well? Gerroff all of you, on the double. We're about to weigh anchor."

"Goodbye, then," Margery said, and I heard the cabin door close and steps retreating. Above, on deck, feet pounded and chains clanked and sailors shouted, and in mere minutes, I heard the ship groan as her sails filled with wind and the tide began to take her.

After what I judged to be a reasonable amount of time, and too late for Patch or anybody else to stop the ship, I opened the trunk and stepped out. I put on my hat and climbed up to the deck, moving quickly to a spot near the rail where I would be out of the way. I looked out at London, at the workers and clergymen and peddlers and buildings and streets. I took deep breaths of the coal and fish and onion smells. I'd first seen London years before as a smudge of smoke on the horizon. Now that I knew her streets and her moods, now that I knew people who loved and struggled and laughed and cried here, I felt as though I were leaving a friend.

The gulls above cried, "On! On!" I turned my face into the brisk wind that filled our sails and relentlessly pushed me away. When Granny Kestrel had asked if I felt the pull of the New World, I'd said no. Ever since her question, though, I'd been expecting to feel whatever a pull was supposed to feel like. I hadn't. But now, safely on board a ship bound away from London, with Patch

(I hoped) banished from my life for good, I closed my eyes and placed my hand over the hip marked with a pelican. I calmed my mind. I sought the waterfall. I dipped in a finger.

And felt a thrumming, insistent tug on my heart and saw in my mind a shining path of light laid like a ribbon, running west from me to a distant point I couldn't see.

Acknowledgements

What sparked Jem's story was a classroom discussion about the American War of Independence. I asked whether the war might have been averted if Britain and America had gotten along better. Out of that conversation Jem was born.

Thank you to editor Mary Ellen Foley, who cracks the whip and works magic with a blue pencil. Without you, MEF, this book never would have become what it was meant to be.

Thank you to my beta readers, Jessi Peterson, Lauren Foeckler, and Kelsey Messner. Thanks to Dan Thiede of Kaze Studios for designing the book and creating the cover.

The heart of a historical novel is story, but its bones and sinews are research. Books that strengthened this novel include *The History of London in Maps* by Felix Barker and Peter Jackson, Kirstin Olsen's *Daily Life in 18th Century England*, *Crucible of War* by Fred Anderson, and *The Brother Gardeners* by Andrea Wulf. Books that helped me devise Jem's conversations with Dr. Franklin include *My Dear Girl* by James M. Stifler and *Benjamin Franklin, an American Life* by Walter Isaacson.

The web site maintained by the Chelsea Physic Garden was not only useful but also a delight for this avid amateur gardener.

Thanks also to the thousands of history and geography enthusiasts who generously share their research online. History buffs will have noticed that I altered some names and dates and invented some people and events to enhance the story. (For example, the *Present Peerages* book entries were invented, the Duke and Duchess of Newcastle had no children, and, as far as I know, the Bishop of Durham never faked a funeral!) In addition, there is not now and never has been, as far as I know, a poison corner in the Chelsea Physic Garden. The tribes of Tara did not embrace the Dark. A final word of caution: do not tattoo yourself with ink mixed with blood.

To make the story more readable, I streamlined period diction that might sound stilted to modern ears. Other than deliberate changes, though, the book is researched down to the date individual words were in use.

If you want to know what Jem encounters in the New World, watch for *Jem, a Novice in Philadelphia.*

Delaney Green, Summer 2016

Discussion Questions

1. Why is the first chapter titled "A Matter of Perspective"?

2. What is "Sight"? Is it a good or a bad thing? Keep track of the 20+ ways Second Sight manifests itself in the book.

3. Look up information about Benjamin Franklin. What was going on in his real life in 1758? How do the events in Franklin's life affect his pupil, Jem?

4. Look up the Chelsea Physick Garden, which during Jem's time was on the bank of the Thames River. What could one find there? Who started it? In what condition is the garden today?

5. In 1758, England was fighting the Seven Years' War on two continents, Europe and North America; in North America, it was called the French and Indian War and was the precursor to the Revolutionary War. How does the war affect the people in the novel?

6. Describe the relationship between Jem and Franklin.

7. What are reasons for and against Jem's returning to work at the apothecary?

8. What famous person might be Jem's grandfather? Why is that a problem?

9. Why do you think Mr. Galt chose Margery to inherit his apothecary shop?

10. Margery doesn't give a good reason for wanting to clean out Abernathy's parlor. What reasons can you think of that might explain why she wants to do it?

11. How does Abernathy react when Jem finally tells him the identity of her grandfather? Why does he have that reaction?

12. Does "the Dark" remind you of anything? Could it be called something else?

13. Granny says in chapter sixteen, "Try always t' be exact in what you say, as a stray word can go off and do damage." Is that true? Can you think of any examples?

14. Based on what Granny says, what's your explanation for "the Light"?

15. Would it be a good or bad thing to have Sight and see into the future?

16. What is the solstice? How do Granny's beliefs clash with Jem's education in their conversation about the solstice?

17. How is the Jem like the cocoon Granny finds on the holly?

18. Explain how Jem's Sight differs from the other women's—for example, Dolly's gift is to communicate with insects and Elowen's gift is the healing of people.

19. Why does Jem decide to accept her Sight despite all the trouble it may bring? What does she see when she stops fighting it?

20. How does the author blend pagan beliefs and practices with Christian ones?

21. Jem must learn to concentrate in order to develop her Sight, which Granny says will become second-nature, like opening and closing a door. What other kinds of doors do people "open" and "close"?

22. Jem writes down her memories in order to tap into the power of her mind. Is that something anybody could do? What is the author trying to say about writing?

23. One of Jem's challenges is to reconcile magic with science. How does living on the moor help her to do that?

24. Describe Granny Kestrel's relationship with her grandsons. Is it like any relationship in your life?

25. What revelation does Margery share about her relationship with Dr. Abernathy in this chapter? Did you see earlier hints in the book?

26. In what ways is the behavior of the hawk moth like Jem's behavior?

27. Granny talks about Jem having a destiny. Is there such a thing as destiny? If so, can it be changed?

28. With whom will Jem stay in Philadelphia? How must she dress there? Why might this be a problem for Jem?

29. The conversations at the wedding show Jem that life in London will go on

without her. Is this depressing or reassuring for her?

30. Examine Jem's conversation with Elaine. At what point in the conversation does Elaine's attitude toward Sighted people shift? What is the author trying to say about tolerance?

31. Why do you think Patch is so talkative when he finally traps Jem?

32. Patch tells Jem he has more than one option regarding her fate. What does he finally decide to do? Why do you think he makes that choice?

33. Does Patch behave as though he owns Jem because he has complete power over her or because he wants to scare her into believing that he does?

34. What does does Franklin's reaction to learning about Jem's magical ability reveal about his personality and character?

35. What does Jem see on the water once her ship is on its way to the New World? What does that suggest about the next stage of her adventure?

Made in the USA
Charleston, SC
22 November 2016